Hurricane Road

A novel of Cuba, the Florida Frontier and the Spanish American War.

By: Roger C Horton

ISBN: 9781728744636

Introduction

Hurricane Road is the first novel in the series of that name. It's a story of Cuba, and the Florida frontier during the years of the Cuban insurrection, and the Spanish American War. A young man and woman, each out of step with the cultures they were born to, meet and struggle to survive the great storms of man and nature. It is a tale of gun running, war, commerce, treasure and unlikely love in a turbulent time. First of a series, it's non-stop romantic adventure on land and sea, an adventure over decades that will stay with you long after the last page is read.

Titles in this series:

1 Hurricane Road
2 Florida Straits
3 Valuable Things
4 A Change of Times
5 Lies and to the wall
6 Implausible Deniability
7 Paths of War

Other Books by Author:

To Stalk the Hydra
Truth and other Precious Things
Racing for Pride and Profit

The Central Northwestern Atlantic

Chapter 1

Beneath an opal dark sky, the steam schooner *Eclipse* fled. The bow of the black ship, sheared waves, exploding them into sheets of phosphorescent spray, and around her, other seas swept coral shoal, exposing it with brilliant rushes of foam. Eighty feet above her deck, Asher Byran, squinted intently at the water ahead, then shifting his grip, he bent to the voice tube, and shouted another course change to the helm. Below him, the ship swung, trembling, with the power of the steam pistons that drove her. Astern, the occasional white of a bow wave, flashed below the red glow of sparks, showing that the gunboat continued to pursue. The sparks had alerted *Eclipse's* crew but outrunning the Spaniard was proving difficult. Profit for a laborious voyage was not guaranteed -- Survival itself was not sure.

Twelve hours before, the *Eclipse,* had approached the Cuban coast , and swung close in on the eastern shore of *Bahia Cochinos.* The captain had ordered the ship slowed and it groped its way along the murky coast. Puffing a cigar, he watched, waited for the blue flares of the *insurrectos.* The Captain was Connor Byran, Asher's uncle. The proper use of signals were one of many things he considered important to the family trade. Others, to mention a few, included: the placing contraband on dark deserted coastline, knowledge of revolutionaries with money, and a familiarity with local naval routines.

When the signal, a blinding blue light, came, it was low and close aboard.   At the captain's shout, *Eclipse*'s anchor plunged to the bottom a mere two hundred yards off the dark line of mangroves. Waves of mosquitoes and other biting insects surged out the jungle marsh. Futilely, men began to swat at them, cursing, as they nourished these winged tormentors. Small boats clustered alongside, and for five hours, the cargo was manhandled over the rail. Cases of rifles, boxes of munitions, hundreds of them, provisions, and machetes were rowed ashore. The captain had paced, occasionally he hurried men at a task, and always he nervously smoked long cigars, one after another.

Even with a lookout at the masthead, and the boilers fired, Connor Byran

worried. The narrow *Bahia Cochinos* was a natural trap and with the Spanish Royal Navy base at Cienfuegos only forty miles to the east, a filabuster might hope for luck but if he planned to live a long life, he must do more than hope. The Byran clan, like Satan, the Devil, had long believed in insuring their luck.

"Stack fire, away south there, Captain," the lookout had shouted.

That had been the warning; the first sign that things might not go well. Connor had pulled his pocket watch and held it to the binnacle. The hands showed it to be an hour past midnight. He'd looked to see what remained on deck, there wasn't much.

"Cut away the anchor boys, she's time to get," he yelled, the volume of his bellow carrying the length of the ship, and echoing back from the shore. "Let's go, men! Dons are a-coming'! Let's go!" He turned and shouted the same to the Cubans, "*Vamos hombres! Pelegro! Vamos!*" He then, crossed to the telegraph, and rang half ahead.

Chopped, the bower splashed before echoes of his words died. Water churned beneath the counter and *Eclipse* had begun to move. Cuban patriots rowed for the mangroves shouting angry obscenities as a portion of their precious cargo began splashing over the side. The First Mate, Thompson,

6

screened the stack, and passed word for the boys to douse any lights.

"Due west," Conner told the helmsman.

The warship had become visible from the deck, a faint shadow at the edge of the southern horizon. *Eclipse,* low and black against an equally black shore, provided no silhouette as she crossed the bay and swung south. The gunboat passed two miles east on an opposite course and was falling astern. Distant thunder preceded the twin fountains of water that rose from the sea a half-mile aft. The captain rang full ahead and watched as the gunboat turned, its bow aligned on his stern. Two more columns of water sprung up, closer but still well astern.

"Asher," he yelled, judging his ship to be out of range by about a thousand yards. Staying out of range that would be the trick. He yelled again for his nephew, and a tall young officer appeared out of the gloom. "Y'all get cha bearings, and get up the mast there. See if you can scrape 'em off on the Garden Banks."

Asher glanced aft at the Spanish gunboat and leaping into the mizzen sheets, began to climb.

Bow aimed toward the maze of shoals known as the Flower Garden Bank, *Eclipse* streaked southwest at over fourteen knots. On board, a few men could claim eyesight as sharp as the second mate, but when it came to the running of shoal water, Asher Byran's talent was rare. Having memorized charts of the Flower Garden on the outward voyage, he was familiar with the sea bottom on this piece of coast, and at the masthead, he alone bore the responsibility for the ship's path as it wove its way across the reef-strewn bank.

The moonless hours had stretched toward dawns glow and his hoarse voice called to the helm, "starboard a point and steady." The bow swung west, toward the shadow of Cayo Rosario. In the shoal water the propeller began to cavitate and

Eclipse vibrated -- the rail, to which Asher clung, quivered.

"By the deep two," the leads man sang from the bow chains, "four fathoms full."

Glancing back, Asher knew that daylight wouldn't aid in shaking the gunboat but he could soon rest. After the hours of coral reefs and tension, Cayo Largo was broad on the port beam and the deeps of the Caribbean Sea lay a mile ahead. He relaxed for the vibration was gone, and there was light enough to distinguish color in the water. It was a purple blue, more than twenty fathoms and falling off.

Peering down, he watched his uncle take a bearing on Cayo Rosario. Connor and Asher's father James had been twins. The old man was a bit more than medium size, and thickened in his years, and was, as his brother James had been, a gentleman, who dressed plain, but neat, always with a starched shirt and a well knotted tie. At Connor's waist hung a Naval Colt revolver and short saber; in the coat pocket, he kept a pipe, tobacco pouch, and a silver flask of whiskey. Each day he stropped a razor, and shaved clean, save for a full and waxed mustache, which he maintained with the same pride that he commanded his ship. To his nephew, he was more father than uncle and Asher emulated him where possible.

Hooking a leg around the mizzen halyard, Asher, slipped quickly to the deck. He stretched and twisted his head to relieve the tightness in his neck, and walked aft to where Captain Byran stood, staring at the stack smoke astern.

"Clear water, sir," Asher reported.

"Well, that's fine. Was hoping the bastards would tear their bottom out before they cleared the bank, but hoping ain't having." He gestured aft and said, "We ain't gained spit on that gunboat, mate."

"I expect they have a local pilot or a turtler aboard there, and he's good sir. Crossing that mess took some doing. Be a

8

straight-out race now," he said with a mix of admiration and irritation.

Leaning back, looking up into the rigging, Connor felt the strength of the wind against his skin and sighed. He looked astern again, thinking, Best get some canvas on this old bitch.

"Asher, y'all tell Mr. Thompson, we'll put on what sail she'll carry — all she'll carry. We'll see if we kin discourage that Spanish hound with a mite more speed," he said brightly. He turned back, but his nephew was already moving forward in search of the first mate.

He stepped into the lee of the house to pack his pipe. Spray splattered the deck, and flew horizontally above his head. For Conner Byran, a chase such as this was no novelty. Having been taught the seaman's trade by his grandfather, he'd been at sea for a lifetime, a far longer lifetime than most Byrans. The smuggling part of the trade was changing. With time and technology what had been at best a chancy craft, was becoming downright dangerous. The Spanish gunboat astern was the fair proof. Warships were gaining in speed and range, while he and his ship were getting old. He could hear the slapping rumble as another sail was hoisted, then a thump as it sheeted home. The ship heeled a bit and steadied. Connor lit his pipe and stepped from behind the house in time to be showered with spray. He grumbled under his breath, blinked the salt from his eyes, peered at the wet tobacco, and then aft again. "Son-of a bitch," he mumbled.

Within twenty minutes, the *Eclipse* wore full canvas and ran due south, trades abeam. With full sail and her boiler pressure pushed past what was safe, the old ship had more than doubled her lead by noon. She continued to pull away, doing one knot better than the Spanish gunboat could match, but one knot is a near thing in a chase.

When Asher came on deck to take the mid-watch, he had time for coffee. The Chief Engineer was in a heated debate with the Captain. Erickson was a thin, grizzled old man, who had started as a stoker forty years back. There was little he'd not seen and done with boilers and other machinery. At present, the old engineer's face was as red as his suspenders. Soot and oil streaked his skin and rancid sweat soaked his clothing. Brown rivers ran from him as he warned, with the tone of a prophet.

"Y'all doan ease off her, somethings gonna fly all to hell. Fly all to hell purty soon here, Captain. Y'all may ah put a new boiler and other parts in her, but some ah that machinery down there's more than thirty-year-old, and it ain't gonna take this," he warned, his head craned forward. The tension in his skinny frame, expressed more than his words.

"Can't ease her much, Gus," he apologized, gesturing aft. "Need the speed if were gonna lose that gunboat. I'm not at all partial to a Spanish firing squad."

"Damn, Cap'n, coal hain't gonna last, this rate neither," the engineer complained, "and a for long yer gonna haft a send some ah yer deck boys down to shovel coal. My gang is about whipped. Plumb whipped, sir."

Connor drew on his pipe and slowly exhaled smoke. "The coal will suffice to outrun that gunboat, Gus, and then I'll still have the wind, won't I now?" he said sarcastically.

He looked aft again, balancing the danger in each course of action. Turning back to the engineer, he continued in a reasonable tone.

"But let's say we do take a little pressure off, Gus. Suppose a little won't hurt with the lead, we got. I'll let y'all know if we need it back." He turned and sat on a hatch, showing no sign of having given in.

The chief grinned, nodded at the captain's back, and hurried below. Asher had removed the sextant from its box to measure the *Eclipse's* latitude at noon, a daily ritual of the

10

second officer. Connor watched his nephew take the sight and plot it. He packed and re-lit his pipe while Asher measured the distance for speed and run.

"Been doing sixteen for an average, sir, good wind abeam," Asher announced, smiling. "Be passing west of Grand Cayman in two hours."

"Be dark in six hours, Ash. Lose them then—they don't give up the chase first." He chewed his mustache and stretched. "Tenacious bunch, that," he added, gesturing aft with his pipe. "Chief took a little pressure off, so call me if they gain on us. A nap's in order at the moment," he said yawning, and standing, he proceeded down into his cabin.

Connor was bone weary with the stress of the night. Added to that was the problems of the voyage in general. He doubted if more than a handful of the vessels chartered to run Cuban arms had avoided seizure in U.S. ports or capture at sea. Better the U.S. Navy than Spain, of course, but it had been a hard chance in any account. Both he and the *Eclipse* were too tired for this, but after the hurricanes had torn up his orange groves, using the old ship for gunrunning had seemed his best chance. He knew more about contraband than he did oranges anyway.

He had been a young man at the time of *Eclipse's* launch, back in 1863. She was one of the first propeller driven ships, Clyde built, 160 feet, fast, low, and designed to run the Yankee blockade. By '65, she'd made fourteen successful runs, and a fortune for him and his brother, James. In 1868, that fortune had been ferreted out by the Federals and confiscated. He and James had left South Carolina that year. Three decades as Florida growers had not seen them prosper. Besides hurricanes and disease, his own children died young, leaving his wife sad and older than her age. Yellow fever had taken his Brother James and James's wife Christine, along with their girls. Asher and he were the last of the Byrans and his own

11

health was becoming poorly.

"And a fine young man, Asher is, and a damn fine officer," he mumbled. "Damned fine, and here I am risking him at running guns." At seventeen, his nephew needed to be in a university, not chased by the Spanish Navy. Christine Wallace Byran would be turning in her grave if she knew that her son sailed on a filibuster. She'd been promised, her son would be educated as a gentleman should be; promised on her deathbed that Ash would be introduced back into the Charleston society she had been born to.

Well, there was time yet. As little use as Connor had for the snobs of the Saint Cecilia Society, he would see the boy got back among his mother's people. Connor Byran had promised his sister-in-law, and a deathbed promise was a sacred oath. His own wife, Fay, had been a Gibbes, and cousin to Christine. If Fay had gotten her way, her nephew would have been in a Charleston school seven years past. He tapped the embers from his pipe and stripped off his clothes, then wrinkled his nose at the smell of his body. Crawling into his berth, he vowed to bathe at the first opportunity. Lulled by the throb of the engine and the water's rush, he let sleep take him.

Thompson relieved Asher of the watch at 6:00 pm. A few rain squalls lay southeast, dark against the horizon. Trade winds, remaining strong from the east, pressed the lee rail to the sea. Ben Bodden, a black Cayman Islander, took the wheel from Gordee Castle. He leaned into it to get the ship's feel as he repeated the course. Two of the engine gang lay in the lee scuppers, letting the surge wash the heat and grit from their bodies. Most of the crew gathered around the cookhouse though, feasting on fish and rice. Now and again, someone peered aft at the black smudge of smoke, which followed.

"Holding our lead, sir," Asher remarked, his nose catching a whiff of hot food.

"Doin' thet for sure," Thompson agreed, "but weren't no

luck they were on us like thet. I'd wager they had our name, cargo, and destination for we left Florida -- just chanced to spy us out a bit late." He grinned and added, "Us running twenty miles ah shoal water in the dark, well hell, thet may have set them back a mite, too. What say?" Thompson chuckled, nudging Asher.

"Yeah, a mite, I spose," he agreed, embarrassed at the compliment. "Sure, are dogging us, though. I'd have figured they'd let off by now."

"Could be, they're supposing' we got men and guns aboard yet. More likely they don't want us doin' no future business. Don't mean to let go whatever the reason". Turning his shoulder to the wind, Thompson put a match to a cigar, and blowing smoke, he turned face to wind. "Back in '64, ya know, was a blockade-runner, a steamer name of *Pee Dee Queen.* She ran aground up off Georgetown, in the Carolinas, ya know, and the Yankees up and armed her as a blockader. A smart quick ship she was, too. We had the misfortune to run up on her one night just a tad south of Savannah, if my memory serves me. Chased after y'all daddy's ship, the old *Gull.* Gave chase for better then three days for we lost them. Good part of the cargo got burned to keep up steam. Was a crying shame, I'll tell ya, a crying shame. And thet thar Spaniard astern, well, he appears about as determined as the common Yankee," Thompson stated with passion.

Asher yawned thinking the situation appeared far from dire. "It looks like we have a good chance of shaking him, sir."

"A chance," the First agreed, but with less faith concerning their odds at losing the gunboat, than young Byran, who had yet to suffer at Fate's calloused hand. Well, he had suffered, but not to a great degree, not to the older mate's way of reckoning. Time would resolve that part of his education, and it might turn out just dandy --

"Long as the wind holds and the boiler don't burst," he said

13

under his breath.

"Time for some sleep," Asher said and started below. He looked astern, then at the squalls ahead, and nodded for his own reassurance, figuring the ship would be into them by dusk, and that would help to muddy things a bit.

Thompson judged the second mate's outlook correctly. The possibility that they might fail to elude their pursuer hadn't been taken seriously, but concerns of death and disaster are foreign to most young men of seventeen. It was not that Asher lacked the intelligence to imagine *Eclipse's* capture, rather that experience had led him to a boundless confidence in his uncle's ability. Asher Byran was not ignorant of death's existence or the menace of man's nature. He was, after all, an orphan and schooled in a hazardous trade. He had encountered storms at sea, in which fellows had been injured or lost. He had seen the ravages of disease, and witnessed the deadly disputes of angry men. On balance though, Their Captain had in the past managed to succeed in such ventures, thus, in his nephew's mind, there resided the logic that he would continue to succeed. This logic, prevalent in humankind, is generally corrected only by painful experience.

Connor woke to a sharp rap on his cabin door and as he sat up, he grunted, "Yeah!"

"Mister Thompson sends his respects, Cop'n," a gravelly voice informed him, "and he is saying, you's might be wanting to change the course about now".

"Tell the chief mate I'll be up shortly," Connor said stumbling out of his bunk, for the ship's heave caught him unready. Bracing himself at the sink, he splashed water on his face to bring him fully awake. He fumbled for his pipe, lighting it before climbing on deck. At the companion hatch, he nudged one of the seamen on watch, sending him for coffee. Facing the wind, he sniffed. The sky was dark; the smell of rain was on the wind.

"Still with us, Thompson?" he asked, looking aft. His eyes were not ready for the black, but his ears heard the mates reply. "Well then, when we enter those squalls, take in all sail. We'll run west in the rain. Call all hands for the work, mister." A cup of coffee was in the captain's hand, without his remembering the taking of it. It was good. He inquired about the condition of the boats and whether they had been provisioned. He then ordered that they be swung out as soon as *Eclipse* was running west with the sea. Time to shoot craps with the devil.

As the rain began to pelt down, *Eclipse* shed her canvas and turned west. The world became black and close, unlit but for the binnacle lamp. Twice in the hours that followed, the *Eclipse* altered course to run within the rain. Her engine slowed to two-thirds, and she slipped along at twelve knots, as Connor Byran debated his choices: a direct run for home or try for a foreign port to wait out the trouble. From this voyage, he had banked several times the value of his old ship. He was old, fifty-eight, with aching joints and pain in his chest -- he was feeling his years. He had outlived all his family, and most of his peers. It was time to come ashore when he was well ahead. He stared into the gloom, debating his future.

It was near midnight; off to starboard, the rain was clearing. Asher came on deck for watch, and as he greeted his uncle, a flash illuminated his expression of surprise. An instant later there was a thunderclap as to starboard, water was thrown thirty feet into the air.

"Hell, and the devil!" someone swore out of the dark, for not a mile to starboard, the gunboat came at them bow on.

"Hard-a-port," Connor bellowed, already pushing the engine-order telegraph to full ahead. Heeling hard, *Eclipse* swung rapidly to the south, and as a second shell burst near her stern, she retreated into the thinning rain.

"Asher, y'all tell the chief to toss a keg of oil in the furnace, and get his boys on deck. We'll be going to the boats now," Connor announced soberly.

Carrying his trousers, a man emerged from the companion hatch in time to see a shell explode fifty feet to port, just forward of the beam.

Shouting this time, Connor repeated the order, "All hands to the boats!"

The ship slipped into a heavy squall. As Connor brought the bow to starboard, an ear-splitting boom thundered, and water fountain-ed aft and to port. Shapes clamored over the rail, dropping down into the leaping boats as spray and rain showered them.

Sliding the sweep between it's pins, Asher bellowed to the starboard boats crew, "Cast off, boys!".

From the wheel, the captain yelled to them, "Fetch me out when I jump."

The port boat cut away. Immediately, it leaped, plunged, nearly capsized. As it swept past the stern, it appeared half swamped. Connor put the *Eclipse* back to port, steadied her, and tied the wheel and as the starboard boat swept past, Connor leaped. He went over the stern rail into the wake just as a Spanish shell struck high on the mainmast, showering shrapnel and splinters. Abandoned, *Eclipse* charged the East wind, her fine bows tossing sheets of spray.

When they hauled Connor gasping into the starboard boat, *Eclipse* was near a half-mile out with the Spaniard close in her wake. Asher ordered the boat's mast stepped, and the men had the longboat under sail before his uncle had time to get his breath back.

"Nor' west, sir?" he asked, glancing downwind, which was the boat's fastest tack.

"For now," the old man groaned. "Had to cut my pistol and

16

sword away. Dam'd iron liked to drag me under."

Leaning back into the bows, Connor rested. He listened as the men hallooed the port boat at intervals. They paused for answering call, but heard nothing. His butt hurt and, putting a hand where it hurt, he realized he'd been pinked in the cheek. He fumed silently at the insult of a wound in the ass, a most dishonorable location. A cousin of his, a sergeant in Pickett's Division, had backed all the way down from Missionary Ridge just to avoid such a wound. His thoughts shifted and he worried about Thompson's boat, but decided the first mate would be running south to the Bay Islands, He had family there. He felt weak and tired -- the mate would deal with this boat. He wanted only to sleep.

Near to 1:00 am., the rain cleared off, and the gunfire ceased. To the east, Asher watched the low clouds flicker orange with the warm glow of flames on the sea below. Each time the longboat topped a steep wave, the black horizon was visible. It was clearly marked by the glittering brilliance of a burning ship. He decided it was a fitting end, a fine death for the old ship. She had been conceived to dance with the devil, and for thirty-two years she'd run blockades, smuggled guns, and contraband over dark shores. That was considerable dancing. Slender and fast, *Eclipse* had outrun the best. It was not as if the old ship hadn't turned an honest dollar, she had, but she'd not had the beam or bulk to compete for honest trade. He understood this as the pure truth of it. He counted six years aboard *Eclipse;* the six years since his mother's passing. He had learned his trade and earned his mate's certificate in the old ship -- her destruction seemed unreal. The abruptness of the ship's loss left him strangely empty. He recognized this as a point where his life would surely come about on a new tack. He felt uneasy with the sudden uncertainty of his future. The longboat dropped into a deep trough. When she rose on the peak of the next sea, all was black in the East.

"Lordie, boys, she's slid away!" Woody cried, standing as he spoke.

"There, Gordee! She gone for sure now," Ben, agreed.

Haywood Crib was mumbling and moaning in the bilge at Asher's feet. He ordered the older man to pipe down.

"No reason for all that moaning, Crib! You're in a sound boat with plenty of rations, good wind, this ain't hurricane season, and there's land no matter which way we sail," he informed in a easy but commanding voice. He said this for the benefit of all hands, using Crib's fear as an excuse to settle the crew as a whole. Asher's face was calm, as he glanced forward. The Captain lay in a deep sleep as the ship's boat bore off toward the Yucatan.

Dawn brought a few light squalls off to the south, but no sign of the Spaniard or of *Eclipse's* port boat. Connor woke in a foul humor, not only at remembering he'd been outfoxed and sunk by the Spanish navy, but due to the pain of their parting gift. The pain of the shell fragment in the left cheek of his ass was troubling. Being knocked about at sea in an open boat was punishment enough for an old man, without adding to it the inability to sit properly. Not that there wasn't room in the starboard boat -- it could hold over twenty -- but it now held only nine men: four seamen, two stokers, the cook, Asher, and himself. Thompson and fifteen others had gone into the port boat, all able men, but God alone knew how they were fairing. Connor was down in his spirits and felt so poorly that he was pleased to leave the directing of matters to Asher, who was in his mind, a Cracker Jack of an officer.

To fix the boat's latitude, that officer, had managed a good altitude of Polaris at dawn. With an estimation of their night's run, he had a reasonably accurate position, placing them a near equal distance of two hundred and fifty miles from

18

Mexico's Yucatan, Cuba, and the Bay Isles of Honduras, even less to the Caimans. To reach Florida, they would have to double Cabo San Antonio, sailing an additional two hundred and fifty miles east. Nevertheless, wind and currents were favorable, and the longboat was a sound Cayman-built, twenty-six-footer. Asher could see no reason why a passage might not be accomplished in a week, give or take, and be there a need; the Cuban coast offered numerous points of refuge.

He set a course to the north northwest, and divided the boat's crew into two watches. At dawn and dusk, rations were doled out, while astern, they trailed lines in the hope of fish. In two days, the boat had covered two hundred miles but on the third dawn, the wind veered, forcing the boat onto a northeast tack. Sailing with a wind forward the port beam, made slow going, and the boat thrashed about in a violent fashion, spray wetting all hands. The weather was cold for the Caribbean, a February front pushing south. Though all hands bitched, none suffered more than the Captain, whose wound had become swollen and putrid. Unable to sit, he had taken to lying on his side or stomach, and due to the boat's antics, this became difficult. By dusk, he was feverish, took only water, and Asher was troubled.

During the night, the wind slowly veered northeast, then east. Dawn found them back on a starboard tack, running west, close on the Cuban coast off Cabo Antonio. The strong breeze now pushing them down light seas was cool but agreeable. The Captain's skin was hot, dry to the touch, and propped on his side in the stern sheets, he rambled. Asher sought to speak with him, but his mind was plainly unhinged. They cut his trousers open, exposing a ragged puncture, which had scabbed over. The area was purple-red, blotched and swollen, with the smell of rot. Although he masked his emotions, Asher was fearful for his uncle's life.

"Sir," Ben whispered softly, plainly acknowledging Asher's authority, "what pierced de Cop'n, it still in him. It what be causing de wound to mortify. It needs be cut out or it do for him. My doddy, he in some barroom scrap in Kingston, he got dis little prick, same as that, small and deep, but yo' see de blade she broke off in there. Take two weeks, for that little' cut to do for him, and all my mama's praying and crying didn't change no thing."

The men waited, observing the young officer, subconsciously evaluating, not his right, but his ability to command. He was not a boy, nor had the drama of the last days brought maturity -- it was born of discipline and responsibility accepted early in life. He was tall and solid for his years, with eyes of a piercing gold hazel, and from them, his gaze was straightforward as were his words. His confidence was tempered by a particular force, a presence -- men tended to do his bidding without question.

"I'm afraid you're right, but it's in there deep," Asher said, "and I've neither the knack nor the tools to go digging. I'm sorely tempted to put in on the coast for a doctor -- if I knew of a near place to put into," he added looking man to man. "Who knows the Cape?"

Woody Burnett spoke, shy, scratching his whiskers, "On the north side of the Cape, mate, there's a little place up in the bay, mouth of the Rio Guadiana. Road to a bigger town about ten miles in the direction of Pinar Del Rio. I've been there, mate, on a turtle boat outta Key West. Was asleep going' in, and drunk coming' out, but a town, she's there someplace."

Asher considered his options. There not seeming to be many, he asked, "Anybody else been on the coast north of the Cape there?"

"Been pass the place regular, mate; never put in," Gordee offered with a shrug.

"That bay, it runs back thirty miles, give or take some. Ships going someplace back there."

Studying the subject for a moment before speaking his decision, Asher figured it would take two to three days to reach Key West, and, in his estimation, Cuba was not such a bad place if you weren't running guns. With this wind, they would round the Cape within the hour, and should be able to make the pull to windward by dark. Twelve hours to land in a Cuban town was a sight better than three days to reach Key West, especially considering his uncles failing condition. Decision weighed on him, and he knew it unsettled men when an officer could not fix his mind. Having chosen a course, he spoke.

"Well then, boys, listen up here. Y'all eat some extra rations and take a good drink. We're going' to clear this cape, and pull for the bay's end." Asher turned saying, "Cook, When it's time to pull, give them each water and a inch of rum, and another inch on the hour, and we'll be ashore tonight, if y'all are willing."

Ben Bodden grinned and spoke out loudly, "That's de style, mate; that's de style."

"Get our feet on de ground," Tailor chipped in, voicing approval.

"Be a long pull, a hard pull, and then we'll be landing Captain Byran," Asher continued. "Can't have talk about what we been about. One loose mouth and they'll have us all up against a wall for shooting. Remember, and when the Captain here's fit, I'm planning to take this boat across the Straits, try for Key West. Y'all start thinking on it; decide if you're with me or staying in Cuba."

North of Cape Antonio, the boat's mast was un-stepped. With grunts and groans they leaned into the oars, six pulling, while one of the two remaining at rest steered. In the lee of land, the sea calmed to a light chop, it flattened, its color shifting to emerald, then pale aqua. The breeze was cool, the sun hot, and Asher served water in triple rations with the rum. The length of the peninsula made for a longer pull than expected, and they were still plying the oars at dusk when the breeze shifted onto the beam, allowing the boat to be sailed the last miles.

Asher guided her between anchored schooners, and ran her aground about fifty feet off the beach. Worn with fatigue, the men slept, lying as if dead, across the thwarts and in the bilges. Water lapped softly on the hull; it reflected light from the village, and carried the scent of fish and sewage to him. The place, though awake, had no cognizance of one more boat on its crowded beach, and as music played in the distance, a woman laughed in the dark. A dog barked, and a neighbor cursed it. Asher sat at the tiller, limp with weariness, silent, unmoving, until a restless groan from his uncle recalled to him, his purpose for coming here.

By the means of prodding and shaking, he managed to transform the men to a state of disgruntled wakefulness, at least enough to beach the boat. Before another order could be considered, they were asleep on the sand, each man where he dropped. Asher returned to his uncle, leaned over, and gently felt Connor's cheek with the back of a hand. The skin was hot, but his breathing was steady. Asher spoke to him, and receiving no response, sighed. On awkward legs, he trudged up a sandy street in search of a doctor.

On the side of a square opposite a market and cantina, was a church. He found the priest playing dominoes, and in Spanish explained his need of a doctor. The priest explained that La Fe had no doctor. A midwife, yes; and there was some old man who prepared herbs, but the nearest doctor was fifteen miles inland at the Guane rail head. With the assistance of the priest, and for the sum of one silver eagle, a mule cart and driver were arranged. Again, Asher shook some of the crew into awareness and made them load Connor. With words of certainty, Asher promised them that he would do his best to return in a day or two. Again, he warned them to mind their business and their tongues. That said, he climbed onto the back of the cart, and set out for Guane. At his feet, his uncle groaned and mumbled.

Beyond the old man's whimpers, there was a still silence that made the land seem empty. The road east was obscured by great trees, which overhung it, providing shade by day, but blocking all light from the sky at night. The air was thick with lush perfumes: flowers, pine, rot and, later as he descended into sleep, the scents of tobacco and cut grass. An hour or so short of dawn, the cart reached Guane. Asher woke and sat up stiffly to check his uncle, who lay staring at the stars.

"I fear they've finally done for me nephew," he rasped, suddenly lucid. "Look to y'all s Aunt Fay now," he charged. "Y'all be as a son to her with me gone."

"A doctor is right up the road sir. A matter of minutes and he'll be putting you right," Asher said, using his most confident tone. "No reason to despair sir."

"Not likely," Connor said and the midst of a fit of coughing, he again lost consciousness.

The cart bumped to a halt abreast the gate of a two-story house, and as a man drugged, Asher jumped down. The driver knocked on the doctor's gate. He whispered to a servant who appeared, explaining about a wounded Yankee, then yawned and waited with Asher for the doctor to be summoned.

The Doctor arrived within moments. Still in his night clothes, he climbed onto the cart. He muttered at the smell of the wound. He inspected it by lantern light, and asked the nature of things, before ordering Connor carried into his surgery. He operated at first light while Asher napped in his courtyard. The doctor found him there, and waking him, explained apologetically that the old man had died. His heart, strained by fever, had not stood the surgery.

Asher had half-feared his uncle might die, but regardless of how poorly the old man had seemed, buoyed by youthful optimism, he had hoped for the best. Now that Connor Byran was gone, the ache of reality burned inside, and a dull loneliness descended upon Asher, clouding his mind.

Connor Byran had been more his father than an uncle. He'd taught him hunting, shooting, and proficiency with a saber. His uncle had taught him his trade, had been his captain at sea; and from observing him, Asher had learned the craft of command and decision. Asher had practiced these arts, knowing the old man watched over him to catch his mistakes. In one fell swoop, Asher Byran had lost parent, teacher, and employer. Life was indeed hard.

Asher swallowed and fought off tears that would have appalled his uncle. As sad as was his plight, he recognized his lot was to become more bitter still, for he must report these events to his aunt. He dreaded the duty of informing his Aunt Fay, but he would not shirk it. That duty would be in the future though, and other obligations were closer at hand.

To the doctor, he promised, as a gentleman, to send payment for the services. With the aid of his cigar chewing *guajiro* driver, he loaded the body and prepared his uncle for burial. He removed Connor's wedding ring, gold watch, silver flask, and a locket. There were a few silver eagles and small change in his pockets, but little else. With the cart parked in front of an open *café*, a nickel bought them coffee and fried plantains. For a casket, two bits to a carpenter; another silver dollar to a young priest, who agreed to provide a plot in the churchyard, and a *Requiem* mass said for the soul of the deceased. A spot was marked out in the cemetery and Asher began to dig the grave. He could have had it dug for a nickel, but this last service was an honor among his people. He was glad to perform it.

The *guajiro* smoked in the cool shade of the cart while

24

Asher dug in the sandy soil. The priest hung about questioning him about his uncle's life. Between sweat and lack of breath, the conversation waned. The priest, recalling other duties, soon departed, and Asher, sweating in grim silence, continued to dig.

Done by mid-afternoon, Asher lowered his uncle into the foreign soil, and mumbled a few sorrowful words of prayer. The *guajiro* poured rum on the grave and crossed himself. Asher looked perturbed. The *guajiro* shrugged.

"My wife is a wise one, a holy woman. She says the saints, they like rum," he explained.

"My uncle didn't take to Santaria," Asher said tersely, and returned the shovel to the church. Walking back to the cart, he noticed several horsemen in gray uniforms. They clustered about the cantina smoking, drinking rum, and toying arrogantly with the whores. Other patrons sat apart, avoiding their eyes and looking uncomfortable.

The driver hissed softly as he returned to the cart, *"Señor, Guardia Civil!"*

"Who?" Asher asked, not understanding the point of the *guajiro's* comment.

"Military police, sir," he replied. *"Cuidado*—'take care'. They are a law unto themselves. These are not placid times."

The remark suddenly pulled Asher back from the haze of his personal grief. It restored his awareness of political realities and the precariousness of his present position. Without further hesitation, he climbed into the cart. "We go," he said quietly.

The date was February 24, 1895. Asher's was a timely departure for, at five that afternoon, *insurrectos* blew up Guane police barrack. Other attacks were carried out in other places -- many other places. The insurrection had begun, but that was some time after they had left town. When the

25

distant sound of an explosion, then gunfire, reached them from behind, the driver looked over his shoulder, concern apparent in his expression. He yelled to the mule, turning it off the road between two hills, and came to a halt in a small tobacco field.

"Bad," he said, "very bad. If you wish, sir, continue, but I stay here tonight. My place is but three miles up this road."

"What's going on now?" Asher asked, half-knowing already.

"The revolution begins. The army will be crazy with anger. Not good to be on the roads, bad enough for a man, who is in his home," he explained, already unhitching the mule. "They will shoot anyone they suspect. Only last month, they took those they thought would become rebels and put them against the wall at Campo Verde. They let them smoke, and then killed them while their women screamed. They raped the pretty ones in sight of their husbands' bodies. It's because war is coming."

"I need to get back to the coast. They got no reason to bother me. How far to walk"?

"A three-hour walk, but in three hours you can be shot without reason." The man continued, "My cousin, he was shot by soldiers in his own field. I was shot in the last revolt -- in the yard of my father's house. Look," he said, pulling his pants leg up to reveal a white scar. "There was no reason. The fear of it killed my mother. Her name was Eva, a name I have always liked -- a name I'll give a daughter, if my wife gets one." He sighed, "It's a cruel world, more so for women -- perhaps I should have no daughter," the *guajiro* said considering aloud. "God does as he wishes and the saints also," the man said finally and became silent. He lit a cigar, puffed smoke, spit and put the cigar back in his mouth. Clearly finished with conversation, he adjusted his hat and began to unhitch the mule.

Asher was more disgusted than apprehensive. He was in

no humor to listen to the man jabber about trigger-happy soldiers. When compared to his recent past or to the death of his uncle, sitting in a field scarcely seemed dangerous. He had men waiting, men he was responsible for, and he needed to be on his way. In addition, he'd not eaten since morning, and had labored hard on that small meal. He was hungry. The possibility of sitting in the middle of a plantation all night with nothing to sustain him had little appeal to Asher's youthful appetite. He noticed a grove of coconut palms against the hillside and went in search of food. The few coconuts on the ground were dried out husks and most were split, but large pods hung in the treetops. In the last light of a low sun, they swayed invitingly. Licking his lips, he put his belt about his ankles and began to shinny up a sixty-foot trunk.

So, intent was Asher on the climb that he failed to notice a fast galloping band of riders until they were almost abreast on the road. They passed, the dust settled, and he continued his climb into the fronds, more concerned with his stomach than horse traffic. He'd already managed to twist several nuts loose, when a second group of horsemen appeared from the east. Plainly, they were cavalry, perhaps thirty men moving rapidly. Three soldiers broke off from the unit, galloping across the field toward the cart. A non-com, by his stripes, reined in his overeager mount, and slid to a halt before the cart.

Asher could hear shouting, but was unable to make out words. The horses danced and wheeled in the dim dusk. The little Cuban, hat in hand, cigar still clamped in his teeth, shrugged his shoulders. The sergeant, in a single fluid movement, pulled his pistol and fired, shooting the *guajiro* in the head. He was spurring his mount for the road before the body hit the ground. A second bullet, fired over his shoulder, put the mule down braying and kicking. The reports, echoing off the hills, seemed almost separate from the act. The soldiers vanished in a moment, leaving only drifting dust and the mule's painful grunts to assure Asher of the reality of what he had witnessed.

"Dam'd, but don't grief and tragedy travel in company," Asher said aloud, feeling more alive at hearing the sound of his own voice. His scalp itched. Again, he was reminded of the tenuous quality of life and the value of wisdom heard, but not acted upon. He had not been preserved by warnings, as a prudent man might have been; instead, his hunger had saved him. Was that fate or mere luck? It was not a bad thing to have luck, but better, perhaps, to have the wisdom to listen to a warning.

He waited, letting dark settle in before sliding down out of the tree. He listened, and then crept carefully to the cart. The man had plainly died before he hit the ground. His cigar, still clenched in his teeth, was soaked in blood, as was the sandy soil where his head rested. The mule, also now silent, had ceased quivering. The smell of blood, and loosened bowels, made Asher suddenly queasy, reminding him of his uncle, and he spit a few times to keep control. Taking the machete from the cart, he returned to the palms and split a coconut. He ate while looking toward the corpse of the mule and its owner.

"Yep, luck and my dam'd stomach saved me this time," he mumbled. "Best get clear of this island before my luck's all gone."

He ate the meat from three more coconuts, chewing with nervous energy as he mulled his situation. The prospect of leaving the cart driver's body in the field seemed improper. The man had been in his service and Asher knew a responsible for him, but burying him could be fatal. The *guajiro* was a small man, not much more than a hundredweight. Carrying him occurred to Asher, but he dismissed it as awkward. Slinging the machete on his belt, he started west toward the village of La Fe unencumbered. He'd gone no more than fifty yards when guilt conquered his better judgment. His upbringing would not allow such disrespect. Returning, he bound the man's head in cloth from the cart, and hefted him across his shoulders.

The first small house he reached was not the man's, but two boys from the place led Asher to it. The *guajiro's* wife waited. She was stoic, calm, as if his death had been expected. Weary of the weight, Asher rolled the body onto a table indicated by the woman. He stood to the side as she positioned her husband by candlelight. Asher watched silent tears roll off her cheeks, and he was again reminded of his own grief. The woman caressed her husband's cheek, and turning to Asher, in a soft voice, thanked him for her husband's body. Holding his hat, he respectfully explained, it was an honor and duty, he had felt obliged to perform.

She offered him a seat and coffee. She watched as he drank, and then spoke to him seriously, saying, "I dreamed of this, but did not know when the time would be. My *Orisha*, he often tells of a thing, but only a part. We are warned, but must wait to know the end of a thing. I dreamed this night; I dreamed of you -- long ago -- dreamed the shape of your days."

Asher's skin prickled, and remembering, he had difficulty swallowing. Her husband had said the woman was a "wise one", a Santaria priestess. As the words came from her, the tone of her voice changed, and she seemed to look past and through him.

"I see you as a soldier, but your path will be the water. You will pursue a woman on horseback and claim a pure love, but the love is washed in blood. I see you gather great wealth, wealth that means little to you. You sire strong children, but death will—"

Unwilling to hear more, Asher bolted for the door, and fled

into the night. It was well known to Christians what befell *King Saul* for listening to the *Witch of Endor*. Unnerved, he walked and ran until the unreasonable fear left him. Then, embarrassed by his biblical superstition, and even more by unmanly reaction to the woman's words, he grinned sheepishly as he continued toward the coast.

Two hours later, a few miles from La Fe, he topped a ridge and saw fires. Unfamiliar with the countryside, and having no clue as to what evil waited in the town, Asher left the road. He followed a ravine down to the river, and the river out to the coast. He covered two miles walking and wading in the shallow river. Out of the dark, the overhanging jungle undergrowth caught and ripped his clothes, and left bleeding lines on his arms and face. Near exhaustion, it was with pleasure that he smelled seaweed and shell.

The scent of the sea had come before the sound. The sound reached him before the sight. It comforted him, like a familiar companion. On a sandbar at the river's mouth, he rinsed his scrapes, almost enjoying the salt sting. With his boots tied about his neck, he moved tiredly along the beach; rock to rock, shadow to shadow, enjoying a vague pleasure in the coarse sand and cool water. He chose a jagged ledge of a rock, jutting into the bay, as a place to sleep and wait for light. He would be safe, out of sight, and from here, he would see La Fe at dawn.

High on the rock, Asher lay motionless in a cup of sand, and it came to him again, how chancy life could be. It came to him that a soul should decide what he wished from life and waste time on nothing else. Fear and superstition should not motivate him, nor should imprudent greed. To survive, a man needed to strike a balance between caution and courage, and he must not be so prideful as to ignore another's words as he had with the cart driver. His uncle Connor had taught him that each man had some knowledge, some ability that was of value, and he only need consider its worth.

Chapter 2

Dawn broke upon the Spanish warship as it steamed slowly east, toward Havana's harbor. Squalls, drifting west along the coast parted, and the gunboat's lookout made out the walls of El Morro. He shouted the bearing, and her bow swung inshore toward Havana's entrance. Flags flying and crew at parade, she approached and signaled. The fort acknowledged the signal and as the ship came abreast, they traded banged off salutes. In the shadow of the Castillo. Captain Vega greeted the pilot, and as the colonial capitol began the day, they docked in the inner harbor.

The family had scarcely gathered for breakfast, when the guns began to fire. Corazon O'Ryan watched as her mother gasped, began to rise, and was stopped by her father, who chuckled as he took her hand.

"My darling Isabel," he said pleasantly, "it will take Louis time to dock. He must then attend to the formalities of the port and speak with his superiors. Sit and eat with the girls and I. Your brother would not wish us to be waiting in a carriage while he is kept at his duties."

"You must understand," she apologized excitedly, "I am anxious." Then, obedient to her husband's wish, sat back and smoothed her skirt, saying, "It has been three years." She glanced at her reflection. How quickly time passed. Her features had lost their softness, deep creases below her cheeks, and a thinning of a long nose reflected more the matron than the young mother. Nevertheless, her hair remained black, and her body shapely, which was more than many mothers of thirty-five could pride themselves on.

A servant poured coffee with milk, while another brought fruits. She smiled nervously and sipped from a porcelain cup. February of 1892 had been the last time she had visited with her brother, Louis Vegas, then an officer aboard the Cruiser *Viscaya*. At that time, he had taken his son, Hermon, to enroll the boy in Spain's Royal Naval Academy.

Though Hermon was her nephew, he was as dear to her as her own son, for she had raised him as her own after yellow fever took his mother. Isabel, feeling pride in the military heritage of the Vegas family, had resolved to be strong, but her proud resolve and her maternal emotions were often at odds. Having an American husband did nothing to sooth her conflicting concerns, for Douglas O'Ryan did not share the Vegas' understanding of nation and honor. Their son, Robert, had been educated in both Cuba and the United States, and then enrolled in a university in France. It was her husband's intention that Robert be well rounded—that he remain unbound by nationalistic emotions. Privately, Douglas disapproved of the military as a career. This was an outlook that Isabel shared secretly for she preferred having her family close about her.

The meal continued with routine. Esmeralda and Corazon discussed the planned activities of the day, and Douglas inquired about them or offered his daughters instruction. Today would be quite different from the normal activities presented on their visits to Havana. The girls were nearly as excited over Louis Vega's arrival as was their mother. Esmeralda, now sixteen and Corazon only weeks from fifteen, looked forward to a visit to his ship. Both had been aboard ships; neither had visited a war ship. The prospect was exciting.

O'Ryan pushed back his chair, signaling the completion of the meal, when his eldest daughter spoke.

"Will Hermon come home soon, Papa?" Esmeralda asked. "It's been forever."

"I doubt it," he said. "More likely, he will be assigned to a ship far from here. You may ask his father. Your Uncle Louis will be far better advised."

"May we go inside the ship, Papa?" Corazon asked.

"If it pleases your uncle, Cori, yes, you may. Isabel," he continued, turning to his wife, "I have business. I'll return within the hour to take you to the harbor."

Leaving the villa, O'Ryan tilted his broad brimmed hat to protect his ruddy skin from the low morning sun, and walked quickly up Obispo to the office of the attorney who acted as his agent in Havana. Papers were ready and he would sign them promptly, finalizing the sale of thousands of acres. He was disposing of his sugar fields and most of his holdings in Santa Clara province. The present value was not high, but he expected the land to become worthless in a few short months. The same money could eventually buy back ten times what he sold. It was obvious that another revolution could begin any day, and this transaction was merely good business. As a boy, Douglas O'Ryan had learned that land was a poor investment when a war was being fought on it. In 1865, his family's Georgetown plantation had been sacked and burned by Federal troops. The fields, with no hands to work them, had already gone back to swamp. Only his grandfather's British investments had given his family the foothold needed to rebuild after the war.

If you were to question honor, the O'Ryan's of 1861 were as gallant and honorable as any family in South Carolina.

Three of his brothers died honorably in the war, a fourth was blinded at Gettysburg. His father had lost an arm at Lookout Mountain, and his cousins lay buried from Georgia to Pennsylvania. As an eleven-year-old, Douglas O'Ryan had dreamed of riding out to join his brothers. By his sixteenth year, the hardships and his quiet observation of the war's effects had given him a pragmatic outlook. O'Ryan had become both cynical and mature. Loyal support of the Confederacy had led to the near destruction of family and fortune, and provided lessons that he had learned well. There was a great deal of profit to be had in a war, providing you did not become personally involved. In the ensuing thirty years, he had, indeed, profited greatly from the national conflicts of others.

Separation from conflict was another of his rules. Arrangements were already made, tickets for his wife and daughter's passage north to Georgetown, South Carolina. They would enjoy the Carolina spring with family and friends, while the island of Cuba engulfed itself in its latest war of liberation.

The reunion with Louis was a pleasant one. They were escorted about the gunboat, before enjoying sweet cakes and coffee in Captain Vega's small cabin. Having pursued and destroyed a notorious filibuster, the *Eclipse,* Louis was in good spirits. The Governor General planned a reception for his officers tomorrow, and these sorts of successes did not harm an officer's career.

"Will your ship remain in Havana, Louis?" O'Ryan asked.

"For a short time only, I am afraid, and then we shall be returning to Cadiz, sailing by way of Bermuda and Madeira." A junior officer approached with a note, and Louis glanced at it and nodded. "We will remain a week, perhaps two, in Havana, replenishing coal and provisions," he said, and glancing at his son's picture added, "I look forward to seeing

Hermon soon."

"Uncle," Corazon interrupted. "Might we see Hermon also?" She continued speaking, ignoring her mother's glare of disapproval. "Robert was with us for the summer, but Hermon has been away so long."

"God knows!" Louis smiled, his eyes looking upward, "In a few months your cousin leaves the academy, he goes to new duties. He will be aboard a ship for two years. He becomes a man and an officer," Louis explained. "Where life will lead him, I could only guess." He paused, smiled again, "A father can only hope."

"Home, I would hope," Isabel said. "Father said often, 'A man, who is well with his family, is well with his duties'."

A steward poured wine, and Louis toasted as they raised their glasses. "Family!"

The O'Ryans had just returned home, for the midday rest, when Carlos Vega arrived from Matanzas with his family. There was a clatter in the courtyard.

"They are here, *Señora*!" a servant's voice shouted.

Corazon hurried past her sister, coming out first into the courtyard to greet her cousins. There was the usual ordered confusion: Grooms attended the horses, the carriage was unloaded, maids took the baggage, and the family women embraced.

"Come first for refreshments," Isabel invited, "then you can all go to your rooms for rest. Louis will be arriving later, so you must take time to look your best."

As at any family gathering, the girls all began to talk at once. Cousin Pilar, very gay, soon commanded the younger girls' attention with her descriptions of the balls and dinners she had attended throughout the winter season. The oldest of the Vega girls, Pilar was the first to enter society, and her father had already been approached by two young men who

35

had begged permission to court her.

"There are so few good families in Santa Clara," Pilar complained. "I wish we could stay in Havana where there is always some occasion of state, requiring a ball." She clapped her hands and gasped, "Wait until you see my new gown! Papa had it sent from Paris. It arrived only this week, and I'll wear it to the Governor's reception tomorrow."

"Oh! Pilar, when may we see it?" Esmeralda exclaimed excitedly.

The very mention of one of the Governor's balls set all the girls to dreaming of the glitter, the elaborate gowns, and the young men who would attend. They would dance the *danzon*, the *guajira, habañera*, and *zapateo*. Corazon, who was not old enough to attend, felt a twinge of jealous anger and succumbed to it.

"Papa says there will be less to celebrate soon," Corazon said matter-of-factually.

Her cousins looked at her perplexed, and Esmeralda openly frowned at her sister, whose comment she felt was meant to dampen everyone's mood.

It's true," Corazon continued in a very superior manner, "Papa said the political problems have become insufferable. I heard him say to Senor Costa that there will soon be trouble. War! All the men will be away fighting then."

Pilar, angry at the unpleasantness callously tossed upon what had been a moment of frivolity, hissed at Esmeralda, "Can't you make her be quiet?"

"You know even mama can't shut her up," Esmeralda complained.

"It's only true," Corazon said stubbornly, thrusting out her chin, "and anyone who marries will soon be a widow, and widows sit around in black. They do not get to dance. I had a dream about it. Pia said the dream meant there would be sadness."

"You're horrid," Rosa said shocked. "We will all have good husbands and we will not become widows -- no matter what some mulatto witch says. It will be difficult for your father, the poor man, to find you a decent husband. You are so unpleasant, Corazon. If you cannot be pleasant, you should leave us."

"Yes, just go," Pilar, agreed, and turned her back.

"I will choose my own husband, thank you!" Corazon snapped, green flecks flashing in her deep blue eyes. "I leave only because I find you all foolish." She tossed her dark hair and marched out, feeling furious. She knew she had no right to feel furious. She had been boorish and ill tempered. It would be impossible to admit this, of course, and she wondered why she did such things. She only spoiled things for herself.

The women soon retired and the house became quiet. Louis arrived and the men sat with cigars in the villa's central garden to discuss business. Above them, on the balcony of her room, Corazon lay in a light cotton slip. Enjoying the cool afternoon breeze, she listened to the conversation of the men. She found what they discussed far more interesting than the drivel offered when the women were together. After all, it was men that controlled the world.

"I must disagree," Carlos was saying, "Spain will never give up her last colonies. In addition, the Army is very modern now. Rebels would not have it easy."

"My dear Carlos," O'Ryan said, beginning to lecture, "They need neither ease, nor success to destroy profits. The disruption is enough. When our fields' burn and workers are not on hand, there is no profit. People fear, they flee, and the value of land falls."

"What difference is the value of the land?" Carlos said.

"We own it and work it. Our wealth flows from the land, not from the land's value. We are the land"

"That may be," said O'Ryan, "but it's far better business to hold the core of your property, and to buy and sell the land around it." He took a drink of iced tea, and continued. "I've sold fifteen thousand acres today. Experience tells me it will hold but a tenth of its value at year's end. I can purchase land again, but when I do, I will be able to buy ten times as much for the same money. Until then, the money will work for me in other ways."

"Land value will never fall so low."

"I doubt I'm wrong, but I won't lose a cent. However, the war goes, I will profit."

"Even if you're correct," Louis said quietly, "it would be dishonorable for me to act in such a manner, to show such a lack of resolve. After all, I bear the King's commission."

"Loyalty to the throne Louis -- what's it to do with success outside your duties?"

"You are not Spanish, Douglas. You have no understanding of honor."

O'Ryan bristled and frowned. He began to speak.

"Wait," Carlos interceded. "No offense is meant. We are from different parts, different countries. There is simply a different understanding of honor, a difference of the heart concerning these things," he said, attempting to soothe tempers.

"This is true, I suppose," O'Ryan said. "Nonetheless, I plan to spend some time in Georgetown until events here become more certain. I don't wish Isabel and the girls exposed to the dangers and unpleasantness of a revolution."

"It won't touch us," Louis said with confidence. "What can rabble do?"

"I was here in the last revolt," O'Ryan reminded him

soberly. "War touches everyone."

Louis argued arrogantly. Carlos, on the other hand, conceded that danger might exist for their families as it had in the Ten-Year-War. Soon conversation moved to other matters.

Corazon's mind raced off in an entirely different direction: Georgetown, visits to Charleston, Atlanta, and the great cities of the North. There would be fine entertainment, different kinds of music, friends who saw things as she did; a world where there was freedom. She much preferred the freedom and energy of the mainland to the island's provincial conformity and strange pinched morality. Here nothing was new; nothing changed.

Esmeralda and Mama would not be pleased. This wasn't speculation on Corazon's part, it was experience. Her older sister and mother preferred the island to the mainland. Her mother whined shamelessly whenever she was away from the Matanzas estate or separated from her Cuban relatives. If the decision were her mother's, they would not even visit Havana; not if it meant parting with the other Vegas.

Esmeralda, eleven months older than Corazon, had already had her *quince* -- her fifteenth birthday celebration. Having joined adult society last summer, she now was considered a woman. Corazon would be fifteen in April, and certainly, her Aunt Samantha would arrange for Corazon to come out in Charleston. Mama would argue, but Samantha would convince her. Corazon held herself. Eyes closed, she pictured Aunt Samantha's home in Charleston. She imagined herself dancing, imagined balls and beaus. Mama would have objections over Spanish tradition, but papa would see that she enjoyed herself. Corazon was his favorite, and she used this knowledge scandalously.

Corazon had slipped into a light slumber when explosions jarred Havana. Shouting and confusion accompanied the scattered popping of gunfire. Down the hall, the cousins were screaming, "and Isabel rushed to Corazon's room followed by a frightened Esmeralda.

Awake and smiling, Corazon blurted out, "Papa was right! It must be a war."

Chapter 3

He woke with the sun well up and in his eyes. Immediately, he shaded them with a hand, and peered toward La Fe, where small buildings, on the far side of town still smoldered. People, could be seen walking, moving here and there. Only one schooner remained anchored offshore. He wondered at the scarcity of vessels at anchor. It was then he noticed bodies hanging from net racks on the beach. He counted at least a dozen. What stunned him was what he did not see: the *Eclipse*'s boat.

Asher sighed. With revolution breaking out, and violent death in the town, it was only sensible that the castaways would make a hasty departure. He blamed them not for leaving, but rather, cursed the circumstance, of not being able to accompany them. Although hungry and thirsty, Asher, was in no way tempted to enter La Fe. He decided to re-cross the river, to make his way east on the coast. He would keep moving until he found another town or a boat, which could be bought or hired. His uncle's gold watch and fob were equal to more than a year's wages to Cuban boatmen. He would work something out.

Putting his back to the town, Asher began a determined march north along the coast. He forded the Rio Guadiana and followed a meandering foot trail up into the hills. Finding a tiny farm in the first small valley, he was able to buy a meal for a few pennies and learn the distance to the next nearest coastal village. Though he was told two small villages, the farmer assured him, Los Arroyos, some fifteen miles north, was the nearest place of any size. Asher continued north, winding through steep hills and crossing several valleys planted in tobacco. A low range of worn mountains spanned the coast, and the road twisted its way up into them. Climbing steadily, Asher reached the crest in late afternoon. Off to his left glittered the clean blue of the sea, and five miles down slope were the tile and thatch roofs of Los Arroyos.

He arrived in the town before dusk, and found it rife with rumors of the insurrection. Talk in the market was both fearful and excited, for Jose Marti and the great generals, were reported to land any day. People held these reports to be fact, even though no one knew exactly when or where.

Smiling and showing their legs, girls flirted from the door of a cantina. Feeling lusty, Asher smiled back but remembering he was in mourning, he continued through the market. Soon he found a vendor who needed a machete, and traded his for several loaves of bread and a few small coins. Consuming a loaf immediately, he purchased a tin can of well-sweetened coffee to wash it down.

Satisfied, he wandered along the harbor front, sipping and thinking about the girls. There were no large vessels at anchor; however, there were numerous small fishing boats moored or beached, boats that were rigged to sail. Tired, he chose a place beneath an overhang of rock and sat. He hung his loaves in a scrap of discarded net, and lay in the soft sand to sleep.

In predawn gloom, he woke. Two small children squatted

in the sand, peering at him. They giggled and ran when his eyes opened. All about the beach, men of Los Arroyos were preparing boats for sea by lantern light. Stretching, Asher rose to his feet, brushed off sand and slipped on his boots. Retrieving the sack of bread, he broke another loaf and munched slowly, using the long part to swat at flies. Barefoot men stood about a lean-to, built against the harbor wall. They drank coffee from tin cans. Asher bought coffee for himself, and as a faint glow appeared in the East, he listened to the fish talk. When there was a pause, he spoke.

"Pardon, but does anyone know of a boat for sale"?

"What sort of boat?" an older man asked.

A tall *pescador* stepped closer, inquired, "How big?"

"Like these," Asher answered, pointing along the beach. "Eighteen, maybe twenty foot," he told the tall fisherman.

"With sail?" a young man asked.

"Sail and oars, good on the wind," Asher specified.

There was a short general discussion, concerning who had an extra boat, followed by a short debate on what boats might be sold. Asher sipped coffee, paying close attention to the talk.

A young man looked over his shoulder asked, "How much will you pay?"

"I want to see it first," Asher, countered.

"I have a good boat, a fine sailor," the young man offered.

"May I see it?" Asher repeated, making a slight gesture with one hand.

The older man spit, waved his disdain at the young man saying, "You're foolish, Lucas, better to keep the boat." He walked away mumbling words of disgust.

Fishermen were wandering away. The sky would become light soon, and they had yet to launch their boats. Lucas shrugged and pointed to the left. He led the way down the beach to where his boat lay, and then stood back while Asher surveyed it by lantern light. It was a good boat, new, nineteen-foot long, with a six-foot beam, and its shallow keel ran full-length. There was an un-stayed mast, with a gaff rig sail and two pair of oars. The un-shipped rudder lay in the stern. He liked its lines and could find little fault with it.

"What would you pay?" Lucas asked, his hand affectionately stroking the gunnels.

"All I have," Asher answered, pulling the fob and chain from his pocket, letting it swing and glitter in the lamplight.

"Gold," Lucas gasped, bending forward to see it better.

"Yes, gold," Asher affirmed. He wiped some of the wax off to bring up the shine.

"You're Yankee?" the Cuban asked, "Why do you need a boat?"

"To get home," Asher answered. "Florida."

"Ah," Lucas said. "Why not take passage from up the coast, Havana? It costs little."

"The revolution worries me," Asher said. "On the road, men can die without reason."

Barefooted in the coral sand, Lucas walked down the boat's side. His face was serious when he turned back. "The revolution is why I sell the boat. I am a patriot. I join Marti."

"A deal, then," Asher said, both wary of, and uninterested in the man's politics.

"A deal," Lucas agreed, and accepting the chain and fob, he moved off across the sand, toward a place where boats lay upturned for repairs.

Feeling a nagging guilt, at having traded away his uncle's possessions, Asher walked the other way, toward the market, thinking that at least he had the watch. The pale light of dawn warmed the eastern sky. It was cool, not light enough for shadows, but already, in the market, produce lay out for sale. He traded some of the boats unneeded gear and nets. With his small coins, he bought a stalk of plantains, coconuts and a few mangoes. He spent only enough for those items and a few of pounds of rice. With a little luck fishing, he expected to eat well enough. He squandered the last Spanish penny on another cup of coffee.

In spite of the preceding week's tragedies, he found a moment of enjoyment, drinking as he watched a pretty girl hang laundry. When a man is eighteen, women are never far from his thoughts but returning to the shore, Asher's mind focused on the Florida Straits.

With the help of Lucas and other men, the boat was launched, and Asher's meager stores, passed aboard. Asher pushed off into deeper water, lashed the oars to the thole pins and shipped his rudder. He hoisted the sail, but the dawn was calm. Standing, he dipped his oars, and thrusting in slow sweeps, began to row out from the beach.

"*Adios,*" they called out to him.

Soon he caught the first of the shore winds, coming off the mountains. Riding them over the calm flats, toward the Gulf Stream, he felt a rise in his confidence. Here, at sea, he understood what he faced. The sea had no concern for man, no awareness of humanity. It was treacherous, but also straightforward. It simply was.

He judged Key West to be some two hundred miles across the straits from Arroyos. After that, to reach Ft Myers, only an easy run up the West Coast remained. He peeled a plantain and ate with satisfaction. Flying fish, in a swarm, left the water pursued by a large predator. The boat cleared the outer reef, and the water turned dark, almost purple. Yellow-orange Sargasso weed spun on the surface, marking the inshore current, and tangling any Portuguese man-of-war,

44

which chanced to drift too close. The trades blew from the east, and the boat sailed well, very well, slipping along to weather at five knots. He caught a nice king-fish, ate some, then cut strips to dry.

That night, in the middle of the Gulf Stream, Asher dropped sail and let the boat be carried East by the current while he slept. He woke nearly thirty miles closer to the Keys -- and to windward at that. During the morning, the trade winds increased, strengthening to a degree that the straits north of Bahia Hondo became purely nasty. The east wind opposed the current, giving waves a short steep crest. With reefed sail, Asher steered north. The wind gusted and he became frustrated having to bail every time a crest broke aboard or the boat dipped a rail under. Down came the sail and out went a canvas drogue.

The boat was being borne east by the great sea current, Held bow to wind by the drogue and pulled by the current, it leaped and plunged all day. Asher napped, bailed when necessary and chewed coconut. When dawn came again, the wind had eased some and veered south. To the northwest, the sky was full of mares' tails, which meant a norther by late night. He believed himself to be south of the western Keys, perhaps south of Rebecca Shoal. With no more than forty miles to the Florida reefs and wind aft the beam, he would be on the banks tonight. If not, he'd be wishing he were.

Several steamships passed far out, for he saw their smoke. He also spied the tops of sailors, bound northeast in the straits. Near dusk, the wind veered around southwest, and built but by then he could see the lighthouse off Key West. When dark clouds and a cold wind, came howling from the north, Asher was holed up in the lee of Sand Key. He stretched out on the sand, thankful of the wind that kept the gnats away. He listened to the surf and considered the loss and the gain of the past weeks. His uncle Connor and the family ship were gone but he was alive and whole.

It appeared to him that life was less a matter of chance, than of choice. Fate was fate, but the proper choices increased the odds of survival, and a soul must survive to succeed. He chooses -- or chooses not -- to accept risk. He chooses to do good, or ill. Asher vowed to remember that to survive and prosper; a man must make thoughtful decisions; no choice was unimportant.

Under a brilliant blue and cloudless sky, Asher entered the harbor of Key West, tacking into a fresh northeast wind. The harbor was thick with sponge boats, many in port due to the blustery weather. The air coming down from them was heavy with the stench of sponge rot. Sailing quickly through the anchorage, Asher was close on the naval station by the time he got to windward of the odious fleet. He took note of the U.S. Navy cruiser *Newark* alongside the wharf, and farther up the line, sailed past the Havana steamer where she lay at her berth.

Eventually he ran his skiff up alongside a tobacco pier. Canvas flapping, Asher hurried forward, tying off to a piling. He had the sail down in a moment, and vaulted up onto the dock with a burst of youthful exuberance. No one noticed. The conclusion of his intrepid voyage attracted no attention. It was merely one more skiff sailing up to the busy pier.

Numerous people crowded the wharf. Wherever he looked, someone was engaged in profitable industry. Amidst the hubbub, a café adjacent the dock attracted Asher's attention, for the smell of food cooking drew him from the wharf like a magnet. At the open kitchen, he parted with the last of his coins, spending the five cents on a plate of eggs and grits, with coffee. Glancing at an open newspaper, his eyes were drawn to an article wired by the Havana correspondent of the *Times*.

'It is known here, that an American ship, the Steam Schooner Eclipse, landed an armed expedition west of Cienfuegos. The Eclipse was reported to have been overtaken at sea, by a ship of the Spanish Navy' and sunk with all hands'.

Asher's first emotion was mirth. "Don't feel dead," he joked with himself, "may smell dead, though." He had, of course, no news concerning of the fate of his shipmates. This brought on a twinge of remorse. Knowledge that he shared a responsibility for them sobered him somewhat. Finishing his meal, he wandered about the docks, inquiring to see if anyone had news of *Eclipse's* longboat. In the process, he came across the steam schooner, *Miriam Valdez*, out of Punta Rasa. It was a vessel, whose owner was well acquainted with the Byran family. She was anchored a hundred yards offshore and returning to his skiff, Asher rowed out to her.

On deck, there was hammering, footsteps, and the murmur of voices. He bumped alongside, swiftly tying the painter off to a chain plate and boating the oars.

Before Asher could hail the deck, a man's angry face, glowered over the rail. He let go a torrent of words, so closely spaced as to offer no chance to address him until choking on his own phlegm, the man hawked and spit, allowing Asher to get in a word.

"Is Captain Wilcox aboard, sir, and if so, might you please pass to him that Asher Byran is alongside and wishes to pay his respects?"

"*Quein,* who'd you say?"

"Asher Byran, second mate of the *Eclipse*. Our families are acquainted, sir."

"Damn! I thought you was a dam shore skiff, here sneaking' rum on board. Only got the crew sobered up, and working dis morning," the mate explained. "I'll tell the Cop'n. Come aboard, if you want."

Before climbing up on deck, Asher wet his hair and beard, running his fingers through it, in order to look less wild in appearance. The captain greeted Asher with a broad smile and a look of pleasurable surprise. Wilcox was a tall man, grayed, with a weathered face. Like the Byrans, he had migrated from South Carolina after the war.

"Ash," he said, "Just read in the papers, y'all were dead. Glad to see it was an exaggeration." He shook Asher's hand, beckoning toward his cabin, and said, "Come, have some coffee and tell me the news."

Asher sat opposite Wilcox, with a mug of coffee and said, "Papers weren't all wrong, sir -- *Eclipse* is sunk sure enough. All hands abandoned her quick like, dark of night in a rain-squall. We were running full steam and dodging shellfire. Lost sight of the port boat, and Uncle Connor caught a shell splinter coming away."

"Not mortal, I hope," Wilcox said, with concern.

"Should not have been, sir," Asher said solemnly, "but it mortified in the longboat. We landed him in Cuba, but he passed on during surgery."

"How did this all come about?" Wilcox asked with saddened voice.

Asher took a deep breath, and for the better part of an hour, related the voyage, describing events beginning at Apalachicola, to his arrival in the Keys. He expressed his wish to break the news to his Aunt Fay, or at least to console her, if she had already learned of Uncle Connor's death.

Wilcox informed him that his ship had discharged cattle in Matanzas three days previous, and had sailed from Cuba with tobacco. Most of the tobacco was ashore already, and the *Miriam Valdez* would depart for Punta Rasa that afternoon. Wilcox would gladly carry Asher and his skiff. Meanwhile, he suggested sending a telegram to Fort Myers. With the newspapers already circulating stories of the *Eclipse*'s loss, Wilcox's suggestion seemed a good one. With the loan of some money, Asher had returned to the island and wired a short message to his aunt.

When on the following morning, the *Miriam Valdez* docked at Punta Rasa, Asher's boat was put off too clear the hatch. Soon drovers were forcing cattle out onto the pier for loading. Asher thanked Captain Wilcox, and accepted a letter of condolence for his Aunt Fay. His beard trimmed short and wearing clean clothes; he boarded his skiff. The wind being fair, Asher sailed the ten miles up the Caloosahatchee in a few hours. He guided the skiff into a creek, three miles below Fort Myers, tying off to his uncle's dock. Looking as presentable as possible, he began the walk to the house. As he walked, Asher practiced what he would say to his aunt.

Shrubbery and grass had overgrown the river trail in the past month. The grass brushed up past his ankles. As he walked, a rattler, coiled somewhere ahead warned, the whir of its tail causing a soft racket. Asher tossed a broken limb into the general area and caught a flicker of motion as the snake retreated into the palmetto. Suddenly, he was in no hurry to reach the house, and picked his way cautiously, finally stopping behind the drooping limbs of a great live oak. A gray-green curtain of Spanish moss screened him from the road and house beyond. Its long, delicate streamers offered the privacy to watch and think a bit before going in. A cool, dry north wind filtered through into the dark shade. A plump black boy ran along the road, rolling a barrel hoop with a stick. His face showed both enjoyment and concentration. Laundry baskets piled around her, his mother yelled at him from the pump house.

"Jinks, you rascal, get you self over here on dis pump. Come on for I tans you hide, boy. Come on, I's ain't got all day

49

for fooling."

"Comin', ma'am," the boy called back.

Spinning abruptly and ducking under the fence, he ran. The hoop continued a way, slowing and toppling in deep grass near the gate. Tess, Aunt Fay's cook, appeared on the porch with a glass and a pitcher of tea. Bending, she placed them on a table and hurried back inside. Asher watched as his aunt appeared through French doors. She sat on a white wicker chair, smoothing her white dress. Promptly, Tess returned with a tray of pastries, and Fay carefully chose one.

She has not heard! Asher knew this subconsciously in numerous ways: her expressions, her voice, the way she moved, her wearing a white dress, not black. He-- must be the one to tell her.

He recognized, in himself that he was a coward in this respect. He found he could not bring forth the necessary vestige of courage to cross the road. He quietly stood watching her as he thought the thoughts of death's inevitability. A profound silence overcame him, and it occurred to him that the unfairness of death laid not with the dead, but with the living. They were the ones duty bound to cope with a changed world, the ones who must adjust, fill the empty places in their lives, and struggle on. He knew it was up to him to tell her, but he could not bring himself to step out of the trees. Therefore, hard put to accomplish his duty, he stood a while longer.

Eventually, mustering determination into himself, Asher strode out onto the road, crossing it in a few steps, and pushing open the gate. Fay saw him then, and a warm smile came to her face as she began to rise. He plowed ahead, as would a doomed soldier, advancing into the maws of cannon.

"Oh, my, Tess, come look," she cried into the house, "it's Asher come home!"

Fay was a far different woman than the girl who had come

south from Charleston twenty-seven years before, yet in her, the demeanor of a southern lady remained unaltered. Her dress was high-collared and crisp, her hair was done up with turtle shell combs, and a gold locket hung at her breast. She advanced with quick steps across the porch, still gracefully erect at fifty but she smiled from a line laced face. These years had been difficult for a woman on the harsh Florida frontier.

"Hello, Auntie," Asher said awkwardly, as he stooped to accept her embrace.

"Ash, dear, come sit and have some tea," she said gaily and turned back to the porch chairs. "I heard no whistles. Y'all have slipped in on us, quiet like."

He sat, as she had, taking a quick breath before saying, "Were no whistles from the *Eclipse*, Aunt Fay." He continued blunt, straight ahead, not allowing his voice to falter. "She's lost, some twelve days past, ma'am, and Uncle Connor, five days after. He's buried in Cuba, ma'am, in the town of Guane, in a churchyard, with a mass said."

He paused as the words settled in her mind. Reaching out, he placed the gold wedding ring, watch and locket on the table.

"I had to trade the watch fob for a boat ma'am. I am sorry for that. Uncle Connor might have mended if I'd thought how to get him to a doctor sooner, ma'am. I take the responsibility for that," he added.

She seemed for a moment not to understand, but cocked her head. Her mouth parted ever so slightly, and he continued, for he must make it clear.

"Uncle Connor's dead, ma'am. Of ship and crew, I'm all that's returned. I'm terrible sorry."

He could not have predicted how she responded to this news. Fay leaned back in her chair jarring it, angrily folded her arms hard against her, and rocked ever so slightly. "I always knew this would happen one day," she said spitefully, "more so when we first married, but then I held the hope of children to comfort me."

Asher sat uncomfortably, uncertain of what to say.

"God's will!" she sighed. "My sweet children were taken, Ash, as were your parents and older sisters. I nursed them, I prayed, and I watched them all suffer and die miserably, and for what?" Her face took on a hard look as she said, "If they were gonna keep to the sea, Connor and your daddy -- they should never a brought Christine and I down to this green hell."

She looked up at Asher and snapped, "Growing oranges in a place where hurricanes and pests do more damage than the cold does further north. God knows, you cannot be off at sea and expect a plantation to prosper. A pure waste is what it has been Ash, a waste of youth, of life, and of resources. The world has advanced beyond this backwater; wonderful things have been accomplished, while I have languished in this wilderness. Your life, too, for y'all shoulda been brought up properly among your own people. If you had been around your mother's people from birth, they would of warmed to y'all soon enough. They would have forgotten your mother eloped and married against your grandpa's wishes. It's separation that makes the heart hard -- separation. You remember that Ash, 'cause going off with unresolved problems is like neglecting the weeding of your garden. Soon y'all can't find the crops for the weeds."

"Aunt Fay," he asked, "Could I do anything for you? Maybe I could fetch Father Paul out to the house?"

"It's no matter now, Ash. Truth be known, I've been a widow each time Connor went to sea." She said this with resignation. "I'm used to it! Least way, now I won't have to worry no more."

"Yes, ma'am."

"You're acquainted with Horace Jackson?"

"Yes, ma'am, he's Uncle Connor's attorney. His place is on the river west of town, just east of Mr. Edison's estate."

"Well, you saddle a horse and go tell him that I'd be pleased to have him here at his first opportunity. If he's not to be found at home, seek him out at the courthouse, and direct him to be prompt. Assure him that any efforts in my service will pay handsomely."

"Yes, ma'am," Asher said, standing.

"And Ash, change into proper clothes. You're a man of eighteen years, and you've become the gentleman of the Byran estate, the last Byran of your line. How you look and carry on your affairs will reflect on the both of us. Best if you'd become more concerned with appearances."

He could only nod quietly and go around to the barn. He saddled up before changing his clothes, and soon was riding toward Fort Myers. Glad for something to do, Asher was, today at least, thankful for someone to tell him what to do. The week that followed Asher's return had all the effect of an earthquake, shifting the bedrock of his life, and tilting him in a new direction. The attorney had arrived at the appointed time on Tuesday past; the will was read, and family finances and interests made plain. Widowed, Fay had far more than her home, and three thousand acres of overgrown citrus plantation. She also had a modest fortune in various stocks and certificates.

Asher's inheritance from his parents amounted to an additional four thousand acres, as well as twelve-thousand-dollars in treasury bonds. All would come to him at his twenty-first birthday. If not a vast fortune, it was a notable sum. Few were favored to start life with as much. The growth of this fortune would depend on his enterprise and abilities.

Fay Byran put her properties up for sale within the week, and made immediate plans for a return to the bosom of her South Carolina family. It would be Asher's responsibility, to see the house closed and the furniture shipped, before taking a train north to join her. He understood that soon, he'd be introduced to the Wallace s, his mother's people, and that Aunt Fay planned to enroll him in a military college where friendships of the right sort would be formed. Fay had counseled that learning to speak less like a cracker, and more like a young gentleman, would not harm his prospects in life either. Asher was also to forget about ships, at least so far as Fay Byran was concerned. Short of outright rebellion, on Asher's part, there seemed no clear way out of Aunt Fay's plans for his immediate future.

With the last of his aunt's belongings freighted out, and the house closed, Asher found himself balking. The prospect of being among strangers, who would make decisions for him, was unsettling. The Wallaces -- certainly, they were family -- but he sensed the reunion would affect his freedom profoundly. Rather than take a train north, he decided to prolong his independence by taking the road. He telegraphed his intentions to Charleston and departed before a return message could forbid a change of plans.

Chapter 4

It was cool March weather, with good winds to blow away mosquitoes, and Asher horse was full of go. East of Ft. Myers, he fell in with an outfit of young cowboys, riding north from Punta Rasa. A wild night in a bawdy house left the six young men sickly and pale but they brightened as the whiskey wore off. Two of the herders were brothers; three others were cousins. With the exception of the sixth man, they had grown up together in the Peace River Valley to the north. The sixth man, Gabe Spear was plainly not kin. He was a blue-eyed carrot top, a touch over five and a half foot of lean gristle that only seemed even tempered. He came from a bit farther, up-state, near Dunnellon. All were employed herding beef down to the port of Punta Rasa, the shipping point for Cuba, and each had Spanish gold doubloons jingling in his pocket. With the Cuban insurrection beginning anew, future employment for a cowboy promised to be regular.

"Ain't gonna be round for a bit, boys," Gabe Spear announced. "Goin' up home, for to visit my folks. Gal up there', I aim to court."

"That's about it, boys," said the cousin, "Old Gabe ain't riding no hundred miles for kin."

"Might do lil courting myself," Mike announced preening.

"Y'all mooning round that Lucy Walsh yet? Ah reckoned y'all was shed of thet hussy."

"I'll thank y'all to shut ya mouth, lil brother."

"Lucy, hear y'all was lickered up, and sporting with whores, she be the one quitting y'all."

Mike swung out with the butt of his whip, knocking his brother's straw hat off.

"Aye! Ya low down dog," he cursed, jutting his chin. "Is it

gonna be you what's telling her, ya low snake?"

"Hey! Was just ragging on ya, hey. That's all."

Asher swung low, snatching the hat off the road. He passed it to the man who nodded his thanks.

"Don't mind that bunch," Gabe called out, "them is naturally scraping all the time."

They crossed the Caloosahatchee River by ferry, riding out into pine and palmetto country. Herds of cattle, being driven south, had beaten down the vegetation. The boys began the sport of popping snakes, caught in the open, with their bullwhips. Asher was invited to give it a try. He provided a good laugh when he cracked his own mount up under the belly and got bucked off.

Twice they passed southbound herds. His companions, yahoo-ed, waving and joking with acquaintances. Asher rode mostly listening to them talk about work and cattle. He picked up more than a little of how the Florida cattle business functioned.

By late afternoon, they rode into Arcadia. The four local boys cut loose heading for their homes, while Asher and Gabe put up for the night in a boardinghouse. Dinner at the long table was plentiful, and afterward, there was a card game at the saloon in which Asher won a little. Moonshine made the rounds and the company was friendly enough, but when the stakes rose beyond comfort, they gave quit to the game.

Walking back to the boarding house, they talked about their destinations and agreed to make the ride as far as Dunnellon together. Gabe, who had ridden up into Georgia a few times, suggested that if Asher intended to travel clean up into the Carolinas, he'd best ride due north, cross the Suwanee, and then keep it to his right. He should get well up into Georgia before going east. This route was not only pleasant but would avoid the Okefenokee swamp and the many rivers on the south-east coast.

Gabe turned in, but restless, Asher wandered up the street. He'd spied a sporting establishment and was looking for some female comfort. He did in fact, entertain so much comfort that Gabe had to kick him awake in the morning. Asher had little to say through breakfast.

While saddling up, Gabe slipped his Winchester into the saddle boot and inquired, "Shoot much?"

"Some," Asher answered.

"Where your headed, It would be right smart of y'all, to carry a pistol or leastwise a shotgun," Gabe said, swinging up into the saddle. "There's more trash, white and black alike, twixt here and there than snakes."

"Be safe enough without, I'd think."

"Ain't no such thing, fella. Y'all being a gentleman, and from other parts, I wouldn't 'spec' y'all to know. Take Marion County where I be from. Ain't safe for a decent woman out alone."

"Why's that?"

"Dam'd phosphate mines." Gabe reined his gelding around. "Boom-towns," he said with disgust. "Four, five years back, was right nice. Some fool found phosphate, and went to digging. Ore started and they digged up the whole dam'd county. Couldn't find 'nu-ff labor fur to dig, so they sent trains all over hell, gathering up whatever no count white trash, drunk or nigger, didn't have no work. Now we got shantytowns all over. Every street got a blind tiger."

"What's a blind tiger?" Asher asked.

"Ain't y'all the lily-white innocent?" Gabe laughed.

"Not entirely," Asher said, feeling a bit put upon, for he was acquainted with some of the world's wicked places, and did not considering himself a Greene. "Just not familiar with the expression," he explained.

57

"Sells moonshine, sells women, has gambling, and is best described as a preacher's nightmare. They operate right in town: gunfights, cuttings, lynching. It's sad; thet's what it is. Sheriff, he runs a big share of it through his kin. Lot-ta money made thar fella. I just druther earn mah wages down this way."

"Well I can see that," Asher said," still men are going to drink and sport; somebody's gonna provide for it. Folks seeking profits for their trouble, it's only normal."

"It's away past that, fella. M'ought be best to see it for yourself, hey."

They camped that evening near Plant City, on a lake adjacent to strawberry fields. The land had gone from flat shrub to low hills and the pines had given way to live oak. They cooked grits, smoked ham, and drank some coffee. Gabe took to boasting concerning marksmanship. With his rifle, he fired off several shots at a stick thrown into the lake. Woods creatures, scampered excitedly, and in panicked flight, hundreds of water birds launched themselves into the pale orange sky. He smiled at the closely grouped splashes.

"Mind if I take a whack at it?" Asher asked.

"If y'all like."

Taking the Winchester, Asher wet the sight, chambered a round and sited on a stick about 50 yards out in the lake. He fired once, the splash was slightly right and below the stick.

"You like duck, I hope," Asher boasted, and correcting, he aimed overhead at one of the wheeling ducks. He led him carefully and fired once, then again; dropping two birds onto the lake-shore.

"Thet's some whacking there, fella," Gabe said appreciatively.

"I used to hunt real regular, but I only had a single shot rifle. It makes you careful."

"How y'all with a pistol?"

"Couldn't hit a wall at twenty foot," Asher admitted. "Never did get a chance to practice."

"Takes practice."

"Ya, I suppose. Mostly, I hunted with shotgun or rifle," he added. He walked over to collect the birds. "I like the taste of duck," he said squatting to retrieve a bird.

It went cold during the night. Twice, Asher dragged logs to the fire, and he woke to a dank, gray day. Continuing north, through low hills and a few orange groves, they lunched on cold duck. After riding all afternoon in the rain, fording the Hillsborough River got them no wetter than the constant drizzle already had. Considering they'd spent the day cold and wet through by the rain, both were ready for a night in a Brooksville boardinghouse. Twice that evening, hard-pressed planters stopped by the boardinghouse seeking labor to burn smudge fires in their groves, but all the willing men had long since been hired.

Dawn was crisp and cold and frost sparkled in the morning's first light. In the chill air, the horses were frisky, taking a while to settle down. Beams of light bore through the great oaks and long shadows played across the leaf-carpeted road. First sign of the phosphate industry was a train south of Inverness. Behind a Tampa-bound locomotive, Asher counted twenty high-piled cars. Gabe informed him that it was nothing compared to what went out to the Cedar Keys.

Not far beyond the rails, they began to encounter stretches of tree-stripped land. Land -- not just stripped -- but scraped ten foot deep. New railroad spurs crisscrossed the deeply rutted road. Piles of half-burned trees lined miles of shallow pits. Here and there on the sites, miners had thrown up shantytowns, but Dunnellon itself was worse than Asher had imagined. With no drainage system, the streets were a quagmire of mud and sewage. Hogs wandered unbothered through the town, competing with dogs and varmints for the ample garbage. To walk without stepping in waste was difficult.

Saturday was a payday afternoon and long lines of workers, most of them armed, stood waiting their turns to purchase supplies from local merchants. A white body hung from an oak in the town square. Segregated even in death, three black bodies dangled across the street. From open doors, music and laughter rose above the noise of freight wagons. Whores waved from windows.

"What y'all think ah my hometown?" Gabe asked sarcastically, as his horse sidestepped a fistfight that had tumbled into the street.

"I can see where a preacher would find this place challenging," Asher remarked, for as he looked up, a bare female bottom began wiggling in a window.

"That was our house over thar," Gabe said, pointing at a modest two-story structure It was now being used as a barbershop. "Ole man, he moved outta here, three year back. Lives couple miles outta town now. 'He's a saddle maker, saddle en harnesses both, and thar's plenty of business here about."

Along the road north of town, about fifty acres of farmland had been dug up, and just beyond, a huge steam-powered digging machine gouged at the earth. Men lay about a cabin near the pit's edge. Gabe reined up, put both hands on the pommel, and called out to a man on the steps.

"Hey fella! Where'd the Sutters git off to?"

The man shrugged. "Dunno. Old man sold out to Dunnellon Phosphate, been a couple months back. Moved on I 'suppose."

Gabe said nothing further, but Asher figured him to be bothered more than he let on. Turning west at a fork in the road, Asher followed Gabe through huge oaks to a large farmhouse. A long barn and work shed bordered the north side of the wagon yard. He waited a short distance back as Gabe hello-ed the house.

"Gabriel Spear," a woman's mature voice called, "about time y'all visit, ya varmint."

"'Lo, Ma," Gabe said easing down off his horse to give her a hug. "Thet's Mister Asher Byran, Ma. Come a piece with me. on his way up to the Carolina's."

Asher, hat in hand, made a slight bow, said, "Pleasure, ma'am."

"Will thank'ee, Mister Byran. Foods about ready, and I'd be proud to have y'all sup' with us. Get those animals tended to, and come on in," she invited. "Mr. Spear's due home any time now."

Gabe was middle son of a large family, and as well as his three brothers and a sister, he had uncles and cousins nearby. Except for him, all worked at the family trade. Only Gabe wandered. The subject of his work came up during the meal. Henry Spear asked him if he was back to stay this time, or just showing his face. It was past time, in Mr. Spear's opinion, that his son take up respectable work.

"Plenty time for thet, Pa," Gabe said good-naturally. "Pay's good herding. No need being worrisome," he said, and took a gulp of sweet tea. He continued, "Leastwise ain't no one chewing at the country side down south. See they done dug up Sutter's place."

"Good riddance to thet pecker-wood drunk. God be praised, that Tim Sutter and his spawn is outer here," Henry Spear trumpeted.

"Doan be hateful, Henry. Till fervor took her, Mary Sutter was a good mother to that bunch. Both Gordon en Hannah, they come out fine young-ins. If' Tim Sutter spoil-t the others,

61

it lay on 'is own soul." Jan Spear said this with the heartfelt conviction of a pure Baptist.

"So, where'd they get to?" Gabe asked, looking at his plate, trying to appear more concerned with food than the Sutters.

"I heard Gainesville," Nathan said, as he reached for biscuits.

"Mr. Byran try some this here sweet potato pie," Jan invited. Looking up, she corrected Nathan. "No, the boys, they gone thet way, but Tim, he's on the other side of town. Heard last month thet young Hannah was with her pa, cooking and such."

Asher, who was enjoying the potato pie, nonetheless noticed Gabe perk up at mention of the girl's whereabouts. He was now beginning to perceive the tilt of family opinion; at least where it concerned the girl. For sure, Gabe was here to court Hannah.

Dinner eaten, the women cleaned up, and Asher accompanied Gabe and his brothers into a large back room. Asher noted a gun rack with numerous weapons. One caught his eye and he inquired about it.

"Special-built shotgun," Gabe said. "Won it playing poker last year. Has lever action and holds six twelve-gauge shells en the stock. Like to use the Winchester myself," he added, "No range with a shotgun."

"Better for birds," Asher said. "How much?"

"Wanna buy it? Fifty."

"Its not made of gold, is it Gabe?"

"Cost a goodly bit more than that."

"I got thirty silver eagles I can spare," Asher offered.

"Forty, and eat a bit less on the road," Gabe suggested.

"Thirty-five," Asher bargained.

"Forty and I toss in a box of shells and a saddle boot. Nice

62

leather work."

"Done, if it's two boxes," Asher countered, and they shook.

"We got no twelve-gauge bird shot here, only buckshot. Come on," he said. "Let's get y'all some bird shot." Gabe dug into a drawer, and pulled out a bag of twelve-gauge shells. "Give her a try with this buckshot." He showed Asher how shells were slipped into the stock against the pressure of a spring and how the receiver picked them up.

"Takes six, you say," Asher said.

Gabe jacked round into the chamber and shoved another round into the stock, "Holds seven this away, hey, wanna give her a bang?"

"I've used a shotgun enough. One shoots about same as another," Asher said.

"Let's go get yer bird-shot then, fella. Hate to owe a debt."

Asher was a little uncomfortable at having spent such a sum of money, but the gun was really unusual. He recognized a bargain when one offered itself. As a guest, he felt a twinge of guilt at having haggled. Well hell, fair is fair, and fair's when both sides are happy.

When Gabe insisted on going to town for the shells, Asher figured he wanted an excuse to search his girl out. They saddled up their horses in the dim light of dusk, and Gabe rigged a new leather boot for the shotgun. It was pitch-dark riding to town, but Dunnellon had street lamps, and it being payday night, everything remained open. They stood in line at the hardware for maybe twenty minutes before the clerk, a young man, acquainted with Gabe, got to them.

"Hey, Tucker, how's about two box ah twelve-gauge bird shot?" Gabe said pleasantly.

"Where y'all been, Gabe?" The clerk asked, pushing the shells across the counter. "Still herding cows down South?"

"Ain't for the moment," Gabe said, exchanging a dollar bill.

Say, y'all know ware ole man Sutter be staying? He up en sold out the family place a while back."

"Damn! Din ya know, Gabe, thet ole trash is staying en the graveyard, dead a week now. Ole son-ah-bitch gambled his cash money away, and then gave Bass Perry markers he couldn't honor. Talk is the ole bastard let Bass take his girl to work off markers, a fore he died drunk. Dead Saturday last, that is."

The words had an explosive effect on Gabe Spear. Asher couldn't have believed a more profound effect was possible. Shouldering patrons aside, the cowboy rushed from the store. Pocketing his shells, Asher followed, nearly running to keep pace. Gabe vaulted onto his mount and galloped down the street. Asher mounted his own horse and tried to keep up. Gabe pulled up at the end of a muddy alley, blocked with tethered horses. He climbed down off his horse, and was checking his pistol. Asher rode up behind, observing men in various states of drunkenness and riotous behavior crowding the boardwalk. He slide down off his mare.

"You're in a terrible hurry, Gabe. You're jumping into a thing that's more than a week done. Are you going to bull in there without looking around first?" Asher said this plainly uneasy in the midst of so many armed men.

"Thet gal, y'all heard tell of, she ain't nary turned sixteen this month. I come back yonder to marry with her." His voice was hard. "She's a sweet, gentle thing. Know-ed her from church meeting when I was just' a young-in, and I aim to take her home."

"Be better if you get the law here, have them with you?" Asher suggested.

Gabe looked up at him, his face filled with a brooding bitterness. "Told ya, Ash, they is the law. Ole Bass is kin to the sheriff. The sheriff owns a piece of the place."

"Well, then, see if you can sneak her away and settle up later."

"If I choose to do what's only right, whatever man has the meanness to try and stop me, will thet man's gonna get sent to the devil for shore. God be my witness, I'm gonna take Hannah Sutter outta there, and take' her out now."

"Only what's right -- I suppose," Asher mumbled. He was feeling ever more uncomfortable with the direction things were taking. He'd seen more than a few disputes concerning women, and most got out of hand very quickly.

"It'll make me proud to know y'all might back me, Ash, quiet-like, you see."

Sighing, Asher swung down out of the saddle with his shotgun, "We've got a better than even chance of getting ourselves killed. You understand that we could wait till things quiet down," he suggested, hoping to change Gabe's mind.

"Can't," Gabe said, turning to the alley. "Dun reckon ya could if it was y'all."

Asher nodded silently, and fumbling with his new shotgun, followed Gabe into the crowd. It was a dim-lit place smelling of spilled liquor, sweat, and tobacco. It sat back against an old hotel that currently served as a bordello. Gabe stood at the doorway, peering inside. The place was packed and rowdy, and the piano was hardly audible over the din of voices.

By pure chance, Hannah saw Gabe Spear in the door. She panicked. So great was her shame at the possibility of Gabriel seeing her that she became sickly weak. Scarcely able to think, she tried to scramble away, ducking behind the piano. She crouched against the wall, dizzy with a dull horror. Gabe only glimpsed Hannah, and wasn't sure, but he walked round back anyway. He saw her reflected in a mirror where she stood. Her back pressed to a pillar below a gas lamp.

She was dressed in a low-cut red dress ruffled at the knees.

65

Her hair was done up and off her face, and her face was heavily made up. When he came closer, he could see a bruise on her cheek, as well as scratches and bite marks on her shoulders. His eyes teared with both tenderness and rage. She saw him at the last moment and tried to flee, but was trapped by the piano. When he pulled her to him, she was too weak to resist, almost too weak to sob. Gabe held her gently. He'd never held her before and he could feel her shudder all over.

"Come now, darlin'," he whispered against her hair, "I'll take y'all on home."

"Can't, Gabe; there's cash money owed, they made me a whore to pay it. Ain't fitting. I'm not decent no more."

She tried to explain, but he wouldn't listen. He was easing her toward the door.

"Please, Gabe," she begged, "they ain't gonna let me go. It'll be a beating shore, if I go out of here." Her voice was small. It quivered.

"Shush, now," he said. "Doan be scared."

"Y'all don't know what all kin happen to folks here, Gabe' -- she didn't finish.

The hand that gripped Gabe Spear's shoulder was powerful, but friendly. Bass didn't believe in discouraging business. He had a wide, ruddy face with a weak chin. He was big. He weighed over three hundred pounds, with a paunch that hung over his belt, and a deep voice with a mean charm.

"Wrong way there, son." He jerked his thumb toward the stairs. "Y'all take thet gal up there," he grinned. "Just leave a dollar with Mattie there."

A fierce, unthinking anger erupted in Gabe. He shrugged off Perry's hand, shifted a terrified Hannah to one side, and snarled, "Ya cob sucking bastard. Only place I'll take this lady is outer that door. God knows who learned y'all to treat decent woman folks like this."

Gabe was so intent he failed to see one of Perry's barmen come up behind him. Hannah screamed. Gabe flinched, causing the club to graze his head instead of making solid contact. Gabe pulled his gun and turned. The club struck his hand and the gun went off, a forty-five-slug taking the man's leg out from under him. A blow from Perry knocked Gabe to his knees as people reacted to the shot. Some scrambled for cover; others looked at the battle. Perry got a handful of Gabe's hair, yanking him to his feet as he pulled his own gun. Gabe's knife went into the big belly an inch above the belt buckle, and ripped upward a foot and a half, spilling intestines onto the floor. Perry gave a deep grunt; his gun fired twice into the pine floor as his knees hit the wood.

The bartender drew a pistol from under the bar and fired at Gabe, even as Perry slumped, bug-eyed against him. Everyone was diving for cover now, opening Gabe up for clear shots. As he yanked a hysterical Hannah behind him, a bullet caught him in the side. A second burned under his left arm. A thunderous shotgun blast went off in the deep shadows behind him, knocking the bartender from his feet, and shattering the mirror. Buckshot from a second blast took another man's legs out from under him, and spun the man's gun across the floor even before glass quit falling. Hannah's weight was against Gabe's back. She was clinging, but her feet went out from under her as he stumbled through the door. He picked her up, staggering toward the end of the alley and his horse, but he fell with her under a street lamp. There was blood, pumping out of Hannah's neck, and more from a neat hole in her upper abdomen.

Gabe groaned, "Oh, dear Jesus! Hannah, they done kilt us."

The girl's body was shaking and Gabe put his ear close as she fought to speak.

"Thank'ee, Gabe, for coming," she whispered, "but ain't

fitting that y'all be taking up wit' no whore----"

Hands grabbed at him, pulling him up from her. He could see her eyes going glassy, eyelashes fluttering, as if her soul were preparing to take wing. Someone yelled that he'd killed Bass Perry -- yelled for a rope. Unexpected, another shotgun blast roared out; wood splinters flew from the planks over the mob's head.

"Back off there, boys," Asher shouted, in a commanding tone from astride his horse. His voice was far steadier than he felt, for he was nauseous and horrified at his part in this. The fact that he had shot three men, probably killed at least one of them was plain to him. It was at the same time unreal, and far worse, he could not alter his train of actions now, for he had made his choice when he fired on the bartender.

"You in the yellow shirt, you put him up on that horse there," he directed trying to keep his attention on the crowd, and away from the slender body of a girl, being trampled into the mud. He reasoned in a forceful tone, "No business of yours here, no sense in getting shot to shit for work the sheriff's paid to do."

Gabe grunted as they put him onto his horse, and leaned forward in the saddle. Blood wet his side, front and back, and up under his left arm where another bullet had passed through. He heard Asher's steady voice through a haze.

"Probably bleed out before I get him to a doctor anyway," Asher called from the street.

He swatted Gabe's gelding as it passed him, starting it into a fast trot up the street, then spun, hugged his own mount's neck, and spurred after it. He'd got no more than a hundred feet before somebody started shooting. He was outside town when his horse slowed and staggered. As Asher jumped clear, the horse dropped to its knees, and fell sideways, blood drenching its side. He swore and yanked his saddlebags clear. The mare had been a two-year-old when his father died and he was uncommonly fond of it. Angrily he stuffed some shotgun shells into his pockets, pushed five more into the twelve-gauge, and, on foot, lit out down the road after Gabe.

He found him about a quarter-mile away, slumped over the saddle of his grazing horse. He mounted behind him and kicked the gelding into a quick walk -- where to, he had no idea. An hour at a steady lope brought them to a rail yard. There were switches to tracks leading off in four or five directions. An engine, pulled up under the water tower, was filling its tanks. Asher checked the sky for direction. The train was headed north. Edging the horse up to a boxcar, he rolled the door back a few feet. Crated oranges filled most of the car, but a small area at the door remained clear. He rolled Gabe from the horse into the boxcar, quickly dismounted and unsaddled the horse. After pitching their gear into the car, he ran the horse into the pines, barely making it back as the train pulled out.

Gabe's wounds had clotted, but he was only semi-conscious. Asher broke open an orange crate, tearing a few oranges open, squeezing juice into Gabe's mouth. He gasped and choked a little but managed to swallow. He even managed a weak "thank'ee," before falling into a deep sleep. As the train rolled North, Asher studied his situation. No doubt, the law would be seeking him. He'd been seen, but no one would recognize him or know who he was. He determined to shave at the first opportunity to be sure. Few, if any, would know Gabe; and Gabe's kin would give nothing away, so this could be a successful flight. He guessed the train to be moving at about twenty miles per hour. If it kept going for no more than eight hours, they'd be out of the state. He'd get them off the train before first light; see Gabe to a doctor and himself to Charleston. Hopefully, no one would think to telegraph descriptions.

With nothing to do but sit, Asher brooded on how quickly a

wrong choice could draw a man into dire circumstance. He'd come close to a sorry end, still could meet a sorry end. He knew Bass and Hannah were dead. Fairly judged, if the barkeep succumbed, he, Asher Byran, would be responsible for the man's death, and as well the wounding of at least two others.

The scene unfolded in his mind. There had been only short seconds once it began -- curses, the club, a gun, a knife, crashing glass, Perry's guts, Gabe hit, staggering, bullets passing through him into Hannah -- all so deadly fast. Suddenly he'd found himself shooting to cover Gabe, then to defend himself. The terrible ease with which violence had found him was as stupefying, as it was frightening. Like a misstep on slippery ground, once you were sliding, there was no way to stop. He was shocked at having killed a man with whom he had no personal dispute. Under other circumstances, he might have found he liked the fellow.

Asher napped and woke to lights as switches changed the train's rhythm. He read the station sign as they rolled through a town. "Gainesville." The crew took water on a siding, and a southbound train passed. He ate some oranges, waited until the train pulled out, and slept again. Gabe's groans woke him. There was a faint glow in the sky to the east. The train was pulling into Jacksonville.

"Can you try walking? Get you off to the side, before some railroad bull shows up. Then get a wagon."

"H ain't no yard bull, gonna mess with that shotgun there."

"That shotgun's been employed more than enough for one day," Asher retorted angrily, rolling the door back with more force than was necessary.

As the train bumped to a jarring stop, the stink of the yards overcame the smell of oranges. He tossed the saddle and bags to the ground and jumped down. Gabe passed him his Winchester and the shotgun, which he laid across the saddle.

70

He backed against the car, letting Gabe roll across his shoulders, stood him on his feet and helped him off into the trees. Within minutes, Asher found a black man with a freight wagon, who was willing to take them to a doctor for two bits. For six bits more, the same man put them up for the night.

Gabe woke to the odd sight of his clean-shaven friend sitting down to dinner with the black man's family. It was unnatural, a white man supping with a negro family.

Next day Asher put up at a sailor's boarding house off Church Street, where he got a bed for the price of two bits a night. On Wednesday, he moved a somewhat wobbly Gabe in with him. The cowboy, though mending quickly, was morose. He spoke little, mostly choosing to sit on the porch, gazing toward the John's River. Asher, feeling it was past time that he attend to his own business, said as much.

"I'm getting on up to Charleston," Asher told Gabe. "I'll be taking the early train tomorrow."

"She's past time, I recon."

"Sooner the better," Asher said. "Feel more comfortable, when I'm clear of Florida, you understand."

"Only natural, after this here mess. Y'all a true friend, Ash. No small thing, y'all taking my part -- most wouldn't of had the hash to stand up that way and I thank'ee."

"Not much chance to do it different once the lead began to fly. Fall in the water, you gotta swim," he added, smiling," besides, a man that don't stick with a friend ain't worth spit."

"I ought paid y'all more mind, come back late," Gabe confessed. "I could a took her out the window or something. My damn-fool temper's the thing, what got my Hannah kilt."

"Seems to me, Gabe, that Bass Perry and the girl's daddy were the root of her troubles. She's not the first, nor is she gonna be the last, their sort treats shabby.

"Swear to Christ Jesus, me or mine won't never use a

71

woman in no place like that," Gabe vowed solemnly. "It never come to me, the pure misery of them girls."

"There's women that choose it, I hear." Asher said this as he stood to stretch, "And ain't all of them forced, you know. And most I've been with, why they appeared to be having a fine old time."

"Hard to see—ain't much of a life," Gabe mumbled unconvinced by the argument.

They sat in silence for a few minutes. Asher broke the silence. "What y'all planning to do when you're fit?"

"Reckon no place 'round here gonna be healthful for a stretch, never thought I'd have to leave Florida, and I never thought I'd be beholden to negros, but I'm leaving, and there I was t'other day, beholden to ah bunch ah darkies. It surprised me some, seeing ya, sit-tin' down to the same table, supping with darkies."

Asher grinned and said, "I suppose, but then I was raised up at sea by my uncle. He figured it a wise course to measure men by ability and character rather than their look. No sense in having false divisions when you're going live or die together. Men come to ships from different clans and in all colors, so you mind a man's worth, not his skin or nation. My uncle Connor used to say, 'all men look about the same once they're skinned out'."

This being a subject of some controversy in his part of the world, he looked a little embarrassed. Running his mouth and spouting opinions seldom made a man popular, so he added, "At least, that's the way my uncle Connor saw it."

"S pose they're might be some small truth in that. Ya did say y'all were a sailor. That the family trade?" Gabe asked, changing the subject.

"Mostly. I apprenticed under my uncle. Yellow fever took my parents, siblings, cousins, and left me. My pa and my uncle Connor were twins, worked the shipping trade since they were boys. Taught by their own daddy, who was taught by his. I think there's been a Byran seafaring since Noah."

Gabe sighed, "I best concern myself with keepin hid, and gettin gone, 'cause I sure ain't go-in home for a spell. Guess y'all need be mindful too."

Asher agreed. "I suppose talk of Bass Perry getting gutted in his own place is bound to last. I swear to one thing, though: I'll not mentioning those events or show my face in that part of the state again. How about you, you gotta run somewhere, so what are you planning?"

"Thought of joining up with the cavalry," he said, "might ought to give it a go."

A dinner bell began to ring and Asher gave Gabe a hand up out of his chair. Boarding house lunch wasn't fancy, but there was plenty of it.

Next morning Asher boarded the train for Charleston.

Chapter 5

When she came over to him it was quite late; the evening was almost at an end. Striking an elegant, royal pose, she placed a china white hand on Asher's uniform sleeve, to get his attention, and leaned close, apologizing in a hushed tone.

"Who but me, Gwen"? He placed a hand over hers. "I'd have felt put off, had you called on someone else, and I hope you'll continue to call on me whenever I can be of help," he said with fond warmth.

"But because of me, you've had demerits at school. Difficulty with Charles, as well." she said this sweetly, if with complete insincerity. Yes, she appeared contrite, but Asher knew Gwen to be not in the least sorry.

"Oh, I'll be marching the yard due to that altercation -- ha -- but then so will he." His smile softened as he began to escort her toward the entrance where departing guests were donning their coats. "Besides, cousin, as a senior I've earned very few demerits this year, thus I'm able to bear the weight of these quite nicely -- for the sake of your honor that is."

"Ash, when Grandpa returns I'll tell him what a noble prince you've been."

He smiled at her words, but laughed inwardly at the thought. Not much anyone could say would improve the opinion of Ian Wallace, where it concerned Asher Byran. He was tainted stock in his grandfather's eyes. Aunt Fay's best efforts had proved futile where his grandfather was concerned. Being reminded that a grandson of his bore the Byran name was irritation enough to put the old man in a poor mood. It was the result of his parents' elopement, of course, for James Byran hadn't been thought a suitable match for Christine Wallace. Her death on the Florida frontier had not helped.

A reminder of his mother's folly that is what Asher knew himself to be. A ruffian and tainted stock, the old man had been reported to say, but then Asher had poured oils atop the flames of his grandfather's prejudice. Headstrong behavior and a failure to adhere to convention, did not sit well with his grandfather. Asher Byran had a record of both. A military education had put a bit of polish on Asher, and rounded off sharp corners and rough spots, but had done little else. His character had been set in stone by the time he arrived in Charleston. Being an early student of life's difficult lessons,

Asher Byran was not easily swayed. Truth be known, he wasn't much concerned with altering the opinions of others.

He did honor his word and because he did, was very careful of giving it. He'd promised his Aunt Fay to attend the Citadel and attend he had, even though he hated the place. Late this spring, he would graduate from what was the premiere military college of the south. He would earn the option of seeking a commissioned officer's billet in the armed forces of his country. It was an option he had no interest in taking, for though unmentioned; his true interest remained a career at sea.

Likewise, unspoken, was the frivolous romantic interest he had once held for his second cousin, Gwen Wallace. Being no fool, Asher had taken care to never address those sentiments, which he had fortunately outgrown. The family would have seen such a match in the same light as a mongrel caught round one of their prize bird dogs.

Acting the perfect gentleman, he assisted Gwen with her coat, then handed her up into the carriage beside her mother. She waved quickly as they pulled away and he began a rapid walk to get back to school for the Citadel was two miles' distance. As officer of the guard, he was to report for duty at midnight, and he remained in trouble enough, without being late for guard duty.

Monday morning found him, with a portion of his class, engaged in saber drill. His smaller opponent was a bit more agile, and held an advantage of speed. Asher was much stronger. Their blades wove, touched, and rasped loudly, as each sought a way through the others guard. Classmates observed the combat with interest, these men being the last two undefeated contenders in the morning's matches.

Ross lunged suddenly but Asher managed to turn the blade, barely sidestepping a counter stroke. Asher thrust, his wrist strong from hours of practice. More agile, Ross Orrell caught his blade, but Asher stepped in driving the basket forward, propelling it against his opponent's chin with the force to knock him from his feet. He leaped forward as the cadet hit the wood floor, blade to the man's chest, crying point. Bitterly, his opponent had cried 'foul'.

"The idea is to overcome one's adversary," Asher defended, breathing hard.

"A point, gentlemen?" Major Tillman stepped forward, his left hand up and repeated dryly, "A point, gentlemen? Hmm," he paused, a finger under his chin and continued. "If purposely done here in practice, Mr. Byran's counter, yes, a foul. If done on the battlefield, victory and survival. Your match, Mister Orrell, but Mister Byran's logic is impeccable. Gentleman, the object of war is to defeat your enemy, and to survive both victory and defeat. You must survive to enjoy the fruits of victory and suffer the shame of defeat. You must survive to exact revenge. War has rules. Survival has no rules -- none! Dismissed."

The following class, one given by Lt. Col. Grey, concerned tactics of an assault with the support of naval gunfire. This was of particular interest because of hostilities with Spain, now exacerbated by the explosion of the battleship *Maine*. Presently divers at the bottom of Havana's harbor were inspecting the wreckage. It was widely believed the report would show the *Maine's* destruction was the result of a mine. Speculation was that if war was declared and a campaign took place, forces would land and advance with close naval support. Examples were discussed, examples such as coastal and river gunboat support during the Civil War. Also studied was the tactics of foreign armies in similar situations, such as the British in Egypt, and allied forces in the Crimea. Toward the end of the class, cadets were in an open discussion concerning the prospects of war with Spain. In general, the opinion was that a war would take place. The hopes of many were to have a part in it.

For decades, American newspapers had printed inflammatory stories, and reports, detailing the cruelty of the island's Spanish administration, the brutality of regime's political defense. Only in the last year, had the policy of the United States government begun to bend to the expansionist doctrine of men like Henry Cabot Lodge. President McKinley had continued to oppose war, even

when factions of his party continued to press the issue. A letter written by the Spanish ambassador, a letter stolen and published in February, called President McKinley "feeble-minded," among other things." This insult caused public outrage. On the heels of this disclosure, the *Maine* exploded, killing two hundred-sixty of her crew. Political balance tipped in favor of the expansionist war hawks and McKinley altered U.S. policy.

Early in March, spurred by newspapers and a war faction, Congress unanimously voted fifty million dollars to prepare the military for the possibility of war. By month's end, McKinley stated several conditions necessary for the Spanish to avert war. The Citadel's Cadets hoped the Spanish would find these conditions unacceptable, for they were ambitious and real wars were not commonplace. On April 11, President McKinley, bending to political pressures, ignored peace overtures from Spain, and delivered a war message. Cadets, only weeks from graduation, began earnest attempts to find officers' billets in what was sure to be an expanding army.

It was in this atmosphere that Asher completed his punishment and restriction. His liberty restored and having free time, he attended a ball at the Newgate Mansion. He'd rather dance than worry about military commissions and politics. He found a great number of cadets in attendance, as well as Naval and Marine Corps officers ashore in Charleston. The general conversation concerned rumors and opinions of war, and just as often, individual plans or prospects for becoming involved. Older men had served in the Confederate Army. Younger men had, for years listened to their endless tales of the Great War, the Cause. Young men now looked on a war with Spain, as their chance for personal glory.

The older women of Charleston also remembered the war. They recalled too well, the war's lonely misery, its privations and the empty homes and beds. There was small enthusiasm on their part. They shared knowledge and a reserved dread, thus were unlike the girls who bubbled with excitement, and allowed themselves to become caught up in the brave, cocky talk of the officers. Drawn like twittering, giggling moths to fanned flames, young women clustered around the men or sought out a special beau.

Asher sat at the edge of such a group of officers, cooling off with a rum punch, as he listened to the discourse. During one conversation, he offered a few comments concerning areas in Cuba that he was familiar with, but the general drift of the talk bored him. Asher returned to the dancing. He had enjoyed himself while dancing with a number of partners during the evening, but only one dance with Gwen. He was surprised when she caught him by the arm and pulled him to a settee.

"Oh, Ash!" she gasped. "Isn't it exciting: going off to battle, conquering new lands. Have you any idea where you'll be assigned?"

"None at all," he admitted, again influenced by some mysterious combination of feminine attributes. Gwen seemed to wield a spell over him, as might an unwanted but potent fairy's dust. "From what I hear, the only positions will be with new regiments. Every vacancy has a dozen officers, who have applied to fill it. Not much chance for brand new graduate cadets to serve in the regulars," he said, though he not at all upset by the situation.

She pouted, sighed, "I should think it would be a disgrace to miss out." She fanned herself looking about. "Why Ash, I know of a half dozen boys in your class, boys who already have the promise of a billet."

"Gwen, as for the boys, who are receiving commissions, I'll wager they have the advantage of well-placed family or friends," Asher said. "With neither, I may just have to remain in Charleston with the ladies," he half joked.

"Asher Byran, what a cowardly excuse," she frowned, her tone one of absolute disgust. "Why, I'd never have believed you'd admit to such a thing. Some are pledging to enlist as ordinary soldiers," she said turning her head away as she spoke, as if unable to bear the sight of so loathsome a creature.

The music had started again. A handsome young man approached, holding a dance card alongside his smiling face. He bowed and took Gwen's hand, leading her onto the floor. Over one shoulder, she gave Asher a forgiving glance as she spun away. Asher watched for a time, admiring her physical beauty. At the same time, he was conscious of a sense of irritation with her. Gwen was a girl of eighteen whose life was so tightly locked into Charleston's social orbit that the world's realities must elude her. Was it only a year ago that he was continuously catching himself waiting on her, seeking her attention, and often stopped just short of embarrassment. Only a few years her senior, Asher now felt like an adult dealing with a silly child. Gwen merely amused him Asher decided, for he now recognized that beyond her ability to entertain, she was quite shallow.

Looking about the hall, the thought struck Asher that most of the people attending seemed childish in many respects. The attitude of the majority of his acquaintances, concerning war, was an excellent example. To them it represented honor, glory and good fun. Asher having experienced killing, knew it to be physically unpleasant, final and indiscriminate.

"There you are. Where have you been keeping yourself?"

The nearby voice caught Asher's attention and he turned toward the speaker. The young woman was clearly addressing another girl. He could not help staring at her with keen interest. After a moment, she caught him staring and turned away with a disconcerted frown. Smiling, Asher backed away and sat where he could watch her in a less obtrusive manner. She was the prettiest girl, beautiful really; no, striking would describe her better. She had a wonderful form and a quick grace. Her dark brown hair was done up high with combs, and her eyes, she had intensely blue eyes, blue with green flecks.

'How could I have noticed that?' he wondered, unable, or at the least, unwilling to remove his gaze from her.

"Ash, old boy," Davy Proust said, stepping between him and the object of his attention. "We had no idea you'd been up against the Spanish. Would you indulge me? Come settle some questions?"

"Certainly, Davy -- if you could answer a question." Looking past Proust, "Who is that girl in the blue gown, the one with dark auburn hair?" Asher asked his curiosity over-coming embarrassment.

"Oh! One of the O'Ryan sisters, down from Georgetown," he informed. Dropping his voice to a whisper he continued, saying, "I don't know them formally, you understand, but I understand their mother is Spanish." Glancing furtively to the side, he said, "Makes it a little awkward under the circumstances. Now," he began again, still wanting his questions answered, he led Asher away from the dance.

Looking over his shoulder, Asher glanced at her again, "Oh Lord!" he mumbled under his breath, not in the least concerned with her Spanish mother.

Chapter 6

Corazon was aware the Georgetown spring had been tranquil. This would have been her fourth Georgetown spring since the O'Ryans' return to the mainland that is her fourth, had she not managed, as usual, to be elsewhere.   Charleston was elsewhere.   Springtime in Charleston, with its rounds of parties and balls, meant gaiety and a certain amount of freedom.   Aunt Samantha always invited them and Corazon relished every moment spent there.   Here among friends, even her mother's gloom, and her sisters worry could not spoil her mood.   Unlike her sister, she refused to dwell on those problems, which did not directly concern her.

The conflict in Cuba, overshadow everything in the life of Isabel O'Ryan, and her eldest daughter.   Esmeralda was as much like her mother, as Corazon was different. Anyone, who read the news, knew of the violence and cruelty.   The inhumanity, clouding every aspect of Cuban life, seemed to escalate daily. Of course, a determined Spain had every right to subdue her rebellious province, but the methods, the cost in human suffering -- well, some considered them inexcusable. Horrors like the re-concentration camps, the starved innocents; were subjects of which her mother refused to speak. Instead, Isabel prayed fervently for peace, and that the good times would return so she might return home to Matanzas and to her family.

It was with the selfishness of youth that Corazon had hoped the insurrection might never end, that is, if it meant returning to live in Cuba. She refused to be depressed by events over which she had no control, or to pray for a situation, which would place her where she did not wish to be. She might be selfish, but she would not be a hypocrite.

When Corazon O'Ryan recalled Cuba, she remembered empty days and dull restriction. Here, her life was interesting. Her days were adventures filled with friends and exciting ideas. Over the years, her cousins, Jenny Ashe and Mary Brewton had become her close companions. These were girls with interests, and a certain daring, which matched her own. She was entertained, called on by more young gentlemen than she could spare time. Arrangements made by Samantha Ashe, had kept her young women engaged in Charleston's social rush. Occupied to a point, Jenny actually was heard to complain that she hadn't the strength for another night of dancing.

In the shadow of conflict, it seemed everyone wished to congregate, to dance, and be entertained. The ball at the Newgate home tonight was no exception, and as the pressing inevitability of war quickened the gaiety in the atmosphere, the underlying excitement lent to an easing of formalities . Most of the young women were swept up by a romantic fever. They were victims of words such as duty, honor, bravery and sacrifice. Already, a rash of engagements had broken out, for perhaps as men began to take up arms, they also sought, unconsciously, the security of emotional relationships.

Corazon did not approve of war. She considered war ridiculous and barbaric. She could not conceive of how a civilized society, a society with the aid of a diplomatic service, could allow itself to become involved in such a wasteful exercise. "If women are allowed the vote there will be no wars," she had told Jacqueline Walsh only this evening. Later, she had overheard the same young woman condemn her as mannish, and a blatant feminist. Another commented that being half-Spanish, a patriotic support of the war really couldn't be expected of her. It was ages since Corazon had been made to feel as an outsider. It angered her to a point that she could have happily pushed their smug faces into a punch bowl. Hot words had risen like bile, but she clamped her teeth, checked the words, and swallowed them as she hurried away. Experience had taught her that an angry retort would not avail her.

Moments later George Ward found her standing by the windows, still fuming. When he asked for the pleasure of a dance, she thanked him, but pleaded weariness, and begged for refreshment, perhaps a rum punch. He returned with punch and they had chatted a bit. She excused herself and wandered through the throng, her temper still burning. Christi, a friend she'd not seen in the preceding year, was walking toward her. Corazon had called out.

"My heaven, where have you been keeping yourself"?

Even as Christi Pace approached, an officer cadet had turned, looking directly at Corazon. Unashamed, he had continued to stare. He had been tall and solid, with sandy hair, and hazel eyes, gold, almost like a wolf, she thought as she turned to Christi. While they spoke, she could not get the man from her thoughts . The image of him had remained strangely clear in her mind, and she found herself drawn to glance back toward him. To her hot embarrassment, he had remained where he was, his gaze still holding her boldly. His eyes had taken her in with such utter assurance — why it had been disconcerting, if not displeasing. She turned away, embarrassed. Still feeling the weight of his stare, she tried to concentrate on her conversation with Christi. After a moment, and quite despite herself, she had looked toward him again, but he was gone.

She could not decide whether she was disappointed or relieved. The unusual eyes, peering out from the strong features of his face remained clear in her mind, and the strangest thing; there had been a tingling up her back. She told herself, she should drink nothing more this evening. Only later had she realized that she had completely forgotten that she was being angry. Though he remained a mystery and she had no clue to his name; she knew that tonight, shet had seen the most disconcertingly handsome man of her experience.

Soon the festivities came to an end, and after a carriage ride home, they returned to their rooms. Jenny was overflowing with pleasure. So well had the evening gone for her that she had been literally bursting to get home so she could confide to her cousins.

"My dears," she had squealed as she closed the bedroom door, and leaning back against it she squealed again, "Tommy Ware actually proposed marriage to me this evening."

"And you declined, of course," Corazon said, smiling as she shook her hair out.

"Why, of course dear, but with ever so much heartfelt confusion." Jenny giggled.

"He's such a sweet thing, but far too dull, to be taken seriously, I'm afraid."

"It's a shame," Mary cried, in mock despair, "the interesting ones never ask, if they do, are penniless." She sighed dramatically. "Having to decide with such a wide field, it's so tiring."

An easy laugh escaped Corazon. Turning her back to Mary to be unbuttoned, she said, "What's fun is the shopping. I am personally in no hurry to buy and lose my freedom."

"Exactly!" Jenny exclaimed. "When you say yes to one, you lose all the rest. Princess to slave with a single, 'I do', and for now, I will not." She smiled wickedly and added, "For now I'd rather conquer, see them groveling at my feet, see them begging for my smallest favor, instead of me begging for a break from childbirth."

"I've heard," Corazon, said cautiously, "some women grow to enjoy their conjugal duties."

"Humph! That's not what I've heard. Lower sorts perhaps, but I cannot imagine a lady finding pleasure in carnality. Laboring under the weight of a sweating man, I find the wretched process troubling, although I suppose it's a burden we must bear. Have you read Mr. Kellogg's tome on the subject. He considers the practice most insalubrious, advises that married couples should not share quarters, except by appointment that is, and then of course, only for the purpose of procreation.

"Poor Tommy," Corazon said, half meaning it. "When shall you free him?"

"Speaking of slaves, Jenny, didn't I see you with one belonging to Gwen Wallace?" Mary inquired mischievously.

"Charles Carol?"

"Oh, not him silly, her cousin, Ash."

"Mary Brewton! Asher Byran may be devoted to that feather-head, but I swear, no woman will ever have him for a lackey."

"Do say, Jenny. Pooh! Gwen draws him like a pistol," Mary said firmly. "Why, I believe Ash Byran's terrified every boy Gwen Wallace has ever felt slighted by. Why — why, a dog couldn't be more obedient."

Jenny's mouth fell open, aghast at such a slur coming from Mary. "Why, Mary!"

"It's true, Jenny, you know it. She even set him on Charles Carol, and Charles is her beau."

"Mary!" Jenny said, wiggling out of her dress. "I swear! You simply must get your gossip right. The Wallaces' treat Asher as an illegitimate relation, and do so through no fault of his. Gwen has looked to him, as an older brother, and I believe he's quite loyal to her in that way alone. Why, Ash Byran's not one who could be made to do anything he doesn't wish to." She tossed the dress toward the wardrobe, and turning back to Mary said, "Not a boring bone in his body, either. And handsome," she added, flashing a quick smile.

"Unfortunately, cousin, he hasn't two thin pennies to rub together," Mary teased.

"Isn't it," Jenny countered with indignation, "unfortunate I mean."

Corazon, who had slipped into a robe, laughed as she cracked the door, peeking into the hall. "I'm going to bathe and sleep, which will suit me far better than listening to gossip concerning strangers and men I care nothing for."

This said, she slipped out and down the hall to her room. She drew a bath and settled into the warm water. She'd enjoyed the evening, even with Charleston's growing martial climate. Why, she had not seen so many men in uniform since a diplomatic reception Papa had taken them to last winter. They had visited Washington, and the two-week visit still unsettled her. It seemed as if Mama had invited every eligible Spanish officer and diplomat in the city to a dinner or to some other function during their stay.

It was then that Corazon, had for the first time, realized how seriously her mother wanted Esmeralda, and herself to marry among her own people. It was frustrating to be treated a child while being considered overdue for marriage on the other. Her sister might bend to such a ridiculous outlook, but she certainly would not. Esmeralda would be married twice over if her mother's candidates had not died in the conflict.

Regardless of how her mother might try to arrange things, she felt secure in the knowledge that her father was reasonable. Marriage in due time was inevitable; she accepted this, but to a man she approved of, not a mere family name or nationality. If a husband were to be the foundation of a woman's life, if his smallest whim was to be her law, then by God, she would choose the husband.

She rose from the water, and hurried to the fireplace, where she dried, savoring the heat of the flames while bundling into her nightgown. She sat for a few moments staring at the fire, pensive. It was so important to choose properly, for there was only one choice allowed, one choice out of countless souls, an instant to speak the vow, and a lifetime to regret misjudgment. She was aware of far more marriages in which wives were unhappy, than of those thought of as pleasant. Corazon had long ago vowed that she would refuse to remain in a situation in which she was miserable. Simple logic provided, it would be better to avoid such a match at the outset.

She climbed into bed, wiggling, so the friction might warm the sheets. Waiting for sleep, she thought of her mother. She suspected that at times Isabel regretted the union with Father. Her mother's marriage was arranged and was a good one; somehow, though, Corazon sensed that her mother could never warm to the culture that had bred her husband, or to his people. To Isabel, her American in-laws were never quite family.

Chapter 7

The declaration of war came on April 24, with a call for 125,000 volunteers. Graduation was moved up a month so senior class-men would be in position to serve in newly formed units. Most graduate officers were already preparing to leave school when stunning news arrived by wire. In a great battle off Manila, the US Navy had destroyed Spain's Asian fleet.

Asher, caught up in personal conflict, vacillated over what he should do. He considered applying for his commission in one of the new regiments, but common sense told him, he would be six months in training. By then the war might be over. Pragmatic, he saw not the slightest possibility of joining an established unit; thus, any attempt would be a waste of six months. This, and he was not comfortable with the military system. Even though he functioned well enough in the military educational environment, he suspected, the military itself would be far different for him.

The early morning summons to the Commandant's office came as something of a surprise. It caused considerable speculation on his part, as he hurried toward the day room to report. He could think of no problems, nor could he think of anything he had done wrong lately. He was sure that he was there for some purpose beyond the routine, but was puzzled as to what. An aide opened the door to the waiting room.

"Please come in, Cadet Byran," a voice instructed.

Asher entered, coming to attention and saluting as the door closed behind him.

"Cadet Senior Byran, reporting as ordered, sir." He barked this, as his hand came up.

"Stand at ease, Mr. Byran," General Webb ordered. "I'd like you to meet Major Johnson." With a gesture to left, he added, "Captain Grisom you may know."

The Major came to his feet, and shook Asher's hand, treating him with greater deference than he had expected from a superior officer. To the side, he recognized the Marine captain who had spoken to him at the Newgate home.

"I understand, Mister Byran; you have more than a little knowledge of the Cuban coast, portions of it at least. Captain Sills, here, was impressed."

"I am familiar with some areas sir, but quite ignorant of most," Asher informed.

"You've lived in Cuba?"

"No sir. I trained at sea as a youth; a family ship, involved in trade with Cuban interests. Sometimes legal, sometimes not, but I've been ashore here and there."

"A filibuster?"

"At times, sir," Asher admitted.

"You speak the language well?" he said, as a question.

"Yes sir. Spanish is spoken quite commonly in the part of Florida where I was raised. A former Spanish colony, and as you're aware sir, there are a lot of Cubans in Florida."

"Well, Mr. Byran, it is Cuba, we're interested in. *Ud. me lleva la ventaya en conocimiento del pais,*" he said testing.

"*No es nada senor, pero soy a sus servirle,*" Asher answered.

"General Webb assures us that you're a competent man, and from your records, we see you did well with signals."

Johnson crossed the room, tapping the ashes from his pipe into a tray. He was a stoop-shouldered man of perhaps fifty, pale with thinning hair. His face was sallow from a life indoors. Satisfied, Johnson straddled a chair, and began to pack the pipe as he continued.

"My command is with U.S. Army Signal Corps. My superior, Col. Wagner, is in need of men with knowledge of Cuba, and its language. We need men who have some ability to move about there. Would you consider a commission, a place with us, Mr. Byran?"

"The duty will be in Cuba, sir?"

"That's correct, but you must understand; you may be involved in the gathering information, communications in forward areas or in places beyond our control. We must attempt to maintain contact between local insurgents as well as with naval support. We plan to pass information, hope to gather information," he paused, turned in his chair. "This is not the sort of soldier's work that young officers envision Mister Byran. It will, I know it will, require a great deal of initiative. Much of your time might be spent evading or hiding from your enemy, but this must not be construed as cowardly. A signal officer must get his signal gear to a high place, pass on what he sees, pass on the signals sent to him, and endeavor to disappear. In fact, constantly flee before an enemy can corner him."

"Under such circumstances, I would do my best to flee, sir," Asher said in earnest. He pictured himself chased by dragoons, and at the same time wondered where his mouth had led him. He had not intended to become involved when he'd discussed Cuba the night before.

"We've gathered several other officers, men with various knowledge of the island. You're actually something of a latecomer to our group, Cadet Byran or better, Lieutenant Byran," the Major said smiling. He rose from the chair, placed the pipe in his mouth, and gripping it firmly in his teeth, extended a hand to Asher, who remained standing at ease. "Congratulations. Your commission and orders will be on hand in the next few days. You will be joining us quite soon," he said, pleasantly informal.

"Sir, might I ask how soon?" Asher said stunned by the speed at which events progressed.

"You'll have a few days. The documents will have to arrive here. Be prepared to travel, Lieutenant. A great deal is beginning to happen and you will be in the vanguard." The Major paused, jotted a few notes on a piece of stationery and said, "Present this to the quartermaster at the Fort. You'll be issued uniforms and kit. "Good day, Lieutenant."

"Sir," Asher said, snapping a salute, and exiting the room in disbelief.

Wasting no time, he carried his letter to the quartermaster. Before noon he had delivered the uniforms to his tailor. They altered one suit as he waited, and wearing it, he presented himself at his Aunt Fay's home on Tradd Street. Expecting Fay's approval, he was taken aback, by her lack of enthusiasm. She looked up as he came through the door, then leaned back in her chair, her eyes taking in the Army officers uniform as her mouth pursed and twisted to one side.

"Asher Byran, what in God's mercy have y'all gone and done?"

She stood and gave him a hug, accepting a kiss on the cheek. Her hair was entirely gray now, and it came to him, her face was more wrinkled than he'd noticed. He felt a twinge of sorrow, for he had always thought of her as ageless, and she was the only family that held him dear.

"Come, sit with me, Ash. Tell me what has happened. I'm gonna hear all of it."

"Well — you can see, Aunt Fay, I've been commissioned, taken into the regulars. My papers and orders will be here in a day or two," Asher said, as he sat across from her.

"Ash," she sighed, "I am amazed that you've let yourself be caught up in this naughty little war. I know! I know, I have insisted on y'all attending the Citadel, but that was for the contacts a man needs to succeed in life. I'd suspected you were canny, least wise enough to avoid a part in this." Fay paused, sighed again. "I lost two brothers and a number of cousins in the Great War. My own dear father lost a leg.

91

Twelve Gibbes' men died for the Cause," she said, and looking askance at him, she continued with her sermon. "And have y'all considered that you've no son? That the family name, the Byran line dies with y'all?"

"Ma'am, I had no real intention of getting involved with the war. I thought I'd have no chance to be honest. They sought me out, after some chance remarks about the south coast of Cuba. I couldn't honorably refuse," he said, and explained what had taken place.

"Well, Ash, y'all could've delayed by pleading personal matters," she complained. "This war will surely prove a short affair. I feel Spain hasn't heart for it."

"Ma'am, they chose me out for what I knew. Having attempted to avoid serving under those circumstances would have been dishonest."

"A little dishonesty can be prudent at times," she scolded. "Any woman would admit to the truth in that, Asher Byran, and you remember it," she added, with pique.

"Aunt Fay, you said yourself that your reason for wanting me here was for social contacts. Can you imagine the censure I'd suffer for avoiding an obligation to serve, while the great majority scrambles for any possible place in the Army? Why, if Gwen Wallace discovered it, she'd have complete shed of me and tell all her friends. You can imagine what my grandfather would think."

Fay leaned her head back in disgust. At times like this, she wished she had the boy attend university anywhere but Charleston. She knew she was a fool for hoping Ian Wallace would relent where Asher was concerned. She hated admitting to folly, but there it was. Asher was more her son than her nephew, and she had such hopes for him. Charleston was simply too stiff-necked and backward. Even she must secretly admit to this, though she did love the city and did love her family.

"Ash, I'm sorry to be blunt. You will never please your Grandfather, nor will the majority of your mother's family accept you. They consider your father's line to be upstarts and trash, and your sweet mother to have been a rebellious fool. They feel absolved by the fact that she came to an early end. There! I've said it."

Asher smiled broadly and laughed. "I'd more or less come to that conclusion quite a while back, Auntie."

Fay rang a bell, and turning to Asher as a servant appeared, she asked, "Would y'all like a glass of wine, Ash? I would so enjoy a glass of wine myself."

"Yes Ma'am."

"Willium, bring some of the red, please," she instructed. "As to your cousin Gwen, what are your intentions?" She paused. When he did not respond quickly, she said, "Be forthright, Asher."

"I admit to having had an admiration of her in the past, Asher admitted, choosing his words. She is attractive and I'd once dallied with the thought of an alliance, but I knew better than to actually express my sentiments. Auntie Fay — I've long since recognized those sentiments as youthful infatuation, and Gwen as a feather brain. No insult intended," he added with a winning grin.

"Well, you have some sense for a fool," Fay told him. She chose her words but did not mince them when she said, "Asher Byran, y'all had as much in common with that girl as a lion with a peacock. Even if the girl did mature to own half a mind, you two would remain ill suited. I point this out, notwithstanding the ill will of the family, which that young woman would never chance. There are others like her too — do you understand what I'm say-in', Ash?"

He was annoyed at being advised of what he'd already

figured out for himself, but all the same, it was the truth. "I said, I knew better than to express my feelings," he reminded her.

"God knows, y'all best take a step further, and put your feelings to rest concerning any young lady remotely like Gwen," she admonished. "That young woman, why, she loves nothing better than the attentions of her circle." Fay twirled a hand near her head, saying, "Even if she or one like her should come to share your feelings, it would be a disaster. You would be a fool to acknowledge such feelings. To involve yourself with any young woman at this point in your life would be difficult." The wine arrived and she was compelled to smile, and calm herself for a moment as William poured.

"To your health, ma'am," Asher toasted, and sucked in his cheeks at the sharpness of the vintage.

"Y'all are the one who needs to be look-in to his health," she warned.

"Ma'am?" He said, his eyebrows lifting.

She snapped, "Don't ma'am me, Asher," and sipped from her glass, taking a moment to think. "I have things that need to be said for your own good. Y'all recall what I said when you came to me with the news of my Connor's death?"

"Not entirely, Ma'am," he confessed, wondering where she was headed.

"I told y'all that given the chance, I'd not ah married your uncle, knowing how things would go. I loved him but he made a tragedy of our lives, when we could just as well have remained here among friends and family, living a civilized life. I dearly loved him, but Asher, love seldom has reason. Someone must have reason, or sweet love can lead to bitter misery." She said this with a profound sincerity. "Young women trust, Ash, and the men they trust, must have the maturity to see where they are taking a wife. It's not a matter of what a man can do, but rather what he should do. Choose you a wife for her abilities, and strengths, in the full knowledge of what your path in life is going to be. Y'all do not choose a racehorse if you need it to pull a plow. Choose a wife for the station in life that she's to fill. That way she will not be a burden, and she will know she is of value to you. See to what's best for her. Listen to her complaints, and remember that children change a woman's priorities. Don't you be surly and jealous when it happens to you. Do you understand what I'm saying, Ash?"

Asher leaned back into his seat, his aunt's words making perfect reason. It was as if he'd always known these things, but never acknowledged them. So true! How could a man guide a wife and rule a family, when he had no knowledge of where he was going? He looked at his aunt.

"I understand, Aunt Fay. Just needed to hear it, I suppose."

"I'd be proud to know y'all are gonna take it to heart," she said, leaning over, placing a hand on his. "I'd be pleased to have your children all about me some day," — she squeezed his hand — "long as the time and the circumstances were fitting."

Asher grinned. He promised, "I'll do my best for you, Auntie, and for the fine counsel given, may I escort you to dinner? You might's well show me off before I get any nicks and scratches," he jested.

"Asher Byran, I do not appreciate such grim humor," she said reproachfully. "Never heard of anyone, man or boy that thought about food so much, or ate so much either, but I would be pleased to dine with y'all. Haven't been out with a handsome man in some time," she announced, with a coy smile.

Chapter 8

The cabin of the old side-wheeler was small, but airy, and with a breeze off Tampa Bay, reasonably comfortable. Asher sat with the door open, observing the transfer of guns and ammunition from rail cars to the *Gussie's* hold. Two companies of the 1st infantry, one hundred-fifty men, had been mustered on the pier and were now boarding. They were to land and secure a position on Cuba's north coast, and hold it long enough to deliver the weapons to a Cuban army.

An officer passed the door, and doubling, back dropped a bag to the deck. "Name's Noland," the lieutenant said, extending a hand enthusiastically; "looks like we share a cabin."

"Byran," Asher said, rising and shaking the proffered hand. "I'm in the top bunk."

Lt. Noland, plainly uncomfortable in the wool blues, wiped sweat from his eyes with a kerchief, "Dam'd hot down here," he commented.

"It's the humility. Actually, it's Cool Season now.

"Your jesting?"

"Oh no. Be a whole lot hotter in a month or so," he said with a juvenile grin. "I was born and raised just south of here. Ft. Myers. I promise, it will be a lot better once we sail," he added, to give Noland a little hope.

"I can certainly look forward to that," Noland said, tossing his gear onto the lower berth. "Be good to get shed of here."

Leaning back against the bulkhead, Asher said, "I've been

here all of three days, and can agree with you completely. There seems to be no end to confusion, and no one in charge."

"Oh, I expect things will be sorted out. They always are, but if you'll excuse me, I'd best see to my men and equipment!"

"Certainly," Asher said, "later then."

"Yes! Later," he repeated, ducking out the door.

A crowd, largely Cuban, milled about on the dock. Some were shaking hands and backslapping with three of their number, picked men of the insurrectos, who were about to embark for Cuba. Off to one side an artist stood, his paint box and easel set up on the railroad siding. He was capturing the scene. Asher, paying the crowd little attention, walked forward to the ship's saloon. A small group of civilians sat near the bar, conversing rather loudly. One sketched in a large tablet resting on his knee. He paused only to knock ashes from his cigar.

"Good afternoon, Lieutenant; can I offer you a drink?" one of them asked. "Its compliments of the press," the correspondent said, and responding to Asher's affirming nod called to the Bartender, "Steward, a beer for the Lieutenant."

A mug, with a good head, slid across the bar toward Asher, and raising it in a salute he said, "Asher Byran, at your service Sir. May I ask, whom do I have the pleasure of addressing?"

"Bigelow's the name, that's Bonsal and Archibald there, and Zogbaum with the stinko. Are you with the first Infantry, Lieutenant?"

"No, sir," Asher answered, seeing Bonsal's hand already moving to his note pad. "I'm only commissioned a week, Signal Corps, un-assigned at the moment. Just around to see how it's done."

"Well, we wish you success, Lieutenant," The journalist

said, abruptly losing interest.

Bonsal's note pad snapped shut, and the pencil went into his pocket. Zogbaum continued to work on his sketch, and Asher sat in a corner seat sipping his beer. When his superiors had briefed him, the day before, they returned to one point repeatedly. Anything you said, and much you did not, would find its way into print. It was best to remain out of the way, and uninteresting to the press corp. Asher intended to do just that, even if the rest of the Army did not.

Captain Dorst, the expedition's commander, entered a short while later followed by his officers. More drinks flowed, as did a steady conversation with the correspondents making occasional notes . Dorst was somewhat acid in his comments. It was plain to see he was more than a little incensed at having responsibility for a secret mission to Cuba that was no longer secret. Because of these journalists, the destination and details concerning the five-million-dollar arms cargo, was printed in every paper in the United States, and known to every Spanish agent in Tampa.

Asher was about to sit down to a game of poker with Archibald, Noland, and Crafton when the *Gussie's* first mate announced to those in the crowded salon that due to machinery problems, they would not be sailing until tomorrow midday.

"Damn sorry spectacle this is becoming," Captain Dorst muttered under his breath.

"Better broke at the wharf than at sea," E Company's Captain remarked. "No advantage at drifting around the Gulf in a busted ship during hurricane season."

"Gentleman," Bigelow said, "Might we not take advantage of the time? Would you be my guests for dinner at the Tampa Bay?"

"Why, certainly," another officer said, slapping down his

glass, "That's very generous of you."

"Certainly is, Bigelow, let one of my sergeants arrange cabs."

"Well, this promises to be pleasant," Lt. Noland, added with his boyish grin.

"Beats cards," Asher agreed and pushing back his chair, he followed the others.

The Tampa Bay Hotel was huge. It was not only huge but as luxurious as anything Asher had seen. Even with the general staff and hundreds of guests, it wasn't filled. Its five hundred rooms sat beneath a silver dome and thirteen minarets. Not only did its six acres hold bars, dining areas, and ballrooms, but a theater, swimming pool, and casino. It certainly outmatched anything in Charleston. Outside the grounds though, there was little more than sand and scrub palmetto, and Asher was amazed that anyone would build such a palace in a backwards place like Tampa.

After a few words exchanged between Bigelow and the maître d, their group was escorted to a large circular table in one of the elegant public dining rooms. Drinks were brought round while they relaxed and ordered from the menu. Another group of correspondents at a nearby table, acknowledged their colleagues with smiles and nods. One waved.

"Zogbaum — Come join us," one called, standing and pulling a chain.

Zogbaum rose, "If you gentlemen would excuse me for a few minutes." He said, and moved toward the other table. "Surprised to see you today Fred, out there on the dock, daubing that is. Did you mistake that old hulk for a horse?" he joked, and the laughter continued around the table as Zogbaum joined in the conversation.

"Fredrick Remington, the artist," Dorst said, leaning close to

Asher. "He's quite the celebrate. He was our guest in the 4th Cavalry some years back, an interesting man."

"No small talent as a writer, either," James Archibald added. "I speak from envy."

"Speaking of envy," Bigelow laughed, "Zogbaum and Davis were on the *Cruiser New York* a few weeks ago, when she bombarded Fort San Severino at Matanzas. Fred was on the *Iowa*, and only found out the day after, when he transferred over. Now that was envy."

"Who's Davis?"

"Richard Harding Davis, the highest paid of our humble profession," Archibald said.

"That's him on Remington's left. What the Journal pays him is obscene."

"Now we hear envy," a slender man said quietly over Archibald's shoulder.

"Hah! Ralph Paine! I thought you'd given up war for the garden page."

"Since war was declared, my career as a filibuster journalist is no longer considered criminal, James. I believe heroic is a more fitting word."

"Come sit with us, Ralph; we'll make room," Archibald invited, signaling for a chair.

Asher and Noland shifted sideways making room as the chair arrived and waiters began adding another dinner service. Great attention seemed to be paid to the every whim of these men, and Asher, began to sense the influence of the newspapers.

"Seems we're residing amidst the royalty of journalism," Asher said to the officer next to him.

Archibald gestured with one hand. "Ralph — may I introduce the bold officers who will lead our first foray onto

Cuban soil? This, on my left, is he who will command, Captain Dorst," he quipped. Then in order, he continued introductions around the table.

As the conversation continued, Asher found himself in need of a visit to the necessary and excused himself. Though he was enjoying the evening, he understood he was out of his element. It was a sophisticated group he'd fallen in with, and the very topics at which he was knowledgeable, and might add to the conversation, were the very ones that should be kept to himself. Though likable, these men seemed to have a singular loyalty: their editors.

He crossed the dining area and turned up a hall, taking note of a striking young woman with auburn hair. As she entered the elevator, she seemed familiar, but with a better look, he realized she lacked the striking qualities he remembered, and only reminded him of that young woman he had seen at the Newgate Mansion. He sighed. Well, he'd had that one look.

Eventually, the very woman of which Asher was reminded, Miss Corazon O'Ryan, would herself recall this night with a fond embarrassment. Corazon did not choose to be in Tampa. It happened that Papa, having pressing business in Tampa, had promised not to abandon Mama, and Corazon had been compelled to accompany them. She had used every bit of her persuasive ability to coax her father into allowing her to remain in South Carolina, but of course, Esmeralda had spoiled it. She would not hear of allowing Mama to make the trip alone while she was upset. How stupid, as if mother were alone in Papa company.

It was news of the battle at Manila that had upset her mother. News of the destruction of Spain's Pacific fleet came as a shock. The lack of news concerning Uncle Louis, who served as second in command aboard the Spanish cruiser, *Castilla*, made it worse.

Tampa was a rude place but Corazon recognized the hotel as excellent. Granted, it was overrun by the army, but this offered certain advantages in an otherwise boring social climate. Each night the young officers provided dancing partners in the ballrooms, and early, Corazon decided to take advantage of what diversions were available. Sitting at her dressing table, she cast a critical eye over her mirrored image and removed a ribbon, exchanging it for one that better matched her gown. She smiled as her sister entered.

"You're going dancing again?" Esmeralda accused. "Haven't you any sense of propriety, Cori, dancing with just anyone?"

"Don't be a prig, sister. They are officers and gentlemen."

"But who are they?" She spoke with a certain note of disdain.

"If they are pleasant and dance well, who cares? I am merely enjoying the evening, not choosing a husband or lover," she said for effect, fully intending to scandalize her sister.

"Cori! That is the most shocking thing to say. I should tell Mama," Esmeralda threatened.

"Don't be a fool; you should join me, have fun, and not pester poor Mama with such trivialities. Besides, Carla hovers when I'm not with mama. How could I come to harm?" Corazon looked at the wall clock. "Hurry," she said, standing; "Papa will be waiting."

"Uuh—you hurry me, when I'm the one sent to fetch you," Esmeralda complained, and followed her sister quickly down the hall.

Stopping before the elevator, Corazon turned to her, in an attempt to be pleasant, and asked, "Did you play croquet again today?"

"Yes — with mama, and Mrs. Ward. She looked impatiently up at the floor indicator. "I suppose you went riding? Did you see the Army at practice?"

"Yes! I saw them practicing at a distance. The cavalry seems very competent and exiting to watch. There are some excellent horsemen among them."

As the elevator door slid open, Esmeralda scolded, "You shouldn't be about with thousands of common soldiers and rabble."

"Stop it -- stop it -- my god, just stop it," she cried, now fully exasperated. "You know Papa has William follow behind me." She stepped into the elevator. "He sticks like a burr — He is my shadow, my dog — I am perfectly safe."

They rode down five floors in silence, Corazon facing the elevator operator. As the door opened, Esmeralda began to say something. Corazon, not wishing to hear, rushed out into the hall paying no attention whatsoever, thus from her point of view, the incident was her very own fault. Out of the corner of her eye, she had sensed a dark blue shape moving toward her. Suddenly she was sprawling onto the floor, her lower limbs exposed in a most immodest manner. Her combs had jarred loose, allowing her hair to fall in her face, and as she swept it to the side, she realized her gown was far above her knees, very far. As she attempted to push it down, her foot became further entangled with that of the army lieutenant, with whom she had collided. He tripped hiking the gown up past her waist.

Returning from the lavatory, Asher had turned to glance at himself in a wall mirror, and collided with the young woman, literally bowling her over. In a humiliating attempt to help her up, he tripped over his own feet, hooked her gown with his boot, and upset a potted palm. As he bumbled above her, he realized she was the very girl he had been so taken with at the

103

Newgate ball.

"Sorry, so sorry," Asher said miserably, as he tried to keep the potted tree from falling on her, but covered her with black soil in the process. "I beg your forgiveness, ma'am. Please! Allow me to assist you," he offered extending his hand.

"Sir — would you do me the favor of leaving me alone?" she whispered.

She was mortified as her sister bent to assist her. She could not look him in the face; her embarrassment was too complete, but she did glance at him. He was a tall man, fair-haired, with hazel gold eyes; familiar those eyes and he blushed. How strangely the thing struck her that such a man, so masculine in appearance, should blush. It occurred to Corazon that he had a fine voice, with a sincere tone, and then she realized she had seen this man before and where, and that the nearness of him somehow weakened her knees.

"May I be of assistance, ma'am?" he said feeling the flush in his face. Another young woman, remarkably similar in appearance, who had helped her to rise, brushed soil from her gown, and directed sour looks at Asher. "I owe you a most profound apology," he babbled.

"Sir, you are forgiven." Her tone was maddeningly sensible, considering her state of disorder. "But please, just go," she repeated desperately avoiding his eyes.

Lacking words and any other viable course of action, he simply nodded and turning to walk away, bumped into a waiter. A tray flew and glass shattered. Asher cringed.

Watching him slink away, Esmeralda said, "*Madre de Dios, que' hombre desmanado,* 'Mother of God, what a clumsy man'."

"*Pero hermoso,* 'But handsome'," Corazon replied absently, as she turned toward the elevator.

Asher heard them and reddened further. So, "*He was*

clumsy, but handsome." He needed to crawl beneath a rock.

Dinner had arrived by the time he returned to the table. Famished, he took his napkin, and was amazed that his hands shook. As he ate, a distinguished couple were seated at the next table. Accompanying them were the same young women he had blundered into. Of course, Archibald knew them, and of course, exchanged cordial words.

Corazon was astonished at seeing the lieutenant again. As they were seated for dinner, one of Papa's journalist friends, an intelligent looking young man, had said hello, and inquired after their health. The young officer sat exactly next to him, where she must sit facing his way. She did not know whether to giggle, cry, or ask to be excused. *"What a poor ridiculous thing I am,"* she thought, immediately bracing herself up, not condescending to look away from him after that moment. He seemed to be uncomfortable, and as her eyes met his, he immediately knocked over a glass. He seemed to lose his appetite and departed early. She thought this fortunate, for now she would be able to eat without fear of choking. The affair was both foolish and confusing, for this" man was strangely appealing. She considered that perhaps she might be morally unhealthy in finding a strange man appealing, but her curiosity of him ended abruptly as she realized, *"My God! How could I ever face him; the man has looked right up my dress."*

As Corazon sat blushing, Asher carefully departed the dining room. Imagining himself watched, he was fearful of further loutish awkwardness. He hired a cab and rode back to the ship, trying to think about how fate might treat him during the next few days. His mind returned to the girl at the hotel, Miss O'Ryan. She was lovely. Strangely, he could recall her features in the smallest detail. Enclosed in the cab, he realized a trace of her scent still clung to his uniform.

"Surely played the bumpkin in that exchange," he mumbled

to himself, and what a shame. God, Jesus, she was a beauty."

Chapter 9

The Gulf Stream lightened with the dawn, changing from a silver streaked black, to a deep purple, then a transparent ultramarine blue. The smell of mangrove rot and smoke drifted out from the faint coast. Puffs of low clouds sailed on the southeast trades, and the rising sun's rose-gold rays alternately painted the *Gussie's* port side with shadow and dazzle. As she steamed south, a man at her stern hauled a trolling line to clear its lure of weed. He gazed to starboard at the flanking gunboats, *Wasp* and *Manning*.

Following astern were two seagoing tugs, chartered, and filled with additional correspondents. Here, so that they might be witnesses to the world, reporting on this most secret expedition. It was May 11, and ahead, in the shadow of Cuba's western mountains, lay the port of Mariel.

Taking his breakfast early, Asher carefully put his field gear together, complete to his rifle, pistol, and a suit of clothes in the Cuban style. Aboard was the consignment: 7,500 rifles, 1,300,000 rounds of ammunition, medical chests, tents, uniforms and other materials, to be supplied to the Cubans. Asher's orders were to accompany the rebel army to which this equipment was delivered, and communicate their activities by any means possible. Though Asher had been a commissioned officer for only eight days, he did have considerable previous experience in the practice of landing guns in a place Where the local authorities did not wish guns landed. Based on his experience, he had seen little in the Army's plans that would instill confidence. If anything, he was becoming somewhat apprehensive.

With his field glasses, he sat atop *Gussie's* deck-house as they approached the bay. He could make out the flashing of heliographs on the Mesa de Mariel and from the coastal mountains. As the morning mists cleared, Spanish infantry was visible, massed on the beaches. On the deck to his left, he noticed James Archibald, who was also studying the coast flanking Mariel.

"Congratulations," he said, putting the glasses back in their case, "it seems the Spanish read your newspaper. Unless, that is, they're enjoying more time at the beach," he added sarcastically.

"Really!", the correspondent said, non-pulsed.

On the bridge deck below, one of the Cuban scouts pointed out in broken English that he no longer had any interest in landing here. Dorst was arguing with the *Gussie's* captain, as the mate studied charts below. Shortly, semaphore signals whipped back and forth between the ships, and the small flotilla swung west on the coast, pursued by Spanish cavalry on the shore. Rain squalls drifted west, occasionally obscuring the land, wetting the deck, and driving Asher down off the house to shelter under the deck.

The mate was swearing at his inability to place the entrance of Cabanas, a port Asher had entered on occasion. As inconspicuously as possible, Asher pointed out a deep notch in a fifteen-hundred-foot, hill behind the bay. He suggested, discreetly that it made a range up to the inlet. The mate looked shoreward, then back at Asher, his face annoyed after being told his job by a landsman, an Army lubber.

"I was second officer on a ship in these waters Mr. Brown.

Been in here twice before. You can anchor within a hundred yards of shore, off Arbolitis Point there," Asher said, pointing at an un-surveyed section of the chart.

"You sure?" Brown said, wanting to believe. "Old man's shy of places he doesn't know. So blind, he doesn't see past his nose no more. Have me skinned if you're mistaken, Lieutenant."

Asher shrugged. Brown took one more look, and had the helm put over. The Captain's voice could be heard on deck to where Asher had moved. He was arguing with the mate. Dead slow was rung on the engine telegraph, and the thrashing of the side wheels slowed. Sounds of the boats clearing, and of troops mustering, rose from below. From the bow, the clatter of the steam winch preparing the anchor; the call of the leads-man: "No bottom, no bottom, by the deep sixteen, by the mark sixteen, and a half fifteen, and a half ten."

The water shoaled and *Gussie's* engines backed. The frothy churning of her big paddle wheels brought her to an awkward halt. Hair blowing in the wind, the mate stood at the forward rail. He squinted at the long white line of surf and a rain squall setting down on them. He let his arm fall, and *Gussie's* anchor plunged down into water so clear, sand could be seen to puff up as it struck. As the crew manhandled the longboats over the side, rain pelted down in a squall so dense that the beach was obscure. The *Wasp*, drifting two hundred feet to port, became a mere shadow.

Asher watched as Archibald crowded into Noland's boat, already jammed with troopers. The rain cleared and the first boat, the one with the Cuban guides, was already pulling for shore to mark a pass in the reef.

Archibald looked up at Asher and yelled over the din, "You coming?"

Asher pointed as the first boat, capsized in the breakers

and he yelled, "Later maybe."

"Don't be shy. You'll miss the fun," the reporter teased, and the officer, in the boat's bow, ordered them to cast off. Archibald shrugged and smiled.

Asher called pointing toward a flat stretch in the breakers, "Looks better over that way."

Three more boats put off, and the landing parties began an exuberant shouting, "*Cuba lib`re!*" He climbed back onto the house for a better view. Zogbaum was sitting cross-legged, sketching feverishly. Steve Bonsal was taking notes. He arrived to see a boat, half filled by the surf, broach on the beach, dumping passengers in three feet of water.

Gunfire erupted out of the trees and the men were immediately deployed; more troopers stumbled ashore. Asher could see sand and water kicked up by Spanish bullets, but no men down. The mixed reports of the American's Krag rifles, and Spanish Mauser s, seemed almost unconnected with the ship, until a random round shattered a spotlight over Bonsal's head. He swore, calling them louts for firing on civilians. One of the officers, he could not be sure which, backed up against a rock bluff, and had two men with semaphore flags signaling the gunboats. Reading automatically as the flags waved, Asher was surprised at how quickly the *Manning* responded. Big chunks of jungle erupted upward; plumes of smoke drifted west across the ridge, and then, just as cheering started, salvos from the *Wasp* begin to burst against the hill. Spanish soldiers appeared, hurrying up over the ridge. When cease-fire was signaled, the jungle became quiet.

Another boat was loading on *Gussie's* port side and Bigelow yelled up, "I'm going ashore, Stephen. Are you coming?"

"No! I'll wait. It's a better show from here."

"Well then, you can read about it," he laughed.

Asher swung down off the house again, and crossed to the starboard rail. He could hear a general commotion below, vigorous swearing, and suddenly a horse erupted from the side port. There was a huge splash, and the animal began swimming in circles. The second mount lunged out, and two soldiers went overboard, entangled with a third animal. While one of the boats was fishing out troopers, the horses struck out for the beach. Soon the men of E Company had to dash up and down in the shallows to catch them.

Watching men saddling horses on the beach, Asher wondered how this was going to work. He knew *Gussie* to be ten miles, possibly more from the planned landing point. Spanish Army regulars were without doubt marching to engage them, and the Cuban force would have no idea where the *Gussie* was. One moment the Cuban scouts were mounting, the nervous horses dancing and wheeling, and then they were gone into the trees. Well, the scout might make contact. For the next few hours, everything remained quiet. The gunboats drifted nearby and the tugs hung close to *Gussie's* stern. There was only the occasional shouting going back and forth. The sun reached its zenith and began sinking west. He went into the saloon to eat, and found Archibald with his left arm in a sling.

"Did you enjoy yourself, James?"

"Really, Ash," the writer said, "it was hardly memorable. Minor hole," he said, "But I will be forced to type with one hand. I was the only man hit, you know."

A steward poured Asher a glass of tea. "Dubious honor," he mumbled, taking a drink.

"His own damn fault," an infantry officer growled. He bit the end off a cigar, spit and putting a match to it, puffed. "Standing in the middle of the beach during a skirmish. Stupid!" The infantry officer shook the match and pointed with the cigar in his left hand. "No offense Archibald, but I believe it's obvious how coverage in the press has jinxed this expedition."

The writer had mellowed some, understandably, as this was his third whiskey. He was a slim man with regular features, except for ears that stuck out, and he seemed not the least upset by officer's remarks.

"Seems to me, J.J.," he said, "that Spanish agents had all of the same information. Just that they wired it and we printed it."

It amazed Asher that the man could actually argue the point. He saw Captain Dorst moving along the deck, looking in the port. Entering the salon, he crossed to their table.

Captain J.J. O'Connell looked up, said, "The Cubans shown up yet?"

"Hell, no," Dorst spat. "Sound recall. We're getting off this damn beach before something serious happens. One piece of artillery on the other side of that hill and we're all fish bait. We'll watch for them from offshore."

"Yes, sir," he said, rising from the table. He nodded, "If you'll excuse me, gentlemen?"

Dorst watched him leave, as he poured coffee from the service. He followed with cup in hand. Bigelow, hurrying into the salon, collided with him, sending coffee flying.

"Oh! Pardon me, Captain; my fault entirely."

"Perfectly all right," Dorst growled, through clenched teeth, wiping chin with sleeve.

"May I have a moment, Captain?" Bigelow asked, his expression showing not the least bit of discomfiture.

Dorst, stepping to the side, took a deep breath — "No!" he said curtly, and stepped through the doorway, still clutching his now empty coffee cup.

"Touch of temper," Bigelow said archly.

Archibald had finished his third large whiskey, and spoke, one hand signaling for another drink, "things don't seem to be going well."

"Be a good story either way. Look, the *Dauntless* is running back to Key West, to the telegraph. You want to go?"

Archibald looked through his glass at Asher. "No! I believe I'll stay and report the whole sordid story, but thank you for your consideration."

Bigelow laughed, "Think nothing of it. Starting for the door he turned, "Will you watch the 1st come back aboard?" he asked.

Archibald winked at Asher, "No I'll just stay here and take my pain killer."

A plate of chicken and rice arrived for Asher. Archibald requested a portion of his own. They ate in silence, alone except for an engineer and the *Gussie's* purser.

"Just what are you aboard for?" Archibald asked, his curiosity breaking the silence.

"Observation," Asher said, and looked down as food fell on his tunic.

"Come now, old fellow! I saw you directing the mate, Mr. Brown."

"Nah! I simply happened in here on a ship once, and remembered the range," Asher said, pushing his plate back and dabbing at a stain. "Not a bad dish," he commented.

"No use to dissemble Lieutenant, the truth will come out."

"I tell it, when I know it."

"A fair answer," the reporter said wincing as he readjusted his sling.

"Painful, James?"

"It aches a bit." He rubbed his arm, and slouched. "You were here. What's inland?"

"I haven't seen much, sugar fields and a lot of tobacco in the mountains. Not rich like Matanzas. Years since I was down here. Be good to see the common man with his own land."

Archibald snorted. "Americans have bought up a lot of the Island," Archibald said. "When we run the Spanish off, we'll buy a lot more. That what it's all about, that, and selling newspapers," he admitted. "Of course, the suffering, the atrocities, they're real, but self-interest rather than suffering is usually the prime mover. The big boys will own the land here. Where have you been, my friend? The world is about self-interest."

"Of late," Asher said, "the Citadel -- Charleston, South Carolina, courage and honor, but I suppose they'll have to add greed and power-lust to the motto."

"Remember the gentleman, next table the other night, O'Ryan, wife and daughters?"

"Oh yes! I remember," Asher, said, his mind going directly to the young woman.

"He was a rice planter from Georgetown, Wynya Bay. Both bought and married into Cuba twenty years ago. The wife is Isabel Vega. The Vegas' have been in Cuba for almost three hundred years, but Douglas O'Ryan is the type who controls their estates these days. It's Americans like him who will profit from this war in the end."

"You're cynical, James."

"Not cynical, Ash, knowledgeable. Wealth and its pursuits guide the world. Businessmen, the commercial interests of a nation is the base of power. Commerce points the way and armies march. That's the way it is now, the way it's always been. When the conquistadors professed to serve God – it's said they misplaced the letter "L" in the word."

Sounds rose up to them, the hiss of steam and the clink of

anchor chain, came from forward. *Gussie's* paddle wheels began to turn and, "Here we go."

"My cabin is where I believe I'll go," Archibald said, pushing up from his seat. He swayed more than might be expected, with the ship's slight roll. "Call me if we sink."

"Why, I'd be pleased to, for a price."

James Archibald laughed, "Why, Ash," he said, "I see a spark of hope for you."

Chapter 10

Soldiers and equipment came pouring in, and Tampa became more crowded by the day. By the end of the forth week one entire side of the city had transformed itself into a red-light district, and with the import of women and liquor, to keep up with the ever-growing numbers of troops, Douglas O'Ryan like other prudent men kept his family far from this social blight. He had taken them on excursions the to the Port Tampa to see the transport fleet, and to Ybor City to observe the manufacture of cigars. She continued to enjoy the dances, and riding remained a pleasant diversion, but they were kept from the city, and beyond card games, there was little else to do at the hotel where the confinement of the hotel became tiresome for Corazon.

When Mrs. Ward arranged a pleasant buffet, and croquet match; it was quite special. Even Mama's mood was improved; in fact, she bested everyone twice, and took to teasing Esmeralda with feathers from her hat. It was three days after the *Gussie* expedition had returned in disgrace, the nineteenth. She remembered, for father had told them all about it.

Douglas O'Ryan thought the affair humorous. He explained how for days, the old steamer had wandered futilely along the coast, dodging shells from shore batteries. Her old captain had finally had enough and returned to port. The Army blamed the press, and the press blamed the Army. General Shafter ordered Dorst, now promoted to Lt. Colonel, to try again. A new transport was being loading, this time in secret, and another as a decoy for the press.

Asher did not find the failure of the expedition humorous, but was relieved to see it return to port. The military cargo was removed from the ship, as were the troops, which left him without a billet. He had no success in contacting Major Johnson, and Col. Wagner was between Washington and Tampa with staff. The prospect of sweating in a hot tent was unappealing. With a clear conscience, he decided to spend the interim period at the Tampa Bay Hotel, taking advantage of its daytime diversions and nightly dances. On his way to a poker game, he failed to see James Archibald but Archibald saw him and called for him to come and sit. Turning, to the calling of his name, Asher saw the reporter beneath a pavilion, where an elaborate buffet had been set. With a wave, he walked his way.

"I see you have a new sling for your wing, James."

"Nice turn of phrase, and actually, the arm is much better." He leaned toward Asher and said with lowered voice, "Between the two of us, it's amazing the amount of attention it gets me. I may nurse this along for some time, God knows, he confided, "the women love it."

"Who are you with?" Asher asked, looking at the empty chairs.

"Oh, that's them over there, the croquet match. The skinny one is Hale, one of our editors; that's his wife with him. Ward there, he owns some of the ships that the army is preparing as transports. That woman in the pink frock, is the Mayor's wife, and you'll remember Douglas O'Ryan and his wife Isabel. Their daughters are on the far side there," he said, gesturing with the banana he was eating, "Corazon's taking the shot, Esmeralda's beside the Mayors wife. Juicy young things aren't they?"

Asher rolled his eyes back as the reporter looked his way. "I'm afraid I've met those young ladies," he said. "In fact, I believe Corazon's the very one I knocked down and trod on."

"You're joking." He was familiar with the incident and smirked with perverted pleasure. "Is that your usual approach to young women?" he laughed, absently tossing the remains of his banana into a hamper.

"You can understand why I might be less than acceptable to Miss O'Ryan," Asher mumbled, seeing very little humor or hope in the disclosure.

Archibald leaned forward, "Seriously, ladies do love being swept off their feet."

"Swept, not knocked."

From the corner of his eye, Asher noticed someone approaching, and turned to see Douglas O'Ryan and his friend Mr. Ward. He rose to his feet and gave them both a firm handshake, as Archibald formally introduced them.

"Where are you from, Lieutenant?" O'Ryan asked, selecting a section of melon.

"Charleston, sir, perhaps you're acquainted with my mother's people, the Wallace's and Hughes? My Aunt was a Gibbes."

"Oh, yes! Indeed, a small world if you're related to Ian Wallace."

116

"My grandfather, sir."

"My own father spoke of him often, served together in the great war, Longstreet's division. As a young man, I was on several occasions, a guest in his home," O'Ryan said pleasantly. "He's still sound, I trust?"

"As of a few weeks ago, sir."

"Well, that's excellent. You must mention me to him," and smiling, bit into his melon.

Ward, who had been pouring himself a drink, said, "You'll be off to Cuba in the coming weeks, Lieutenant?"

"Actually, I've just returned, sir. James and I were shipmates on the *Gussie*."

Ward took a drink, "Unfortunate affair," he said, swallowing. "The next expedition will be more successful, to be sure."

Sitting again, Archibald said, "It will be a ship belonging to Mr. Ward that you're traveling on, Ash."

Reminded of the press' blatant disregard for confidence he looked askance, and Ward, an observant man, correctly read his expression, chuckling pleasantly.

"Don't be concerned, Lieutenant. General Shafter promised to cancel press privileges for indiscreet correspondents."

"Can't type regardless," Archibald complained, making a sorrowful face.

"When will the *Florida* be ready?" O'Ryan asked.

"The Master informs me, in a day, perhaps two at most," Ward replied while taking a seat. "Besides her boxed cargo, she's to carry horses, mules, and wagons. Five hundred volunteers, new soldiers for General Garcia, and it takes time to construct bunks and stalls."

"Be glad to see some movement in the situation. This conflict has put quite a strain on business. Much of our cane's been burned in Matanzas, and for weeks I've been unable to move a thing out of Banes." O'Ryan put his feet up. "Mining could be halted through summer."

"You have interests in Banes, sir?" Asher asked.

"Oh yes," O'Ryan's face took on a satisfied look. "It's over twenty years, I've been involved there. Americans have substantial holdings in the area, and I promise you, we will have more. Very pleasant countryside," he added changing the tone, "although I don't see much of it — Isabel prefers Matanzas," he smiled. "You know how women are — about being near family that is? She's been away from them for years now, and the war has been quite a trial for her." O'Ryan held out a wine glass for the steward to fill. "As I was saying, I prefer the scenery and climate around Banes," he said.

"Speaking of women," Ward interrupted, "I believe ours are in the offing."

The ladies came from the game in good spirits, and as they collected around the buffet, Asher was politely introduced. He noted that though Isabel bore strong Iberian features, her daughters had inherited a slightly wider face, and softer features from their father. They both had his blue eyes, though Esmeralda's hair was lighter auburn, and Corazon's was a dark reddish-brown.

As the party helped themselves to the buffet, their hosts put questions to

Asher and Archibald, concerning the *Gussie's* sortie. During this pleasant small talk, Asher found himself singled out by Miss Corazon O'Ryan, who made no mention of Asher's previous awkwardness. Miss O'Ryan smiled at him as they conversed, and after lunch, she challenged him to croquet. Later he promised to accompany her for a morning ride along the bay.

Corazon had been surprised to find her father, and Mr. Ward conversing with the very same young officer, who had unsettled her the week before. Everyone, having been introduced, they were left to fend for themselves, both with the food and the conversation. Lieutenant Byran: she thought she knew the name, and of course, he turned out to be the very same one that her cousins had been discussing after Newgate. She was sure she blushed when introduced, but during the following hour, she overcame her embarrassment. Not only did she speak with him, but also, she had particularly enjoyed conversing, for he proved to be a pleasant person, asking her opinion, and listening carefully as she spoke it. She had purposely broached the subject of riding, stressing how she hated ridding out alone. Of course, he had offered to accompany her. She was inwardly smug at finding him so easy to maneuver, until it occurred to her that he had the same objective. This was all very forward of course, but after all, he just kept appearing out of air. Once he had gone, she found herself thinking of him more than favorably, even fondly, and later Corazon overheard papa comment to mama that young Byran's family had close ties with his own.

An early morning telegram, on the following day, put all such thought from her mind. The messenger had arrived after breakfast, and she knew something was dreadfully wrong when she heard Mama sobbing. Esmeralda stood pale behind her and Corazon understood without hearing, that Uncle Louis was dead. Before noon, they departed for Georgetown, and Corazon was aboard the train before she remembered her missed riding appointment. It seemed sadly unimportant.

By telegraph, papa, made arrangements with agents in Manila for the transport of Louis' remains. From the far side of the world, his casket would travel to Cuba. Safe with her family in the Carolina s, Corazon worried about her other family in Cuba. She knew that she had been selfish and thoughtless. It was truly frightening that a war would reach to the other side of the world and snatch a loved one. It was an epiphany that a war could so personally affect her. This should have been no revelation, and she was ashamed that it had taken so long for her to understand and accept the obvious.

Chapter 11

When Archibald excused himself, Asher regretfully departed with him, and they finished the afternoon playing poker at the casino. After the game broke up he found orders waiting for him, and checking out of his room, ordered a cab for the port. On the pier, he was strutting a little, thinking of Miss O'Ryan, and his morning appointment. A wiry corporal, sporting a handlebar mustache approached him, snapping a salute.

"Sir, y'all wouldn't be Ash Byran, now would ya, Lieutenant?"

"I would be," Asher said.

"I recon y'all might member me sir — back a spell when I was called Gabe Spear."

"I'll be damn, Gabe. I never did recognize you."

"I weren't sure if it was y'all, neither. Scared to speak up, y'all bein' an officer."

Asher took his hand, shaking it vigorously and said, "I remember, you were joining the cavalry weren't you Gabe. Let me buy you a dinner and a drink. Three years, you can tell me where and what you've been up to."

They ate at the Los Novedades, chicken and yellow rice. Gabe, who was going by the name of Strong now, had seen three years' service in New Mexico and Arizona. He was presently of the 1st cavalry. To hear it, after three years, he remained a wanted man, still sought in Marion County. He admitted to being uneasy, so close to home. Asher touched on the fact that he had gone to college as intended, and had been commissioned only a month earlier. He described his voyage to Cuba on the *Gussie*, and he told Gabe, he was due to depart again. They discussed getting together in Cuba, and after dinner, went to one of Gabe's haunts for a drink.

Asher could not remember how the fight started or how it ended. He did recall singing in the back of a freight wagon, and he remembered falling down the *Florida's* gangway. He had no memory of how he got back up, and the ship was underway when he woke. When his riding engagement with Miss O'Ryan came to mind, he groaned, for he had no way of sending his apologies. Miserable he went back to sleep.

Two days found the steam ship *Florida* south of the Bahamas Bank, her engines pounding away, prow chopping waves, as she plowed east against the Trades. The horizon glowed peach and expanded toward the poles. Low clouds took color; and the sun lifted above the sea, its dazzle blinding the lookouts.

During the night, the lights of the Havana blockade had passed off to starboard; Cay Sal bank was astern at dawn. As the ship pushed east, it was alive with the mixed sounds of land and sea. Horses nickered, mules brayed, and men gathered aimlessly about the decks, talking, laughing. On the officer's deck, strong coffee and cans of milk sat on a table crowded with maps. Major Federico Diaz sat across from Asher, his feet on the rail, sipping the *coffee con leche,* "coffee with milk".

"Carahatas is there," the old man said, pointing a thin finger southwest. "I was born near there, a slave." He smiled adding, "but that was long ago."

"You're going back after the war?" Asher asked nodding shoreward.

He shrugged, "For me — nothing is there now. The butcher — Weyler, he killed my children, my grandchildren. *Reconcentrados* 'civilian prisoners', they starved in the camps."

Asher drank his coffee, relaxed. Diaz was responsible to General Garcia for transportation of materials. For ten years, the old Mabisi had fought alongside General Maceo in Oriente province. He knew of every road and trail. A runaway slave, Diaz had become a soldier in 1868, surviving battles, capture, and torture. He had been before the firing squad in 1877; shot and left for dead, yet here he was, resigned but not bitter.

"We hold most of the countryside now. Only the big cities are in Spanish hands. The end will come soon," he said without drama.

"Success, then," Asher said, lifting his cup in the form of a toast.

"*Cuba Libre*," the old man said, with a smile that showed few teeth. He drained the cup and reached into his pocket, producing a long fat cigar. "Would you like *Teniente*?" he asked, holding it out.

"*Gracia, no, Señor*," Asher thanked him. "And if you'll excuse me, sir, I believe I'll walk about for a while." Already lighting his cigar, Diaz nodded and he left him, walking forward.

He had been acquainting himself with the Cuban officers for two days now.

It surprised him that they considered the war all but won. Some, for a fact, were even wary of the United States, concerned that they could be trading one oppressor for another, now, when the prize was all but in their hands. On the main deck the canvas laid stripped back from the hatch gratings, and he looked down into number two hold where a squad of the 2nd Cavalry and some Cuban teamsters were feeding and watering the horses. He watched a game of dominoes, and listened to the Cuban soldier's talk, his ear regaining familiarity with the backcountry Spanish dialect. Eventually he became bored, returning to his quarters. He sat alone, brooding over his part in the scheme of things.

In theory, Asher understood the concept of war but his involvement in this war seemed surreal. Perhaps it was because he had no group of comrades, no routine or firm objective. They had casually cast him adrift with instructions to observe and communicate. He was out here on the chance that he might see something useful, and relay it. If he disappeared, how many years before someone besides the paymaster would notice? He was a ghost. Who would know, who would care? The sound of water slipping by the hull was reassuring. There was no doubt in his mind that within months this conflict would be resolved. He'd resign and see himself back at sea, or would that be a mistake. His stomach growled and looking at his watch, Asher realized it was mealtime. The clearest communication was that of the body. There were many automatic signals of the body: hunger, cold, pain, fatigue, and of course lust. These were but a few, and the body seldom erred. It was a shame that the brain's intellect could not be error-less in recognition when non-physical issues demanded decisions. His stomach went towards the saloon led by his appetite.

Throughout the day and into the night, the coast swept past without incident. Asher slept soundly, waking at dawn with the decrease of the ship's engines. The transport slowed and entered the twisting gorge that led into Bahia de Banes.

The passage was torturous, and a longer ship would not have made the bends, but the channel soon opened Into the bay. Within the hour, the *Florida* lay alongside the wharf and people began to come down to the port. Music, a Spanish-African mix, underplayed with drums, burst from the warehouse. Workers danced for joy and residents rushed onto the wharf, rapturously welcoming the passengers and crew.

A ragged troop of cavalry, led by staff officers belonging to General Garcia, rode up within the hour. Officials exchanged documents, and things began to move. The stock was ashore before noon, and the *Florida's* cargo began its transfer to wagons. They backed the battered cars of an ore train onto the wharf late that afternoon. What materiel could not be loaded, was warehoused. Amidst this bustle, several small groups of Americans had arrived, women and children mostly, who petitioned Col. Dorst for passage. With the master's permission, he had them taken aboard.

Asher's duty lay with the cargo, and he put his kit together and prepared to leave. He offered his respects to the colonel, and to his acquaintances among the officers. During the afternoon, he disembarked with his gear, and a good horse, riding toward Macbi with Diaz. It was a miserable night of rain and bugs that he spent bedded down in a shed behind headquarters. At dawn, he joined the small army of General Mendez which he was to accompany on a march southwest toward Holguin.

They were to skirt the mountains, and then turn east along the plain of the Rio Cauto. Another American officer, a Lieutenant Rowan, had traveled undercover through Spanish-held territory with messages for General Garcia. That correspondence informed that the American army would first attack the fortress city of Santiago. To support them Garcia was now moving his armies to the base of the Sierra Maestra, and into coastal mountains adjacent that city.

The march began well enough, but then it rained. For two days, it rained, and it continued to rain. Under a tarp stretched between two trees, cooks spread food on a folding cot: rice, beans, chicken and plantains. Those officers without kits ate from banana leaves held in the palm of one hand. The ground beneath their feet was ankle-deep muck, and the sucking sounds of their feet in the mud created a strange accompaniment to the sucking sound of men eating without implements.

"Do you like it, *Teniente*?" Major Cruz inquired, concerning the seasoning.

"Very good, sir," Asher replied, speaking with his mouth full.

"More rum, perhaps?"

"Thank you, no."

Cruz poured rum for himself and took a sip; he hissed, showing his teeth.

"We had wine until a few days ago. The Spanish left a great deal of it in Bayamo. They had little time to remove things when we drove them out. They left many enjoyable things, some with two legs," he laughed, winking at Asher. "April twenty-eight, a good day," Cruz grinned. "I was not there. Machado, he was there. *Gato*," he called, "come, tell the Yankee about Bayamo."

A slender cavalry officer of medium size, and cocky in his walk, approached carrying his meal. He was close before the shocking scar on his face became evident.

"A pleasure to tell it," Muchado said with a flourish of his free hand. "It was a good plan. We cut them off from Santiago by a small fight at San Luis. Some of Bayamo's garrison was sent to take us from the rear, but the full army fell on them along the open road. Garcia moved on the city from the west and used cannon on the strong points. On April 28, they fell back on San Luis, using the way García left for them. For very little trouble Bayamo, it is ours." Machado said this, and took a swallow of rum. "Las Tunas was more difficult, but we took their guns at Las Tunas," he said with a wolfs grin.

"A large victory," Cruz agreed. "We took more than eight hundred rifles and a hundred horses, a good supply of bullets. Now we fight them with their own bullets," he laughed.

A rider dismounted and approached Major Cruz with a dispatch pouch. They exchanged a few words, and Cruz directed him to the thatch hut where the General was. He turned back to his food with a somber expression.

Machado asked softly, "Bad fortune, Juan?"

"God knows. He hears the fleet of Spain has come to Santiago," Cruz said solemnly.

"The United States has ships, too," Asher reminded him.

"I know little of ships," Cruz said, "except that these have great guns are here now."

"A small affair," Machado laughed, "they cannot come on the land."

"Truth," Cruz agreed, with a tilt of his head .

From the General's tent, a man hurried splashing through the mud to advise Cruz that his presence was required. Asher munched another piece of chicken and slapped a mosquito. He wondered if rigging his tent for the night was worth the trouble. Perhaps he should try to sleep on his poncho. He sat on his poncho and leaned against the tree. The hanging flap of the tarp gave him some shelter, and the mud was soft. All night the mosquitoes droned.

Chapter 12

Any consideration of an assault on San Luis had ended; now they marched through the mountains. Below, on the plain, the trade winds swept endless fields of cane, causing moving streaks, spears of white, as it undulated below the gusts. Above clouds sailed with the wind, like islands. Their blue shadows darkened the sweet grass and shaded laborers, who drove cane laden ox carts toward the rising smoke of mills. From the mountainside, Asher made out a railroad track, and a telegraph line that ran between the foothills and the river. Beyond the river, haze dimmed the white walls, and red tile of a large town that lay against the side of the coastal mountains.

"San Luis," Machado pointed. "It guards the west of Santiago, four thousand soldiers, perhaps more, around the city. They are regulars in the large part, but there are also the *guerrillas*, 'Cuban militia', who are mostly cavalry." Machado spit, "Whores! Cubans who give their loyalty to Spain, and when they are taken — we kill them. We kill them with machetes, as they do our wounded in our hospitals," he growled, his face taking on a hard smile as he spoke.

Machado had once taken a bullet through his cheek. Asher thought it gave the man a sinister grin. When Machado smiled, his face stretched to one side. Machado's home had been Holguin City, where he had been a lawyer and it was rumored that his family were taken, all of them. They were all executed when the Spanish re-took Holguin in 1895. Machado was believed to be a better soldier than lawyer -- a matter of passion.

On May 30, a night march south was planned by General

Mendez. This was in order to cross the plain between the Cauto and Mayare rivers unseen. The men were to march in two columns, keeping the pack trains of mules toward the rear. Ahead, Machado's cavalry would provide a screen. Some men slept in the shade of the mountain forest. Others lounged, played games through the afternoon, or made music, using drums of steel, or whatever served to make a sound. Asher chose to learn from Machado the use of the machete against the saber.

"Shorter and heavy at the end, one must swing for the hilt of the saber, you see. Even if the saber is not beaten aside," Machado explained, "if you get inside the guard, you can hack or stab." He demonstrated.

Asher backed quickly, blocking the attack deftly, and countering with what could have been a killing thrust. "That is," he said, "if you let someone inside your guard."

Machado smiled, "You are skilled Yankee, but men pressed close on horseback cannot back away with such haste."

"Guess in a melee, there might be an advantage," he admitted. He understood the lesson, but did not entirely agree. "But," he suggested, "With a pistol in your other hand, the advantage is not so strong."

Machado shrugged, "Few have great skill with sword or pistol, my friend. For us, the machete is well suited."

"And if you miss, *Teniente*, when you shoot your pistol," a thin Negro sergeant said, "you may lose the hand that holds it."

"Yes, Charro, show him," another man shouted, while several others began to smile or laugh openly.

Charro held up a stump, where his right hand had been. He grinned toothless. "I have learned not to miss with my left hand," he boasted, amid the laughing.

Smiling at the grim joke, Asher sheathed his saber, and slid

128

it into its sleeve on his saddle. He moved his horse some distance, to where sunlight had fed the grass. He gave the gelding water and tethered it, so it could graze. His mount was a solid bay, roman nosed, with black boots. It wasn't a good-looking horse, but it was strong, fast and well trained.

It was twilight when a black soldier nudged him awake. He said, "*Vamos, señor*," and placed a coconut with its top sliced off in his hand.

Asher rose and drinking as he went, walked toward the small group of officers that surrounded Mendez. The coconut milk was cool and sweet. A light breeze rustled leaves overhead, muting the voices until he drew near.

"Awake, Yankee?" Mendez asked.

"*Si, General, a sus ordeñes,*" he answered.

"Good!" Mendez gestured toward Machado. "Would it suit you to ride in the vanguard, ride with the Cat?"

"Sir, an honor," Asher answered and made a slight bow.

"Well then, luck to us all," Mendez said. "We go."

As they advanced, trees on the plain appeared as islands of darkness. The moon, low already, would soon be gone. Below them, the dim hills sloped away toward the rivers, flattening and becoming lush grass and tall cane fields. Preceded by a half dozen scouts, they rode scattered in an uneven crescent, covering a half-mile. The infantry columns followed at a quarter mile with the pack train at their rear. The air was moist, almost cool; hooves no longer clicked on stone, made soft plopping sounds. There was the swish of grass, the creak of leather and the occasional clink of metal. Vague shapes, walls, deserted buildings, would loom suddenly out of the night. At intervals, Machado signaled a pause. They listened -- they allowed the infantry to come close.

"We are half way, my friend," the cavalry officer told him as their horses stood beneath a mango tree.

Asher's bay stretched. Head down it munched on fallen fruit. His voice low, he said, "You'd think the country was empty of Spanish."

"Uuh," Machado made a grunting sound. "Not empty here my friend. We have pushed them back to here. Now they are very many in this small end of Cuba. They only move in force, and enjoy the use of block houses and trenches." Machado's saddle creaked as he twisted, looking back for sign of the infantry. "And their Mausers fire very rapidly," he added, "with excellent range. In ambush and defense, they can be difficult. We must use maneuver and stealth to succeed against them. Spanish cavalry fight well, but the loyalist guerrillas — they, as we, are Cuban. They know the land and even if they have no honor they fight hard." He paused; spoke softly, "Never surrender to them — they have no mercy."

Asher swallowed from his canteen. He heard a horse blow nervously nearby. "Why such venom, isn't one bad as the other?"

"Law my friend, is not always justice," Machado said. "Men must have just law, equal law. Those who would oppose just law; they strike at the roots of justice. They are beasts. The Spanish *soldado raso* 'common soldier', he is paid little and sent here without choice. The loyalist is different; he fights because he wishes, he chooses to maintain the evil."

A low whistle out of the dark snapped the Captain's head around. A mounted shadow pointed back to the approaching column. Machado signaled an advance.

Asher walked his horse over a grassy, rock-strewn hill. He followed a goat trail, angling down toward an expansive area of cane fields. At the bottom his horse lunged, and clamored across a gully. Narrow cart tracks cut the high cane, and intersected a dirt road that crossed the route of march. Some rode directly into the cane; other filed down the cart tracks. The track Asher followed branched. He reined to the right,

130

advancing a hundred feet before it ended, forcing him to push into the cane.

"*Mierda!*" The soft curse drifted from the left with the sound of a stumbling horse.

Abruptly, Asher's horse pricked its ears, its head up and to the front, nostrils flared, it hesitated. He spoke to the horse softly, nudging it with his heels. The bay pranced in place, tossing its head, irritated with his stupid rider. Letting the gelding settle, Asher listened carefully at the same time un-holstering his pistol. He thought he could make out a series of metallic clicks over the faint brushing of horses against sugar cane.

"*Fuego!*"

The shout burst out of the dark, clear, and abrupt. It preceded a storm of rifle fire. Green leaves snapped and rustled as bullets cut through the dense cane. The air close by hissed and whined, so crowded was it with bullets that there seemed to be a continuous whistle. Over the din, Machado's voice: "*Ala derecha, Lopez*; 'to the right, Lopez', to the left, Charro; *rápidamente, hombres.*" Noise: the scream of horses, crashing cane, grunts, and hooves on the road, metal rasping on metal, all mixed with the firecracker chatter of gunfire.

Asher reined to his right. Leaning forward, he eased the reins, and dug his heels in simultaneously. The bay exploded forward, running blind through the cane. Leaves whipped at him. He could hear another rider closing on his right. He laid reins against the bay's neck, and it cut to the left, suddenly breaking into the open, leaping over a ditch and onto the road. Several horses ran ahead, at least two rider-less. Others of Machado's men galloped behind or crashed through the cane, out of sight of the entrenched infantry.

The Spanish cavalry that emerged from a cart trail immediately ahead were surely as amazed as Asher, who, having nowhere to go, rammed a Spaniard mounted on a small dun. The big bay slammed horse and rider to the ground. Pulling up, he leaned away from a slashing machete and fired across his saddle into the man's chest.

Horses lunged and wheeled, blades flashed. Men on both sides fired rifles from the saddle. Asher fired again, inches from his target. He switched the revolver to his left hand, and drew his saber, only managing to stop a machete slash by parrying a man's hand. With no time to aim, he back handed a dismounted soldier with his revolver and urged his horse ahead. The bay lunged and struck another horse in the flank, staggering it and throwing its rider, a man who had been cutting at Machado's back.

"Thank you, my friend," the Captain yelled.

Asher was engaged on his right by a sergeant whose small agile gray pressed against the larger bay. So closely did the pony press him that the Spaniard's blade was inside Asher's guard. Only by driving the basket of his saber, like a steel fist, into the man's temple, did he prevent himself from being sliced in the ribs.

Wounded men crawled and horses lay kicking in the road. Those yet on their feet struggled to break free, dash after comrades, who had managed to disengage. Asher, cutting back north along a cart track, overtook two of Machado's men as they rode clear of the cane.

Mendez, having ridden forward with Cruz, and others of his officers, was conferring quickly with Machado. Officers galloped back along the column shouting, and men were running forward in silence. A company from each column flanked the fields. The night became still with the exceptions of distant screams.

Asher dismounted and dispassionately replaced the spent cartridges in his pistol. He examined his horse. The feel of the animal, the nervous heat of it, strangely calmed his own rapid pulse. He was rubbing a greasy ointment into a groove in the bay's flank when Machado jumped down from his black mare.

"Hot work," he said, "Engaging both infantry and horse."

"An unpleasant surprise," Asher commented.

The Captain took a swig of rum from a flask, and then poured some more over a cut on his thigh. "I am running out of blood," he laughed. "I see you are not new to killing, Yankee. You do it well."

"Only new to war," Asher said laconically.

"Ah! You have fought for your honor, then?" Machado said.

"Why are you called 'Cat'?" Asher asked, changing the subject.

Machado sat -- he lit a cigar -- smiled in its glow, and replied, "I see well in the dark and have been, at times, quick."

He puffed on his cigar with enjoyment. He watched the Yankee. This Yankee lieutenant was a steady man, who had little hesitation and no brag in him. Machado liked that in a man, liked it even more in an officer. Along the earthen bank, men were working themselves into comfortable fighting positions.

"They're holding the road. What now?"

"Feel the breeze on your face, my friend. Look for a warm glow behind our foes."

Asher looked south beyond the road. The wind was driving flames toward

them, flames that consumed the cane.

"How?" he asked.

"Charro," Machado answered. "The Spanish, they will come to us driven by the fire."

They did -- running -- some firing -- others choking, blinded by smoke, they came from the flaming fields into a wall of bullets. The insurrectos collected more than one hundred fine rifles from the smoking earth before marching south toward the sea. Asher's opinion had not changed. He didn't care for war. One moment there was a future that held: women, fortune, life, and the next moment: pain, blood and the earth. A poor form of employment, which was for the moment his, and he was feeling uncommonly shaky.

Chapter 13

In the remaining dark, they climbed. Before daybreak, Mendez had ordered camp made in dense forest that spread along a low bluff. The wounded were attended with the resources available, and a meal of rice and horse-meat was cooked. Even dead horses had value. Asher rigged a piece of blanket over the bullet furrow on his horse, and dressed a few other small injuries. He was out of the oats he'd carried in his saddlebag, but secured some corn meal. If the bay's performance in the fight was any indicator, the difference in strength between a grass-fed horse, and one fed on grain was impressive.

He slept through the morning and was still sleeping when the soldier sent to wake him shook his hammock. Mendez had his men and mules on the march again. Asher, now in the column's rear, followed a narrow switchback trail further up into the coastal mountains. In darkness, they encamped on a long mountain ridge. There were trees but no heavy undergrowth and a good breeze blew. No sooner had he lain down than a rain squall swept the camp, soaking everything. Grumbling, he crawled under a ledge to sleep. Again, he woke with the sun high. From his perch, he saw the blue dazzle of the Caribbean Sea spread across the southern horizon, and to the west Santiago's rooftops. To the east, Guantanamo Bay glistened beyond a hilly plain.

Looking for the headquarters tent, he wandered through the camp. Instead, he found Major Cruz sitting barefoot with a tree at his back, as he consumed a bowl of beans.

"I see you have a new Mauser".

"Spoils of war sir. I plan to place a target, and adjust the sights to my eye at the first opportunity."

"Beans and coffee," the major offered, pointing to a cook fire some hundred feet away. "Compliments of our oppressors."

"Good! I could eat a horse."

"Horse we eat again tonight," Cruz said, and laughing at his own humor, he choked and coughed up a bean.

Asher got himself some food. He wolfed down his beans, but drank his coffee slowly. He noticed for the first time his blood splattered uniform blouse. As he contemplated searching for a place to wash it, Cruz spoke.

"Come Lieutenant'," he said, getting laboriously to his feet. "I become old," he added, walking on stiff knees.

Rising, Asher walked after him, to the edge of the ridge, and took his field glasses from their case.

Cruz pointed down slope; "We are above the Spanish defenses," he said. "Below us, near the sea, they have block houses. There are trench systems at the villages of Siboney and Daiquiri, also along the highway, and the railroad west toward Santiago has strong defenses. There are blockhouses east, at the ends of Guantanamo Bay. These are small, of no consequence, but an army of seven thousand, with artillery, holds Guantanamo. We cannot assault such a place, and Santiago is even stronger." Cruz paused and lit a cigar; he smiled with it sticking sideways between his lips. "They

135

cannot venture out, though. When your army comes, this will change. General Garcia gathers his army in Santiago Province also." Cruz sighed, "It will be soon," he said.

Asher raised his field glasses to his eyes. He could not make out details of the coast, although he did see the railroad. Off Santiago, several ships steamed slowly. Whose ships? An American blockade possibly, like the one off of Havana he thought. "War ships?" he said, passing the glasses to the major.

Cruz looked; he passed the glasses back. "I know nothing of ships," he said, unconcerned. He snorted. "Did you know, before last year, I had not seen the sea?"

That afternoon, Asher informed General Mendez that he required a heliograph. Mendez said there were none; none that he was aware of anyway. The Spanish used them regularly, and Asher refused to believe one hadn't been captured at some point. He mentioned this to Machado.

"Two more ships steamed in from the west," Asher said over dinner. "My orders were to pass information. All I've been passing," he complained, "is beans."

"That is also soldier's work," Muchado said, and men sniggered. He had a large cigar stuck out the side of his mouth, and took a gulp from a bottle of rum without removing it.

"You could blow yourself up that way," Asher warned, and scratched at a bug bite.

"*Es verdad*, 'it's true'," he agreed, "but life has many dangers, does it not, and many are pleasant. Dominoes," he called out expectantly, "who will play?"

Machado, gone in the morning, had returned to camp in the evening. With his scarred face bearing a self-satisfied grin, he had presented Asher with a heliograph. It was battered; blood smeared and had suffered a bullet hole through its case, but was perfectly workable. Asher, as pleased as a birthday boy, had immediately acquired those other things he required for a signal station.

At twilight on the morning of the fourth, he was working his way through scrub and scattered trees, using an old cattle trail. The ridge of the high plateau angled toward the sea. His information was, it would lead to a number of small but high hills on the coast east of Santiago. With him were four men. They led a burro loaded with gear, and one man swore to knowledge of an area perfect for Asher's purpose. A hillside gap, overgrown with brush and small trees proved excellent. It was not obvious from the summit, and nearly invisible when viewed from the sides or below, yet it faced the sea. There was even drinkable water within a half mile.

They quickly cut away a small space for sleeping, and stretched a tarp between two trees for shelter. Asher placed the heliograph where the light would strike the mirror, and began the adjustment necessary to sight the signal glass on the ship nearest him. He reviewed his notebook and began to send. Twenty minutes had passed before he received a reply. Then for two hours, he transmitted information, constantly readjusting the heliograph as the sun and ship changed position. There were questions about Guantanamo's lower bay, for which he had no answers. There were other questions he could answer, and he agreed to a schedule for daily communication with the fleet.

He secured his device, and leaned back in the shade to cool off, then leaned forward again and stripped off his uniform blouse. The wool was far too hot for the tropics. Even stripped to the waist, he was wet with perspiration. He took a drink and relaxed; spoke to his companions, telling them, things were well. Asher grinned in satisfaction for this was the first time he'd accomplished anything useful as a soldier. He felt much better about being in Cuba. Up to this moment, he'd considered it all a waste of time. Of those in his graduating class, he was probably the man least interested in becoming involved in the war, yet he had preceded the entire army in fighting it.

He didn't consider himself a soldier, but on appraising his ragged comrades, he realized himself to be better trained as one than the majority of those he traveled with. He supposed the set of a man's mind, and the depth of his determination, to be factors that turned a man to a trade. Beyond that, the level of expertise, and natural ability developed over time. His success in the cane field skirmish was predicated on talents acquired over a lifetime. Other than the use of his saber, he had fought using skills originally mastered for reasons having nothing to do with war. With that *ménage* of abilities and luck, he had survived. Fate had it's own logic.

The Navy put into lower Guantanamo Bay on June 6 and the cruisers *Yankee* and *Marblehead,* chased a small Spanish gunboat into the upper bay, their shellfire kicking up the water on all sides of the retiring ship. Their guns were then trained on a blockhouse to support the landing of a hundred Marines. They held off the Spaniards for the better part of a week, until reinforcements arrived from Key West. The US Navy had swiftly acquired a secure coaling station for the fleet. Occasionally that fleet, blockading to the west, shelled Santiago's harbor fortification. Inland, the Spanish continued improving the city's defenses while their fleet remained at anchor in the fortified harbor. The trapped population trembled, and wondered when the US Army would arrive.

Asher, who had been actively prowling up and down the coast for two weeks, was becoming ever more efficient at finding his way around the Spanish positions. His field pouch was crammed with drawings and notes describing the disposition of enemy troops and their defenses. Unfortunately, the heliograph was unsuited to send much of the information.

He was alone, for on June 14, General Mendez had marched to Guantanamo on instructions to assist his compatriots in the harassment of those enemy defenses. Only a few ragged companies remained east of Santiago. He had to forage for meager rations of fruit and rice, and the area had been picked nearly clean by the Cubans before they departed. He had made the decision; he would request that the Navy disembark him. If that couldn't be arranged, he would sneak past Spanish pickets, and into the Marine camp, south of Guantanamo. It appeared to Asher that Admiral Samson was far more concerned with harbor fortifications and the Spanish fleet than with the disposition of Spanish troops.

His opinion proved correct, for the next communication from the *Cruiser New York,* requested that he direct naval gunfire on the harbor fortifications. He acknowledged the signal and picked his way up through the scrub to a hilltop, where he climbed a tree. From it, he could see Santiago, but not the fortified peninsula south of the bay. On the ridge to his west were blockhouses and Spanish picket posts. This left only a few high hills to their rear. From those hills, he would be able to see and to signal, but the Spanish would also be able to see his signals. He surveyed the area and studied the problem. It could be done but more likely he'd be caught or killed, or both. He climbed unhappily down out of the tree, descending the hillside to his camp. He was hungry and for Asher, being hungry made focusing on subjects other than eating difficult. Within minutes the heliograph was dismantled and in its pack. With it and his rifle slung on his back, he hiked back through the trees, and up to the plateau where he tethered his horse. Rain fell daily and there was plenty of grass, but without grain, the bay was losing weight. He supposed the horse didn't like guavas any better than he did.

Late in the afternoon, he saddled up, and began working his

way north, down off the limestone ridge. He rode through scrub brush following gullies to keep out of sight. A mile south of the river Aquadores, he turned west between two steep hills, emerging where the Laguna road met the San Juan River. Here, Asher watered his horse and concealed it within the low dense jungle.

He ate a coconut and a couple of mangoes, and slowly chewed some uncooked rice. Uncooked rice was not particularly tasty or satisfying. If he could get up into the mountains tomorrow, he promised himself that he would try to shoot a goat — if the insurrectos had left one uneaten.

In the scrub jungle, mosquitoes became insufferable near twilight. He moved cautiously south, parallel to the Laguna road. The undergrowth clutched at his pack and clothing as the horse moved under and through the tangle. With the cover of dark, Asher climbed the coastal escarpment west of the river, coming out of the trees onto a semi-barren hilltop. Before him lay the sea, and across it glared the spotlights of the US fleet, their beams illuminating Punta El Morro and the harbor entrance. He saw no one; he heard nothing, other than the rush of the trade wind, and yet he had an uneasy feeling. Using his machete, he quietly cut brush and wove it around a lone tree, forming a blind to conceal him and the heliograph. He lay down, thankful the brisk wind kept mosquitoes from the hilltop.

From somewhere below, he heard music, laughter, and later a roll call as the changing of the guard took place. He felt unexpectedly lustful and wished for a warm woman to share the night. It had been some time since he had indulged in female comfort. It was lonely here, and Asher realized that if it went badly, he'd die alone.

"Dead is dead," he told himself, but dying seemed an easier thing to do with good company. Well, any company. He'd do his best to avoid being killed, and he had a good route of retreat, with a horse waiting. That, and he was a crack shot. Doubt entered his mind though, and he decided to write a letter to his aunt. He put it in his pouch on the off chance. He thought about Charleston, school, and his somehow distant relatives, and he wondered what Gwen would think of all this. For a fact, he didn't care. When women came to his mind — the sort of woman one married, Miss O'Ryan's image came to him now. It had been long since he thought of or pictured others. Perhaps he would meet her again.

Asher had no sense of what time he fell asleep but the sun was a good hour above the horizon when the smell of cooking bacon woke him. Punta El Morro and much of the harbor were visible, as were the ships of both fleets. To his horror so was a block house, no more than five hundred yards downhill to the east where soldiers were hanging laundry.

"Dam-it," he muttered, cranky from weeks of sleeping in the open, itchy from feeding bugs. He scratched with vigor but only itched more. He opened his canteen and took a drink, then splashed some in his face before going to work. It required only minutes to adjust his mirrors. Using his field glasses, he picked out the *New York* about four miles offshore, and began to flash his recognition signal. He received a reply within moments and returned, "All ready." One of the battle ships was easing inshore, and he aligned his mirrors on the ship just as smoke erupted from its forward guns. The shells cleared the point, exploding three hundred yards inside the bay. "Three hundred long," he flashed. The next salvo burst on the beach. "One hundred long," he sent, and so it went, for perhaps thirty minutes.

So, intent was Asher, on the transmission of signals and events to his west that he was unaware of the soldiers until one walked between him and the battleship *Oregon*. Asher, who happened to be reading the Oregon's message at that

141

moment, hunkered down and cursed his luck. It was now evident that they had climbed the hill to watch the bombardment. Their backs were to him, five men, perhaps more beyond the curve of the hill. He slipped his field glasses into their case and picked up his rifle.

"*They aren't going to see me*," he thought, but then one decided to stand in the shade. As he walked toward the tree, Asher saw his eyes widen and shot him in the chest.

Three of the men, who had walked up the hill, were without their rifles and ran away. The other threw himself down, opening fire and rapidity emptying his clip in Asher's direction. One of his wildly fired rounds grazed his scalp. It burned furiously. Asher's second shot took the soldier in the forehead, and the man slumped over his rifle. Jumping up, he cursed, and began running down the backside of the hill. Behind him, a bugle called assembly.

"Cavalry," he swore aloud. "Damn!"

Blinking blood out of his eyes, he ran all the faster. The first shots came from his right, from off the shoulder of the hill, three hundred yards. They skipped and sang off the rocks, none closer than a few feet, but threatening enough for him to jump into a gully. He paused, catching his breath and appraised the situation. They knew he was alone and on foot. Surely, he was flanked, but in this wash, he could move downhill without exposing himself. It would take only minutes for cavalry to overtake him, but if he could reach the trees down slope unseen, he might reach his horse. Turning to his left, he glanced at the wash twisting down into the scrub. Blood and sweat blurred his vision. He wiped his eyes, and fighting off a wave of dizziness, studied how the wash disappeared into the trees beyond the base of the hill.

He began a skip and jump decent, being careful not to show himself. There was a great deal of rifle fire now, but most directed high up the hill. The trees thickened and he ran along

142

what appeared to be a narrow trail as the ground became level. He ran unencumbered except for his weapons and field glasses, but the undergrowth thickened and slowed him. "Minutes are what I've got," he panted out loud, "Run the road or I may not find my horse." He cut to his right and within a few moments slid down an embankment onto the Laguna road. Turning again, this time to his left, Asher ran northwest on the hard-packed dirt.

Hooves and the clanking of metal soon came from behind, and he plunged into the undergrowth again. The road was running beside the river now, and he knew he must be within a hundred yards of his horse. He was out of breath, but the slower pace forced by the jungle helped. By pure luck, he blundered across his own tracks, finding the horse a hundred feet further. Shouts and voices from the road alerted him that the cavalry were guerrillas, and that infantry would be coming up behind him. He was between them now. Well, they didn't know he was mounted; they had just run their mounts two miles at a fast pace. He replaced the rounds he fired from his Mauser, adjusted his tack and mounted.

He would cut the road, cross the river, and ride east into the mountains. Astride the horse, he felt more confident, even if he was a better target. He walked the bay ahead, pulling up at the edge of the road. It was quiet. Asher leaned out, looking both ways; he saw nothing. "Well, horse, I hope you feel like a run this morning," he whispered to the bay. He reined around and smacked it across the rump. The big gelding launched itself nearly across the road and straight into the shallow river. The bay was half way up the far bank when shots were fired.

Asher runs for it.

The leaves made slapping sounds as bullets passed. Asher saw horsemen. They were well upriver on the west bank, and then he was into the trees, vines ripping at his clothes. The bushes were head high and he bent low, letting the horse pick a fast walk. Behind him was a bugles blare and shouts. He pictured them running those horses up that road, their officer spreading them out, sending a squad racing upriver and around the hill to head him off. He headed the bay up slope; the underbrush thinned, and he broke out onto a narrow road. The hilltop was clear of growth, and a barbed wire fence bordered it. He took the road uphill, and left it riding cross slope at the end of a fence, into a dip, then onto a second hill to the right. Near the top, rifle shots told him he'd been seen.

They were riding fast uphill as he topped the crest. Urged the bay into a gallop at the top, they raced northwest down a gentle slope, and into a gap leading northeast between two steep hills. Forced to slow to a walk by the thick forest, the horse was weaving among the trees. The jungle became so close he had to pull his feet from the stirrups, and cling with his feet over the horse's rump for a few hundred feet. When it thinned, he urged the bay into an easy lope toward the northeast. The group of four riders, coming at him from a shallow valley on his right was a surprise.

He was sure the Bay could outrun them, but if they ran into any troops ahead, these would come up behind. He didn't want to fight these men, but he was not being given a reasonable option. He rode into a ditch and jumped to the ground with his rifle. He hit the first horse at five hundred yards; the second two went down inside of four hundred. Not having time to adjust his sights, he aimed at the chest of the fourth horse and hit its rider instead.

Hands trembling slightly, he swung back into the saddle. The guerrillas, enraged at losing their mounts, were putting down a stream of rapid fire in his direction. Bending low, Asher trotted along the ditch, keeping high ground between him and the rifles, and then cantered across a green hillside toward the Seco River. East of the river, the land rose slowly, rolling hills and scattered palms. From a hilltop, he saw them coming over a crest far behind. They were scattered now, some horses already spent, but perhaps a dozen that were holding up, and they were gaining.

Asher pushed the bay into an easy gallop, holding his lead to over a mile. His head ached where the bullet had creased it. Sweat trickled down his spine. Sweat burned his eyes and his shirt stuck to his side. He reined in at a small ford to let the bay drink. Only then did he notice new wounds. Small holes, in and out of his side, five inches apart, just above his belt. The wound had begun to burn a little, not really much pain. If he had to be shot that was as convenient a place as one could ask, and then the lack of pain surprised him.

145

He mounted again, continuing to push the pace, and slowly circled to his right, climbing up into the mountains. By three in the afternoon two riders still followed. They would keep up, stay in sight, long enough for others to arrive with fresh mounts. The bay was still strong, but he did not intend to run it into the ground. The bullet hole, which had seemed so minor, now hurt something awful. Ahead was a depression between a ridge and hilltop, a kind of bowl with a rocky ledge on the far side. Asher crossed it at a gallop, and dismounting, led the bay behind the rocks. He was hurting too much to make running acceptable anymore, and if they wanted so badly to kill him, well, they deserved what they got. "*God's will*," he thought, and knelt in the shadow of the rock.

As they cleared the crest, he waited. He could smell his own sweat, his own blood. Biting flies settled, distracting him. He sighted and remained still, ignoring the insects until his pursuers were no more than forty yards. It took five shots because one soldier swung behind the roan he was riding. He had to drop the horse in order to get a clear shot at the rider. He wasn't sure of his shot because the Spaniard had gone down behind his horse, and couldn't leave the shelter of the rocks without exposing himself. Feeling bad about the entire situation, he sat and waited. After a while, he was sure the man was hard-hit, for his rasping, attempts to breath were audible. A miserable guilt bore down. Asher knew the man was dying. He wanted him to die, wanted it over. He didn't want to listen to his dying. After a few minutes he did die.

Getting the field glasses out hurt, for his side had stiffened and his head throbbed. He looked back down into the valley and saw nothing. He was alone, and realized he was hungry. The men he killed were not big men, and even shot-up, he was able to drag them against the bluff. Prying at the bank with one of their rifles, he collapsed some earth over them, and said a prayer. He prayed forgiveness for himself, rather than

146

his victims, and finished saying, "Lord, I had no ill will for these men, but I wasn't the one doing the chasing."

Crossing himself, he went to his horse, intending to get rice to chew. "To hell with it," he said aloud, and put the bag to the horse's mouth, to give it what rice remained. Pulling the machete from his saddle, Asher walked out to the roan's carcass. Looking down at the dead horse, he thought, "Better me than the vultures," and swung the blade downward into the warm flesh.

Chapter 14

Under a clear and cloudless blue sky, wind from the northwest blew cool from the mountains. Beneath the wind, the shallow water of Mahomilla Bay teemed with birds, and reflected the palms that lined the south shore. Asher though, was in no state to appreciate local beauty. From a hill to the west, he had spotted several small fishing boats and aimed to commandeer one. He would need it to cross the mouth of Guantanamo Bay.

A few of the fishermen ran when he rode in, not at all strange, hostilities being what they were. He spared no time in asking who would ferry him to Camp McCalla. No one spoke up, a likely reason being that the Marines had taken to shooting at anything that came close.

"Who will accept my three double eagles for passage?" Asher asked, this time holding coins in one hand and his thirty-eight-service revolver in the other. Three of the men stepped forward, each ready to fight the other for the fortune offered.

"A coin for each man," he said. "I'll pay another coin to the man who cares for the horse."

Stiffly he dismounted, pulled his rifle from the boot and leaned against a boat. He was hurt, dizzy and feverish. His wounds leaked, and even his trouser leg was wet. He wanted to get to where there was a field hospital. He wanted to eat, to bathe and to sleep in a bed. Other dam'd fools could have his place in the war.

A boat was readied within minutes, but he made them mark a large "U S" on the sail with charcoal, then tie rags to a pair of sticks so he could communicate by semaphore. With his rifle and map pouch, he climbed into the bow with his rifle. Exhausted, he sat.

"*Vamenos*, 'We go'," he said.

"*Donde, Señor* ' where, lord'?" asked the old man at the tiller.

"Go to them," he pointed, speaking of two ships anchored side by side, a collier and the battleship it was bunkering.

They pushed off. Once the men had rowed out into the channel, the wind became fair. The old man at the tiller sheeted the skiff's sail tight and, with wind abeam, bore up into the anchorage. The skiff heeled and slipped along smartly under his skilled hand. Details of the east shore became sharp; tents and shitters were evident.

A mile off, Asher stood. He was painfully weak, so he put his back to the mast as he began to wigwag a message. "US Army officer, request to board." A half-mile out he read a reply, a man sending from the after turret, "Come aboard," the semaphore read.

Asher managed to climb from the boat to the deck of the battleship *Texas*, and to report that he had intelligence to pass. He was not aware of how bad he looked, nor was he conscious of stares drawn by his slate-pale complexion, smell, and his ruined uniform.

"Here, make way there," an ensign said, as he cleared a passage leading Asher toward the Captain's dayroom.

"Careful there, sir," an old chief said, and steadied him when he slipped in the stairwell. He was dizzy; he concentrated to hold himself steady as he gave the pouch to Captain Phillip, and briefly explained what it held. Asher had no memory of sagging to the deck, but he did remember a cool hand on his head.

"This man's been wounded," a voice said, and someone called for the surgeon. After that, he must have slept.

The first coherent conversation was with a doctor.

"Fractured skull and loss of blood," The doctor told him. "You've not been yourself for several days. That was the fever of course, but it's broken and another week aboard *Relief* will have you fit."

The wards of the hospital ship *Relief* had already begun to fill. Bedded down in double bunks to both sides of him, were wounded men. Asher was not quite oriented, but was acutely aware of a sharp antiseptic odor. He realized that an orderly was swabbing the deck behind the doctor and the smell was ammonia. His stomach growled and he asked the doctor what had happened.

"The landings have occurred Lieutenant and the first battles — you'll have to excuse me now," and he walked toward a frantically waving nurse at the far end of the ward.

Asher's bunk was alongside a window, and he eased himself up so he could see out. A half-mile away, laid the village of Siboney, now filled with troops and supplies. Anchored offshore were transports. Lighters shuttled back and forth. A trooper in the next bunk motioned.

"Sheess!" he hissed, "y'all ain't got some tobacco, by chance?" the man whispered. "Ain't had none for more in

149

four days. Don't allow for it in here neither," he said, his face screwing up in disgust.

There was subdued conversation, the clink of glass, sound of leather on tile as a nurse walked down the aisle, not a silence, rather a lack of noise. Asher was weak, but did not feel ill. Putting a hand to his head, he realized someone had shaved a strip down the middle where the bullet creased him. He imagined himself looking a little like a skunk. There was a dressing on his left side, but it was an unblemished white, and It seemed probable the wound was healing.

A little later, a steward rolled a cart along and doled out beef bouillon and corn bread. Before the cart had moved ten feet, Asher swallowed his portion like a greedy hound, and asked for more. Coffee came later and an orderly showed him where the sanitary facilities were. Through the day, he could hear artillery fire, and asked his neighbor where the fighting was.

"Near Santiago, I spec." He gestured at Asher bandages, "where'd y'all get yours?"

"Had my hair parted on the coast south of Santiago, but I can't say just when I got it in the side. I was doing my best to out ride some cavalry, and got so beat up in the trees that I didn't really notice."

"I know how 'tis," the man said. "Indians plunked me some years back. So busy I didn't pay it no mind 'til my boot filled up".

"How'd you get that?" Asher asked, pointing at the dressing high on his inner thigh.

"Las Guasimas, with the first foot cavalry," he said. "Dam'd fool army shipped us in without our horses. Dam'd near shot my wedding gear away. First Volunteers and the Tenth took that ridge, serving under old fighting Joe Wheeler. Hell, my pa was a Confederate Cap'n with him some thirty year ago. I will say — that was one hot little fight. Put sixteen boys in the ground, and half a hundred on their backs. Bullets were thicker en flies 'round a dead cow. Say! My name's Baggett," he introduced, "Sergeant First Class Carl Baggett."

"Asher Byran, lieutenant; and pleased to know you, sergeant."

"Likewise, sir," the sergeant said. A nurse accompanied by an orderly approached from behind his bed, and when they stopped, he turned to face them.

"It's time to change your dressing, Mr. Baggett," the nurse announced.

"Oh — Now, ma'am — y'all did do that the other day. Can't ya leave off picking at me?"

"Don't whine sergeant," the woman barked, motioning for the orderly to help Baggett to his feet. "You took that bullet in a nasty place, and we wouldn't want the doctor having to do any additional cutting down there, would we?"

The orderly helped the grumbling Sergeant out of bed and toward surgery. Asher lay back, comfortable but drowsy and napped. He woke to cool night air, and an awareness of activity. The ward had become more crowded while he slept. The electric lamps were turned down, and the newly wounded, groaned in the near dark. He thought back on the preceding weeks but had no way to judge if he'd accomplished anything useful. He had directed, perhaps twenty minutes of navel shelling, reduced, by some minuscule percentage, the number of the enemy. Somewhere there would be orphaned children, women grieving. That was, after all, the duty of a soldier; still, what difference had his efforts made?

From below deck rose muffled screams . He conceded he was alive and whole, which was as important a consideration, as needed to be dwelt on. He had done his duty, done what he could and had survived. What would come next? Boredom, he hoped. He wouldn't fret. After he convalesced, someone would assign him to something. He became aware of mild cramps and climbed from his bed to sway awkwardly toward the toilets. Covering fifty feet of deck was as much of a problem as he wished to deal with. Tomorrow, yes tomorrow, he would find someone who could inform him as to what was happening.

The information came to him directly across the poker table as the Major said, "I swear, boys, they're near to marching up to headquarters, and putting the tar brush to General Shafter. Why, we've been looking down the Spaniard's throats for over a week. We've been letting them improve the defense while ole fatty negotiates."

"Well, gentlemen, from the way fever's taking hold, we won't have any boys left for fighting if the talking don't do it," prophesied another of the poker players.

"Your deal," Asher said, pushing him the cards.

"You're correct," a captain said, as he tried to scratch inside his cast. "My company had near a third of its strength on sick roll. Boys are falling off quick — hum — 'll take two cards."

One," Asher said, keeping his face blank, as he looked at four kings.

"Pat," said the captain.

Others at the table drew or folded, leaving Asher and four others to raise, see and call. In the end, he beat a full house, ace high, to win the equivalent of two months' pay.

"Lucky bastard," the Major swore, tossing down his hand. "And you'll give your fellows no chance to recoup," he complained.

"No chance, sir," Asher grinned. "Tomorrow perhaps," he said excusing himself, and climbed to the bridge deck to visit. He and the *Relief's* second officer had struck up a friendship, and the mate was a prime source of information via the Navy. He found him gazing aimlessly at the water, and asked if there was a change in negotiations.

"We're to bombard the city again," he, said, "Unless they surrender, that is. General Linares is conferring with Madrid. The latest offer is, they surrender the city, and we transport their Army back to Spain. That's with their arms, you know. Dons feel strongly about their honor. Hell, our boys destroyed Cervera's fleet last week; it broke what resolve they had. I suppose they've been praying for a hurricane to come along and wipe us out, but that isn't likely now. Linares just has to find an honorable way to give up. A matter of time I'd say." He crossed to the chart room, pouring a coffee from a pot perched above a candle. He gestured to Asher. "Help yourself," he invited.

"How soon do you think?" Asher filled his cup and added milk from a small can.

"Soon," the mate said, and in his slow manner, seemed to be less than interested. He sipped his coffee before answering. "Tomorrow morning and the Navy moves in shore. Capone's in charge of what artillery Shafter has. My guess is it won't come to that."

"Fire-eaters want to assault the defenses -- I've seen them. I personally wouldn't care to."

"Not much chance. My belief is, Santiago will be surrendered tomorrow."

"I hope you're correct," Asher added truthfully. "I expect to be pronounced fit shortly, and would prefer to see the place pacified before I visit again. No profit in getting killed prematurely. I look forward to filling the earth with my prodigy before going to my just rewards."

The mate chuckled, and bent forward to answer a whistle from the voice tube. He was called to attend the landing of some shore boats and excused himself. Asher descended from the bridge level and reclined in a deck chair. To date, most accounts of the invasion were in conflict. The telling often depends far more on the correspondent's wish for a good story than troublesome facts. What men saw or knew to happen, seldom determined the writing of an article. Even the men who engaged in the battles often disagreed on what had taken place.

The old Confederate, General Joe Wheeler, had begun the fight by pushing the Dons out of their fortifications at Las Guasimas with dismounted cavalry. This initiative enraged General Young, who considered himself usurped, and complained to General Shafter. Thus, during the week that followed, the Army did little other than get itself ashore and skirmish. The actual assault on Santiago's outer defenses did not take place until July 1, and as in most battles, few things happened as planned. The Spanish artillery proved not only to be superior, but invisible with the use of smokeless powder. Their Mauser rifles not only fired more rounds than most American weapons, but also used smokeless powder, which helped conceal Spanish positions. Shafter's army was marked by clouds of white smoke every time troops pulled a trigger. For hours, the U.S. forces lay exposed to enemy fire, awaiting orders to advance.

Frustrated, three officers at different points took initiative, attacking almost simultaneously and without orders. Of these, Lt. Jules Ord, was killed as he reached the top of the hill; another was wounded. The third, Col. Theodore Roosevelt, once Assistant Secretary of the Navy, and now the darling of the press corps, well, he came through unscathed, and was now the hero of the day. Medical facilities were overwhelmed, ammunition ran low and so the Army clung to the hilltops, knowing that on that first night, it wouldn't take much to push them back off. By the second night, they were entrenched and reinforced.

Admiral Cervera received final orders to take his fleet to sea. On July 3 they charged out the narrow channel into the combined fire of the US Navy's Atlantic fleet. By dusk that day Spain's fleet had been destroyed. Since, that day the Armies had sniped at each other, negotiated, sickened, and like all armies, complained. There was a great deal of complaining, particularly about the transport for wagons and mule trains were proving insufficient to move enough materiel from Siboney to feed and supply Shafter's Army.

Asher looked blandly out toward the pale line of the Sierra Maestro, wondering about the Cuban armies he'd marched with. From what men said, there had already been a number of misunderstandings between the allies. Presently there was little respect for the Cubans as soldiers. He had seen them fight, and he felt it was a matter of style. They did what worked for them. The Cuban army on the eastern end of the island was mainly black though, and Asher thought that the root of prejudicial opinion lay in the color of their skin.

"Lieutenant Byran."

His name, spoken so near, startled him. He looked up to see a dispatch corporal. "Yes, Corporal," he said, rising to face the trooper as he approached.

The corporal said, "Orders, sir," and offered an envelope. "If you're fit, sir, you're to accompany me to General Wood's headquarters immediately. He's taking all unattached Spanish speaking officers into his command."

Asher tore open the envelope and read. He was to report to the Second Cavalry Brigade on receipt, etc, etc. "My gear?" he asked.

"Draw what you need from the quartermaster ashore, sir. If you'll meet me at the number three boat, sir, I have two other officers to collect."

"I've a few people to thank. I'll be there shortly," he said, perturbed. For a fact, orders were quick in coming. He would have sworn that excepting for a few doctors and nurses, his existence was unknown. Going below, he managed to find two of his nurses and thank them. The doctor was in surgery, but they promised to tell him of Asher's appreciation. He saw the mate as he was preparing to board the shore boat. They shook hands, wishing each other good luck. Then he was heading for the beach, and wishing he'd grabbed something to eat before departing.

Chapter 15

The hill country between mountains and sea became a slick, slippery quagmire with each cloud of rain. The terrain remained damp and slimy, until the blazing sun of midday caused the earth to steam and crack, as it baked it to the hardness of bricks. Buzzards drifted in the hot sky, circling high up, above the old city. They were plain to see long before the military party traveling the twisting Camino Real, topped the hill, and descended the slope toward the red tile rooftops.

A day after the surrender, General Leonard Wood, who had been named Military Governor of the city's narrow streets at the head of a score of staff officers. Everywhere they turned, they saw emaciated and ragged people who crowded into any available patch of shade. Mounds of garbage and the rotting carcasses of animals lay heaped against walls and often half-filled streets. Open sewers, blocked by this debris, were clogged with filth and excrement, and overflowed, making narrow ponds between the stained stucco buildings.

From what Asher was observing, the General and his staff would not have much free time. The full gravity of what they faced did not strike him until they reached an area of open ground where a river entered the bay. Here, many thousands of women and children, mostly of the poorer classes, had gathered, seeking what shelter they could. Exhausted, exposed to sun and rain, they had starved and weakened. Having only polluted water to drink, disease took them in droves. The sick lay with the unburied dead. In fact, the dead lay not only here, but were piled around the cemetery and throughout the city, uncollected and bloating, in streets or under rubble where they fell during the navel bombardment.

In a hall of the Governor's Palace, General Wood had addressed his officers. He outlined their task with a few simple sentences, saying, "Gentlemen, in this order we must proceed: provide food, bury the dead, nurse and care for the sick, clean up the city. My first orders will be immediately drawn up." He pointed to a map of the city. "Become familiar with this map. You will be dispersing with squads to various quarters of the city. I will want written and verbal reports by dark. I am concerned with conditions, and want your reports to draw attention to any critical circumstances. Within the hour, My adjutant clerk will provide each officer with individual orders. Gentlemen, you are dismissed."

The human suffering, the sights and stench of the city were nearly overwhelming. Asher's orders were to inspect, then to report on conditions at the prison. He found it overfilled and without food. They had packed political prisoners into cells with captured soldiers and felons. Many had served out their sentences long before but were forgotten. Records did not exist. In a room used for interrogation, several mutilated bodies lay rotting in the heat. Overwhelmed by the stench, he swallowed to keep from gagging and slammed the heavy door. As he hurried into the better air of the portico, his sergeant offered him a cigar but he waved it away.

"Helps against the smell, Lieutenant — ought to try it. Good cigar," he continued and shrugging his shoulders, slipped the cigar back into his blouse as clouds of smoke wafted from the cigar in his mouth. "Only three guards left in the place, sir. Lopez says, only reason they're here yet, is they got no place else to go."

"Put men at the gate and on the wall there," Asher ordered. "Let the prisoners out into the courtyard where they can at least get at the well." He absently swatted flies away from his face and said, "Have Lopez talk to them from the wall. Tell them we'll get rations in here by morning." He spit and held a kerchief to his face, wanting to leave the place and its hollow-eyed inhabitants.

"Ain't but ten of us, sir, what if they try to bust out?"

"Why, hell, Sergeant, just let them run. The way I see it, they will most likely be released. Damn — Not many can do better than crawl anyway," he said venting his disgust at the conditions.

The staff meeting lasted a couple of hours; General Wood, who invited discussion in some instances, regarded each report he received. Staff foresaw the need for food as the most critical need, and a transport ship loaded with military rations had been piloted into the harbor. Already, the Army had begun to cart food to relief stations for distribution by the quartermaster corps. Asher, a junior second Lieutenant, gave his own report briefly stating his estimate of the prison population and conditions. "It's my belief sir," he had said, wrapping up his report, "that most of those people don't belong in there."

Wood nodded, thanked him, and the conference continued. It could have been past midnight before Asher slept. He hadn't checked his pocket watch. Stretching out on the floor of a reception room, he had fallen to sleep in moments.

Wood needed even more men who were bi-lingual. In the next days, he stripped Shafter's army of Spanish-speaking officers, and attached them to his new command. His old Rough Rider command, the 2nd brigade, was placed under the command of Col. Roosevelt. Arrangements to communicate with General Colaxio Garcia's rebel army were a priority. Most of the Cuban force had separated itself from the Americans. There was no doubt of how General Garcia felt. His army had been forbidden entry into Santiago, and the American flag, rather than the Cuban, flew over the city. Garcia had been so incensed, so deeply insulted that he had remained away from the surrender ceremonies. Further, he voiced a refusal to stand in the same building as the surrendering Spanish officials. Wood felt it imperative to repair the relations with the Cubans that had been so badly damaged by Shafter's staff.

Asher had not attended the ceremonies himself of course but he had been amused, when he learned what had happened to a journalist of his acquaintance. The journalist, inflamed at being ordered to leave the palace roof during the flag raising ceremony, had thrown a punch at General Shafter. The adjutant threw the reporter in question into the local prison for the night, the very hellhole that Asher had inspected a day later.

Though taken by the humor of this one small incident, Asher had been ignorant of the policies and politics played out, and of bad blood fostered between the allies. Kept out of Santiago, Garcia ordered his armies west and north against Holguin and other Spanish-held cities. Asher and three other officers' received instructions to accompany the Cuban armies as liaison. Staff assigned them dispatch riders with orders to

159

communicate daily with Governor Wood. As chance would have it, one of the Spanish speaking riders was Sergeant Gabriel Strong.

"I swear it, sir," he said, having arrived from Santiago, "They're stacking bodies up in heaps wit' grass and kerosene. Burning a couple hundred at ah shot. Dam'd gory a thing as ever I saw. General Wood, he hired every cart in Santiago for hauling bodies. Two, three hundred, maybe more folks dying every day. Getting caught up is giving the General fits."

"He is the man that will get it done, and it sounds to me like being in the field is not half bad, considering." Asher took a pull from a bottle of rum and tossed another green branch on the fire. "I can't say Gomez's people are as friendly as they used to be, not that I blame them."

"Women friendly 'nuff," Gabe smiled and scratched.

"I'm talking politics," he mumbled drunkenly.

"I got no head for that."

"Well, they're starting to suspect we may want Cuba for ourselves," he said.

"They're poor, but they're not stupid. Got a right to be rankled. Ain't such a poor place, and I spec we could steal worst," Gabe said, searching his crouch for an offending insect.

"Well, yeah, but it won't happen. The people with real money will just keep buying up Cuban dirt. They may have their independence, but Americans will own the place. Hell — I sat in Tampa listening to our wealthier citizens discussing how it worked."

"Well, sir, me being just a yellow leg Sergeant, y'all word on that's good enough, but spec it works that away about everywhere, now don't it? May buy up some lil bit ah Cuba for myself. It surely is cheap enough these days." When Asher didn't comment, he continued, "If y'all don't' mind, sir, I plan to wander down there and see if there's any friendly women to be found." Gabe stood stretching. "Dam'd saddle stiff," he said. "All the killing going on, there's more than a few lonely widows needs consoled sir. Better than cuddling up to that bottle," he added, sincerity in his voice.

"Not in the mood. You might consider washing up for the widows though. You smell like horse sweat."

Headed down hill, Gabe left him, his laugher still clear, after he had disappeared into the dark. Asher leaned back, took another drink. In the morning, he'd feel poor for the rum, but he'd sleep well for it tonight. He was camped on high dry ground, with few mosquitoes, and he pitied the troops in the lowlands around Santiago. Half were down with fever, dysentery, or both. Be more men dead from bugs and bad water than bullets before long. The US Government seemed to fear that the returning army would carry yellow fever back to the mainland, and driven by this fear, they appeared ready to abandon the army. It was a bad circumstance, unfair to say the least as Asher judged, but then who wants the opinion of a junior officer. A last pull from the bottle, and he closed his eyes, letting the drunk and the sleep take him.

When Asher, now a First Lieutenant, had finally been ordered back to Santiago to report personally to Governor Wood, the political landscape had changed radically. Cuban forces, under Gomez, were executing all guardia soldiers, as well as any civilians believed loyal to Spain. This was a serious concern of the military governor.

As Asher reached the cathedral, he saw columns of troops marching toward transports in the harbor. Many of the soldiers marched on wobbly legs, or far too sick to walk, rode stretched out in wagons. He spotted an acquaintance, Captain Luna in a café with fellow officers and dismounted.

"On their way home?" Asher asked, pulling off his

gauntlets.

"Wish I was," Luna replied tiredly. Turning toward a pair of fresh-looking men, he gestured, "Ash, Lieutenants Brown and Hefner, Seventh Cavalry's healthy replacements."

"A pleasure," Asher said, shaking hands as they rose from their seats.

"Same," Hefner said, with a pleasant smile. "We're another batch for the fever."

"Not so bad if you take care of yourself," Asher said raising a hand for a waiter. "I've spent most of my life in the tropics, born in Florida, and I've done well enough, but it seems to take those who are already worn down or otherwise unhealthy. Coffee, please," he said to the waiter. Turning back to Luna, he asked, "When did the orders come to return the army?"

"Haah! Now there's a story," Luna grinned, a sudden spark in his sunken eyes.

Asher could see he was perspiring and pale, no doubt a touch of malarial fever.

"Shafter called a meeting of all his officers, brigade commanders and above, to deal with the health of the army. That was on the 31st. Roosevelt instigated what amounted to a mutiny of the general staff and wrote a letter stating that if the army was not returned to the mainland, it would be destroyed by epidemic." Luna smiled, "Made sure the papers got a copy under the table. It took about three days to embarrass the government into action. Teddy ought to ride that one into office when he gets back to New York."

Coffee came and they continued to talk. The first American troops were now ashore in the Philippines, and the Army controlled the south of Puerto Rico. Luna informed him that Spain was trying to arrange a peace, and the army was preparing to set up six military areas like Santiago, seven departments, each with a general and his staff to govern. "I was under the impression that the island was to be independent," Brown said. There was surprise in his voice.

"And I," Luna said with a shrug. Grinning at Asher, he added, "But I believe we, the linguists, are soon to be divided up and parceled out. To where, I don't know."

"Who cares," Asher said, with an unaffected look of satisfaction, "duty, friend, duty."

Chapter 16

While Georgetown was not comparable to Charleston on the level of its social activity, it did have its own busy calendar. Another six months of abstinence in order to mourn was madness. It was not fair that she sacrifice all social intercourse for so lengthy a time. True, in Spain, where Mother's people had come from, it was the custom but that did not necessarily make it so here. She had been fond of her Uncle Louis, and she had grieved, but he was dead and she was alive. To wear black, avoid society and to mourn for years on end seemed mere show to her, and Papa agreed. She was sure Papa agreed, but he would do nothing to upset Mama. Corazon stormed inwardly, pacing in her room. Her father did not suffer to sit in a house, imprisoned day after day, by an outdated foreign tradition.

Independence Day had been an uncomfortably strange day: the entire country celebrating the destruction of Spain's Atlantic fleet off Santiago, while her mother and sister wept.

Father had found pressing business outside the house. Feeling herself American rather than Spanish, she had sat alone on the terrace watching the fireworks. Two of her cousins from father's side of the family served in the US Navy. Would it be better if they died than her Spanish cousins? The entire war was a ridiculous exercise. She refused to support either side, and only wished for its end.

When news arrived, that Hermon had survived the destruction of the Cruiser *Viscaya,* that he had made his way home to Matanzas, they had all been happy and relieved. It had changed nothing with mother though. The house remained in gloomy mourning through July and into August. When on August 9, the war ended, it came as a great relief, and within the week, Papa announced plans for an immediate return to Cuba. The casket containing Louis Vega's remains would arrive in a few days and with the hostilities at an end, it was critical that he be on hand to transact business. They packed for a quick departure and arranged for the bulk of their possessions to follow. Corazon traveled with uneasy feelings. Visiting relatives was one thing; remaining to live in Cuba was another. Her brother Robert's arrival improved her mood though. Sporting a beard when he met them on the dock in Havana, they hardly recognized him. Not only did the beard make Robert seem quite mature, it tickled when he hugged her.

Disembarked, only six hours from a British steamer, Robert had been busy. He announced a special dinner at the Inglaterra, and directed them toward a carriage. They ate in an alcove off the main dining room, the cuisine was excellent. Robert entertained them with stories of travels in Europe, and highlights of the voyage from France. Isabel made a great fuss over her son, and complained when he and his father retired to the bar for an after-dinner smoke.

Next morning, they boarded the train for Matanzas. The

carriage was in poor repair, and as they traveled east, it became difficult to ignore burned buildings, and clusters of emaciated people passed. Though everyone was aware, no mention was made of these scenes. Corazon thought that to speak of what they saw, was to acknowledge the reality of the suffering. This was a reality; her family was not yet prepared to recognize. At the station, Uncle Carlos awaited them with a carriage and wagon. He embraced them, each in turn, as they stepped down from the train, and directed his servants in the loading of their baggage.

Like Havana, the town of Matanzas was untouched by the war, but had become shabby and unkempt because of it. Spanish soldiers, in their odd straw hats, wandered the streets and lounged about the plaza. There was a seeming listlessness to the town, a dull despair, and she was pleased when they left it. Passing into the countryside, her mother chatted with Uncle Carlos as the carriage bounced and swayed down the rutted road. Corazon leaned back on the cushion and gazed at her family. She was less apprehensive now that she was actually here. The countryside itself seemed little changed, and she did look forward to seeing everyone, yet the stillness and isolation of plantation life had never fit her nature. She had a need for movement and change, the change that one found in ideas, in great cities or in travel. This was why she loved the seashore: its constant, restless change.

She looked forward to walks on the beach behind her family's home, for her father's villa sat on the north coast, overlooking the Florida Straits. She dozed and woke, surprised that they were approaching her uncle's home. The sight of the barbed wire and blockhouses that surrounded the mansion, and its centro to the south, sobered Corazon's mood. What the fortifications said of life there silenced Isabel's chatter.

Saddened, she finally asked her brother, "Was it so bad?"

"At times, my dear, it was. "Many planters paid money to the insurrectos, tax money to keep them away. A tax," he laughed. "As a matter of honor, we did not, and the fields were burned. Men were hired to protect the house and mill, of course."

"I had no idea," Isabel said, "how terrible for you all."

"Not to be concerned," he said with a wave. "We had the governor's ear, and the support of the military. It was nothing."

"Have you begun to plant?" Douglas asked.

"In a fashion brother, there is difficulty with labor. We can speak of it later perhaps."

As Carlos spoke, the delighted squeals of the women, pouring out of his house, almost blotted them out. For the next few hours, there was laughing, stories, gifts and the showing off of new babies. Carla and Angeline, both younger than Corazon, were mothers. Gracia was betrothed to the Spanish colonel who commanded Havana's artillery. She chattered excitedly over plans to live abroad. That a girl here would marry early, well it was expected. What else was there for a woman but a home and children?

Dinner was a lavish affair, with all the fruits and foods she had known as a young girl. The scents, the taste, the language all merged to move back the wall of years that had separated her. Soon she joined conversation between friends and family favorites, and became acquainted with new members of the family. She spoke with her cousin Hermon, who introduced her to his particular friend Tomas. More time with Hermon would have been nice, but he was much in demand. Tomas, a stranger to the house, became overly attentive to her, a situation for which she did not care, and she excused herself to visit the lavatory. Later, she came from the veranda and a talked with her great aunt Rosa. A hand touched her elbow, and she turned to face a young man, short and slight with a

166

winning smile.

"Cori, you are looking lovely, come sit with me."

"Fedrico," she said with obvious pleasure, kissing him on both cheeks. "I am so pleased. I spoke of you with Aunt Consuela only minutes ago."

Taking her arm, Fedrico led her to a bench and asked, "Did she say I was a poor son?"

"Only that you have grown more stubborn than tall. You have tormented your mother?"

"Never would I do such a thing—except she wishes me tethered nearby. I refuse to remain at home. I've decided to study law, to study abroad." He leaned forward and whispered, "Not in Europe, but in the United States. I prefer English law to Roman, Boston to Madrid."

"And your father, cousin?"

"He refuses to speak of it."

"How then?"

"Why, I've conspired with Uncle Douglas," Fedrico said, his eyes taking on a boyish openness. "Arranged when he was here last November. I will work for him when I've earned my degree," he confided. Leaning close and speaking quietly, he added, "I trust you to be discreet Cori."

"I will," she promised, "When though?"

"I had hoped this year." He shrugged, with a disgusted look on his face. "The war and another year wasted. I'll be eighteen before I begin." He was silent for a moment, then brightening, asked, "Have you seen Natan?"

"No, but I've spoken to Gracia, and Angeline. Is her baby boy not darling?"

"It is a baby like others," Fedrico said unimpressed, and not wishing to change the subject. "Natan though, he's much the same but changed. He fought as an officer with the volunteers, and is one of the few who escaped both Santiago and Holguin." Fedrico paused for a moment, "he doesn't show it, but he has a great deal of anger for Americans, anger for everything. He and his fellows hold hate for the entire world I think, but most for the Americans."

"For me?" she gasped, ready to accept Fedrico's comment as fact.

"Never," he laughed, as if she had suggested something as ridiculous as flying pigs. "Cori, you share the same blood. It's for their government, their military, it's for the very fates that they reserve their anger. Foolish girl," he whispered. "I only want you to understand how it is with them. Moreover, Natan, I think he still dreams of your kiss. You remember you gave him a kiss?"

Embarrassed, she complained, "I was a child, a little girl of thirteen and he's my cousin. He was like my brother. The idea of it is ridiculous."

"Angeline has married her cousin."

"Hector is a cousin?"

"Yes, from Aunt Rosa's side."

"I didn't know." Corazon said her eyes large. "I know nothing of the family, it seems."

"Luck," Fedrico said. "I know too much of the family, but then a lawyer must learn to keep secrets," he joked. "Ah, excuse me, Cori, there is Miss Nunez, and I must flatter her next."

Corazon gave him a little slap, and smiled as he hurried away, but then Gracia grasped her arm, and took her to meet her colonel. Outside, there were drinks of rum, lime, coconut and champagne. At dark, a bonfire burned and a whole bull roasted on a spit. Some of the men gathered, talking of the war and politics. Others conversed with the women or spoke on more pleasant topics. On a wicker couch behind a trellis, she listened to what the men discussed. It was wise for a woman to listen, to be concerned with what men said among themselves.

They spoke of reprisals and raids made on villages suspected of feeding rebels. Raids regretted, because between Wyler's camps and their own raids, much of their labor force had been killed. They spoke of their parts in the war, memories that were fresh. Natan Vargas, who had fought in Holguin and Orient province, was only two weeks from the fighting. Blood was fresh in his mind, and he feared what the mambis might do as the army fell back on Havana. Most of his men were shot or hacked to pieces when Holguin fell. This was a thing for which he was bitter, even though his guardia volunteers had always executed rebels in the same manner.

Hermon described the sortie of the Spanish fleet from Santiago, the running battle with the American Navy as the Spanish ships sought to escape. He related how great shells had struck the *Viscaya*, and of his captain's desperate attempt to run her on the beach. She burned as she ran, her guns still firing. So hot was the flaming ship, her sailors blistered at their stations. The captain had ordered the magazines flooded, and with the sea pouring in, he ran *Viscaya* hard on a reef. As she settled outside the line of surf, men dove overboard, wading onto the reef for safety, but rebels on the beach opened fire on them with rifles. Sharks drawn by the blood swept in over the shallow coral, tearing at sailors struggling waist deep in the bloody water. Some men clung to the bow of the burning ship, roasting as the fire blistered paint from steel, burning rather than suffer the sharks. Hermon had told them, it was only by the grace of God, he managed to swim to the high rocks without being bitten. He like most of those who lived were those rescued by the American's boats. He confessed it was a dreadful thing to watch.

The conversation had soon turned to politics and business, questions of when the Americans would occupy the West. Her father had answered many of their questions concerning occupation of the island, but to many, he could only shrug. It became late. Guests departed; others retired in various rooms of the big house. The last coals of the fires grew cool, and the place became quiet. Corazon lay restless, unable to sleep until nearly dawn. Though she was pleased to see everyone, she felt strangeness, a separation. Three and a half years gone, this no longer was home.

Chapter 17

At the end of hostilities, General Wood brought as many Cuban Army Officers as possible, into Santiago's municipal government. Because of this, the region began to settle into a routine of life. Many of Wood's officers moved on released to other units. Asher found himself assigned to General James Wilson's staff, in what would be the Department of Matanzas and Santa Clara, and after traveling half the length of Cuba, sat, hat in hand on a porch. Dripping perspiration, he waited, watching a troop of the Seventh Cavalry at practice parade drill. A slight breeze within the compound did little to cool, but carried mixed smells of hay and horse manure to him. From inside headquarters, through glassless windows, Asher listened to the cursing of General Wilson, who was venting his wrath on an unlucky officer.

"What this damn fool report is good for is ass wipe, Major. I ask you, sir, did you ever leave your office to collect your information? I would gather not. This is a mere expression of opinion, and reprehensible opinion at that. I will expect facts before me by week's end, sir. Facts," he growled. A loud, "Dismissed," followed.

The hapless officer passed Asher. Looking neither right nor left, he hurriedly crossed the parade ground. The general had begun dictating a letter. The scratch of his secretary's pen was audible as he hurried to keep up.

"Lieutenant Byran," the orderly's voice pulled Asher out of a half stupor. "Colonel Morse will see you now."

He dried his face on his sleeve, and followed the sergeant into the building, entering the Colonel's office through double doors. He saluted saying, "Sir, Lieutenant Byran reporting as ordered, Sir."

"Be seated," Morse directed, returning his salute and accepting the pouch holding Asher's orders. He leafed through them quickly, making comments as he went, "Citadel, hum — observer Cuban Army — forward observer for naval gunfire before landings — independent gathering of intelligence provided before the Daiquiri landing — wounded, and while engaged in unsupported combat with a superior force — Wood's staff and liaison duty, recommended for further promotion." He looked up from the papers and smiled at Asher. My, you have been busy, Lieutenant. Humm! Five months in Cuba now and still fit. Have any problems with fever?"

"I survived yellow fever as a child, sir. I've not been bothered by malarial fever."

"You get on well with the Cubans?"

"I get on well with most men, sir, Cubans included."

He was wondering if, again, he was about to find himself hanging around the camps of the now inactive rebel army.

Other than taking revenge on particularly hated officials or informers, the insurrectos had little to do these days. If he were to spend time with them, he would have even less to do, and he groaned inwardly at the prospect of sitting in the countryside swatting bugs.

"Lieutenant Byran," Morse began forcefully, "the army has to govern this province, and we're strangers, ignorant of its problems and needs. General Wilson is an administrator who takes his duties here seriously. His intent is to gain a grasp of the essential needs, and problems of this sector as well as the sentiments of its population." Morse bit the end from a cigar, and struck a match lighting it. "We are not here to fight, but to govern, and there is a whole lot we need to know. You'll have twenty men from Captain Bar's "D" troop. I'm afraid few of the enlisted speak Spanish, although Lieutenant Dryer, the surveyor, does. You're to tour your sector and command will expect a reasonable survey and census.

General Wilson is interested in industry, agriculture, roads and conditions among the population. Visit, talk, record and report Lieutenant. You're to have responsibility for one of forty sectors in this district." Morse handed over a map case. "It'll be the eighth area we've started in this district. I've provided some maps, and a list of landowners and such in the pouch. Moreover, Lieutenant, keep in mind, technically, Spain still administers here until New Year's day. They may be sitting on their backside swatting flies but technically, they are still the government. Step lightly." Walking around his desk, he said, "Questions you have, bring them to me tomorrow."

"Understood Sir," and standing, he shook the Colonel's hand.

"Good, pleased to have you with us, Byran." He pointed to a non-com in the orderly room. "Sergeant Diny will arrange quarters, and provide you with a roster of your men."

Asher snapped a salute, which Morse returned carelessly,

his mind already turning to other business. He departed the office in search of his quarters and the cookhouse. After lunch, he read his papers briefly, and later arranged with the Battalion Sergeant Major to have his own sergeant transferred up from Santiago. Although Captain Bar was in command of "D" troop, he was presently away, so Asher went to choose a mount on his own. Taking the advice of the Master Sergeant in charge of remounts, he chose between three geldings. Satisfied with one, he rode it about Matanzas in the late afternoon as he acquainted himself with the place.

With its dirt and hunger, the city reminded him much of how Santiago had been in July. The central plaza with its cathedral was clean though, and he noted a theater, the Sauto, at which billboards promised a concert within the week. There was also a pleasant looking café. Dismounting, he passed the reins of his horse to one of the young boys outside and entered.

"A seat, sir," a waiter offered, speaking only slightly accented English.

"Yes," Asher answered in kind, and sat near the wall, facing the bar. He asked in English, "Do you serve a fish and yellow rice?"

"Yes, and a wine, perhaps, sir."

"I prefer coffee with milk."

"As you wish," the waiter said, hurrying off.

There were a few gentlemen seated, and many Spanish officers at the bar, or occupying tables facing the plaza. He paid them little attention, and sat thinking his own thoughts, as he waited for his coffee. A boy brought it on a tray, moving with a quick ease between the tables. He stumbled at the last moment, causing the coffee to crash onto the tabletop and splatter Asher's uniform. Leaping up from the floor, the boy begged forgiveness while blotting at the coffee with a towel. Several customers seemed quite amused, and the proprietor rushed up, chastising the boy in Spanish.

"But I was tripped," he cried, also in Spanish.

"Shush," the man hissed, motioning for the waiter.

"So sorry, sir, we must apologize for the clumsy fool," the waiter told Asher. "I will have another coffee here in a moment, and we would be pleased if you would allow us to pay the cost of laundering."

"Thank you, no," Asher said. "It's not a problem."

As the waiter moved quickly away, Asher caught the remark of one of the overly amused young men at the next table.

"Arrogant dogs," one of them said, "how can the Yankees expect to accomplish anything here when they are too stupid to even learn the language?"

The coffee and food came together. Asher ate slowly, enjoying the meal, listening to the conversation around him. In the conversation, he heard uncertainty, anger, outrage and a strong displeasure at his presence. He finished and glancing at the man, who had tripped the boy, placed money on the table. He pondered on how to answer the affront peaceably.

"Look," the man said to his friend. "He must know, and has not even the courage to acknowledge the insult."

Hearing this insult, Asher decided how to answer the affront peaceably. With an innocent smile, he stood, placing his hat under one arm. He made a polite nod to the adjoining table, saying in perfectly clear Spanish, *"Caballeros, no es verdad*, 'gentlemen, it's not true' — my courage and my sword are reserved for fighting enemies of my nation — Are your nation and mine not at peace; have our leaders not put away war? I am only here to enjoy a meal."

He smiled at the suddenly uncomfortable men, and coming to attention, he bowed. Turning, he walked out of the café.

He took the reins of his horse from the boy, and flipping him a coin, mounted. Riding slowly up the street, he thought, 'No doubt it would be a while before some people become civil.'

Chapter 18

In the countryside, days passed into weeks. Asher leaned into the brisk Northeast breeze, and gazed toward the Florida Straits, six miles to his north. Far out, a four-masted Barque sailed west on the fair breeze, and he watched it with a distant longing. From this hill, he could see most of his sector, an area between the coast and the railroad, stretching east 26 miles from the Canimar River to another river running into Cardenas Bay. Well over 500 square miles and most of it in ruin and starvation. Only the large plantations had merited protection.

On the summit of the highest of the Tetas de Camarioca, there stood a high pole placed for the surveyor. On the previous afternoon, it was hauled up the slope between a pair of mules. They had set it in place this morning. Lieutenant Gene Dryer, of the Corps of Engineers had marked the spot with numerous bearings. He would now use it as a reference in mapping the low ground extending for miles in every direction.

During the past three weeks, he covered much of the easily accessible area, and spent a few days in Cardenas when it had rained. It had taken a while to organize his information. A series of notebooks, one general, and several dealing with specific subjects, seemed to do the job. At least with trooper Harwell on hand it did the job. Pax Harwell had taught school in New York, until in a fit of patriotic fever he had enlisted. As an avid polo player, he had little trouble joining the cavalry, but to his disgust, he arrived in Cuba after the fighting. To Asher, Private Harwell was a treasure in the form of a secretary. At the end of each week, he wrote a report in legible handwriting from notes and a rough outline provided by Asher. Gabe Strong had joined "D" troop only a few days back, and speaking respectable Spanish himself, he made Asher's job even easier.

Asher ordered his men off the crest. They struck the tents, saddled the horses, and his sergeant soon had the detail mounted. He swung up on his own horse, took a last look toward the sea, and lit out, downhill toward Matanzas. They crossed an area bordered by newly planted sugar cane, and passed cattle grazing near the burned ruins of a centro. Crossing the Canimar River on a rickety bridge, he halted the detail to take a better look, and record its condition in his notebook. The river was low today. It was plain to see the bridge pillars were undermined. He closed the notebook, slipped it into its pouch, and continued toward Matanzas.

They cleared the top of a low hill, and from the opposite direction, a party approached on the narrow road. He reined to the side, signaling his men to do likewise. There were two young ladies on fine horses, and a young gentleman between. Two armed men followed at a discreet distance.

"Good day, sir, and ladies," he greeted in Spanish, while lifting his cap.

"Is that you, Lieutenant Byran?"

"Why yes, ma'am," he said, holding up the hand with the cap, to halt his detail. "Why, Miss O'Ryan, I'd never have expected to come across you and your sister so far from home. Why, never in a million years."

Miss Corazon O'Ryan was mounted on a gray mare, a well-bred little Arabian that capered, dancing and tossing its head. Seeming to pay no attention to the excited mare, she sat the horse with a straight-backed ease, a dauntless grace. She wore a black outfit; a high-waisted jacket of the Spanish fashion, over a ruffled silk blouse, with a split skirt to match. Her dark hair was done up under a flat-rimmed riding hat, showing off the graceful line of her neck, and he said inwardly, *"My God, if she is not the worlds loveliest woman!"*

Miss Corazon O'Ryan

"Not far, Lieutenant Byran, why my father's estate is north of here, not a half-mile from where the Canamar enters the bay."

"I had no idea," he said. "I'd thought the majority of your father's properties were near Banes."

"Properties, yes, but we have our home here. My mother was born not far from this place, as I was also," she informed. Then bringing her hand to her mouth, she said "Oh! I am rude. Lieutenant Byran, may I introduce my cousin, Fedrico Vega."

"At your service," the young gentleman said, sweeping his hat off, lowering his head.

"Very pleased to meet you, sir," Asher replied, nodding.

"Lieutenant," Corazon called over her shoulder, for her mare, refusing to settle down, was flashing her hooves and prancing in a circle. "If your duties are not pressing, might I invite you to our home for refreshment?"

"Miss O'Ryan, I'd be delighted," he said accepting. "Give me but a moment," he continued, and wheeling his horse to face Gabe Strong, he said, "Sergeant, proceed to the barracks with the detail, and inform the duty officer that I am detained until this evening."

"Cori," Esmeralda hissed as this was taking place. "How can you invite this—man?"

Eyes narrow, brows knitted, Corazon answered under her breath, "He is

known to papa and has been introduced — His people are known to papa's people and I find his company pleasant."

Fedrico overhearing the exchange laughed to himself and waited quietly. He observed as the officer moved to one side, and his men rode off behind the sergeant.

"You have you been to Cuba before Lieutenant. You speak well," he said.

"Yes! Many times, but I learned the language in Florida."

"Ah yes, a Spanish possession for centuries, and many Cubans there. I have wished to travel, but have not been as fortunate as my cousins."

"You wouldn't care for it, Fedrico," Esmeralda said sharply. "It's a crude place."

"It has many parts, ma'am," Asher said, "and there are some pleasant parts."

"Well, before this wretched mare wears my arm out," Corazon said, "may we go? I for one have an appetite for lunch."

They rode back across the river and north through open country, Corazon's gray setting the pace, and Asher's big bay refusing to fall back. Corazon glanced at Asher and he caught the challenging gleam in her eye. With a flashing smile, she cut from the road, putting her mare over a stone wall, and into a field of young cane. Asher followed; racing her through the wind bent cane. Uphill, they sped abreast, she urging her mount, and together they flew over a palmetto hedge. He stayed with her, plunging wildly downhill, clattering across a shallow stream, and side-by-side up a rocky ridge, he riding recklessly to keep up.

Glancing back, Asher could see the others, all far behind on the road, except for a lone guard a few hundred yards back, whose horse struggled to keep him in sight of the young lady. Ahead was a large house, a villa built on a ridge and backed by the sea. They pounded toward it; she was leading him now, and laughed as she tossed a glance over her shoulder. The joy, the pure clarity of it reached him above the sound of hooves, the breath and leather.

As the trail curved, he cut through a field of guinea grass, and burst out onto the road abreast her, and they raced up through the gate, the mounts matched stride for stride. As they pulled up before the stables, boys ran to hold the blowing horses.

Asher dismounted, flipped up the stirrup and loosened the girth.

"Thank you for the escort, Lieutenant Byran," Corazon said, ever so pleasantly, and coming up on tiptoes, peered back the way they had come. With a mischievous lilt to her voice she added, "My own escort, it would appear, could not keep up."

"Miss O'Ryan," Asher said with wonder, "winged Pegasus would do well to keep pace. You're a natural rider."

She smiled, appreciative of the remark, and caressed her horse then stepped back so the groom could walk it away.

"They will care for your horse, Lieutenant. Would you take me to the house? My sister will not leave the road. So, I expect them to be delayed for some minutes."

A neatly dressed servant met them at the door, taking Asher's hat.

"If you'll excuse me, please, Luko will show you to the garden. And Luko," she added pulling pins from her hat, "please tell Father we have met Lieutenant Byran on the road and invited him to lunch."

She hurried up the stairs to wash and change. Her own forwardness shocked her, though she regretted it not in the least. She had enjoyed drawing him into a chase, and had discovered a little about him by doing it. There were many things about him that interested her, not in the least of those that he was good to look at, but more, she sensed a form of confidence in him, as if he saw himself equal to all persons, all difficulties. Was she mistaken? Possibly, but it would be pleasant to see, to be around an American at the very least. Besides, she was frustrated at being treated as inferior by men. At least in Tampa, this man had spoken to her as if she had a mind, had opinions equal to his own, and his presence strangely thrilled her.

"Who did she say, Luko?"

"Lieutenant Byran, sir."

Douglas O'Ryan searched his memory for a moment, finally touching on him. Yes, he recalled, the young officer with Archibald in Tampa, Ian Wallace's grandson. Strange, he should turn up, he thought, but then when one has daughters—From below, he could hear Esmeralda calling to her mother—Fedrico's laugh.

He said, "I will be down shortly, Luko," and began shuffling his papers into a drawer. He sighed. In the next weeks, he would spend a great deal of money on the purchase of land, very inexpensive land for the moment, but would the venture profit? European production of sugar beets had already depressed the market. A great deal would depend on politics. Who would control the economy? Should he concentrate on Banes and fruit, or strongly re-enter sugar?

The garden was cool, open to the Gulf of Mexico and the sea breeze. Wicker chairs sat about a tiled floor, shaded by a vine-covered trellis. Asher leaned back, enjoying the breeze. He sipped from a glass of cool sweetened tea and admired the house. It was a beautiful house, with a beautiful view, not the least of which was its women. The circumstance seemed strange, unusually so, that he would see a woman, one he found exceedingly attractive, and then meet her in such a succession of times and places, far flung places. He found it mysterious

A memory came to him from his youth. He recalled a woman's words, spoken in a candle lit room, she standing by her husband's body. *I see you as a solider, but your path will be the water. You will pursue a woman on horseback, and find pure love.* Asher was uneasy, pleasantly uneasy, but even so, chills ran up his spine.

"Lieutenant, how good to see you."

Asher was startled at Douglas O'Ryan's words. He stood quickly and stepped to meet him, extending his hand, smiling.

"And you, sir. You have no idea how surprised I was to meet your daughters on the road."

"Well, the island seems to agree with you. Here," he said pointing, "have a seat."

"Thank you, sir," as they both took a seat.

"Tell me, what brings you to this part of the island?"

"I was transferred from Santiago and assigned to General Wilson's department, sir. For the moment, I'm doing census and survey. The Army would like to have a notion of the district before Spain withdraws."

"A large undertaking," O'Ryan said, leaning back into his seat. "Been at it long?"

"I've been at it for a few weeks. In fact, your estate is in my sector. My responsibility is to survey an area from here to about seven miles east of Cardenas and south to the rail line, a large area but only one of forty in this district, sir."

"Perhaps one day you would be good enough to explain how it's being carried out. I'd be pleased to have you visit when you're in the neighborhood."

"Thank you, sir, I will, but if you could excuse me, might you direct me to the lavatory, sir?"

"Ho—certainly. Demi," he called and rang a small bell. A houseboy appeared, and Douglas said, "Show the gentleman to the lavatory and wait on him. I'll be in the parlor."

"Thank you, sir," Asher said, turning to follow the skinny black.

The lavatory was tiled with porcelain and brass conveniences, running hot and cold water. He removed his weapons and uniform blouse, washed quickly and toweled his upper body. He'd shaved yesterday and putting his blouse back on, he inspected himself in the mirror, judging the whiskers to be within the limits of respectability.

Upstairs, Isabel was fuming as she said, "Corazon, I cannot understand how you think. Have you lost your mind daughter, inviting an American officer? If anyone hears, they'll be shocked."

"Father's American; I'm an American, what should they expect?" Corazon said in a huff of her own. She stepped away from the maid who was toweling her back, in order to choose from her wardrobe. She jerked a dress from the hanger.

"He's not family, daughter, and feelings are very strong. I would never have considered inviting a Spanish officer to our home when we were in Georgetown. Everyone will talk. People have strong opinions. The war is fresh."

"And I suppose I should ask him to leave."

"Don't be insolent."

"Oh! I'm sorry, Mama, but the war is over and he—Lieutenant Byran is a very pleasant gentleman," she said. She was into her slip and struggling with the dress. "Please, Mama, button me. Resa is so clumsy!" Isabel began to do the buttons, and Corazon could tell from the quick little yanks that her mother was not mollified.

"You don't understand how much bitterness there is here. Women must do what they can to calm their men. To keep them from being stupid," she sighed. "At times like this they are wounded and very touchy. It's best to keep them apart. Only last month these men were slaughtering each other. We must take care that they do not continue to do so."

A tight anger filled Corazon, but she smiled, and refused to let it show. Her mother saw problems everywhere, but people seemed to be interested only in getting on with life, and putting the years of war behind them. Were they not at peace? "I'll be sure to keep him away from everyone, Mama," she said, repressing an urge to say more.

Isabel looked askance at her younger daughter, wondering

how she had gone wrong in raising her. It must be the influence of her father's family.

"Oh, Corazon," she complained, "Why couldn't you try to be more like your sister?"

Chapter 19

Under the worst leaks, clay pots sat, receiving water that poured through the tile roof. The common room of the officers' barracks smelled of wet clothes, stale tobacco and the mildew brought on by days of steady rain. There were a dozen officers in the room. Six played poker at a round table, cluttered with smoldering cigars, and a near empty bottle of rum. The others engaged in friendly practice bouts with sabers. Asher, occupied with writing a letter to his Aunt Fay, looked up with irritation when Dryer placed the end of his saber on the table.

"Would you mind a few passes, Ash? I seem to have worn Bar and Gleason down."

"Waste of effort," he said frowning, and pushed the blade away from his paper.

"Come on," Dryer said breathing a little hard. "It pays to keep one's hand in, old fellow."

"All right, a few passes, and you promise not to pester me," Standing, he stretched. He twisted his neck and arms, unbuttoned his blouse, and drew one of a number of practice sabers. The saber, purposely dulled, had its point filed off.

They saluted and stood still for a moment, very slight movements as the steel tapped, then Dryer's point flew straight at Asher with flashing speed. Just managing to turn the point, he back-pedaled; Dryer, small and inconceivably quick, whirled about him. Riposte, parry, counter, riposte, parry, parry, Asher's guard barely managing to hold him off, until finally, in a drive to the wall, he found the point at his chest.

"Touch," Dryer said.

"You're quick; I'll give you that one."

"One of the best in my class, I've seldom been bested," he boasted.

"I did well enough, but I've been told my form was ruined by my first teacher."

"How so?" Dryer asked enjoying himself and always ready to pick up an advantage.

"My uncle," Asher laughed. "Told me fighting was to win. Life or death, survival was the only rule. He taught me to fight in the fashion favored in the mercenary brigades."

"Oblige me," Dryer said smugly amused.

"Sure," Asher accommodated, flashing a smug grin of his own, he grasped a leather hat in his left hand.

Again, they squared off and Dryer lunged in yelling, "He ya!" There were parries, clashing thrusts and turns so fast, it was hard to follow; and again, Asher falling quickly back. He suddenly parried with a powerful stroke, a stroke that swept Dryer's point far to the side. It would have opened Asher up to a killing counter thrust, had he not spun, twisted sideways, the hat pressing Dryer's blade as he threw his left elbow into Dryer's jaw, knocking the man off his feet.

"Point," Asher said, flicking his saber under Dryer's chin. "Was I obliging enough?"

"Damn—you near broke my jaw," Dyer whined. Sitting up, he spit some blood. "I believe you've loosened my teeth."

"Sorry," Asher said, not meaning it but giving him a hand up.

"That was brutal and unfair," Dryer complained and worked his jaw.

"That's what Major Tillman said. He was my fencing instructor at Citadel. He would have also pointed out that dead men do not generally complain much. Can I pour you a drink, Dave?" Asher asked, arching his eyebrows.

"Sure," Dryer said, a little ill humor in his voice, and still rubbing his jaw.

A player's chair slid back from the table. "I'm stripped," he announced, standing.

"Say, gentleman, do you mind if I sit in?" Asher asked.

"If you don't mind losing," another laughed.

"He doesn't mind losing," Dryer said with a wry face, "not that he intends to lose."

Asher took a seat, giving Dryer a silly grin over his shoulder as he slid his chair forward. It was Holland's deal, but the cards were not there. Asher folded his first hand. Lieutenant Thames threw down after him with disgust, complaining he could get no cards.

"Happens," the man across said, discarding. "Two, please."

"You enjoy playing with those pig stickers, Byran?" Thames asked, nodding at the sabers.

"Gets the blood up is all," Asher said, "keeps you quick. I'd rather a skirmish with a pistol, but I'm not much with a pistol, either. Best use a saber and shoot a more proficient opponent left-handed. Truth be known, I'd rather play poker than fight."

"Swords don't run out of ammunition or misfire, though," Dryer called from across the room. "They impress the ladies too."

186

"That's true, I suppose," Thames admitted. "The Dons sure as hell like cutting each other up with 'em. I've seen two spats this month. Serious stuff mind you. Those boys got thin skins where their honor's at issue."

"Duels, you mean."

"Somebody ended up dead, whatever you call them," Thames said, scratching an itch. "Damn bugs! We got more suffering bugs in these quarters than the whole of Virginia."

"They're a little backwards about slights, injury to their honor." Asher said, "Touchy as hell, actually. Lot like it used to be in the Carolina s, but not many outings there since the '70s."

"You talking or playing?" Holland asked, "Your deal."

"You in a hurry to get rich, Captain?" Asher said, and gathered the cards.

He shuffled; placing them in front of Capland for the cut, then took them, dealing smoothly. Men glanced at or studied their cards; he looked at his own, and laid them on the table. Thames smiled, threw in his ante. Others followed. Capland took two, as did Holland. Vespa and Hanny took one, Thames raised, Hanny saw and raised. Asher matched Hanny. Vespa folded; Holland called and put down three aces.

"Damn," Thames said, spreading three tens.

Asher spread three fives and a pair of eights, raking in the pot amidst grunts and groans. Hanny dealt and the game went on slowly, the cards flowing, money changing hands. Faces reflected emotions: stress, nonchalance, ill temper and sly satisfaction. Capland totally betrayed himself with an intense eagerness that showed in his face, when he had the luck of the draw. Asher played always with a friendly soft smile that changed little with the cards. He lost several pots, won, then lost again. After an hour, he dropped out, roughly breaking even. Somehow, the cards, the probabilities of the game seemed out of balance. Holland and Hanny were the primary winners so far. Asher suspected they were playing to each other but really didn't care. He had lost nothing, so he wouldn't make it his business, but he'd keep it in mind. He considered himself warned, might even use it against them in another game. Having perceived a man's true character, it was better to own him than to make an enemy of him.

The rain had let up and he walked outside for some air. It was wet and sharply fresh. He could smell the sea, even a trace of weed or fish on the air. A storm, possibly a late hurricane, must have passed south of the island. Not much wind but plenty of rain, and good for the farmers. He sat on a rough plank bench, leaned on the wall and put his feet up. He noticed his boots needed polish. He knew he should go over his notes, and get Harwell started on this week's reports, but his mind was not really on work.

He'd been giving some thought to investing in Cuba. Property was cheap; he could easily pick up a couple of thousand acres with no more than his army pay and poker winnings. On the other hand, he had no real interest in planting sugar. Gabe had been toying with the idea of raising cattle and horses here. That might be fine for Gabe, but was not something that appealed to Asher, the prospect of running cargo between Cuba and ports in Florida — that was a prospect that appealed to him. In the last month, he had spent a good deal of time talking to merchants and planters. With the end of Spain's restrictive colonial policies, trade would boom. He had enough contacts here to do well. He knew he could do well, very well. His inheritance would come to him in a few months and give him a start. He would be out of the army and a free man, actually accomplishing something, working, beginning to build his fortune.

He functioned well enough as an officer, but the army held

no pleasure for him. Time weighed. He would have already resigned had it not been for a certain status attained with rank. To be honest with himself, he must admit, it was an excuse to be in the area and around Corazon O'Ryan. He had lately found himself altering his plans, neglecting his duties, and seeking any flimsy pretense to be in the neighborhood of the O'Ryan estate. All other circumstances of life he approached with a calm logic. In her case, he was neither calm nor logical. She had his mind so occupied, he could scarcely concentrate long enough to add two and two, which left him frustrated, agitated and aggravated with himself and those around him.

He had accepted an invitation from Douglas O'Ryan to play polo on Saturday. Polo was a sport for which his ability was barely adequate. He would be there of course, willing to humiliate himself, in order to see her. Not wishing to appear a complete fool at the game, Asher had even gone as far as asking trooper Harwell for a few pointers beyond the basics.

Two weeks past, he'd gone riding with Miss O'Ryan and her father, while that gentleman was inspecting some property. He had also danced with her at the Ambassador's Ball, a week before. The effect of whirling about the floor with Miss O'Ryan in his arms, her face tilted up to him, the excitement in her eyes, well it was difficult to describe. He found a certain possessiveness affecting his behavior, sharp pangs of jealousy when she directed her attentions elsewhere. Knowing logically that he was being unreasonable, Asher smiled, conversed and tried not to glare or gnash his teeth while she spoke or danced with other men. He was determined not to act like a mindlessly smitten male, however close to that state he might be. Turning up the lantern, he laid out some paper, and began a summary of his notes. Tomorrow, maybe, he would sneak in a little polo practice.

Chapter 20

Because of the rains, the Canimar River was high, its bridge swaying in the brown current, but the big chestnut gelding never paused while crossing. It had a black nose, black mane and tail, with four black socks. An elegant animal, powerful and compact, it had been bred for endurance and agility. Thursday night, Asher had dickered for the horse with Jeb Rice. It had been the Captain's private mount, but flayed at poker, the Captain was compelled to sell the horse to cover a marker. After hearing from Harwell that the animal was previously a polo pony, Asher had decided to take advantage of Rice's penury.

It was a brilliant Saturday, cloudless after the Tuesday rains, and cool as Cuba sometimes becomes in late fall. He enjoyed the ride out, and despite his apprehension, he fared better than expected in the polo match. Douglas O'Ryan placed him on his own team, riding with his son Robert and others of his household. It was mostly a family affair, with the opposing team consisting of in-laws; still, by any standard, the match was hotly contested.

Having played only a few times, and that more than two years back, Asher failed to realize that the level of aggression focused on him was far higher than competition required. Good reflexes and a superior mount had not only saved him from serious injury, it had made him look good. He had been crowded and at times taken hard hits, even from Carlo and Louis, members of his own team. In one melee Asher's mount, feeling crowded and put upon by three riders, bit

Tomas Milane's dun on the flank, causing Tomas to be bucked off and stepped on. In another press, Asher's horse had quite of its own accord, rammed Natan Vargas' bay, knocking horse and rider to the ground, and kicked Rico's gray in the belly. Asher was dismounted twice, and then on a remount, provided by O'Ryan, he had been rammed. The sorrel had rolled on him, causing him to think, he would never breathe again. He had been elbowed, kicked, sticked, trampled and clubbed. He couldn't remember the last time he had so much fun. It had been a bruising good match.

"You've a fine horse for the game," O'Ryan said, as the riders walked up from the stables. "If you should ever be interested in selling, I'd appreciate the opportunity to buy."

"I'll be sure to give you the chance, sir."

"You remember that promise," he said quite seriously.

Someone was calling. O'Ryan excused himself. Within a short time, the men had washed off the blood and dirt. They changed into fresh clothes, joining the others. Thin wisps of smoke rose from the pit where a pig had roasted through the night. Beneath a great poinsettia tree, a large table had been set, and food served on wooden-handled plates. Carrying two of them, Asher led Corazon to a row of small palm-shaded benches. She took one of the benches, setting a wine bottle and glasses beside her. He offered a plate.

She took it saying, "Thank you. Oh—sit where I can see you, Ash. Sit on the chair," and she smiled at him warmly as he sat. She tossed her head to get her hair over her shoulder, for the breeze blew strands into her face, and she said, "This wind—I should have pinned it."

"With the wind in it like that—it becomes you."

"But it also tickles me," she laughed. "Would you uncork the wine please?"

He reached across, grasped the bottle and pulled the cork,

savoring the red's aroma.

As he poured the wine, she said, "You were quite ferocious in the game today. You were always in the thick. I'm surprised how little damage you show."

"I've a hard head and defending your father's goal, why, a privilege, ma'am. Good sport, too," he added, holding up his glass to the light, and feeling her attention to be a fine thing.

"More like re-fighting the war, or so it appeared. You must forgive the fervor of my cousins. I'm afraid your image is still that of an enemy. The war, Spain's defeat, it's fresh."

"But I'm friendly and unprejudiced," he said, grinning, "benign to a fault."

"On the field this morning, you seemed not the least friendly. Nor was your horse," she laughed.

He laughed with her, a deep contented laugh. "I must apologize for my horse. It has an ill temper, and a far better love for the game than I."

Corazon sipped her wine, and watched him attack the food on his plate. He went at it with the same gusto, and directness that he had gone after the ball during the match. He had a good-natured determination, the ability to recognize obstacles, and the confidence to deal with them. She suspected that neither victory nor defeat would much affect him, a trait in men that should not be underrated.

On the field, she had watched him, one khaki clad Yankee, beset on every side by a swirl of Spanish uniforms. Through the dust, sweat and motion, his reckless grin flashed out to her. She had watched Natan and his friends attacking Asher on the field, at times being not at all subtle. He had shrugged them off, wasting no effort on defense, only playing the game. It was obvious to everyone who saw, they meant him injury, but he had neither acknowledged it nor shown offense. Mother of God, but he was glorious. She had thrilled to watch him, and never had she known quite so powerful an awareness, a heat she did not yet recognize as desire. Corazon felt an insanely fierce pride in him, wished to see him overcome all that came at him, but at the same time, she worried.

She had grudgingly accepted that her mother was correct concerning the temperament of the men. The circle of her father's friends here, and the men of her mother's family, all were gentlemen, but all were of an older culture. Under their soft-spoken courteous veneer, lurked tempers that burned hot over matters of honor, and could flash to killing rages. An offense could smolder for a lifetime, or demand instant vengeance. They seemed so civilized, yet in personal matters, matters of pride, they were coldly savage. She had no doubt that Asher was resented, and was determined not to lend fuel to the resentment. She was quite careful about keeping him from disagreeable situations. How much simpler this would be if she were back on the mainland.

"No appetite, Cori?" he asked, holding his now empty plate.

"Oh!" she said, caught in her thoughts, "my mind was elsewhere."

"If you can excuse me for a moment, I'm going for another plate. I'm starved." "Go," she said, picking up a rib. She watched him walk toward the house, long strides, not graceful, but smooth. He glanced over his shoulder, caught her looking, grinned, and she stared down to her food. She was a little annoyed at being caught. She knew that was foolish, for he must know by now that she found his company pleasant, no, she found it desirable. Still, she would have been scandalized if he even suspected how strongly he interested her.

The crunch of leaves brought her head around and there was Natan. He smiled nicely but she could tell he would be churlish today. His eye was puffed, turning black, and he wore

193

an arrogant expression that she knew from experience, meant rum and trouble.

"Cori," he said, sliding onto the bench next to her, "I saw the Yankee had gone off to oppress someone else. I came to gain sympathy for my wound," he said, pointing to his eye.

"Oh! My poor dear," she crooned, and reaching out, caressed his hurt. "Is it bearable, the pain? Shall you die?" she teased. Teresa Pantoja was passing, dragging her small brother and Corazon called to her, "Teresa, *venga aqui*, 'come here', see poor Natan's eye," she said.

"Oh, that is awful." Teresa let go of the little boy's hand to inspect Natan, and the boy ran back down the hill. "Ah! God forgive me, but I could choke the breath from him," she complained as she looked back at the escaping child. She turned back. "Oh, Natan," she gasped, "we must put something on it so it doesn't close." She said this with a sincere gravity.

"No, it's nothing," he replied testily, and looked back to Corazon, whose face now held an expression of great concern.

"Oh, yes, Natan, she's right. I'll come and we'll find Mama," Corazon said, standing and tugging on his arm.

Asher had just filled his plate when the girls passed him leading Natan. He looked back to his plate, and then went to the nearest seat where, with a discontented sigh, he began to eat. He had almost finished when Fedrico found him.

"Ash, my friend, have you a moment? Uncle Douglas is speaking with friends, and he wondered if would care to join them?"

"I'd be happy to," Asher said, genuinely pleased, and followed Fedrico upstairs.

The room held over a dozen planters, mostly middle-aged, though Robert, and a few younger men were present. Asher leaned back to the door-frame, listening quietly as one or two of the older planters voiced their concerns. They seemed to be far less worried about the United States remaining in Cuba than being subjected to a government controlled by Cuban revolutionaries.

Armand Alvarez sat back, speaking softly. "The treaty was signed in Paris three days ago, and the army will begin to leave on the first day of the year. Can we be sure the United States will remain? Without the Americans we are at the mercy of the rabble."

"It is my belief they intend to remain," said Palma. "They made attempts to purchase the island for a hundred million only sixty years ago, and have been favorable to its annexation ever since. Why should they let us slip through their fingers now?"

O'Ryan stood, "Gentlemen," he said, with voice strong yet not loud. "Unfortunately to the declaration of war, an amendment was attached. Article IV, if I'm correct, disclaims any intention to exercise sovereignty, jurisdiction or control over Cuba, except to establish peace. With peace established, they are bound to leave the island to govern itself. They are bound by law."

Several men began to speak at once, some loudly. O'Ryan remained standing, palms up, making a mute request for silence.

"Gentlemen, please—" Robert said strongly, not quite a shout. "May he continue?"

The words faded to low mumbling, and the elder O'Ryan said to them, "I am acquainted as you know, with a number of businessmen like myself on the mainland. I have spoken at length with senators from my state of South Carolina, and with members of our Department of Commerce. I feel that there are strong moves being made toward annexation of Cuba. Influence is being exerted, both financial and political, to find a way around the Teller Amendment." He paused,

195

gesturing with a horizontal movement of his hand. "If, gentlemen, those supporting the island's independence prevail—well—I expect a certain amount of oversight—that is to say, mechanisms for control of Cuba's government will be established before the United States recognizes a government."

"You mean a puppet government," Fluentes said, cynicism in his tone.

"No, I feel it's through treaties and the wording of a constitution that they will exert influence. To hold and profit from our properties, we must begin early to attain a position of strength in whatever new government is brought into being."

"We are not politicians, Douglas," Jose Mortez pointed out.

"Politicians may be owned, Jose."

"A king, and a few officials, men whose price is known—more-simple," the old man reflected with a sad smile.

Diego Mendoza stabbed his cigar into the dirt of a potted plant. "This is all fine for the future, but what is of concern now are the armies of Gomez and Garcia. They occupy most of the island, armed and intact; they already govern what they hold. If they decide to burn our fields again, shape a government to suit themselves, what then?"

Silence, and then Carlos Vega spoke, "A good question. The rebels in the Philippines are already at war with the Americans. They now aim at uniforms of a different color."

Douglas gave a nod and a sigh of sorts. "It's true," he said. "But there's no Teller Amendment to disclaim the Philippines. The American intent to govern there is clear. As for our protection, by the army, why don't we ask Lieutenant Byran's opinion?" O'Ryan, looked Asher's way with a smile, lifted his brows. Some of those in the room turned toward the doorway. "Would you mind, Lieutenant; perhaps you could ease our minds, clarify a few points from the standpoint of the Governor General's staff and even the insurrectos. I believe you've some direct contact."

"Well, sir," Asher said, unwillingly caught, but seeing the need to be forthcoming yet discreet. He wished to impress his host, specifically because he was Corazon's father, and goodwill could carry a man far. "I may be of help. I can't speak with any kind of authority, but perhaps I can shed some light on what's to be policy."

Douglas looked at him fondly, "We will appreciate anything you feel free to offer Ash. Please—continue."

Asher stood away from the door, composed his thoughts, and said, "What Mr. O'Ryan told you is correct. For the moment, the Army intends to remain and govern the island. The plans for the transition have been in effect for months. The army is presently over forty-five thousand strong. The Island is divided into several districts, each with a military governor. How each will function, I cannot say for it will depend on the discretion of the particular Governor. I do know General Wood is bringing the officers of Garcia's army into civil service. He disbands the army, and provides competent administrators at the same time this way. There is talk of offering money for guns. Governor General Wood has already offered employment for guns.

"But," Palma asked, "what of Matanzas, Lieutenant? Is it not different in the west?"

"Different, yes," Asher said, "for General Brooke, commands from headquarters in Havana, and he is very conservative, very different from General Wood, and very different from Wilson. These two are political, Wilson and Brooke wish to move quickly and expedite. Both would see Cuba annexed. General Wilson has just returned to the Army. His business is railroads and I'm sure as businessmen, you can find common ground." He paused, "Gentlemen, I'm not

197

familiar with the other generals. All I know of Brooke is that he seems to worry about the Cuban armies. It may be that he won't allow more than an honor guard into Havana for the ceremonies. I understand there has been trouble already between loyalist and rebels, some killings. Brooke, I think, will try to disband or suppress the Cuban army. Wilson, I believe he will concentrate on rebuilding the economy, improve agriculture. There are already plans for new roads, public works and the attracting of investors. General Wilson hopes to arrange a customs union between Cuba and the United States, with free markets. The economic bond would create a political merger." Asher shrugged his shoulders. "I offer no opinion, gentlemen, other than in a few years, things could become very good. What happens in the interim, I couldn't guess."

"Gentlemen," O'Ryan said. "My belief has been that things must improve with peace, and I agree completely with Lieutenant Byran's summery." He moved to a humidor and removed a cigar as he spoke. "I believe that if we join, form a consortium, unite resources, economic and political, we will prosper." He paused and lit his cigar. "Thousands on the mainland are looking to invest. Don't let yourselves be locked out of what will become a boom."

Asher listened as the conversation continued, learned a few things, and grasped what O'Ryan was attempting to put together. A fortune could be made if it were a success, but it was not his sort of endeavor; he would be no more suited to life as a sugar baron, than his father had been as an orange grower. His mind and heart were elsewhere. Unnoticed he slipped out with hopes of finding Corazon unoccupied.

The women had retreated to various rooms, and corners to rest or exchange gossip; children were running about the place, emitting screams and squeals. One of the housemaids was scolding a small boy as she pulled him dripping from the fountain. Overhung by palms, a rock ledge extended toward the sea. Asher walked toward it, savoring the breeze, while his eyes took in the surge of swells breaking on the reefs. He sat, leaned back against a palm and stretched his legs, which were a little tender from the slamming they took between running horses. The afternoon sun warmed his face, and he closed his eyes, smiling. He must have dozed, for he started at the sensation of smooth hands, cool over his eyes, a familiar scent, and the soft words.

"Guess who!"

"Esmeralda," he said teasing.

"Hah! You hound," Corazon said, jerking her hands away.

He smiled drowsily as she moved around in front, the scent of her perfume, again, coming faintly to him on the breeze. The light of the low sun silhouetted her form within the material of her dress and he spoke.

"I find you the most beautiful woman of my experience," he said, the words escaping before he could even think to keep them to himself.

For an instant, there was stillness so sharp that all seemed frozen. He noticed that she blushed as she turned away with a look of consternation.

"You flatter me, Ash."

Her voice had an odd flutter, so much did his words affect her. No! It was not the words, rather the tone, and the expression on his face. He rose easily, taking her elbow, but she couldn't look at him, not and contain the unfamiliar rush of her emotions.

"Would you walk with me, Cori—along the shore?"

She nodded and moved with him down the steps toward the beach, looking at the ground. "I thought you were with Father, talking of serious matters," she said. "From the balcony, I saw you were out here, napping instead."

"I was there," he said, and jumping down off a rock, he lifted her lightly down, looking directly into her eyes as he did. "I came looking for you."

The pupils of her eyes had become large, and he sensed an anxious excitement in her. Together they walked east. The surf, driven by a north wind, roared and pushed high onto the beach; salt froth blew past their feet.

"You gave up very easily," she said, stepping around a beached man-o-war.

"I didn't want to create a scandal," he said, "bursting into one room after another, shouting your name."

She giggled at the thought, "I have sand in my slippers," she said, changing the subject. Steadying herself on his arm, she slipped them off, one at a time.

"Here, let me take them," he said, and slipped them into his pockets.

Flocks of terns were running along the water's edge, and taking flight as the seas crashed. Several dolphins surfed swells, coming over the reef. They were quick dark shadows against the translucent breaking crest. He pointed to them, and she laughed with surprise, never having noticed them before. A wave pushed further than others, swirling around his boots. He laughed, and she squealed, dancing back, and holding her dress up from the water.

"You seem very at ease with the sea," she said over the roar of the surf.

"I'm actually a seaman," Asher said, looking from the waves to Corazon. "I'm merely disguised as an army officer," he said bending his head, for the wind was in her hair, blowing it against his face. It pressed her dress to her, causing it to ripple in her lee, to shiver like a castoff sail. "I'm the son, of a son, of a sailor, raised on the bounding billows, a ship's officer at sixteen, and a good one," he bragged.

"Really, Ash, and next you'll be telling me you were a pirate."

"No! It's true. I was second mate of my uncle's ship. It went down in ninety-five, south of the Caymans, and my aunt packed me off to school when I returned home. The uniform is real enough, but I've always felt as if I were a pretender. Fact is, I plan to resign my commission first of the year."

The sand had narrowed and come against a rock that jutted out to sea, trapping logs and weed at its base. Asher sat straddling the bleached, trunk of a huge mahogany, stranded by some long-forgotten storm. Corazon sat near him, tucking her skirt under her feet, keeping it from blowing, thinking, "Two weeks, so short a time and then where?"

"What will you do?" she asked, looking away from him to the water. His looks somehow unsettled her, but when his eyes were this way, it was even more so. She recalled the first time she had seen him, that long-ago moment, he staring at her so boldly. It was his eyes she remembered then, *more gold than hazel, a wolf's eyes, calm, deep, yet the eyes of a wild thing, independent, un-collared.*

"Return to Charleston," he said. "I'll visit my aunt, my mother's family, and I have business—I plan to purchase a ship. Eventually, I hope to have more than one."

"I would so love to return to the mainland myself," she said, "but just now, it's difficult." She sighed; the days would be much less enjoyable; no, the days would grow dull with him gone. She looked directly at him in the realization that it was more; she would truly miss him. "Perhaps later," she said wistfully.

The sun was low as Asher swung his leg over the log and stood. Reaching for her hand, he said, "It's growing late." Then—"I'll miss you. I've stayed longer than I'd intended, because it's become difficult—that is—it's become painful to leave Cuba rather—well—I've put off going because I didn't

201

want to be away from you, Cori." 'There—I've said it,' he thought, but what did I say?

"Ash are you telling me that you have feelings for me?" she asked. She spoke, far more calmly than she felt, for it was not the surf that caused a roaring in her ears, nor the wind that made her tremble. "Ash?" she repeated.

"Yes," he walked a ways with her, a startled silence between them, "since I saw you last spring at the Newgate ball, the day has not passed that I haven't closed my eyes and seen you." He looked straight ahead, as he spoke. "Each time we've met, it's become more difficult to think clearly, and now I find I can't put two thoughts together without you being between. I apologize if I'm acting the fool," he said.

"No more than me," she said, just above the wind. A swift warm current flowed within her, a defiant happiness, as she spoke. "When I see you, Ash, I want to smile; when we speak it's with an understanding, and when we're together I have feelings not proper for a lady to mention."

"Good," Asher said, squeezing her hand, and releasing a contented sigh that eased a tension he had not realized was in him. "Do you mind if I speak to your father, Cori?"

"I would mind if you didn't," she laughed, nudging him with her shoulder.

"Are you saying you'd marry me?" he blurted out.

"You have yet to ask," she whispered, and looked up through her blowing hair.

Stopping dead in his tracks, Asher looked down at her upturned face, and in the most serious tone said, "Corazon, would you be my wife?"

She heard the word, "Yes" come out of her mouth, and she filled with a hot, giddy rush of thoughts, each disconnected from the other. His arms came around her, his strong hands, the salty pressure of his lips on hers, and she would have fallen, had it been up to her quivering knees to support her.

"I love you," he murmured against her cheek, then brushed his lips against her neck, as her hair blew around him.

The most scandalous sensation shot down from her neck, and through her body, causing her to press her knees together and catch her breath. She pushed away gently shocked at the sensation.

"My love," she sighed properly, "we should go."

They hurried, now in the dim dusk, and climbed the steps from the beach.

"My slippers," she said at the top.

He pulled them from his pocket, watching as she put them on. From beyond the crest, they could hear voices and laughter, and she held to his arm with both hands, giving him a small shake, astonished at her own forwardness, but not in the least contrite.

"I want the world to know. You'll see my father tonight, right now," she said, a trace of excitement in her voice, for her mind still focused on the sensation that had swept her in his embrace.

"I'll go now," he laughed.

"Kiss me first, and then go," she said softly.

Leaning to him, emboldened, her hands went to his hair; she pressed her body to him as they kissed.

"Look! Rico, Tomas," the voice, very near, startled them. The words were slurred. "See, my cousin Corazon, she plays the whore with a Yankee."

Corazon felt herself propelled abruptly to the side, saw Natan, his face shaped by a surly smile as Asher stepped forward.

"You said what, sir?" Asher's voice was a stranger's voice, cold hard ice.

Instantly aware of what was beginning, Corazon thrust

herself between them, crying out, "Pay no attention, Ash. He's drunk, he meant nothing, ignore it."

"Whore— Natan repeated, his jaw out-thrust, and in his fever, he stepped forward, spitting full in her face.

It was if she had been struck; the smell of rum was in it, and both her hands flew up to wipe it away.

Asher moved; he brushed past her, furious, striking Natan a vicious backhanded blow, which jerked his head sideways, causing him to stagger against Ricardo Villarosa and fall to the ground.

Natan sprung up, and straightened himself; his face was pale, save for the red handprint that burned his cheek. Others were drawn to the commotion; several had heard the exchange of words.

"Sir, you take liberties—you dare to strike me. I will await your pleasure behind the customs house, dawn, with blades," he said. Bowing a stiff nod, He turned and pushed past his friends.

"Damn," Asher said under his breath, his temper hot, but back under control.

"Ash don't fight him," pleaded Corazon. "It's the moment. You will both apologize in the morning—for me you will apologize—promise me—oh, please, don't fight him—I accept the affront," she cried, her voice quavering now, and in spite of her best efforts, tears were running fast. She turned her face to his shoulder, and said between sobs, "Please—you must apologize."

"What is this about?" Robert O'Ryan said as he approached, pushing past onlookers.

Corazon, trembling over the horrid turn of events, turned to her brother and cried, "Where's Papa?"

"He's gone to Havana with Mendoza, Cori." He saw the tears in her eyes; he had never seen tears in her eyes; not one, so he asked again, this time softly, "What's this about?"

"Robert," Asher said, "Natan made a remark I couldn't allow to pass. I'm afraid I lost my temper and struck him."

"I see," Robert said, suddenly cool. "I feel it best that you leave, Lieutenant. A man will be sent to saddle your horse. If you will excuse me, I must see my sister to the house."

As they walked away, Robert had her firmly by the arm, and when she glanced back, Asher caught a glimpse of a face full of misery. The young men still stood about, though quiet, they were not friendly; a walk to the stable seemed prudent. As he waited for his horse, he reflected on how quickly a precious moment could turn disagreeable. Mounting, he rode out, his mind seeking a solution to an impossible situation. The only solution seemed to be Corazon's. He would apologize even if he had no call to. The last thing he wanted was the blood of Corazon's cousin on his hands, but even an apology required certain formality. It registered finally that he would need someone to go with him, and he thought of Dryer and his constant talk of dueling. "He's bound to know the formalities," Asher thought.

Chapter 21

In the courtyard, beneath a great banyan tree, four men waited in silence: Natan, his friend Ricardo, Hermon Vega and a doctor. Ricardo Villarosa walked toward the Americans as they arrived. His boots clicked, the sound of his walking echoed from the old walls.

"Good day, gentlemen. Are you prepared?" he asked with formality.

"Sir," Dryer spoke. "Possibly this affair can be settled peaceably. My gentleman is willing, even determined, to offer an apology."

"No! It won't do, I'm afraid. Mine insists that only blood will serve for a blow. If your man is ready, might this be settled?"

Dryer nodded his assent and Villarosa returned to Natan, who was removing his coat.

Natan was no mere cantina bravo. Natan was an Army officer who had survived years of war as well as previous outings. Asher understood that the man would not be hesitant in his killing and recalled his own battles. He felt no pride in them, no satisfaction other than the fact he had survived. This fight concerned an extraordinary woman though, a woman he would have as his wife. It would have more bearing on his life than the conflicts his country had involved him. At least it seemed so from the perspective of a young man in love. Asher striped off his jacket.

"Well," Dryer said under his breath, "I wish you success."

"Gene, there are two letters in my pocket." Asher said quietly.

"I understand."

As they walked toward the center of the courtyard, Asher smiled. He said dryly, "At least they won't hang me if I survive."

Dryer had pointed out that dueling remained acceptable under Spain's legal code, and therefore was within the law until January 1st. "Legal like war, only a little more personal, a little briefer. With the weight of the sword in his hand, he flexed and stretched, wishing he'd practiced more lately. He faced his opponent. Both Natan's eyes were blackened, and his cheek discolored in the shape of a hand. His silk shirt, open at the neck, fluttered a little in the breeze, but his expression was still as stone.

"Gentlemen," said Villarosa, "are you prepared?"

Natan made the sign of the cross, and kissed his blade. Asher nodded, going on guard.

"Begin," Villarosa, said.

Natan flicked his sword, lunged suddenly, and with only the most desperate effort did Asher turn the point, and then only to have it reverse and slash at his head. It actually brushed his hair.

Natan's attack had a reptilian speed, if not the strength of his larger opponent, and he pressed him, allowing no respite. Asher fell back, evading quick low lunges, feeling the power in his own arm as he parried. "He can't keep this up," Asher thought, but then the point rose, flying for his throat. Asher blocked, dropping to one knee, and slashed at Natan's middle, cutting his shirt and nicking his side.

Natan countered, cutting Asher's ear on the backstroke. Now both men bled and circled warily. They joined again, steel clashing at speed, first low, then high, and as Asher blocked a high cut, Natan disengaged, and dropping, cut at the back of his ankle. Asher leaped over the blade, felt it take part of the heel from his right boot, swept his own blade back only in time to halt Natan's counter stroke.

"This is not a practice," Asher told himself. It was stupid and he had no wish to injure Corazon's ill-mannered cousin, yet Natan had no such reservation.

Relentless, Natan changed his attack to a series of lunging thrusts. The swords met, whirling, rasping with such speed that the eye could not follow. Finally, Asher caught his blade up in a thrusting spiral that sent it flying from Natan's hand and across the pavement. Asher disengaged as Natan scrambled after his weapon.

"Both of you bleed," Villarosa said. "Are you satisfied?"

Even as Asher's lips formed the word yes, Natan spit and charged, engaging recklessly at a run. Asher looked into the angry face, the burning eyes, and realized he would have to kill or disable him, perhaps a thrust through the thigh. The next thrust sped at Asher's chest, past his guard and he twisted with it, feeling it cut, even as he drove his left elbow into the side of Natan's head. Blood stained his shirt from a short slice, while Natan staggered to the side, blinking sweat from his eyes.

Clench-jawed, Asher went after him with a string of powerful jabs and slashes. Perceiving a weakness in Natan's arm, he drove him back to the wall, cutting him twice, and taking a scratch on the arm. Both were breathing hard now, pausing between passes.

Stamping his foot, Natan made yet another wild, rushing engagement, only to feel his blade brushed aside, as Asher's steel entered his body above the breastbone. Coughing, Natan sat solidly on the ground, blood pouring from his mouth, and stared for a moment at his sword hand. He looked up at Asher, who stood motionless. His seconds and the doctor were running to his side.

"I believe you have killed me, sir," he whispered, blood and foam spraying from his lips with the words.

"It wasn't my wish, sir," Asher said sadly.

He wondered if he were a contemptible dog for wishing to live. He had held no lasting enmity toward Natan Vargas, at least none he would have pursued with such severity. To wound Natan mortally in preservation of his own life was not odious. He determined it would be hypocrisy to regret what happened. He had not wanted this, but he couldn't have functioned in this society had he not acted within the structure of what was considered moral here.

"Let me see your side, Ash," Dryer said, pulling at his shirt.

"A cut is all," Asher said, shrugging him off.

Ricardo Villarosa stood, turning to Asher, "He is dead, sir."

Hermon Vega rose beside him, anger and grief on his face.

He said, "Sir, understand that you are not to be tolerated. I believe you can understand why you would no longer be welcome on the lands of this family."

"I'm afraid I'll have to be told by your uncle, and by the young lady, not you, sir."

'You doubt me, sir?" Hermon said, the veins on his temples

standing out.

"I care nothing for what you say, sir."

"You feel that you can take liberties with our women and not be confronted?" Hermon said, his voice rising.

"I take no liberties, nor do I need give explanations to you, sir," Asher growled.

"You think not," Hermon, said red with anger.

"And I will not be forbidden access to the O'Ryan house by anyone other than the master of that house. Do you understand me, sir?" Asher said, becoming frustrated.

"You are impertinent. You dishonor me, sir," Hermon exclaimed, rigid with fury.

"No," Asher said; "I dishonor your stupid, stiff-necked perception of honor."

The slap came so fast that Asher's cheek burned before he saw Hermon's hand. The crack and the intake of breath, by both Villarosa and Dryer came almost simultaneously.

"I will be at your service. At any time, you wish, sir," Hermon hissed.

Asher had suffered enough of their pride. He was determined to end the stupidity and said so. "Now—now, sir, seeing as we are all here, and I believe the choice of weapons falls to me."

"Your pleasure, sir."

Turning to the others, Asher said, "Fists gentlemen."

"That is not possible," Vega said with disgust.

"Pardon," Dryer said, "but there are precedents."

Villarosa was shaking his head, "He's correct, my friend; on many occasions, it has been done."

Hermon tore off his coat; snarled, "So be it, then."

They faced off and Dryer backed clear of them saying, "Gentlemen, you may begin."

210

Hermon, rage in his face, came in with a windmill right. Asher, ducking under, struck a powerful right of his own, deep into Hermon's stomach, and as he bent, drove a stiff left hook up under his chin. Hermon hit the ground, glassy-eyed, and lay still.

"When he comes to, tell him I'm satisfied," he said to Villarosa, "and please convey my regrets to Natan's family. You must be aware I wanted none of this." Placing the tip of the sword on the pavement, he stomped on it, breaking the blade, and he pitched the upper portion against the wall with extreme violence. "I'll be dam'd if I ever involve myself in this sort of stupid butchery again," he swore. "So help me god."

Asher turned, and picking up his coat, stalked out of the courtyard. At the barracks, he found the surgeon on his way to breakfast, and got himself stitched. Doctor Taylor had raised his eyebrows at Asher's wounds, but asked no direct questions. It being a Sunday, Asher decided to wait and not bother Colonel Morse. Morning tomorrow would be soon enough.

He was tired, very, very tired. He cursed the waste caused by false pride and for allowing himself to be drawn into a duel. In his room, he rid himself of his bloody clothes, and as he washed the blood from himself, the hollow coldness diminished as if the anger rinsed away with the blood. He pictured Corazon, how she looked, and recalled how it was with her in his arms. He knew this would pass, only a matter of persistence and patience. He would have Corazon O'Ryan for a wife, sure as god's judgment, he'd have her, but her people were going to take some getting used to."

Chapter 22

Smoldering, Corazon sat in her room. The curtains lift and fall on the night breeze. The house was somber, still, and not even the muffled voices of servants or the sound of footsteps reached her. At noon, Ricardo Villarosa had arrived, bringing poor Hermon, with his broken jaw and news of Natan's death. During the afternoon she had heard arguing and, on occasion, the sobbing of her sister from the next room. Now there was silence.

A tray with her dinner sat, partly eaten, near the open window . At least she had an open window. The door, it was locked. Even the open window had a man sitting below; a guard to ensure that there would be no foolishness on her part. Corazon was imprisoned in solitude that she might contemplate her guilt, so she might suffer remorse, and consider the consequences of her bad behavior.

Her mother failed to realize she neither experienced guilt nor wanted company. The stunned terror she experienced on the previous night had become righteous anger by morning, and seething outrage in the afternoon. She was outraged at the accusation of her responsibility in Natan's death. Natan bore the blame for his own death, brought about by his vices: arrogance, jealousy, hatred, pride and rum. These were the relevant factors. These were vices borne by her cousin, Natan Vega, and not by her.

It was useless for her to argue further; she would not condescend to it. How dare they condemn her; she had done no more than kiss the man to whom she had become engaged. It was as if she had been plunged into the middle ages. Imprisoned, locked in her rooms like a child, and she was no child. Her twentieth birthday was only three months away. When Papa returned, there would be an end to this. She would demand to return to Georgetown, or better, to Aunt Samantha's in Charleston. Ash would be there; they would marry and live in a sane society.

Looking down from her window, she could see William, his chair tilted to the wall. Walking back to her tray, she took the pitcher of tea, and carrying it to the window, carefully poured it down on the un-expecting man below. Jolted from sleep, he toppled from the chair, cursing softly. Backing away from the window, she felt better at having struck a blow, at having physically expressed her agitation.

Undressing, she lay on her bed, worried about Asher, and wondered when she would see him. Certainly, it would not be before Papa returned, and at least not until after Natan's funeral. It was possible that he would not be received at all. She rolled on her side, and through her window, watched clouds racing across the moon. "No matter, they can't keep me locked up here forever," she muttered under her breath, for unconsciously she had made a choice.

The dull rapping on her door brought her abruptly awake. The sun was high and reflected brightly off the polished wood floor at her window.

Corazon, open the door," spoke Douglas O'Ryan's deep voice.

"A moment, I'm not dressed," she cried, and rolling off her bed, she snatched her robe. Out of spite, she had locked the door from her side. She slipped the bolt and stepped aside.

"Good morning, Cori," her father said as he closed the door behind him. She saw that the lines on his face had deepened, taken on a hardness to which she was not accustomed. "Do you realize that you've placed the family in a position of ridicule?" he said dryly and without preamble. "You've placed me in an insufferable position, at exactly the moment I was

213

trying to bring together the efforts of months of work. What value is my advice, they will say, when I cannot manage my own family? It's a humiliation I will not allow."

"I did nothing wrong," she cried, shocked. "Will no one listen to me?"

O'Ryan sat, gesturing with both palms up. "Certainly, I'll listen," he said acidly, "explain."

"Asher Byran and I, we only spoke," she told him. "He asked me if he could speak to you about marriage and I urged him to. When we kissed, Natan called me a whore. He spit in my face, Father. Before people with whom I'm acquainted, he spit on me," she cried. "That's the reason Asher struck him. Natan was drunk and disgusting. He deserved the slap."

"You miss the point entirely," O'Ryan said sharply. "It's what allowed the incident. We are dealing with appearances. People will say she went off alone with a man. She was discovered alone with him in the dark and in an embrace. No matter it was innocent Cori. It has caused the fighting of duels. These were not simple affairs, not merely outings, where an outsider met discreetly with men of your family. No! This is seen as political, a heated mortal combat. Spanish officers, dueling with an American officer, political, and at the most awkward time for all parties involved. Now do you understand?"

She did not respond. Shocked beyond words, she did not respond. She heard—but this—from her father. It was beyond understanding.

Taking her silence for docility, he added, "What gave you the notion, young Byran would be an acceptable husband?"

"I assumed you thought well of him," she said, finding her voice, controlling it.

"Of course, I think well of him, he's of good family and intelligent, but that lends nothing to his value to me as a son-in-law. He has little more than a good name, certainly no advantages to me in Cuba. He's of no use to me whatever."

"Use to you," she blurted, color rising up from her chest, white encircling her eyes.

"Of course, Cori; are you so childish to expect I'd allow a union with the first poor beggar who caught your eye?" He laughed warmly. "You and your sister will have husbands acceptable and useful to me, in the same manner that your mother married a man who was of value to her father." He grunted with irritation. "That's if anyone will have you after this unfortunate disaster. Perhaps with time the affair will pale."

"You're repellent," she said, immediately regretting her words, for she recognized more would have been gained with a subdued response. She was far too angry though, and it was not in her nature to keep her mouth closed.

"And you're foolish," he said, standing. "Understand now. There will be no more of your lieutenant in this house or elsewhere. Truth is daughter, he should find his feet on the mainland very quickly, and I have little doubt, before long, the charms of some other wealthy young woman, will have replaced yours. Resign yourself, Cori. It's finished"

So amazed was she, hearing the things her father had said, Corazon could only blink. When he turned in the doorway, informing her, she was to remain in her room for a few days, she was silent. He told her, in a matter-of-fact way that Resa would be up with a tray.

"Let her know what you require," he said.

She had never viewed her father in this manner before, yet she had never before found herself entangled in his dealings. She had been along on business trips, enjoying herself, while father involved himself in trades, sales and manipulations. Never did she anticipate he would someday treat her as a commodity to, be dealt with, mere trade goods. Father had seemed strong willed and aloof, often quite distant, but never cruel or ruthless. Corazon become conscious that until this morning, she had never really understood her father.

Corazon walked to the window and looked down. Below, another of father's men sat in the shade of his straw hat. She turned to her bed, grabbed a pillow from it, and threw it across the room knocking over a vase. The crash of porcelain suddenly saddened her, for she had loved the vase. Her chin puckering, she fell onto her bed and wept, a thing that would have astonished those who knew her best. For the first time in her life, Corazon knew precisely what was important to her, and it was denied her. Indignation, the thought of being told whom to marry, it mingled with the impotent rage of being caged. She had never imagined her parents would imprison her in her own home.

"Asher? What had father meant? She wondered, what did he mean about Asher leaving, his being on the mainland?" A knock on the door interrupted her thoughts. Resa brought breakfast, and whispered her sympathy, then cleaned up the broken vase and left quietly. Corazon heard Luko's key turn in the lock, and looked at her food gloomily. "Hopeless only for the moment," she decided. Calmer, she considered poor Natan, dead for nothing after surviving three years of bloody war and only because of his own hateful, intolerant pride. "Death was the only permanence. Outside that, all is possible," she decided, and began to eat with enthusiasm. "What are a few days in a lifetime?" she asked herself.

Chapter 23

His first words had been, "Byran, what the hell were you thinking?" Before Asher had been able to answer, Colonel Morse had continued. "General Wilson received letters from both General Brooke and the Spanish governor. Duels," Morse growled. "My God, two duels over a woman. Two duels in a single day, and I'd thought you were an officer with some common sense, but then you are from South Carolina," he snorted.

"Sir, if I may," he said handing him an envelope.

Morse snatched it, and briefly scanned the contents, "Resignation uh. Just as well," he said in a less severe tone. "This would have ruined your career regardless, and you would have made captain within the year. You're damn lucky Brooke wants this incident to quietly disappear."

"I regret the incident extremely, sir, tried to avoid it. I even offered my apologies."

"Did it occur to you to simply not show up?"

"It wouldn't have been possible to associate with these people if I hadn't obliged them, sir, privately or professionally."

Morse put Asher's letter back into its envelope. He picked another envelope off his desk, and handed both across to him. "Aren't going to be associating with them anyway, Lieutenant. Your orders," he offered. "You're to be escorted to the port, escorted forthwith, to where you're to be put aboard the transport *City of Baltimore*. On arrival Tampa, you will be assigned to a unit presently in the Philippines. Headquarters personnel in Tampa will accept your resignation, if you still wish to submit it. You'll have a few minutes to gather your kit."

"Sir, I own a personal mount. Might I arrange to have it stabled and transported? Only a word with my sergeant."

"Only that," Morse allowed, and then in a lower voice, out of hearing, "best of luck Byran," and he winked. "I understand she is an extraordinary young woman."

"She is, sir," said Asher, who completely agreed. Saluting Morse, he went out into the orderly room, where Lieutenant Thames and two troopers waited for him.

"Ready, Ash?"

"Except for my personal belongings and a word with Sergeant Strong concerning my horse."

"That's a bad luck animal if there is one," Thames said, as they left the building.

"Brought me good luck," he said buoyantly. "I'm going to be married."

"Well, then, Thames said, "let me congratulate you, Ash," and he slapped him on the back. "Shame about all this other mess. Hell, Arizona, where I'm from, ain't nobody's business what goes on between men. I can't say as I agree, with the dam Northeastern notion of kiss and make up." He spit disdainfully and said in a raised voice, "Ain't right, hanging a man over a fair fight."

Gabe Strong had a detail mucking out the stalls. He promised to see the chestnut gelding to a good stable, until Asher decided what to do with it. While checking the horse, he slipped him a letter for Corazon.

"If there's a way, you get this to her," he said.

"Spec that might be ah difficult thing, but I can try," he offered. "Y'all ain't gonna just disappear now?"

"Hell, no! I'll be back, just wearing another suit," Asher said lightly. "See you soon."

"I'll be looking sir, and don't worry about this here nag,"

Gabe said, pushing its head around to keep from suffering a bite.

Moments were all it took for Asher to put his belongings together and toss them into a wagon. Several of his friends shook hands and saw him off. The harbor was only minutes away, and he was on-board shortly, with the two troopers at the gangway, ensuring he remain on board. The *City of Baltimore* had only been at sea an hour when Asher entered the salon and found Gene Dryer.

"What are you doing here?" Asher asked with surprise.

Looking up, Dryer smiled awkwardly. "Traveling to the Philippines," he said.

"This is sudden," Asher replied.

Dryer shook his head slowly. "No," he said. "Not when one assists in a political indiscretion. The army functions with dispatch when embarrassed."

Suddenly realizing why Dryer was there he apologized. "I'm dam'd sorry, I'd have never guessed this would happen to you."

"The good of the service," Dryer said, with a wave of his hand. "And I've always fancied visiting the Far East." He pushed back a chair with his foot. "A seat," he invited.

Asher sat. "Have me on my way to Manila too, but I'm resigning my commission. I'd planned to resign first of the year anyway. Be back in Charleston for Christmas as it stands."

"I'll try to make it to St. Louis myself," Dryer said, and went back to his food. "Lamb's not bad," he added, speaking with his mouth full.

"I'll take your word," Asher said, signaling the steward.

Within minutes, his food arrived and they spoke congenially over drinks, going on deck afterward. A strong northeast wind blew against the Gulf Stream causing a short, steep sea. It set the ship up for one nasty roll after the other. Nevertheless, the sun was bright and the sky clear, rim to rim. Salt was on Asher's lips, the air cool, and as he leaned on the rail, he felt free. Life was good.

His years up to this instant, he realized they were merely a preparation for the life he wished to make. School, even the Army, was a time of focus and the development of his talents and reason. It had been a learning time. Now he felt the presence of will, of a direction. His heart was high. He was in love with a woman, and she was in love with him. Asher knew what his profession would be, and his intention was to succeed. He would prosper and provide for Corazon O'Ryan in a manner that she deserved. He would seek his fortune on the sea, win it, and lay it at her feet.

He sat, foot braced against the roll and relaxed; his eyes closed, savoring images: Corazon at the Newgate Ball, the "catch me if you can" look as she raced her horse through the cane fields, the sound of her laugh and the taste of her kiss. He stretched and perceived, as lovers do, that he was the most fortunate among men. He would telegraph her from Tampa to tell her so. For no reason, a memory, a recollection came to him, a tear-streaked voice in candlelight. *"You will be a soldier, but your path would be the water. You will pursue a woman on horseback and claim pure love, a love bathed in blood. You will gather great wealth that would mean little."*

The memory and the truth of the half-forgotten prophecy were nagging in their accuracy, and he was suddenly glad he had fled from knowledge of the rest. *"You will have strong children,"* was the last he had heard of it. Not a bad thing he decided and perhaps—to have heard the rest—no! A man should not know his future, not beyond the knowledge that death is certain.

The *City of Baltimore* took her pilot at dusk, but it was late by the time she passed Egmont Key, running up the bay. Most of her passengers slept aboard, Asher among them. The process of separating himself from the army proved a simple one. Before noon, he had caught a train that would have him in Charleston by the morning. The miles of pine land clicked away, becoming rolling hills and live oak, and before dark, pine forest again. In Jacksonville, he changed trains and slept through the night in a Pullman, waking to a dawn in Charleston. Low gray clouds raced east, and a cold damp wind promised rain. He'd hired a carriage, given the driver his aunt's address and spent the day talking.

Upon mention of Corazon, Aunt Fay had placed a finger to her temple, "Why, yes, Ash," she had said, "I believe I recall the very girl—from the hospital bazaar last year. She and Samantha's daughter, Jenny Ashe, had a booth; oh yes; I so look forward to meeting her. Will she return here soon?"

"Not soon Ma'am."

It was at this point he hesitantly related the rest of the story, the telling of which had left Fay aghast. This sort of affair was once quite common, why the very thing when Fay was a girl, but she had not heard of an outing in fifteen years. Why, the last legal duel she knew of was when Col. Cash killed Col. Shannon over inheritance in 'eighty. She was certain such things still occurred, but these days were kept very quiet.

"Oh, God, Ash," she said, "A story of this sort will ruin a girl, two of her cousins at one outing Asher. Oh my—it'll all come out," and she knew, most certainly it would come out, and it would do Asher no good whatsoever. She knew it.

Rain and to sleet began by early afternoon, but she had an invitation to attend a tea at Gloria Butler's, and did not intend to miss it, not now of all times. William would drop her there and drive Ash to the haberdashery to purchase clothing and a winter coat. She must be the first to divulge the details of what she would put as, "the horrid way young Miss O'Ryan had been treated by her Spanish relations." She would stress how hatred borne of the war had prejudiced them against the brave young American officer, a hero of Santiago, whose wife Miss O'Ryan promised to become. Why, the tragic story of *Romeo and Juliet* would pale when compared to Fay's version of events, and with the war so recently ended. The moral superiority would certainly be hers.

Why, even if some chose to see otherwise, the issue would be so confused. As she began her delicate social manipulations, Fay remembered the days of her own courting. My God, youth was such a desperate time.

By New Year's, Fay's campaign had borne fruit. Even Samantha Ashe, had called to learn the truth surrounding Lieutenant Byran's defense of her niece's honor. "Isn't it shocking, the way war's bitterness overflows a society's common good sense," she told Samantha. "To be so warped by bitter hatred that a family can be destroyed by sweet love."

"Oh Fay, Fay, how strange you say that," Samantha gasped. "Why, this whole affair has brought Mr. Shakespeare's tragic *Romeo and Juliet* to mind."

Fay refilled Samantha's cup, a serious concern deepening the lines of her old face, "How true, dear, and we must all aspire to a wisdom that is above the common. I can only imagine how your sweet niece has suffered for doing no more than giving her heart to my brave nephew," Fay said, in a broken voice.

"I only wish she was with me now," Samantha said, patting Fay's hand.

The visit continued well into the afternoon. Fay listened to snippets about Corazon's time in her aunt's home, and regaled Samantha with descriptions of Asher's heroic exploits in the Cuban war. They parted late, with warm feelings and tears of friendship. Fay whispered to herself, "The boy will never understand the trouble I've gone to."

During the week, Asher occupied himself, spending time with Mr. Cox, a surveyor he had employed to inspect various ships for sale along the coast. When Fay awoke Tuesday morning to find Asher disgustingly drunk on her divan, she was both surprised and agitated. Fay summoned Willum and Tess to put him to bed. She bent to pick his coat up from her hall floor. She grunted, and bent again, to retrieve a telegram that had fallen from the pocket. "God and the devil," she swore, dropping the coat that she might grasp the telegram in two hands, as she read it a second time.

"Asher dearest: I find I am unable to reconcile myself with Natan's death and the breach with my family that any union with you must now cause. STOP: *I can no longer consent to marry you.* STOP: *Please forgive me. Corazon:* STOP:

"My poor boy," Fay said sadly. "My poor, poor boy."

Chapter 24

Since that instant, the moment when he received his telegram of rejection, Asher had become the absolute epitome of unflagging industry, excepting of course, the first two days. The first, he spent getting slobbering drunk, the second recovering from being slobbering drunk.

It was Mr. Cox, the surveyor, who had heard of the *Gracia de Dios*. She was a one-hundred-and-eighty-foot, three masted topsail schooner. In September, a colleague of Cox had done the survey for her underwriters.

The vessel, with a cargo of mahogany, had driven on Triumph Reef during a squall, bilging herself. Hog Johnson, a Key West salvor, had bought her from the underwriters' right where she sat. After lightering a portion of her cargo, he had towed her north to Jacksonville. The lumber sold to a furniture company, and the schooner now lay in the mud above Green Cove Springs. The damaged ship could be had cheap.

The schooner was built in Livingston, Guatemala and Cox was impressed with her construction. He pointed out that she was all Honduran mahogany and live oak, fastened with bronze bolts, and a great number of ironwood trunels, all costly materials. Except for minor damage to her forefoot, and several stove planks at the turn of her port bilge, she was sound.

After some haggling with Key West Salvage, Asher acquired her for sum of three thousand dollars. He hired a gang of thirty men and Pappy MacArt, a presently retired, but bored shipwright, to run them. On the old man's shoulders fell all the labors of the refitting. His countenance was joy itself, as he set about with oakum, tar, iron and lumber. Pappy careened her to starboard, then to port. He had her floated, and to stiffen her back, had balks of live oak banded in place as a keelson. Under old man MacArt, the ship looked the model of industry, covered with stages hung out over her sides, and men caulking and painting. The old man knew of every bargain on the Johns River, and the location of every cast-off piece of gear. He stretched the dollars farther than Asher had any right to expect, but the cost was still shocking, and the refit ran to more than the ship's purchase price.

Cox recommended an underwriter, and slowly, Asher began to choose out and hire a crew. His bosun, Benjamin Swallow, was a Caiman Islander of vast experience while the mate, Rolland Floyd, was a man nearer Asher's own age. Born in Portland, Maine, Floyd had served in schooners since the age of fourteen. He was reported to be competent.

It was these two, with a pair of Bahamians, who got up the rigging while Pappy set up steam donkey engines to power the winches. Near the end of January, the refit was complete. The schooner was towed down to Jacksonville, where she was renamed the *Miss Fay Gibbes*. Docked near the foot of Main Street, she was prepared to take a cargo when cargo could be had.

One of the brokers Asher had spoken with a few days earlier had a partial cargo. It was a load of rice, consigned for Havana out of Fernandina. On January 27, the schooner loaded several small items of cargo for Key West, and with a crew of ten, slipped down river. She had the tide and a brisk northwest breeze.

When they brought her round to nor' nor' east, off the jetties, the schooner proved so tender in ballast that, for all her free-board, the starboard bulwark was submerged. Bosun Swallow rightly cast off the main halyards, sending both sail and gaff abruptly down over the boom. The mate, who was supervising work forward, ran aft looking pale, while Ben Swallow and all hands, save the helmsman, hurriedly furled the main and secured the gaff.

"Mite tender," remarked the pilot laconically, and as he looked back toward the jetties, it appeared as if he thought, he might be better off ashore.

"No doubt I'll be putting some additional ballast in her at Fernandina," Asher said, his pulse a little quick.

He told Rolly to double reef the fore and mizzen, and get the main back up with a double reef. He gave the orders, feeling far less confidence in his abilities than he had ten

225

minutes before. "Four years since I stood a deck watch," he thought, "and then as mate. Need to get my mind back into what I'm doing, begin to think like a Ship's Master. Be a poor job to sink a good ship -- more so in sight of port and in fair weather!" He promised himself that he would compute the schooner's stability figures again in Fernandina.

He had driven himself all month to get the ship ready, and that had helped to occupy his mind. Still, with maddening regularity, his thoughts returned to Corazon O'Ryan. His preoccupation with her made it difficult to concentrate on his duties. This didn't excuse his present failings as Master; rather, it lent to them, and he chastened himself for his failings.

By twilight, the *Miss Fay* heeled moderately, making good a steady eight knots on a port tack. She had white water all down her sides and a broad wake. The wind had veered north, requiring a more nor' easterly course, which put her twelve miles east of Fernandina's light. Asher ordered the helm put down. As the bow crossed the wind, he called for the jib sheets to be cast off and hauled. The schooner carried forward two hundred feet, her luffing canvas clattering, then heeled to port, and became silent as her sails filled.

The pilot was napping, slouched behind the deckhouse, and he toppled over as the deck angle reversed itself. He rolled and slid a few feet, fetching up against a bollard, from which he glowered red-faced at the helmsman.

"Mr. Pilot," Asher said, "If you'd like, there's a bunk below. I'll be heaving to. With myself and the crew being unfamiliar with the ship, I'd rather have the light. We'll enter at dawn."

It's y' all ship, Captain," he mumbled acidly, pulling himself up from the deck. "It suits me just fine if it suits y'all." He dusted himself, producing a small flask, and before taking a nip said, "Y'all be sure to gimme a warning, a fore y'all do anything—uh radical—me being below decks and all."

The cook came weaving aft with coffee, leaning into the deck's cant. Asher accepted the cup and had the cook show the pilot to a cabin. He paced up and down the windward side of the chart house. As they closed the coast, he took a bearing, now and again, on Fernandina's light. Gib MacArt came aft to relieve the helmsman, who sang out his course.

"Helm relieved, 280°, wind abeam," George Wallace called out.

"280°, wind abeam," MacArt repeated. He clutched the spokes; she wandered off for a moment. He found his notch and steadied up.

"George, we'll tack shortly," Asher said. "Pass to the bosun we're to heave to. I'll want the jib sheets held to weather and the foresail down."

"Sure' tell um, Cop'n."

A three-quarter moon was high, and in its light, the deck forward was plain to see. He saw Swallow step out onto deck, stretch and move to the fife rail.

He called forward, "As we come up, drop her, Mr. Swallow." Then over his shoulder he said, "Right rudder and bring her through the wind."

As the schooner came into the eye of the wind, every line and block aboard shook and rattled, and canvas flopped loudly. Halyard blocks began to squeal, and the jaws of the foresail gaff slid down the mast. As suddenly as the confusion of sound and motion began, it ended. The schooner lay to, nearly motionless, with her head sails backed, and when Rolly came up for his midnight watch, *Miss Fay Gibbes* had moved only a mile to the east.

Asher yawned and rubbed his face, "Have her inside three miles when you call me Rolly, and call the pilot, too," he added. "Turn the cook out early, so the crew can eat before

227

we start in. Tired," he sighed.

"A lengthy day, Captain?"

"Aye," he said starting for the hatch, "We need a second mate before we leave Fernandina. We'll run ourselves ragged sailing watch and watch like this."

"Truth in that, sir."

Below, he kicked off shoes and trousers, and fell into his bunk. The moonlight weave up and down with the ship's easy roll and he slid off into a deep sleep. The cook woke him at five, but it was the smell of biscuits that brought him to his feet. He ate one hungrily as he slipped on his britches, and two more dripping butter down his chin as he put on his shoes. Once on deck he looked about, getting his bearings, and sent for coffee. The mate had set the foresail and brought her about, and *Miss Fay* ran inshore with a northeast breeze just aft the beam.

Pipe clenched in his teeth, the pilot greeted him. "Fine brisk morning Captain; carry the last of the ebb to shore, I'd say."

Asher nodded and ducked into the chart room for a quick look at the channel. Fort Clinch was broad on the port bow, and the swell was breaking to the sides of the channel ahead. Hurrying back out, he turned the ship over to the Pilot, and sent word to the bosun for the anchor to be broke out and set on the brake. Nervous as a new mother, he stood by, trying not to fidget as the pilot ran the channel.

Off Crompton's wharf, *Miss Fay Gibbes* anchored, and warped alongside with her winches. Stevedores were putting bagged rice into her by noon. Asher quickly shaved and prepared to walk up to the harbormaster's office for a look at the bulletin board. He didn't care for the prospect of sailing again with the second mate and carpenter's berths empty. He planned to search out suitable men immediately. "No profit in putting things off," he thought. He might also pick up more southbound freight, be it by work or pure chance. It took but a few minutes to find the office, and entering, Asher stood looking up at the many notices pined to the board.

Chapter 25

"You must realize Fedrico — eventually I will leave — with or without your doing this favor. It will come to the same end," Corazon said with persuasive certainty.

"I would never be forgiven," he complained, apprehensive and looking very unhappy.

"No one would know, cousin. Certainly, you don't believe I would even hint as to the identity of the person who arranged my passage."

She smiled with such a soft beauty that Fedrico looked away, and pacing back and forth, frowned and fidgeted uncomfortably, for he was chosen to keep an eye on her. He was in fact her father's spy and was to ensure that the very thing, she was asking, did not occur. Fedrico was glad she was his first cousin but she was too beautiful to deal with, even as a cousin, but it did help when he remembered her foul temper.

"It would be disloyal," he said snappishly. "I am to be employed by your father. He's my benefactor."

"You are being tedious," she scolded and stretched on the

divan.

Fedrico said nothing, but continued to look uncomfortable, refusing to meet her eye until she stood abruptly, and with anger plain in her face, waved the telegram under his nose.

"This is the man you are loyal to, If so this is the sort of thing you must expect from him, lies, black lies and tricks. My father tries to manipulate me, his own child with this. And Rico, it is obvious that your conscience suffers from pangs of loyalty."

Fedrico backed away fearfully. She was in a high state of temper, worse than during the week they had kept her locked in. He again chose to stare at his feet rather than meet her eyes. He had no doubt she would find a way to leave for she made no secret of her feelings or intentions. She and her mother did not speak, and Esmeralda — after Corazon shook her by the hair, her sister avoided her. Oh, and poor Hermon — him, she treated with absolute chill. "Perhaps," Fedrico thought, "her absence would be acceptable in the interests of tranquility."

"Departure through Havana would be a simple thing, I can arrange a ticket," he offered.

She sighed, her face exhibiting an expression of condescension as she spoke, "You astonish me, Fedrico. Without doubt, I would be caught. I must sail from Cardenas."

"Cori, I don't know. Only a few small ships come to Cardenas, and to find one sailing for Charleston, who could say when?"

"Any port will do," she informed him. "I have sufficient money for train fare, for meals, for any contingency, once my feet have touched the mainland."

"Must it be now?" he asked, downcast, hopeful that a delay might soften Cori's outlook, and make reconciliation possible.

"Yes, or sooner," she said passionately. "I'm determined to

follow this course, and at the first possible moment. I assure you, this is the kindest thing you can do."

"Very well," he said, looking her in the eye, "I'll go to Cardenas today. I'll do what you wish cousin — even if it must come to a poor end."

"You'll be discreet," she whispered apprehensively.

Fedrico bristled with irritation. "Just because I'm idiot enough to do this for you, it doesn't mean I'm a complete fool," he said testily.

"You have a dear, kind heart, Fedrico." She spoke, stepping close, and paying no attention to his gloom. "You're my favorite cousin," she crooned and leaning over, placed a warm kiss on his cheek.

It was two days later when he informed her. A cattle transport, the *Western Sea*, would depart from Cardenas at high tide on the following afternoon. Corazon immediately arranged to go riding in the morning. With her door bolted, she began sewing her jewelry into the seams of her riding clothes. Well past midnight, she slipped out of bed, and crept into her father's study, removing the colt 38-caliber pistol he kept in his desk. She would not be thwarted.

Elated, Corazon returned to her bed, and dawn came, with clear skies and a cool mist over the valleys. She was usually up before the other O'Ryans, and this morning was no different. She sent Luko to have her mare saddled, and to advise William, she would be ready in a few minutes. Breakfast was fruit and a slice of cold ham eaten quickly. As she left the house, she looked down; self-consciously assuring herself, there was no bulge, for the pistol was pushed into the back of her left boot and taped. William was up in the saddle of his horse, a big thoroughbred. Antonio held her gray mare. The Arabian gray tossed its head, nickered as she approached.

"My Pepper," she whispered against the mare's muzzle,

"Today, my friend, you shall run to your heart's content."

Gathering the reins, she grasped the front edge of her saddle, and swung up before Antonio could move to assist. Hurrying, he leaped onto his black, and with William, rode behind her up the south road. Armed escorts for noble women, was an ancient tradition of the Spanish culture, and were now more than prudent due to kidnappings and killings made common in the war. However, she and each of these men understood they were not merely her escorts, but her keepers. They also were aware she was not of a mind, or a nature, to be kept.

The little Arabian was restless, anxious to run, and Corazon let her go, setting the fast pace that was her habit when riding alone. Twice, she pulled up and pointed or asked simple questions of William and Antonio. She judged the condition of their mounts, noting that Antonio's black had begun to lather, and that both of the big horses were starting to blow. At a point where the road made several curves, she bent low, and let the gray have its head. She raced toward the Canimar Bridge and Matanzas. Coming out onto a straight section of the road, both men, suddenly realizing what was happening, came after her, William riding hard, Antonio holding back, pacing the black.

She crossed the bridge, going fast uphill, but as the road curved and entered the trees, she left it, cutting sharply south. Circling the hill, Corazon doubled back to the river. She walked the mare across a wide shallow ford, urged her up the bank and rode back to the east, toward Cardenas.

She let the Arabian pick her gait. Men working the fields looked up in surprise as she passed. In the village's chickens scattered and barking dogs tried to keep up. Corazon was filled with a soaring elation. She wondered, "How far did those fools ride toward Matanzas, before they realized they'd been duped? How long before they found someone who'd seen me?"

She rode up the shoulder of one of the Tetas, saw Cardenas and she laughed, long and joyously. As the last miles passed, she thought of her horse, what was she to do with her Pepper? Coming into the city, the Arabian gray pranced and side stepped, twenty fast miles and still fresh, how Corazon loved her.

The road leading to the wharf cut through a mangrove swamp, and cattle from the port crowded up the narrow causeway toward the high ground. Flies, drawn to the cattle became troublesome. She pulled the gauze veil from under her hat to protect her face, directing the mare with her knees as she did so. Corazon wove her way through the crowding cattle, finally smiling happily at one of the vaqueros who opened a path for her. The way clear, she galloped down the pier to a small ship. Although the cattle ramp remained down, the men were preparing to hoist and secure it as an officer stood by.

"Sir," she called as her gray pranced in place. "I have a receipt for passage to Punta Rasa aboard this vessel. Can you accommodate my horse also?"

"Why, Ma'am," he said, whipping off his hat, "don't concern y'all in the least. Got all the room in the world, we do."

"Why sir, could someone help me bring her aboard then?"

"Ellis," he bellowed, "Get this lady's horse aboard ah here."

The mare shied and backed at the sudden shout, and the mate blanched.

Oh! Now, sorry, ma'am," he cried, his eyes growing large with shame. Abashed, he pressed his hat to his chest with two huge hands wringing it like a wet towel.

Laughing, she swung to the ground, taking the gray by the hackamore. "She forgives you sir," and rubbing her cheek

233

against the mare's velvet nose, looked up asking, "But whom sir, may I be addressing?"

"Thatcher ma'am, Claudius Thatcher, first mate at your service, ma'am."

"Pleased, Mr. Thatcher and I am Miss O'Ryan," she said softly, with her sweetest smile. She passed the reins to Ellis, who started the mare up the ramp; she called after him, "You will rub her down, Mr. Ellis? Not too much grain or water until she's cooled."

"Yes 'um," the sandy-haired boy called back.

"Would you see me aboard, Mr. Thatcher?" In her most helpless tone she added, "I know so little of ships."

"Why, right this way," he said, pointing toward the gangway, and noting the lustful eyes following her, he growled, "and y'all, Pikens, Harps, the rest of y'all, get thet ramp in."

Thatcher assisted her on the gangway. The stench of foot deep manure covering the length of the cattle deck reached Corazon's nose, which wrinkled, and when he saw her put a perfumed hanky to her face he apologized. "We'll be washing her down soon as we clear the pier ma'am. Smell should be sweeter then," he promised.

The pistol Corazon had bound to her leg rubbed now, for it had slipped down against her anklebone. She found herself limping as she entered her quarters. The cabin was a small cubby but very neat. He informed her of an invitation to eat with Captain Henry, as the ship had no dining room.

"One thing, Mr. Thatcher," she said, with a tone of concern. "Two rather offensive men, one a large red-haired brute, the other a mulatto, have been asking after me. I would appreciate it if you would advise the Captain that I wish my boarding to be a private matter."

Thatcher's broad face broke into a wide smile, exposing the

absence of some front teeth. "Don't y'all fret none at all, Miss O'Ryan," he beamed, "not at tall. I'll sure tell the Captain, and bust the head ah any ah the boys what shoots his yap."

Closing her door, she sat on her bunk, and pulling up her skirt, un-taped the pistol with relief. The ankle was sore and she massaged it. Pulling the curtain back from her port light, she peered out at the dock with both joy and a nervous apprehension. "At the worst," she thought, "they might learn I'm aboard and try to remove me. Well," she told herself, fingering the thirty-eight. "They can't shoot me, but I can, and surely will, shoot them."

Fortunately, the tide rose, and with lines cast off, and with no sign of William or Antonio, the *Western Sea* steamed out of Cardenas Bay. The captain, an ancient bearded man, was delightful, and she found dinner with him pleasant. Pictures of his wife and family covered the bulkheads, and he explained that his wife, Mrs. Henry, had sailed with him, storm and calm, for forty years before her passing. Having a cultured woman at his table was a sorely missed pleasure, and Miss O'Ryan was more than welcome, she was a blessing.

Weather was fair, the Gulf calm. Steaming at a steady ten knots, the *Western Sea* was laid on the wharf at Punta Rasa by the following noon. Though Corazon offered to pay the freight for her mare, Captain Henry had chuckled and called the horse baggage. Someone had saddled the gray, and the steward gave her a bagged lunch. Thatcher arranged for a pair of Ranchers to ride with her to Fort Myers, and wished her a pleasant trip.

Both of her escorts owned cattle land on the river near Belle Glade, and as they rode, they exalted the wonders of the climate, boasted their wives' cooking, and told terrible lies of their prowess as anglers. They remained with her in town while she inquired of the train schedule, and of a carriage to the Charlotte station. Afterward, she was shown to a reputable hotel boarding house, one accepting only decent women, rather than the hotel with its rowdy Yankee Sportsmen. Mrs. Bond, the proprietress, took Corazon to the town's only proper dress shop, a small but elegant place, where she purchased two traveling outfits and a bag. After dinner, she joined in with the women in a musical, playing the piano and singing.

Her freedom was intoxicating; her adventure fine, and at the end a wonderful man would make her his wife. Thoroughly satisfied with herself and her condition, Corazon slept soundly and rose early for the ride to meet her train. Mrs. Bond, for a small fee, had offered her yard boy, Orville, to drive Corazon up to the Peace River in her own carriage. They ferried across the Caloosahatchee, and with her mare tethered to the back, were on the road north by 9:00AM. The trip proved tedious but she met her train.

It was more than a full day to Charleston, and as the train rumbled north, Corazon, with time to consider, began to worry. She had Asher's letter, a letter passed to her God knows how, by a servant, Resa. He planned to return to Charleston. He'd had no choice, except to leave the island, but he would return before long. The part she loved best, she would read each day:

"My darling Cori, I worship you in every thought. I suffer each moment of cruel separation. Until we are together, I send all my deep and burning love, Asher."

"My God, how romantic," she thought, "but will he be in Charleston when I arrive?" Numerous doubts assailed her. Should she chance a telegram? Would her father have men there to meet her? Would Aunt Samantha assist her, or turn her out? Then, two different men, Yankee tourist fishermen, made rude comments to her in the dining car. That night she slept only fitfully, with her revolver under her pillow.

Stepping off the train, the cold wind cut through her summer dress like daggers, and she hurried into the station house to check the public register. She found the address of Asher's aunt, and tipped a porter to fetch a closed carriage. The Widow Byran's house appeared pleasant and comfortable. Corazon paused; for long moments, she looked out at the house. Her heart pounded with wild excitement and intense apprehension. Never had she approached an unknown residence without escort or invitation, but she had come all this way to do just that. What should she say? "Here I am with a dowry of a horse, a pistol, three dresses and some jewelry?" Finally, straightening her back, she stepped from the carriage and paid the fare.

There were four steps and a portico. She yanked the bell cord and waited, trying not to shiver. A large old man, a mulatto wearing a fine black suit, answered the door. "Miss O'Ryan to see Miss Fay Gibbes," she announced, managing to keep her voice pleasant, and her teeth from chattering.

He nodded, stepping aside, "Why, come in from de cold, missy, and sit y'all self here; it's far too cool to be dressed so light." He closed the door, saying, "I going to tell her this minute."

"Oh, my dear," she heard from down the hall, and she turned to face Asher's aunt. The old woman approached with her arms out and a winning smile.

"How could you possibly have gotten here? Oh, Corazon— may I call y'all Cori? Here now, give me a hug," the old woman said warmly.

As they embraced, the carpetbag dropped from Corazon's hand. A dull thud and a sharp report echoed through the house, splinters flew from the door, and smoke drifted up from the bag. Both women screamed and William backed against the wall.

"Oh my," Fay gasped. "What was that, child?"

237

Corazon, pale as porcelain, managed to find her voice, "I'm so sorry," she squeaked. "Please forgive me, but I'd forgotten my pistol was cocked."

"God and the devil," Fay exclaimed, laughing, "A cocked, loaded pistol. I advised that boy to find himself a wife that was his like," she said, amused. "God knows, he has, child." She took the young woman's hand and led her toward the parlor and its fireplace. "Now tell me, Cori darlin', what in God's name have y'all been up to, child?"

Chapter 26

"Willium, toss more wood in the fire," Fay said, "and do look to see if Fontaine is back with the fool horse. I want him to check the telegraph office again." Impatient, Fay's foot tapped; she was looking forward to visiting a downtown dress shop before lunch, and for a certainty, it could not be put off. Corazon had but three summer dresses to her name, two of those burned and shot full of holes. "Such a blast," she smiled again, remembering. "Why, Willium could have passed for white." She heard the thump of the kitchen door and the quick light step her ear had learned to associate with Corazon O'Ryan.

"Have y'all gotten your horse?" Fay called.

"Yes, Auntie," she answered, sweeping across the room, kneeling before the fire to warm her hands. "My poor Pepper's never known the cold. The whole night in an open stall at the receiving yard, I'm so upset with myself. I don't know how I could have forgotten her."

Fay coughed to clear her throat, "She won't be the first animal that spent the night under the sky," she said, poking a hole in the girl's guilty mood.

The girl's laugh was a pleasant thing to hear and like now, it came easily. She had a temper, no doubt, but also the intelligence to control and direct it. That was certain from what Fay had heard of the past month. She watched the girl rise, turn and sit facing her.

"*There is such a fluid quality to her,*" the old woman thought. "*Moving or at rest, she pleases the eye, and God knows she owns spirit and courage to match her looks. Her name, Corazon, 'heart' in Spanish, it suited her. It is no wonder Ash killed a man over her. No strange thing at all.*"

"Forgive me for being so foolish about the horse," Corazon said, stretching languorously. "I suppose someday I shall pamper my children as well. I look forward to it."

"Fontaine will be round with the carriage before long Cori. Would y'all like something warm before we go, child?"

"Oh yes, coffee would be splendid thank you," and as Fay reached for her bell, the girl came up out of her chair, and placed a hand on hers. "I saw Tess upstairs, Auntie. It'll take me only a moment," she promised, almost skipping toward the kitchen.

The carriage was round shortly and as they visited the shops, Fay insisted that Corazon have this and that, enjoying the same pleasure a mother might when dressing up a precious daughter. She had found a warm dress that fit perfectly, and was trying coats, when Fontaine arrived with a telegram from Asher's agent. Bound for Fernandina, his ship had departed Jacksonville only that afternoon.

At hearing it, Corazon's face lost its smile, and she cried, "Oh! I've missed him, then."

239

"Not at all, dear. Fernandina is just down the coast. It's only four hours by train."

"Will you travel with me?" she begged.

The old woman smiled in an approving manner, "I expect I'll have to. There are plenty of those around here already have bees in their bonnets over y'all. Hump! Y'all aren't to be out of my sight till the "I do's" are said, young lady."

Corazon had her fingers laced, and out of pure happiness was rising up and down on her toes. Fay thought, *"She still has some of the little girl left in her."* Touched by it, Fay hoped to God, the girl could hold on to that youthful spirit for a few good years, life being so unfair.

"When shall we leave?" she asked, her hands still clasped as if in prayer.

"First train in the morning will be soon enough. First, we're going to call on y'all Aunt Samantha this afternoon, just so everyone knows how matters lay," Fay said plainly. "And I'll say this. She'll be more than happy to hear y'all are under my roof rather that hers."

"Why, Samantha would never hesitate to have me," Corazon said defensively.

"I never said she would but she'd be in an unenviable position, child. Y'all surely see, with the way Douglas has set himself against your marrying Ash — well — you understand, this will allow her to remain neutral where her brother is concerned."

"Well, I suppose," she, conceded, having herself been troubled over the very same thing while on the train north. "I've looked forward to seeing her, and I do hope Jenny will be in," she said, brightening.

Samantha, having received Fay's message, that she hoped to call at 1:00 PM was fully prepared to receive her. Seeing Fay accompanied by her niece was an unexpected shock. Only yesterday, she had received a telegram from her brother explaining that Corazon had disappeared, and she was to be on the watch for her. By the wording, Douglas was in a fine rage.

Within moments, Corazon explained her circumstances, assuring her aunt that she had wired her father this morning. "I explained my situation," she said, "and reminded him that I had promised to leave at the first opportune moment. Contrary to his wish, and true to my word, I did leave his house and do not intend to return. I will marry Mr. Byran — blessing or not."

Though the bend and sway of the matter did not leave Samantha Ashe speechless, it did leave her a little breathless. She had the tea set aside, and served some pleasant Madeira in its place. Jenny, discovering her cousin in the house, had appeared, causing an animated conversation, during which the topic of wedding plans became central. Samantha became markedly silent. Jenny, a young woman, just turned twenty-one, and very much her own mistress, insisted on accompanying them to Fernandina. It would be both fun, and a show of support.

They babbled enthusiastically, and Fay watched Samantha fidget in near silence, worried no doubt, about family politics. Samantha, sensing a storm in the offing, was trying to decide which sails to set fly. Fay smiled smugly and thought about the courting days of her own youth, and the trials surrounding poor Christine's elopement with her brother-in-law, James Byran. The picking of sides had been wrenching for all concerned.

Well, thirty years had not changed much in the way Charlestonians thought, but thank god she was a far wiser woman now. Old enough to do socially outrageous things, and get away with them, is what Fay was. She sometimes wondered if the approval of such a stiff-necked community

241

was worth the trouble, but it was a way of life with certain advantages.

Wind out of the east, weather the next morning more temperate. On the train ride south to Fernandina, it became warmer still, and the women were carrying their coats when they walked down the platform toward waiting carriages. The driver helped them aboard and as he took the reins, Fay, for many years, a captain's wife, called out, "Harbor Master's Office."

****

Dropping his eyes from the bulletin board, Asher glanced out the window

and found himself, looking directly at Corazon. She was sitting, engaged in animated conversation with two other women in a hired buggy, while leaning left and right over her shoulder, to better see ships moored on the wharf. The driver jumped down and one of the women with him seemed to be directing him into the office. To get a better view, Corazon stood and turned around with an ease of movement that was as familiar to him as it was beautiful. Asher blinked and bolted for the door.

Corazon, looking side to side, was twisting back around to face her companions when her eyes swept past the opening door. Her face turned back to the shadow with a look of doubt, and then with the most extreme look of delight, she called his name as he came off the porch. She gathered her skirt, stepped over her companions' legs and leaped from the carriage, her toe catching on the side. Her momentum sent her flying forward, fortunately into Asher's arms. He quickly kissed her astonished face, and placed her on her feet.

"How — Cori — I mean — I am utterly at a loss." His hands were at her waist, and he pushed her out at arms' length to see more of her. "Darling, I can't believe you're here," he said very aware of her perfume and the warmth where his hands touched her waist. "After the telegram, I could only hope that you'd change your mind," he said.

"Ash, that telegram was not sent by me," she said, reminded of her father's deception, and freshly irate. "I received a similar correspondence that I'm sure you had nothing to do with. Ash darling, you have no idea. There's so much to tell."

So, intent were they on each other that Fay found it necessary to reach out, and tap him sharply with her parasol. "Asher Byran," she said sternly, "Haven't I shown y'all better manners?"

He turned quickly, "Ma'am," he said. and except for his deep tan would have reddened as he apologized, "I didn't notice, Auntie, and Miss Jenny please forgive my neglect!"

"Y'all may take us to lunch and be forgiven, Asher," the old woman dictated, feigning grumpiness. "All this way and not even a 'How-de-do,'" she grumbled.

Jenny was laughing, Corazon smiling happily, and he bowed, "Ladies, my pleasure." He lifted Corazon into the carriage and stepped up, sitting opposite her. "May I first show you the ship, ladies? Only a short way down the pier, I promise."

"We'll have a look from the carriage," Fay said. "Don't y'all fiddle with my stomach."

They came up on her bow, and Fay, seeing the name became teary-eyed. She made Asher lean forward and gave him a kiss on the cheek, then looked away. Jenny commented on how sweet it was to have named the ship after Fay. Corazon studied the tall masts, the maze of rigging, thinking it quite beautiful.

Fay, having been to Fernandina on occasion with Connor, knew of a restaurant that was to her taste and directed the driver. Though the place with its rough tile floors, and crude

243

plank tables, was not pretentious, its menu varied as widely as the patrons. Crackers and seamen were seated with merchants and gentlemen. The girls, who had looked askance at so rough a place, soon became relaxed. Asher was advised of the arrival of his horse, and the ill-tempered brute had bitten Fontaine.

As they spoke of this and that, Corazon, quietly content, sat holding his hand, and played absently with his fingers. *"I'm really here with him,"* she thought. She looked to his profile, enjoying the moment in a way she could not describe. That she must appear a lovesick fool — it mattered not in the least. The seafood was fresh, and they devoured countless oysters, washing them down with pitchers of beer, so much beer that the women became quite giddy. Asher felt it prudent to hire a buggy and see them off to the Hotel Carlisle. He promised to be along as soon as he had attended to ships business.

Walking along the waterfront, Asher approached the schooner with a glad heart and a spring in his step. The beer had very little to do with his high spirits. Adding to the already wonderful occurrences of the day, he had received a consignment, two hundred crates of machinery parts and tools for Havana. It gave the Miss Fay a full cargo.

A slender Negro, standing in the shade of a straw hat, leaned on the schooner's gangway, in conversation with bos'n Swallow. His clothes were loose sewn and patched but were neat. He turned and removed his hat as Asher drew near. A thin hawkish nose, solidly planted over wide thin lips, split the man's face. The hair on his head was going gray, but he had clear eyes and a direct, honest look.

"Cop'n Asher, sah," the man said, taking a step forward.

"Yes," Asher said, coming around to face him.

"Been told you's needing a mate fo' dis here schooner, Cop'n." He spoke with eyes level, and confidence in his voice. "Mah names Tros Banks, Cop'n, and ah'm seeking to be dat

244

mate."

"What have you served in, Mr. Banks?" Asher asked with a genuine interest. The man's level-eyed directness impressed him. It was a trait uncommon, and particularly uncommon in a black man, society being what it was.

Four big mules were moving a freight wagon alongside, and they both moved out of harm's way as Banks spoke.

"I been in de sponge boats five year, and was cop'n of turtle schooner. Was on dis here very same ship, as first mate. Dat was back when she was de *Gracia,* and sailing from Roatan. Been a wrecker for' last six year, now cop'n, but dat work, it become poor wit' de new lights long de coast, yo' see." Banks looked up at the sky and grinned, showing a gold tooth. "Can sail by recon, cop'n and I know de wind and weather. Been to all de near places you see, and ah'm knowing this here ship."

Impressed, Asher gave the man his due. He said, "I'm inclined to take you, Mr. Banks. By your eyes, you're a sober man and truth be known, you've far more experience than I. Expect, I'll be asking for that experience from time to time." He took a deep breath and warned, "I won't tolerate drunkenness among the crew when at sea, nor fighting and I'll expect you to keep your watch to their duties. Introduce yourself to the first. His name is Rolland Floyd, a New England-er if you're wondering." He extended his hand, and Banks shook it firmly, "Good to have you, Mr. Banks."

"Thank'ee, Cop'n," Banks said, with apparent joy on his face. "With your permission, ah'll be getting mah chest."

Banks left, hurrying down the dock. Asher boarded, dodging gear and stevedores. He found Rolly sitting by number-two hatch, using a clicker to tally bags coming aboard. He told him to expect Banks, and that he wanted the crates at the bottom of number three hatch.

Asher washed, shaved, put on a clean shirt, and hurried back to the hotel. The ladies had not come down to the lobby and he paced, read the paper, and agonized for an hour, before sending the bellhop to let them know he was waiting. He was pleased that his aunt and Jenny Ashe were long-time acquaintances, and that the women got on well, but he longed to spend some time alone with Corazon. Five week of suffering uncertainty, while being unable to speak to her had near driven him wild. Now, with endless things to say, he found himself in the same building, and she was probably taking a nap.

A lizard darted along the windowsill and froze, transfixed, then with a lightning lunge took a fly. Asher watched two small boys running a barrel hoop along the boardwalk; the grocer waved them away from his fruit with a broom. Men hitched a draft horse to an automobile that had stalled across from the hotel; and the barber seemed to be closing for the day. He glanced at the wall clock, again at the stairway, and there she was, beginning to descend below the dome. He walked over, offering his arm when he'd rather have embraced her. There was an atrium between the lobby and the dining area and a porch swing, in which they sat.

"I'd be pleased to kiss you," he said, softly holding her hand. They sat a little apart and facing, their legs touched as the swing was propelled.

"I'd love nothing better," but with a look of concern, confided, "not in public though."

"I would have been to see you in Cuba next week," he said, his eyes following the movement of the material around her legs as she pushed the swing outward. "I was ready to go to you, to speak to your father. I was determined."

"You would have been driven off," she said knowingly. "I badly misjudged my father, and failed to understand his motives. Can you imagine, me being locked up for two weeks like a miserable child," she said, looking away. "It was humiliating to be watched," she said, her temper showing. "I know everyone was set to watch me, to keep me in as if I were a prize mare, awaiting the proper sire to be bred. If I had not stood for myself, it would have been no time before the house filled with suitors. I would have had more obnoxious men to deal with than good Queen Penelope," she said in a huff.

With the back of his hand, Asher reached and caressed her cheek, causing her to look at him, and he whispered, "Cori, I was hardly about to wander for ten years, as did Ulysses."

"You'd have found the gates guarded against you, Ash. Moreover, slaughtering all those men, as Ulysses did, and in my mother's dining room, no, in our enlightened society it would not have passed as acceptable," she said with a smile. She wanted no bravado from him in these circumstances.

Suspecting a double meaning in her comment, he said, "I did as you asked with Natan. I apologized; I allowed him have his weapon back when —"

"Hush — shush — no need," she said softly, bringing a hand to his lips. "My cousin — the war made him bitter, hateful; death was in him, with him; he sought it. If not you, another, and Hermon," she smiled wickedly, "I believe he's grown sick of soup."

"Soup?" he said, with a quizzical expression.

"Oh!" She gasped. "How could you know? His jaw was broken. Until the spring perhaps, soup and pap, only what he can suck between his teeth," she explained.

He put a hand over hers. "You mean," he said impishly, "I'm not likely to be invited to dinner."

"Oh, Father's not nearly as angry with you as he is with me. Actually, he admires you, but you're poor, and without the proper Cuban connections. As he put it," Her voice deepened to parrot her father's, "He is of no use to me." Her look became serious then. "It's me, he was furious with," she confessed, stiffening unconsciously, as fury rose in her again. "Why, he accused me of not acting above reproach, my God! I should have been more like my sister. My wretched sister, who is ever so proper — she, is in fact docility itself. The last time she opened her mouth to me, I snatched her bald," Corazon hissed, her eyes snapping.

Amused by her temper, he chuckled at her, and half-serious, said, "Well darling that cuts the wedding list down. Perhaps we should walk up the street and find a preacher right now."

A wide smile broke out on Corazon's face, and she looked off to the side as color filled her cheeks. She whispered, "Asher, you're wicked." Trying not to show the idea tempted her, she said, "Your aunt would have a fit, and I'd not get to parade you in front of my friends. And I do so want a priest, and a party and gifts," she said. "It's a memory a woman always clings to, Ash."

"Well, you'll have it," he promised. "It's going to be Saturday before my cargo's aboard. If we take the train back tomorrow, we can have the first banns read on Sunday. We'll marry when I return from this voyage," he said, suddenly aware that he had no home to take a wife. None other than the termite-eaten ruin he had inherited in Fort Myers. He would need to make arrangements; perhaps he could rent a townhouse.

"Ash," she said, leaning toward him so that her forehead touched his shoulder. "I was the guest of a fine old gentleman for dinner, a Captain Henry." Corazon leaned back a little, tilting her face up to him. "His wife sailed with him for forty years; he told me she was with him calm and storm. Might I sail with you?" she said her eyes wide. "I'll be ever so obedient. I'll be no trouble at all," she promised.

248

"Of course," he said, "but it can be very uncomfortable, and you'd have no friends," though even as he spoke, he was selfishly thinking that nothing could be more perfect.

"Cori! Ash," Jenny called from the edge of the lobby, "we couldn't imagine where you'd gotten to. It's growing dark already, and Fay is inquiring as to dinner," she said, walking their way.

"They have an excellent dining room here," Asher said pointing across the atrium, "and over there a hall, and aren't those musicians?" he asked with a teasing tone.

Corazon sprang from the swing, and by the hand, pulled him after her, giggling, "Come along sir." Gaily leading him toward the door, she tossed her head round to Jenny. "You may dance with him once or twice," she laughed, "but only because I'm so very fond of you."

The return to Charleston was without incident. And after arrival, he retrieved from his aunt's vault a box containing family records and his mother's jewelry. He removed a pendant composed of an emerald set amidst blue sapphires, and visited a reputable Broad Street jeweler. He gave them the pendant, with instructions for a ring set. Later, he made a visit to the church. On the following morning, in a state of contentment, he caught the train south to Fernandina and his ship.

Chapter 27

Veering rapidly, the winds of the frontal system, came clear around to the northwest during the night, and increased to near gale force. As the wind had shifted fair, *Miss Fay Gibbes* had lost no time. Being under the lee of the Keys in a northwest gale was no bad thing in itself. However, as day follows dawn, a northwest gale veers northeast in the Florida Straits, and the straits curve to the north. That was hard truth, for a strong north wind in opposition to the four-knots of Gulf-stream current create great, steep, tumbling seas. A northerly gale in the straits meant a dangerously unpleasant time for any ship caught there. Asher had a cargo of coffee beans for Charleston, a cargo that required no great hurry, but on his own account, he had purchased bananas and pineapples on speculation. Of course, any delay would spoil them. Reaching across a thirty-five-knot breeze, with four knots of current fair astern, the schooner flew. With the fair current, she is plotting fifteen knots over the bottom, and put Fowey Rocks astern by dawn. The last of the fore-topsail was taken in at dawn, as well as the number one and two jibs.

The topsail-schooner Miss Fay Gibbs

So hard did it blow that night that sand was carried a mile to sea, coating the schooner as she rode on double anchors. The wind moaned, tearing at anything not secured, but close in, to lee of the island, the sea had only a frothy chop. Trapped by the weather, Asher worried, and paced anxiously. It was cold, forty degrees and that was good for the fruit. He had only six days to reach the port of Charleston though and to be late was a far more serious matter than losing the fruit. Today was Saturday, February 29, the date originally set for his wedding, but it was a date that had been moved a week to March 6.

The women had chosen the first date arbitrarily, and it had suited him fine. He had made a jest though, that he would have to remember his anniversary only every fourth year. Horrified, the women had altered everything, even to the reprinting of invitations, and in the process, given Asher the opportunity to complete another voyage.

The *Miss Fay Gibbes* had made a rapid first voyage, returning with a cargo of coffee for Jacksonville, and had run back down to Matanzas with cases of bolts, railroad spikes and bagged oats for the Army. They were delays in getting rid of the army cargo, and although the bagged coffee was loaded quickly, time was becoming short. *"If the weather doesn't turn, I'll arrive late at my own wedding with a load of rotten fruit,"* he thought. He turned to see MacArt, and the carpenter, coming up through the companion hatch from the captain's cabin. The smell of varnish rose with them.

"It's about done as its gonna get Captain" the carpenter announced. He pinched his nose with a hanky and snorted. "That's six coats ah varnish on it. Dry up in a day or two."

"That's fine; you did a fine job on those cabinets, too, first class accommodations, a liner couldn't compare."

"Thank'ee, Captain," the old man said, "thank'ee kindly. It's a mite chill with this wind blowing up. Recon I find a warm place in the cook house."

"Go on now," he said, and then looking aloft he touched MacArt's shoulder as he passed; "Gib, get on up on the main cross trees, and throw some more lashings on that topsail before the wind has her loose. She's starting to bag out already."

He watched the youth for a moment as he climbed, red hair blown to lee of his head. Satisfied with the task, he ducked into the chart house to get some sleep. He turned down the lantern in the dim light and he kicked off his boots. He lay back on the settee, pulling a heavy blanket up to his chin. He was near to sleep when the door opened and Banks stepped in.

"Port anchor, she is dragging ah lil', Cop'n. Set up again now," the mate reported. "Got Goose to watching it."

"Good ground here," Asher said tiredly.

"Very good. Foul to de east dere. Lot a coral, old wrecks, some even say there's an old Spanish wreck. Gold ship, dey says."

"Gold," Asher said, waking up considerably.

"Dat's de tale. Say, there's gold been found, 'long de shore after hurricanes. Dey churns up de bottom you see."

"Anyone look?" Asher asked, propping himself on one elbow.

"Hah, ha, ha, no," Tros Banks laughed. "All mons seek treasure, Cop'n, but treasure, she don't give she self-up. I am from Long Island. You know, down dere at Clarence Town. To de south of dere, in de Ragged islands, is Water Cay. It well known dat a treasure galleon, she strike dat reef. Three hundred-year dey be knowing it, but no mon ain't never got but a coin here in dere. Dey saying she have twenty ton a silver and half dat in gold." He chuckled again. "I was seeking dat treasure for whole month one year. De sea, she don't give

253

it to me, Cop'n. Just tease me, wit' a lil' coin here and dere."

"Hum." Asher lay back and sighed. "*Gold*," he thought. "Man could do a lot with ten tons of gold." He heard the door click as Banks went out, the muffled sound of the winds, whine in the shrouds, the slapping of lines on wood. Lulled, he slept.

Sunday dawn found the wind moderated and around east nor'-east at twenty-five. All hands turned to the capstan to heave out the anchors, and under plain sail, single reefed, the big schooner rounded West End. Close hauled. *Miss Fay Gibbes* charged boldly from behind the big island.

Puffs of spray, rising at the starboard bow, swept the galley house and wet the deck forward. A heavy swell began to lift her bodily as she passed Indian Rock, and the seas began to wash across her waist, as she cleared Little Bahamas Bank. By dusk the wind was steady, south of east, the seas light and aft the beam. At twilight Monday morning, an altitude of the North Star had them north of thirty-two. A sun line provided a running fix at eight o'clock, and showed them to be only sixty miles south of Moris Island light.

As they came in sight of land that evening, the wind went south and to airs. Cold and damp, a fog came in the night. Shortened up off Charleston bar, the big schooner rolled slowly making only steerage-way. The bell and foghorn sounded in turn; others answered out of the mist. He woke near dawn to a building vibration. He sat up abruptly when he heard the mate howl, "Port cha helm," and then, "all hands." The ship's bell began ringing violently as he leaped up, reaching for the door. The ship staggered. There was a crash and the splintering of wood forward, and as he thrust himself through the door, he looked toward the bow to see a great wall of steel rushing past, lit by a hundred port lights.

"Son of a bitch," he cursed as the stern of the liner passed.

High on her counter, he read *City of Bristol*. He hurried

toward the bow, where the crew was pouring on deck. The bowsprit was gone, as was the figurehead. In fact, everything back to the stem post was sheared off. The wreckage trailed aft along the starboard bow, bound by the fore and bob stays. The foremast was under a tearing strain with its forward support gone and the wreckage dragging it aft.

"Swallow," Asher, yelled. "Clear those jib halyards and winch them down to the cat heads. Quick, before we lose the topmast."

Banks had arrived. Shoeless and without a coat, he hung over the starboard side seeing what he could.

"Can you strap the wreckage to the shrouds, and hoist the sprite enough to clear the rigging away?" Asher asked hurriedly.

"Can do it quick 'nuff." He glanced aloft; "Best get dat canvas in for you's come 'round."

"Soon as the bos'n juries me a forestay," Asher said, and hurried aft. "God damn liners, full ahead in fog," he mumbled under his breath. "Rolly, how long can we run downwind like this?"

"Twenty minutes most, Captain, we'll be about a mile north of that last position on the chart."

He ducked into the chart house, glanced at his position, and stepping back out yelled, "Get forward and furl that topsail. Soon as it's in, let go the port anchor, one shot."

He had the helmsman steer a little more east to ease the motion, and stood nervously listening to the racket and shouting forward, as his crew struggled to lessen strain on the foremast. He could picture the liner snapping past in his mind's eye, and thought, *"Ten foot further along, and it would have taken the stem off, would have sunk us for sure, a close thing."*

They lowered the topsail yard down to the cap, its sail

gathered into the bunt-lines. Asher ordered the helm a-lee. With no pressure forward, the *Miss Fay* spun up into the wind and coasted. He heard the anchor go and saw sparks fly from the wildcat. The bos'n and a couple of the men dropped the foresail, then the main. Tackle squealed forward and the thump of the bowsprit against the hull ceased as it lifted against the bow. Adrenaline began to drain from his system and he, realizing his stocking feet were cold, went to the chart house in search of his shoes. He slipped them on and taking a pen, wrote in the log.

"0550 March 2nd, 1899, Position six miles east of Moris Island light, hove to. The SS City of Bristol, steaming at an observed speed of twelve knots, struck our port bow, carrying away the bowsprit and figurehead. Crew members were observed looking down on us as she passed. The SS City of Bristol did not stop. This ship made no attempt to hail or assist. Miss Fay anchored at 0600. Crew making emergency repairs. Captain Asher Byran."

He opened the lamp and blew out the flame. It was becoming light and they'd soon have her sufficiently jury-rigged to reach the harbor. He would hire a tug off Ft. Sumter and tow alongside. The harbormaster and his underwriter: he must contact both, and the steamer, of course, would pay. Eventually, the steamer would pay, but in the meantime, he would pay. *"Close,"* he thought, *"very close."*

Chapter 28

Ugly as a heron with a broke beak, the schooner lay on a wharf off Concord Street. The brokers with their fruit wagons had come and gone, and the coffee was passing into rail cars. Corazon sat watching as Asher climbed about the bow with a surveyor and a second man from the harbor master's office. She twirled her parasol and found another position to sit in. Both the horse and driver were asleep, as was Mary Brewton, and her foot began to tap. She fidgeted despite her best efforts to remain placid.

She had dressed hurriedly and rushed down to this harbor. She had arrived at this smelly dock, expecting to be swept-up, attended to and taken to lunch. He had pecked her on the cheek, pleaded for a few minutes to settle the business of his cargo, and to a problem concerning his being bumped by another ship. Well, that had been three hours past. That dam'd ship! She wished it would sink right where it was. She'd not seen him in over two weeks, during which he'd spent every day with the ship, and he should, she thought, have the common courtesy to pay her at least some attention. Her eyes teared.

"Stop this immediately," she whispered to herself. "I refuse to be childish," she mumbled, and looked up onto the bow again. He was shaking hands. "Finally," but she would wait until he was actually walking across the cobblestones before she nudged Mary.

Plainly uncomfortable, Asher stepped up to the carriage and said, "I'm truly sorry for keeping you but it couldn't be helped. Regulations require, I report a casualty immediately on arrival and the damage is severe. You'll forgive me," he said hopefully.

"I suppose," Corazon began, "if —

"You take us someplace pleasant," Mary interjected, fighting a yawn.

"One day Ash, you will be waiting for me," Corazon said

tersely, "and when you become impatient, you'll be reminded of this. At the very least, you could have at least invited us aboard for refreshments."

"I realize I was thoughtless," he confessed. "I'll improve, you have my word," he promised, and reaching up he nudged the driver. "Balores, on Water Street," he told the man. What he was thinking at that instant was that the last thing he wanted was for her to see the cabin he built for her. It was to be a surprise.

The late lunch improved Corazon's mood entirely. Afterward, they strolled down Church Street and through the oaks and palmettos of the Battery. As they talked, they watched the Cooper and Ashley Rivers converge, and sea birds dive in the swirling eddies. The air became cool and a mist began to rise from the water, obscuring ships in the harbor and chilling the women. At the edge of the park, Asher hired a carriage he found waiting on the end of Murry Street. He helped the women in, and gave the driver his Aunt's address. Their lunch had been so late that the sun was not far from setting. Soon streetlights would be lit.

Fay was obviously upset when no one wished dinner. She grumbled graciously and had it set aside, offering everyone wine in the sitting room. Sharing wine, they sat by the fireplace and filled each other in on the last weeks. Asher described his voyage, leaving out the more sordid episodes, while the women happily described the planned details of the wedding. Later Corazon played a duet with Fay on the piano, and Asher attempted the violin. He had not picked it up in over three years, and the women applauded when the E string broke.

At eight, Fontaine hitched a horse to the buggy and drove Mary home. Shortly after, Fay excused herself and retired to her room. The young couple sat on the sofa looking at the fire. She kicked off her shoes, and tucking both feet under her, she snuggled under Asher's arm with a small sound of contentment.

"Have you thought where you'd take me on our wedding trip?"

"Yes."

"Where?"

"I thought you'd like to be surprised."

"Yes," she said confounded, "But —"

"You do like surprises?" he interrupted with mock concern.

"Of course, Ash. It's just I have no idea of what clothes I should pack."

"But, darling," he said mirthfully, "why? Why would that be of any importance?"

What he said made no sense at all, and she said nothing. Then, catching a hint of his meaning, she sat bolt upright. "Asher Byran, what a shocking thing to say."

"What do you mean?" he said, feigning innocence.

"Well—you know," she said confused, suddenly doubting her assumption.

He reached over, running the tips of his fingers through her hair and said, "I had another surprise, but if you rather talk about clothes —"

"You purposely frustrate me," she said becoming brisk, "and I shan't be baited."

"Patience, then," he whispered softly. "Close your eyes."

She closed her eyes, her face composed and holding the slightest smile. He lifted her left hand; she unconsciously pushed her tongue against her teeth, holding her breath. The ring slid on her finger.

"There Cori, your surprise," he said, raising her hand to his lips.

A single emerald sat within a cluster of diamond sapphires, and she gasped as she saw them on her hand, whispering, "Asher, it's so very beautiful." She leaned into his arms, and listening to the slow steady beat of his heart, said, "I love you so," and rubbing her cheek against his shoulder, she watched as the gems glistened in the firelight.

Separated as they had been the night of their engagement, and either chaperoned or in public since, there had been no moment alone to repeat their one passionate kiss. As she looked up, he gently kissed her, his hand moving up behind her neck. Their lips parted, his forceful, her's supplicant, in a first hesitant response to the sensation of his tongue. It touched her lips and was gone. He nuzzled her cheek and kissed her ear, kissed below it, and the hollow of her throat. Without thought, her knees came up and she curled against him, and again he kissed her mouth, only more deeply. Her breath became ragged; his hand stroked her back and then her thigh, and she became conscious he was caressing, touching bare skin, the back of her thigh. She merely clung to him, swamped by sensations she never knew existed. She became aware of the clatter of pans in the kitchen and panicked.

"Oh, stop, my God," she gasped ashamed by the low nature of her reactions, and at suddenly remembering, they were neither alone nor behind closed doors. She had never imagined, how easily she might be swept by carnal impulses, and hoped he did not comprehend, she owned such base impulses. She blushed and he pulled her against him, kissing her deeply, while his hand slowly ran back down the length of her leg, returning to the outside of the cloth, and pressed the small of her back. As the kiss ended, he shifted, holding her back from him.

"I should go," he said laughing softly, for he knew what precisely he'd been doing.

Corazon trembled slightly, and words, not seeming to serve her at this moment, she nodded her agreement. He stood and easily pulled her up on her bare feet.

"Will you see me to the door?"

"Of course," she whispered and wondered, *"Why am I whispering?"* She saw herself in the mirror next to him and thought, *"I look so small next to him,"* and, *"God, my hair, how did it get in such a tangle?"*

At the door she asked, "When will I see you, tomorrow?"

"You won't see me tomorrow, darling. I have endless labors to perform before Saturday. I'm sure you'd rather have me to yourself after that," he said in a tone that embarrassed her. "Besides, I'm under strict orders. I've explicit instructions to remain unseen until we meet at the altar."

"Who?"

"Who else?" He grinned, pointing a finger upstairs. "And she's right; I'm much too lusty to be proper company before Saturday, but after that—" He snatched her bodily from her feet, lifting her over his head quickly, then lowered her slowly, kissing her as her face came level. When her feet touched the floor, their lips had parted. "It won't matter," he continued, his breath against her ear.

Tingling was what her skin was doing, and she knew this could not continue. *"This was why chaperones were truly necessary for some girls,"* she thought, sensing the weakness of her own will, and felt appalled that she was of that sort of girl.

"I love you. I will miss you terribly," she added, looking at her feet, for her face had colored.

He opened the door. The cool air washed over her and she stepped back.

"I love you, too, Cori and particularly the part about missing me terribly," he said playfully. "Saturday," he promised with a soft smile and closed the door.

She heard his feet on the steps, and parted the curtains, watching his back as he walked down the street. Her cheek pressed to cold glass, she watched him to the corner. Returning to the parlor, she pulled the screen across the front of the fireplace and turned down the gas light. Retiring, she found that her room was cold. Pulling her dress off, she slipped into her nightgown and jumped into bed, hurrying to get the covers over her head. She began to warm and poked her nose out. If anything, Corazon loved a cool day, but hated being cold. She imagined cuddling warmly on cold nights. The physical sensation that had raced about her body came to mind, and she wondered how she could possibly sleep with that going on, how anyone could sleep. Perhaps that is why so many couples had separate rooms. Perhaps Mr. Kellogg was correct.

Corazon rolled on her back, eyes on the dim ceiling. She knew nothing, she realized, beyond the most basic bits of information about men. Although a great deal was alluded to, much of it seemed contradictory, and no one ever told her anything concrete. As a young girl, the nuns had impressed on her mind that though her soul belonged to God, her body belonged to a husband. The duty of a wife, sworn before all, in holy vows of marriage, was to submit to a husband, suffering the distress of carnal lust in order that she might experience the joys of motherhood.

Corazon recalled, hearing for the first time what the act of submission entailed, when at the age of ten, an older cousin explained the process to her and her sister. Living on a plantation, she had witnessed the breeding process consummated by various species of animal. Somehow, she had failed to understand that the same act would apply to people, would in fact apply to her. Horse breeding had been going on at the time, and poor Esmeralda had actually burst into tears that evening.

Nothing useful could be extracted from her mother on the subject. She informed her daughter's that a refined woman must refrain from the discussion of such unpleasant duties, must hold the assurance that though unpleasant for women, the demands of a husband were not unbearable. Society accepted that men reveled in the act even though women found it distasteful. Through social observation, she'd been given the impression that though men might have dutiful intercourse with their wives to ensure their progeny, they often visited other women to have their fun. Some wives thought this to be an act of consideration on the part of a husband. Others swore that men simply preferred whores.

This had never made sense to Corazon. Why would a mistress, or to be frank a whore, be able to provide a man with more pleasure than the woman he loved? The question, previously academic, now began to worry her. Was it because some women experienced unnatural sensations and actually enjoyed the act that they were drawn to whoring? Was this why they could better satisfy a man, or was it that they had acquired certain learned talents? What if she fell short of Asher's expectations? The very possibility of him with another woman in his arms — it was enough to bring tears to her eyes. The prospect that he might come to believe her a wanton shamed her, but she must risk it. If it were through some lack, some fault of her own that he fell prey to a whore she would be devastated.

There were books, books that proper women did not read. She'd seen Robert with French novels that were reputed to be scandalous in their content and description. She wished that her French was good, but it was not and that was that. If these mysteries could be known, she had an open mind, and a firm desire to learn of them, but from whom? The answer suddenly occurred to her. So simple, it was ridiculous that the solution had not occurred to her immediately. As a married woman, she would have more freedom in some respects, and with a little discretion, could certainly use that freedom to educate herself. First, she must seek a book, something French but in translation. There was always a portion of a bookstore reserved for men, and if she called at a quiet time? If that did not suffice, she would continue directly to the source. If men went to the trouble of seeking indecent pleasures, pleasures for which they were willing to pay certain women, she would certainly be wise to apprise herself of the exact nature of what they were purchasing. Discretion would be of the highest importance. It was a very incautious step — still — if a woman was curious about those mysterious talents, which drew men to courtesans, who better than a courtesan could answer her questions.

Corazon wriggled around in bed, finding a comfortable spot, and sighed sleepily, satisfied with herself for having thought this out.

Chapter 28

Some wedding guests walked; others had left buggies hitched at the edge of the park; most arrived in carriages. Asher saw none of it from the dressing room adjacent to the altar. His head ached after the drinking bout that his classmates had put him through at the "Horse a Hound." His roommate from school, Frank Waring, sat face in hands at a desk nearby. Noticeably unwell, Frank was to stand as best man and Asher fervently hoped Frank would be able to stand.

Corazon's Uncle Brant had left them only moments before, to take his place on the bride's side of the aisle. From there, he would be called on to give her away. The front pews reserved for family, were glaringly empty, with only Samantha's family and Fedrico. The only guest to come up from Cuba was Fedrico Vega. Asher spotted him sitting at the end of the second pew, looking alone.

Among the Wallaces, there was a fair turnout, even though his grandfather Ian was absent. Quite a number of his old school chums were in attendance, and he counted five of the ship's crew at the rear of the church.

When the organ music changed, Waring sat up, "Is it time?" he asked miserably.

"You've got the rings, Frank?" Asher asked a bit too loud.

Waring held up his left pinkie, showing the rings. "Calm down."

The priest came in, trailed by two chubby-face altar boys. He smiled pleasantly, and said, "No second thoughts, Captain Byran?"

"None Father."

"Well, then," the priest said, and walked toward the altar.

As the ceremony began, Asher observed in a state of weightlessness. The priest eventually turned from the altar to face the guests and motioned for the groom and the maids of honor to take their places. As the march began, Asher saw none of the hundreds of faces, only that of Corazon O'Ryan, floating toward him on a cloud of lace. They knelt before the alter sharing the wedding mass. He noticed the fine hairs above her gloved hand, the freshness of herbs washed into her hair, even heard the softness of her breathing beside him as the ritual wove them. Bells jarred! They stood. He was aware of the priest's voice.

"Who will give this woman?"

Her Uncle, answering, "I do, Father."

He was aware of the placing of Corazon's hand on his own. All but her veiled eyes became a blur until he heard, "Corazon Catherine O'Ryan, do you —" and the priest's words flowed, stating the ancient contract, and her voice in its pure clarity answered.

"Yes! With this ring I do thee wed."

A few more words, Asher's, own glad vows, and he was lifting her veil, a kiss, and a hand in his for the rush past rice-tossing, well-wishers to their carriage.

The reception was as most, a swirl of dances and toasts, until at the first opportunity, the couple vanished. It was a disappearance expected and hardly noticed midst the revelry. Their suite was on the top floor of the Victoria, only six floors above the music and noise of the reception hall, but for them it could have been beyond the mountains of the moon.

The bridesmaids had hurried the bride away early to be bathed and changed. When Asher arrived a short time later, he found her waiting by the fireplace in a flowing gossamer robe. It covered her, neck to toes, but concealed little. Asher said nothing but stood gazing at her for a long moment, mesmerized. Even in the dim light, he noticed she was blushing, and as he approached her, she trembled. He swept her up into his arms, turned to a large padded chair, and sat holding her in his lap. She snuggled against him, her face pressed against his chest.

He slipped his hand from beneath her knees, and caressed her cheek saying, "Mrs. Byran, I find you lovely beyond words, and I find you're welcome to be far warmer than any husband deserves."

"I wished to please you," she told him, "but when you came in I — I felt so brazen—Oh, you don't think me immodest?"

"No! No more than you would think it of me. You're an

unusually beautiful woman, Cori, and I shall cherish every moment that I gaze on you. M mm," he muttered, "and you've certainly given me more to gaze upon. Why, you might even find you enjoy looking at me. I find your robe particularly attractive," he said, and ran a finger along the fabric and of course her thigh as he did it. "In the Bible, you'll remember, it mentions women dancing before their husbands in thinnest veils. Seemed like proper attire to me."

She tilted her head, and they gazed at each other, a smile coming to both their faces.

"I love you Asher, I love you beyond all reason and if you wish — wish me to dance."

He placed a finger on her lips. "Will you toast our marriage with me?" he asked. "I've champagne."

"Oh, yes!"

"Let me up, then," he said, slipping out from under her, leaving her in the chair. "I'll be back in a moment."

There were several bottles of wine and a couple of champagne, one on ice, in the bedroom. He pulled the cork and found two glasses. His robe hung by the door. Seeing it, he took a moment to slip out of his suit, and put it on before returning to the parlor room.

He pushed a hassock close to Corazon's chair and sat, handing her the empty glasses. He poured and placed the bottle on the lamp table. She held her glass in two hands before her face. The blue and green of her eyes gleamed, reflected in the wine, as their eyes met and held.

"Long life and many children," he said.

"Long life and many children," she repeated.

They drank together, throwing the glasses into the fire, and leaned together, kissing almost chastely, Corazon kneeling in the chair, her fingers touching his cheeks. His hands went to her waist, and as the kiss lingered and broke, he drew her toward him. His lips pressed her throat, and as the material slipped to one side, kissed the hollow of her shoulder, moving to her breast, encircling the nipple. His arms slipped around her lithe body and he rose with her. Corazon was dizzy, overcome by a giddy weakness, and as she was carried across the room, she giggled, thinking that she could not have walked anyway.

Asher placed her on her feet by the bed, and kissed her again as she felt the ties of her robe loosen. He brushed it aside and it fell open from her shoulders, hanging from her arms at the elbows. An otherness took her for a moment, as she stood eyes closed, stood as if she were dreaming this moment.

"Darling, my robe," he whispered softly.

Corazon's eyes opened, Asher held her gaze. Her hands pulled at the sash. It loosened and she was drawn to him. The warmth of his flesh, the texture of the hair on his body, the sweet salty scent of him, the bulge of his genitals light against her thigh, each sensation separate yet part of the whole registered in her mind.

The robe slipped away, as he moved her against the bed and laid her back. Her eyes followed the contours of his body, as he stood above her, shrugging the robe from his shoulders. His muscles were lean and hard, and scars puckered the flesh, where lead and steel had struck him. The hair of his chest was tawny and tawny below his waist where his partially engorged penis protruded from a wreath of curls.

A strange calm had settled on her, and the sight of his naked body affected her with a pleasing curiosity, though the size of the genitals surprised her. Corazon had diapered babies. She had come upon her brother and cousins, when they were young boys, swimming naked. Her memories, her expectations, were of the small stubby member of a prepubescent boy. As he lay down beside her, she felt its heat against her leg and a drawing within her body. With both longing and apprehension, she found herself trembling.

"You're frightened," Asher whispered.

He pulled her closer so she reclined partially on top of him. Her head rested on his shoulder and her arm across his chest. The feel of his curly body hair against her smooth skin seemed strange, the hands moving over her, possessive. He stroked her back and held her hand to his mouth, kissing her fingers. He softly told her there was nothing to fear, and she felt herself relax again. He smiled when he felt her nuzzle his chest, her lips making small kisses. Her fingers explored his side, touching his scars, skimming over the ripples of his stomach, lightly circling the hard knot where a bullet had left his body.

"Did you suffer a great deal?" she asked softly.

"No," he said bringing his hand to her face, pushing her hair back. "At first nothing; later it burned and ached. Not too bad, I suppose."

"I've never been hurt badly," she said, "Though I have fallen from a horse. Ordinarily one doesn't think of being hurt until it happens, and then there's nothing to be done." She said this, fearing at that moment another hurt, one that she had been warned of long ago.

"I expect that's true," Asher said, and shifted on his side to face her.

He filled the silence by kissing her lightly, then when she responded, more strongly. His hand cupped her breast, the thumb caressing the nipple until it hardened under his touch. His lips moved to her neck and her ear, and he felt a silky smoothness as instinctively her leg slid up and over his own, her knee near his groin. She sought his mouth again, and felt his hand move downward past her stomach, gasped as fingertips began caressing, probing the delicate folds with a feathery light touch. As she was kissed, she moaned, and spread her knees slightly. She arched her back, and stretched at the same time. All thoughts of propriety, of modesty were forgotten as a burning heat filled her. She found herself on her back, his mouth on her breasts, his fingers parting her, dancing with a maddening frequency.

"Oh! Please," she gasped. "Ash, please," she cried, not really thinking of please what.

When he moved over her, parting her legs with his knees, she knew what he would do. He knelt before her lifting her knees, spreading her thighs wide as he moved between them, and she saw he'd become larger, straight and rigid. A helpless weakness swept her, and as his weight bore her down, there was no strength in her. She felt his fingers find her, hold her apart, open, and the soft pressure that grew as his hand came away. Her heart pounded, as her bent knees were forced up and further apart. She gasped when he began to push into her, to pull back, thrust painfully and thrust again. She felt a dragging friction, a sense of being stretched, torn, a sharp burning, an awareness of being filled by both scalding hurt, and an odd, aching pleasure.

She realized her arms were pinned, and as he released them, she clung to him. He remained, hesitating still, looking down into her eyes. He kissed her softly, her neck and then her mouth again, and in time began to move within her, hurting her at first, but not stopping, and slowly her discomfort eased and the pace quickened. She found her body relaxing. Her body grew pliant, moving with him, responding, as a wave of pleasure built inside. She was awed by the power of it as her whole body absorbed the jolting impacts. Consumed by a passion, she heard herself crying out. For long minutes, internal spasms caused her hips to move of their own accord. They moved in ways she had not imagined, as they attempted to match the rhythm of the body joined to hers. When the pace began to slow, her husband's thrusts seemed to come with all his strength, hard, slow, until suddenly he stopped, becoming rigid over her. As he relaxed, he kissed her, quick light kisses; he brushed the hair from her face.

"I love you, Mrs. Byran," he murmured softly against her ear.

Corazon said nothing; overcome with languid warmth, she felt as if she were melting into the bed. Her husband's arm dug under her, and he rolled, leaving her reclined atop him, still joined.

"Ash," she breathed softly, enjoying what he was doing, for his hands were on her bottom, slowly kneading her flesh.

"U mm, sweetheart," he mumbled contentedly.

"Is it really true that a woman is more — I mean, do some women find this more pleasant after the first time, I mean, do they begin to enjoy it more as time goes on?"

"From what I'm told, it's often the case," Asher said running a finger slowly up her spine. "Why?"

"If it's true," she murmured dreamily, "I shan't mind doing this at all."

Chapter 30

Palm fronds swayed in the warm breeze, sweeping sun bright coral sand, with purple-blue shadow. On the eastern border of Biscayne Bay lay Soldier Cay, a low coral Island, tiny with its hundred-yard ring of beach and deep coral ponds.

Abandoned by the tide, a small centerboard sloop lay on its side; twenty feet beyond, stood a pavilion, it's red-and-white strips, partially shaded by a palm.

For a woman, Corazon could run extremely well. She had begun giggling though, which made running more difficult. She squealed when Asher leaped over the log, and dodged to the left. He missed her and tripped, but his hand closed on the fabric of her dress, and as the buttons popped, she ran right out of it. Never having run naked before and in fact never having run without the support of a corset, the sensation of bouncing breasts was disconcerting. She glanced back and he was up and gaining on her again. She ran around the boat, eluding him by dodging from end to end, until he scrambled over the top, and caught her by the ankle as she fled past the tent. He yelled, and they rolled naked in the sand as he struggled to control her kicking and squirming.

"Ash, stop it, Ash," she squealed, for he was sitting on her back, tickling her foot.

She let out a long shriek and managed to heave him off, but he stood still maintaining his hold on her foot. Laughing, he hauled her into the water by it.

"Never tease a man you can't outrun," he advised, and began rinsing sand from her.

The washing soon turned salacious, and the couple tumbled into the tent,

ardently consummating their desire on a large down quilt. In fact, they had celebrated their marriage quite often since their arrival on the shores of Biscayne Bay.

Monday morning, they had left their train at the village of Miami, taking a buggy to Coconut Grove. They had spent three days at the Peacock Inn, renting a beach cabin and a sailboat. The atmosphere was open and unconventional, the community a mix: socialites, artists, characters, and dreamers.

The honeymooners had risen early, sailed, explored, joined in the lively dinnertime discussions, and embarrassed anyone who passed within hearing of their cabin in the night.

It had been her idea to camp on the Cay. Swimming and cavorting, nude as a water nymph, she had lost every trace of bashfulness where her husband was concerned. Corazon had come to a personal opinion that the Victorian view of a woman's relations with her husband was insane. Similar views, on a variety of social morals, seemed taken for granted by the Grove's residents. When people spoke, they apparently said what they wished, even if what they said was outrageous. The women she had met held themselves to have opinions equal with their husbands, and exercised their equality as a matter of course. She loved the freedom of the place. It seemed to her an idyllic tropic frontier, with its scattered homes, rail-head and pristine bay. By the time they caught the train north on Saturday morning, they had agreed to purchase a one-acre lot that lay atop the Coral Ridge near the tiny yacht club. Not only was it a lovely place, but there was an enormous amount of capital invested in the development of Miami. Flagler's railroad, the Royal Palm Hotel, and the dredging of the ship channel were only a beginning.

During Asher's absence, the mate had seen to business and repairs to the ship. The schooner had been repaired a week before, and modified to carry a yawl boat on great davits astern. Mr. Floyd had gotten the cargo in her early, and she had lain on the transit wharf two days, awaiting her absent Captain. Asher, with his wife in tow, arrived directly from the station before seven and boarded. He spoke to Tros Banks for a moment concerning the manifest, sent Wallace forward for coffee, and took Corazon below to see the Captain's stateroom, telling her to close her eyes before he opened the door.

"Well, kitten, still want to go to sea with me?" he inquired with a knowing smile.

"Oh, Ash, this is so very nice," she gushed and turning, threw her arms around him. "You know I do," she added in a throaty voice.

"You'll promise to pay attention Cori, to do as the captain commands?" he asked sternly.

"Why, my Captain," she said going to her tiptoes as if to kiss him on the cheek, and instead, nipped his ear. Don't I always do as you command?" she crooned in that ear."

He laughed, and rubbed his ear lobe, "You misbehave Cori, I swear, I'll tie you up."

She arched her eyebrows and backed into the cabin giggling, "Would you, would you really, Ash? Don't say it less you mean it." She smiled, glancing toward the gimbal-ed bed.

"Yes," he said, trying to look serious and failing miserably.

Changing the subject entirely, he stepped to the cabinets, and began showing her how everything fit together. She laughed at the porcelain toilet mounted over the scuttle chute, and Asher pointed out that no one would be under there looking up. She was delighted at how the settee hinged out to reveal a bathtub, and how the design of the bunk, allowed it to remain level as the ship rolled. The cook arrived with a pot of coffee, hot biscuits and jam. She shared a short breakfast with her husband, for the first time in what was to be her new home.

"This will be such a pleasant adventure," she told him. Collecting crumbs with her napkin. "I'm truly excited."

He slid his chair back, said, "We'll have to hurry," and suddenly business-like. "The tide will be high a little after noon, and I have to be out on the ebb to save paying a tug. You'll want to choose what you want to bring with you."

"Oh, I need to say good-bye to everyone," she gasped as he

held her coat.

"We are coming back someday," Asher, informed her, cheerfully trying to hurry her off the ship. "How about if you send invitations, and have them come see you off?"

"Yes! Yes! What a perfectly wonderful idea," she said, delighted. "Asher, you can be so sweet," and stretching she gave him a quick peck on the cheek.

"I know," he mumbled absently, and hurried her down to the dock.

Fay was pleased to see them, but obviously irritated when she grasped that Asher intended taking his wife to sea. This was the first she'd heard of it. She showed none of her pinch-faced displeasure to Corazon, but to Asher she delivered a rancorous speech in private. It entailed the dangers of the sea and how thoughtless, inconsiderate and selfish it was, to spirit his wife away, and leave an elderly aunt alone. Asher plead the tide, and escaped further tongue-lashing. Three trunks, feather pillows, linen and an oriental rug needed hauling aboard, and it was early afternoon before they could herd Corazon's guests ashore.

Finally, with her lines cast off, *Miss Fay* was worked out into the Cooper River with the aid of her new yawl boat. The current ebbed strong by the time she cleared Folly Island, and they made the channel in one tack on a light northerly breeze. The weather held fair as the schooner reached southeast, crossing the Gulf Stream on a course that would carry her east of the Bahamas. They entered the Trades on the third day and raced across that river of wind, logging two hundred miles noon to noon. Isla Mayaguana rose on dawn Thursday. West Caicos passed abeam by noon, and Inagua was astern before dusk, as the schooner ran west-southwest. Passing Punta de Maisi and into the Windward Passage, she surged and rolled. Wind astern, white foam poured down the face of black seas, crests rose, whooshed under the counter. The schooner, dead before the wind, went under fore topsail and course alone, all fore and aft canvas, furled to save wear.

Asher sat on a gearbox, back braced against a yawl boat davit, Corazon reclining against him, gazing into the wake, phosphorescent with fire fly points of light. The moon came and went under low racing clouds. George Wallace had the wheel, and he sang softly to himself, swaying and tapping a foot. The wheel kicked and he mumbled under his breath, chastising the ship for not behaving, as she should under his hand. From forward a lookout called out.

"Red light, she's fine on the starboard bow."

"A point to the right, smartly now," the mate barked.

Moments later a small Haitian ketch passed to port in wreaths of spray, as she beat up toward Cape du Mole. Watching the ketch, Asher shifted himself and Corazon immediately snuggled closer.

"This is so wonderful," she sighed, "so beautifully romantic."

"Port by tomorrow evening," Asher reminded her, at that same moment, thinking of her soft bottom as she moved in his lap.

"Oh, but then we'll sail again soon," she said, gazing dreamy-eyed at the moon.

"Tomorrow's going to be a busy day," Asher stated. "We must run up into Santiago, dock the ship, and then paperwork. I'll also need to find a cargo."

Knowing, full well, how pressed he would be, she asked, "Can you show me the city?"

"I suppose I can find the time or make it," he sighed.

Twisting around to face him she whispered," I love you Asher."

"I love you, too, Cori. More than words are worth, I love

you," he said in a hushed voice, before gently kissing her lips.

"U mm," she murmured against his neck. "I'm so tired," she uttered, pushing back from him and stretching, fully aware, he was prepared for more than sleep.

"Maybe we should go below," he suggested, trying to look serious.

"Um-hmm," she agreed slipping to the deck and padding barefoot toward the companion hatch.

Asher walked behind, eyes on her hips as she swayed, compensating the ship's roll.

Punta Maisi loomed to starboard as Tros Banks relieved Rolly Floyd. Chops relieved MacArt at the wheel, called off the course.

"Best stand over here to port, Tros," Rolly hinted.

The second mate glanced at the skylight, smiling knowingly, "Dey turn in fo' de night?"

"Been at it like shoats," Rolly complained.

"Ah, de harmonizing, you say." Banks looked up at the sky, "Could use a bit a sweetening myself long about morrow night, you know."

"Been to Santiago before?"

"Oh, yes," Banks assured him, "many times. Fine harbor and de women s dere is hot, ah'm tell-in' you dat. Good place for ah sailing mon, I'll tell you about de — and as Tros continued his dialogue, the ship ran on, a pale shadow before the mountains of Oriente.

Moro Castle's ochre walls lay warm, tinted saffron rose against the faint blue of a Sierra Maestra dawn. Propelled by flower-scented airs the schooner ghosted inshore, signaling for a pilot, as her crew launched the yawl boat. Its sheaves jammed, the engine was troublesome, and copious cursing rose up from below the transom. Hans received a sharp elbow in the side from Gib, who noticed the pretty face of the Captain's wife peering over the tariff rail

"Pardon, ma'am," he bawled, "but this here machine is a plague on my soul."

Uri, looking over his shoulder at Mrs. Byran's shapely bottom, allowed the

bow to wander up to windward two points, and Mr. Floyd bellowed, "Mind your course, dam'd you." His face went from a glower to a weak smile as Corazon turned. "Excuse me, ma'am," he mumbled.

Asher put an arm around his wife, whispering in her ear, as he hustled her below. She returned to deck several minutes later in a baggy, pleated dress with sleeves and a high collar, to sit primly on a bench forward of the chart house.

A launch put the pilot aboard, and the schooner negotiated the corkscrew channel, gliding over the harbor. The sails came down in rapid succession, and the yawl boat towed her alongside. During the next hour, all seemed confusion and paperwork, but things calmed, and soon the agent was on hand, and promising that, the stevedores would begin cargo after the heat of midday.

Other than some sugar, a few tons of coffee, and perhaps again as much tobacco, there was no cargo to be had. For two days while the schooner's cargo came off, Asher inquired, but there was little agricultural production yet in Cuba, and little to ship. "Perhaps Cienfuegos," they told him.

Chapter 31

Two days out of Santiago, the *Miss Fay* anchored off Cienfuegos. Bos'n Swallow got the longboat over, rigging its sail, and he, with two men took Captain and Mrs. Byran ashore. The men's instructions were to remain with the boat while he conducted business. Asher had only just walked out of the cargo broker's office when a voice called to him.

"Lieutenant Byran, could that be you?"

Asher turned, and squinting into the glare, he cried, "Machado," as a man advanced. "You appear prosperous my friend."

Holding up his arms to show off his expensive suit, Muchado replied, "I have become once more an attorney and one must maintain appearances."

"May I introduce my wife, sir?" Asher said. "Corazon Catherine O'Ryan Byran, may I introduce my comrade-in-arms, Orlando Xavier Valle, Captain and hero of the revolution."

"At your service, Señora," Machado said, bending slightly at the waist. "You have a truly beautiful wife, my friend," he said turning to Asher.

"Thank you, sir," she said, acknowledging the compliment. "You're too kind."

Hearing her, he blurted, "You're Cuban! I had assumed you were American, *Señora*."

"I am both, sir. I was born in Matanzas. Though my mother is Spanish, a Vega, my father is a North American. I find myself at home in both countries," she explain.

"Ah," Valle replied. "I'm familiar with the name now. O'Ryan. Your father is a man of substance," he said with polite caution. "You are here for a visit? You will lunch with me. I insist on inviting you."

"Thanks, Orlando," Asher said. "We'd be honored."

"There's an excellent restaurant by the Teatro Tomas Terry. It has air and a fine view of the plaza. May I show you the way?" he offered, extending an arm.

The food was tasty and the view pleasant. Valle was involved in clearing up property disputes caused by the war and clearing titles on property, not to mention his involvement in sales. In addition, there was politics, for he was very involved in politics.

"And when did you leave the Army, my friend?" Valle inquired over coffee.

"Why, in December," Asher said with a sheepish smile. "I'd planned to resign after the official transfer of authority, but the Army suddenly wished me off the island," he said.

Valle's eyebrows arched and Corazon said, "My family believed by removing Asher from the island they would also remove the possibility of an unwelcome suitor."

"Ah, ha," Valle burst out. "I had heard the beginnings of a certain matter, but not the outcome. Gossip seldom provides details. I had no idea it was you, my friend, but I congratulate you both," he said sincerely. "And your new venture, it prospers, I hope."

"It's early yet," Asher, said noncommittal. "Success comes when it wishes."

"Things improve," Valle offered. He placed his napkin on the table. "I must beg you to excuse me," he said. "A previous engagement."

"We thank you very much for your hospitality," Asher said, standing with Valle.

"You will be in Cienfuegos long?" Valle asked.

"Only until tomorrow unless a cargo is to be had."

"If it's permissible — I may visit this afternoon, say five," he

280

said. "Perhaps I should learn a little of ships.

"I would be honored to have you, sir."

"The *Miss Fay Gibbes,* you said."

"Would you like me to send a boat?" Asher asked.

"No! No! I will hire a fisherman's boat. Until later, then."

As Orlando Valle departed, Asher sat and returned to his coffee.

"You were together long?" Corazon asked, naturally curious about all things dealing with Asher.

"For only a few weeks, but there were difficulties enough during those weeks for one man to take another's measure, time for respect and friendship. Orlando was a cavalry officer with Garcia's army. He was known as Machado then. I tell you, he is an able man. He thinks before he acts and he acts decisively."

"His family is here?" she asked.

"All executed at Holguin in 1895, killed when Spanish troops retook the city."

"How cruel it must have been for him," she said, saddened. "Let's not speak of war."

They strolled the plaza, entering the Cathedral of the Pure Conception. Within, the light of afternoon cascaded through stained glass in rivers of exquisite color. For a time, they sat upon ancient oak, as a choir practiced in the loft.

On return to the harbor, the serene mood was spoiled. Asher found the boat waiting but the crew drunk. He had Corazon wait some distance from the seawall while he harangued them and got the sail up. On board, She went below, complaining that something had disagreed with her stomach. Asher advised the mates that the ship would remain at anchor for the night on the chance of something from the broker next morning, and ordered Rolly to attend personally

281

to the drunks sprawled happily laughing, in the bows as the bos'n was one of them.

Concerned about his wife, Asher went below and found her folding clothes. Blushing slightly, she informed him that her discomfort was a common problem among all women, and would clear itself up in three or four days. Certainly, he had something to do elsewhere for she planned to take a nap. Asher, who recognized a dismissal, went to the chart house, and opening his books, began going over his accounts.

Of the fourteen thousand dollars he had begun with, eight thousand had gone into the purchase, refit and provisioning of the ship. He made a combined profit of two thousand one hundred from his first two voyages, but spent one thousand fifty on repairs required after the collision, and another three fifty on the yawl boat. His wedding and wedding trip consumed nearly four hundred, and three hundred for the lot purchased in Coconut Grove.

His balance was over five thousand, and he would collect on his claim against the *City of Bristol*, but he had hoped to do better. This ship must maintain herself and pay for a better one. He would also have to haul and paint her before the summer months and he must plan, build and furnish a home.

Closing his ledger, he leaned back in the chair. Turning a substantial profit was not as easy as he had assumed, and just holding one's own would not do. He thought of the homes and lavish style of life, his wife had nurtured in. The fact that Corazon never made mention of it did not help or sooth his conscience. He wanted the best for her. There must be methods, tricks to discover and corners to cut. Possibly he could pry a little wisdom loose, share a bottle of rum with Tros Banks. He needed contacts ashore who would toss him a plum from time to time. He'd heard his Uncle Conner say countless times, "It ain't the work; it's the workings!" For a while, perhaps, he'd best make some friends for he'd begun to suspect a considerable difference in the talents required of a businessman as compared to a captain. Unfortunately, he was new at both.

Orlando Valle arrived shortly past five, and they sat aft, beneath an awning by the chart house. Sharing a bottle of wine, the conversation touched on Asher's in-laws, and they spoke of subjects in general, until the Cuban was ready to broach the actual nature of his business. He mentioned the maneuvers of various political factions. He said that those who had fought and supported the revolution were in danger of being cut out of, not only the new government, but the forming of the economic structure as well.

"To compete we must have funds," he said. "Everything we had was spent on guns. We have guns supplied by your government, guns we bought, and guns we captured. Thousands still in cases never opened and ammunition. We have many tons of ammunition." Valle paused and lit a cigar. "You are aware there is great pressure to disarm and disband the Cuban army."

"Yes, General Brooke, well, most of the staff was concerned. There was talk about offering a mustering out fee, seventy-eight dollars per man."

"Well, it may happen soon, but we have cached over six thousand rifles and more than a million rounds of ammunition. We also have the artillery we took at Holguin. Alas—the military government suspects it. There is a buyer for these arms though," Valle said, and paused as he lit a cigar, allowing the information to settle in.

He knew there was a point to all this and waited, saying nothing.

"Did you not tell me your family had a tradition of smuggling guns?" Valle asked quietly. "Were you not an officer aboard a filibuster that ran arms into Cuba?"

283

"Yes, in fact far more places than Cuba," he admitted, beginning to see where this might lead.

Valle drank, leaned forward. "Would you consider smuggling guns out of Cuba?"

Asher, who need not give it too much thought, said, "It would depend on the details and where they were to go. If the risk is acceptable, and the reward is sufficient, my answer is yes," he agreed. "My name and the name of the ship, they must remain between you and me, my friend. And I'll need to know of the details."

Valle smiled, looking more like the Machado of old. "There is a large consignment of drilling equipment to be shipped to Mexico. To the port of Vera Cruz," he said. "A ship with such a cargo might drop south from Tampa and take aboard cargo, other cargo not on the manifest." Silent, Valle puffed his cigar.

"If it could be loaded aboard lighters," Asher proposed, "concealed in mangroves, with yourself and a few men to ensure its safety. Unload the lighters, tow them to Mexico and repeat the process. We conceal the lighters in the lagoons, and no one will know where, until your money is sure. This way, my vessel doesn't enter ports with contraband."

Valle said nothing. He scratched his chin. "It has merit," he allowed. "Do you know of places?"

"Some. I'm sure others can be found." Valle said nothing, so Asher continued. "Where on the coast are we speaking of, and how much will you pay?"

"To the west of here, Bahia Cochinos," Valle said. "You know the place?"

"I know the Bay of Pigs," he said unenthused. "Not a lucky place for my people."

"But it's a good place — is it not a good place?" Valle

questioned.

"It's fine so long as no one knows," Asher said cautiously. "And the money?"

"Five thousand," Valle offered.

"Not possible," Asher said, bargaining.

"You also have the profit of carrying the cargo from Tampa," Valle pointed out.

"My ship is worth ten thousand easily -- you're a practitioner of the law -- you know my insurance is void if the ship is seized smuggling. There is also the matter of extra money for the crew. I insist on ten thousand in the bank before we load, an additional two thousand if we're successful.

"You ask too much," he huffed.

"My experience tells me it's very little, considering the risk."

"It will be difficult to get that much money," Valle complained.

Asher wrote the name of his bank and the account number on a card. He passed it to Valle. "If you accept and I receive the Mexican cargo, I'll inquire at my bank before I run south. No deposit and I'll sail direct." From the chart house, he retrieved a chart and opening it, marked a position. He said, "Conceal the boats here."

Crow Tibbs began ringing the galley bell. Asher said "Dinner," and smiled. "Beans, rice, ham and biscuits, would you care join me?"

"Thank you, no," Valle said impatiently getting to his feet. "Perhaps another time, and if this is decided, I'll send you a telegram with my name and a date." He Passed Asher a card with his name and address. It was proceeded by Colonel.

"A promotion?"

"It means little now. The war is done."

"Well colonel, you might have to wait," he, warned him. "I can't guarantee the wind. We could be delayed a few days, perhaps longer."

"We would wait," Valle assured him.

It had grown dark. Asher saw him over the side. Orlando Valle's boat had not gone a hundred yards before it was lost in the gloom.

"Well," he thought, "this may not be the most judicious course to follow, but it'll be a financial coup if it succeeds."

He went below and woke Corazon, asking her if she would like something to eat. She nodded a sleepy yes and stretched sinuously.

"Did Mr. Valle come?" she asked.

"Um hum."

"What did he have to say?"

"This and that there is the possibility of a cargo," Asher evaded. "He told me a little about local politics, and that soon there's likely to be another revolt in Mexico."

Chapter 32

Four days of fair wind brought the *Miss Fay Gibbes* to Tampa Bay. Only hours had been required to discharge the meager tonnage taken aboard in Santiago, but as Asher had hoped, a telegram awaited the ship, a telegram confirming that a cargo would be arriving from Pittsburgh via rail.

He sent a telegram to Charleston, with instructions that his mail to be forwarded. When it arrived, the following day, he discovered, the owners of the *City of Bristol* had agreed to payment of his claim. It amounted to four thousand dollars, a sum which covered damages, demurrage and legal fees. A signed release was necessary, and Asher thought it a convenient way to remove his wife from the ship. He had no intention, of having her aboard to risk the sort of dangers that running arms might involve. A Tampa lawyer drew up a 'power of attorney' for Corazon and Asher signed it. The document, duly witnessed, was stamped and secured in her purse. Outside the office, she threw her arms around Asher, giving him an enthusiastic kiss.

"What was that about?" he said, as they started down the stairs.

"Because, my dear husband, it makes me feel so wonderful to be trusted," she said, putting her cheek to his arm. "You'll find I'm quite clever about business. My mother had no grasp of finance. I handled all the household accounts while we were in Georgetown, you know."

"I'm acquainted with an excellent Cuban restaurant in Ybor City," he suggested. "Are you hungry?"

"Um, yes," she said eagerly.

"Well then," he said, hoisting her into a livery buggy, "we're on our way."

The aroma of rich Cuban coffee and salsa filled the place. Corazon devoured her stuffed snapper with an unfeminine gusto, while he battled with his steak and lost. It had smelled wonderful, but proved impossible to chew.

"Florida beef," she laughed. "I've heard, between it and starvation, starvation was the clear choice."

"It's not so bad stewed or bar-be-cued," he defended and waved for the waiter.

"May I get you something, sir?" the waiter said as he came to the table.

"You can take this," he said indicating the steak "and throw it out back. It'll give the dogs something to chew on for a week. We'll like dessert then, the apple pie."

"Can't we have the cheese cake instead?" Corazon suggested longingly. "It looks delicious and it's my favorite."

"Certainly darling," Asher agreed. "Make that the cheese cake, with coffee and apple pie please." Asher looked up at his wife with shock, for she had dropped her slipper under the table, and was delicately rubbing her foot up his leg.

"I love you," she mouthed with an innocent smile.

He was becoming rapidly aroused. "For God's sake, stop it," he whispered, "or I won't be able to stand up." Mortified, he clamped her foot with his knees. She looked to the side as if nothing were happening, stretched and wiggled her toes. Asher scooted his chair back, and grabbed her ankle. He tickled her sole under the cover of the tablecloth, until she gripped the table, white-knuckled in an attempt not to burst out laughing.

"Peace," she entreated through clamped teeth; he agreed, letting go of the ankle.

"Ash Byran, how have you been?" a man called as he entered the dining room.

Asher turned to see army blue and captain's bars. "Why, Chad Noland," he said, rising only partially to shake Noland's hand and holding a large napkin in front of himself. "May I introduce my wife? Cori, this is Chad Noland, a comrade in arms."

"A pleasure, ma'am," Noland said, and turning to a slim curly haired girl added, "and might I present my fiancée, Miss

288

Eva Mott."

"My pleasure, ma'am," Asher said nodding his head. "Please, would you care to share our table?"

With the introductions made, they sat and ordered. Corazon advised against the beef, and Eva frankly admitted to having made the error only yesterday. Eva discovered Corazon had lived in Georgetown; she had school friends from there.

"Oh, do you know Grace Waring?" she gushed.

"Why, of course," Corazon replied, "and her cousin Christiana Bower. We were in school together," she said, and the two fell into that women's pastime: whom do you know?

"Congratulations on your promotion," Asher said, acknowledging the captain's bars. "When did you get back to Tampa?"

"Never got out, would you believe it? Came down with typhoid fever and by the time I was on my feet, the Dons were whipped."

"Sorry to hear it"

"It worked out well enough. I'm with the quartermaster's corps now. Trying to sort out where all the equipment went and trying to get it back. Unbelievable mess, with everything sent to the Philippines now. Aguinaldo's army giving us far more trouble than the Spanish did. We've lost over five hundred already, I hear."

"Well," Asher said cynically, "I don't suppose the Filipinos want to be Americans any more than they wanted to be Spaniards. I saw enough of war to decide I didn't care to participate. A personal choice, I've always had another career in mind."

"So, if you don't mind me asking, what are you up to?" Noland asked, curious.

"I'm Owner and Master of a ship, coast-wise trade."

"Good timing," Noland said, "and the army is about to begin a great deal of

shipping to Cuba. I wish you success. Ah, and here comes our food."

It all arrived, both the entrees and the Byrans' deserts. Corazon finished her coffee, and Asher made his excuses, explaining the need to get back to the ship. The women exchanged addresses while he settled his bill, and they parted cordially.

Months of heavy use had rutted the roads, and it was a slow drive back to Port Tampa. The winter air was cool but the sunshine filtering through the pines was pleasantly warm. Corazon, leaning against her husband, and seemingly lost in thought until she suddenly sat up straight.

"When will you finish loading your cargo?" she asked abruptly.

"It won't have all arrived; not for a few days. Maybe five days," he answered, not giving much thought to her sudden interest. Suddenly suspicious he said, "Why do you ask?"

She smiled, turning sideways to face him, excitement in her face. "Because," she said, "I can leave early, take the train in the morning, and have three days to attend to your business. I can visit and still be back in time to sail with you."

He grumbled inwardly, trying to think how to derail his wife's plan and settled on guilt, saying, "Thought you'd enjoy time with Fay and your friends. Fay will be offended if you don't stay longer."

"Three days will suffice," she assured, "then back to you, my love."

"I don't think it would be fair to just pop in and out. Everyone, Aunt Fay in particular, will be hurt if you don't spend more time once you're there," Asher said, pushing her guilt.

290

"Oh! Stuff," she swore. Then her voice became soft. She rubbed his knee and said, "I can't imagine sleeping alone anymore, darling. Five days is quite enough and Vera Cruz—do you know that's where Cortez landed? He burned his ships there, chose to conquer or perish, and Asher, volcanoes! There are volcanoes thousands of feet high, Asher."

She was quiet suddenly, and Asher, not able to think of anything useful to say, remained silent.

"I am not about to sit in dusty old Charleston while I could be with you in Mexico," she finally announced in a petulant tone.

'Well, I'd rather you visit in Charleston this time. As your husband, I think it best."

She looked at Asher in confused silence, wondering what was possibly

going on in his head. She remembered stories told of men alone in foreign places, of women that sought them out offering mysterious exotic pleasures, pleasures of which decent women knew nothing. A white-hot wave of jealousy swept Corazon, jealousy so intense as to blur her vision.

"Asher, what is going on? You don't want me with you suddenly . You—you—have you grown tired of me — Is it that you simply want variety in your women?" Her eyes began to tear.

"Holy hell, Cori, don't be absurd. If that isn't the most preposterous thing I've ev—"

Crack! Her slap stung and his hat flew off.

"Don't curse and demean me, Asher Byran," she bawled. "I shan't stand it. If not women, what is it? I'll not be lied to, dictated to, nor will I be treated as less than an equal," she sobbed.

He reined in, bringing the horse to a stop, and wore the irritated look of a caught thief on his ordinarily pleasant face.

Corazon stood and cocked a hand to take another whack at him, but standing, Asher caught her wrists and forced her arms to her side, so stepping back, she kicked him. Although she had meant to kick him hard, she had not meant to kick him there. He released her arms and sort of fell sideways out of the buggy. Except for a grunt, he made no sound. A cold fear sobered Corazon. *"My God,"* she thought, *"I've ruined him. I'll never have children."*

She screamed, "Oh, Asher," and jumped to the ground to help him. So, panicked was her cry that the startled livery horse lurched forward, running off with the buggy.

She threw herself down beside him, pulling his head into her lap, sobbing, "Oh, I'm sorry. I'm an ill-tempered bitch. I deserve to be beaten," she wailed, truly contrite.

"Don't worry," Asher squeaked in a small voice. "Be all right in a moment."

For another minute, she kissed his head and cried, and then he managed to get up but remained hunched over. Corazon ran and fetched his hat, offering it to him as a supplicant.

"Where's the buggy?" he asked, peering around, a pallid cast to his face.

Corazon looked up and down the road, the very picture of wretchedness and woe, and whispered, "The horse ran off when I screamed. Ash— I'll run after it," she added plaintively.

"No! Come here," he said, easing himself down on the deep carpet of pine needles.

Corazon hurried meekly to his side and sat. She put a hand on his knee, but failed to meet his eyes. He looked at her, feeling very tender toward her knowing, he needed more than anything to bring her into his confidence. They, above all else, were natural allies and regardless of disagreements, truth must be paramount with them. If they argued, at least they should both know about what they were arguing. To disagree would be all right as long as they trusted each other. Asher put his fingers under Corazon's chin tilting her face up to him.

"I love you above all other women," he said softly. "You're the only one. Never will there be another that I'll have. I apologize for being less than open with you about the voyage to Mexico." He was silent for a moment. Tears were running down her cheeks and her nose was about to run. He could not imagine a more beautiful creature in the world. "I know you didn't mean to kick me."

Corazon's chin quivered, "But I did," she confessed wretchedly, shaking her head up and down.

"I mean there," he said.

"Oh no, I didn't aim," she said shaking her head rapidly.

"I know, darling."

"Will everything be all right?" she worried.

"Yeah, I think so," he said hugging her and kissing her tears. He pulled out his shirttail and wiped her nose.

A freight wagon came by several minutes later, and gave them a ride to Port Tampa where the horse and buggy had preceded them to the livery. They were aboard the ship a few minutes later and Corazon got Asher undressed and into the tub. She sent Chop Davis for a block of ice and poured Asher a glass of whiskey. The night was quiet, except for the occasional groan, when Corazon changed her husband's ice packs. She had no idea a man could swell up like that. She had several stiff drinks before midnight, and on her knees before God, she promised never to lose her temper again.

If God heard, he probably chuckled, for some promises cannot be kept.

Meeting with the Charleston attorneys was a formality, and outside of tea and pastry, it took only a few minutes to sign the documents. By the end of the second day, it seemed to Corazon that she had spent sufficient time with everyone. She missed Asher terribly, and had barely slept, and then, only after three or four in the morning. *"This is a dreadful way to live,"* she thought.

On Wednesday, Fay had shown her treasured photos of the family, some as old as 1858. Fay happily named names and told histories. Corazon had not realized Asher was the last of his branch of the Byran family. She was shocked to learn, most of the men, including Fay's husband Connor, had died at sea, many of them violently. She saw paintings, photos, Asher as a boy standing with his uncle over the name board of a ship. The *Eclipse*, it read.

"Oh, that's familiar," Corazon, said trying to recall the name. "He told me he'd been mate of his uncle's ship."

"Yes," Fay said. "Connor had him out on that ship from the day his mama died. He made him second officer on her, before he was sixteen. Both Connor and Asher's daddy come up out of a family that dealt in fast ships, honey. The Bryans were privateers in the British and French wars, and smugglers in between. They were blockade-runners during the Great War. Always sneaking something in somewhere on a dark night," she chuckled. "Oh, my, to see them light up when they were planning some foolishness. They were good men, y'all understand, just lived by a different code." Fay sighed, "God knows Asher's bred true to his line, and Connor surely did nothing to change the boy's nature. Y'all' husbands got smuggling in his blood, just like my poor Connor had." She pulled a photo from between two pieces of tissue, "This is the *Eclipse* up in the Panhandle, January of 1895. A few weeks after that photo, she was chased down and sunk. A Spanish warship caught *Eclipse* landing arms on the south of Cuba. That's when my Connor died."

Corazon's face became a deathly pale, and tears formed in the corners of her eyes.

"What's wrong, child?" Fay said, leaning forward.

She shook her head and turned away, unable to face her aunt.

"Don't take on so, honey. Connor's gone these five years," Fay said, trying to console her.

Corazon was too horrified to speak, for she had just realized how she knew of the *Eclipse,* why the name was familiar. She had sat with her family, celebrating the destruction of the *Eclipse* aboard the Spanish man-a war that sank her. She could hear the toast on her Uncle Phillip's lips.

"Tell me now, child," the old woman said, moving beside her on the hassock. She put her arms about Corazon, and when she made her tell, Fay said with melancholy. "My, what a tangled world. Ain't God's fault, y'all know. If we did as the Lord asked, there would not be much sorrow. Men make sorrow for each other and lay the blame of it on the Lord." She gave her niece a squeeze. "Let's pick this mess up," she said with a sweet smile.

Asher received a telegram on April 7. "*Machado 04-13-99.*" He telegraphed his bank the next day, and within the hour received a wire stating his balance. The first mate was on deck when Asher came on board, and he instructed him to muster the crew aft. It took only a short time.

"You know we're bound toward Mexico," he said. "I may have a little something for each man, but you'd be expected to keep the reason to yourself. It's business but business that's of little south of legal. Last time I shipped on a venture of this sort there was loose talk, ship ambushed and sunk, men lost." He paced a little, leaned on the binnacle stand, and said, "Should be an easy piece of work. Still, even calm weather has its squalls, boys. If there's a man here who'd rather not get in the sticky, let me know. Always have a place for him when we come back."

295

Asher gave a pull on his watch fob, held up the watch and said, "Mull It over. Tell me if you're not for it." He looked at the time and added, "If I'm to replace men, I'll need to know right off."

He walked forward to the galley shack, poured a mug of coffee, sniffed the cream and added some. He strolled aft, taking his time, and sat in the chart-house. He thought about the money. He'd be able to build a modest home, and put money toward an auxiliary schooner. What would be lost in cargo space he'd make up with time saved on a regular run.

"Excuse me Cap'n, I'd like a word," Rolly Floyd said, dispersing Asher's daydream.

"Yeah, Rolly, what is it?"

"Afraid I'll have to beg off this venture, Captain. I've a wife now and new babe. I'm not of a mind for problems in foreign places, not with a married man's duties."

"I expect you'll do well enough," Asher told him, thinking he would make Banks chief mate. "Had the chance of Captain's berth, on a Johns River packet. That was before I took this," Rolly said. "Less money but be home every few days, get alongside the wife regular, you know."

Asher grinned, chuckled, "That can be a blessing and a curse," he philosophized.

"One more thing, Captain, Gibbon MacArt, he's rated AB, but he's ready for a mate's certificate. Little short on his numbers yet, but he's fine on dead reckoning and chart work." Rolly said this, a little embarrassed, for he was recommending kin. "Married to his sister, but that ain't the ticket. I'd put a word in for him if he weren't. Hell, Captain, you know his granddaddy."

Rolly went to pack his gear. Asher saw Chop peeing down the side of the bulwark and gave him a cuff, causing his aim to spray off in a zigzag arch as he tried to get away.

"I swear, boy," he growled, "I catch you pissing on deck, I'm gonna tie a knot in that noodle of yours. Go fetch me Mr. Banks and the bosun. Quick, now," he shouted giving him a boot on his way, and mumbling to himself in irritation.

Both men came up out of the hold, and followed Asher down to his cabin. He told Banks he was to sail as first, and that he was considering MacArt for the second mate's berth.

"He knows de work, Cop'n," Banks offered. "Ain't saying he kin make de fellas jump. That we hafta see."

He nodded, "Both you been on the coast here for a good long while. Know a lot of men." He paused, looked at them both and said, "I need three or four more hands. They need to be, strongmen, good with boats. Be best if they've worked by moonlight before."

Swallow laughed and snorted, "I am knowing a few dat working dis ere very wharf. Good boys if you's hide de rum, Cop'n." He turned to Banks and asked, "Tros, you knowing of Tom Grasse dere, and I think Green Billy?"

"Grasse is fine," Banks agreed, "but dat Green Billy French is a poor sort. He is surly and quick wit' de knife when he in de cups. Cop'n Asher, he not a good sort at all."

Ill tempered, the Bos'n mumbled, "We ain't needing no Sunday school teacher."

"Know one good seaman here," Banks said. "He work for Sheriff Broward on de "Three Friends." Other filibusters' a for dat, Cop'n, but de Tampa law got him now. Caught sleeping with a pretty whore dat was de wrong shade, if you take my meaning. Name's Ben Bodden."

"Hell! I know Ben. Sailed with my uncle on the old *Eclipse*," Asher marveled. "Have to see if I can bail him out. See if French and Grasse will hire on, and get the cook's stores list. I'll want fifty gallons of fuel for the yawl boat, along with your list, Tros. All stores aboard today and sail tomorrow late."

"Be done, Cop'n Asher."

"And Mr. Banks, send MacArt. I'll see him before I go into town."

As Asher drove, a buzzard was hanging in the sky. Occasionally, he saw it through the treetops. Birds fluttered over the palmettos and from time to time, rabbits and various critters made a dash in front of the horse. Clouds patched the bright blue of the sky, fair weather clouds. No rain to make the road worse than it was. The county jail was on the west side of town, just off the Port Tampa road. A young cracker deputy stood on the stoop, his shotgun in the crook of his arm. He touched his hat as Asher pulled up.

"Afternoon," he said, jumping down from the wagon.

The cracker turned his head to the side, spit tobacco juice and said, "Hey!"

"You got any labor for hire?"

"Some! Y'all ought to speak a mite with Homer Bellis, inside there. The good labor's gone. Mostly pore piddling sorry things is what's left."

Asher rang a hand bell and waited. A fat man waddled out of a side room, smiled.

"G'day, sir."

"Are you Homer Bellis, sir?"

"I am he."

"I hear you've got a buck in here, name of Bodden. He's a skilled seaman, and I'm badly in need of one. I'd like to buy him out," he stated, beginning a negotiation. "That's if the price isn't too dear."

Can't do it," Homer said. "Got caught with one of Nel Coam's girls, pretty little blond that the sheriff his self-favored. Sheriff, ain't gonna let that slide. Gotta draw a line. Bad 'nuff a whore, next thing the niggers be nosing round decent white women."

"Well, hell," he complained, "you saying I came all the way up here for nothing."

"Yup!"

Asher looked around and asked, "Looks like a tight place. Ever have any bust-outs?"

"Been tried more than once. Just did shoot a bootlegger what killed one of our deputies. Guard shot him going over the fence," Bellis said, winking knowingly.

He slipped two tens out, rolled them, and put them in Homer's pocket. "Guess nobody would ask about a black boy, who tried the fence," he said, tapping Homer's pocket.

"Spose not," Homer agreed, licking his lips, his watery blue eyes dancing. "Course the guard needs a little something for shooting a prisoner. Y'all understand how it is."

"That's fair," he said, and put another five in his pocket. "Buckboard's out front."

"Well, bring it round by that fence. There's a door there now." He pointed out the window. "Kin y'all see it?"

"Yes! I see," he said stooping."

"Well, I'll be a minute." Billis stopped and turned back to Asher with a touch of worry on his face. "Y'all are gonna get that boy off to sea now. Wouldn't do to have the sheriff see no resurrected nigger round here."

The fat man's words were sarcastic but serious to a point.

"Gone forever," he smiled, and went to his buckboard.

The door opened and a puffing Homer waved. "Lend ah hand here, Cop'n. This here buck weighs a ton," he gasped.

A tall rawboned guard was dragging Bodden by the feet. Asher got hold of him under the arms, and together they tossed him in the back of the wagon. He had been beaten head to toe, all knots and welts. He was naked as a babe, and smelled like an old diaper.

"You aren't giving me much," he grumbled to Homer, mostly for show.

"Well hell, Cop'n, he's spose to be dead now, ain't he? Sides, I told y'all the sheriff had a hissy, now, didn't I?"

Asher tossed a tarp over Ben and climbed up on the seat. "Git up," he said and snapped the reins. He made the trip back to the port in an hour and a half, stopping once to check Ben and give him a little water. As he drove, he wondered why it was that the worst seemed to come out when men got a little power. He determined to keep a check on himself, and not to foster feelings of superiority. "Man's a man," he thought. "Difference is in what he does with himself."

Four of the boys hauled Ben aboard, and half gagging, washed the jail stink off him. They put him in a foc'sle berth, and Swallow dabbed iodine, here and there, before tossing a cover on him. When Banks asked after him later, Swallow laughed.

"Be just fine dere, Tros. Few days, yes, for ah few day dat mon, he gonna be stiff-legged, but fine in de end." He chuckled again. "Wonder if he lose he taste for white meat now?" He hooted, and made obscene gestures and thumped the rail laughing.

Asher sent a man to return the rented rig, and then ducked into the chart-house to make some entries in the log. He went from chart house to his cabin, meaning to rest. Opening the door, he groaned. His wife had returned and was sleeping in an elegant sprawl upon the settee. "Why," Asher pondered, "did Providence place so many hurdles in a man's path?"

Chapter 33

Near twilight, the *Miss Fay* came about, and bore north from Cayo Piedras into the *Bahia Cochinos*, 'Bay of Pigs'. The land was low and the coast deep behind a mix of sand beach and mangrove forests. The trees grew to the edge of the shallows, where the bottom dropped like a cliff. With no moon, the shore was black-on-black as the schooner closed the east side of the bay. Asher stood in the mizzen tops, on the starboard spreader. He could see surf and called down directions to the helmsman. She was very near. He had ordered sail area reduced, and she slipped along with bare steerage-way. The leadsman chanted forward, "No bottom," and they were so close to shore that men moved, uneasy. "By the deep six," the leadsman yelled excitedly.

"Let's go starboard two shots," Asher called out. "Cast off your sheets, Mr. Banks." The clatter of the starboard wildcat ended. "Let go the port anchor one shot," he ordered and listened to the splash and the rattle of the chain as the schooner stopped, swung right, and fell back on her anchors.

He slid to the deck on the running back-stay. He checked his watch by the light of the binnacle. "Mr. Banks," he called forward.

The mate, who had been coming aft from the anchor windless, startled him when he answered from a few feet. Asher took him into the chart house and marked the exact position. A deep undersea crevasse ran inshore through the mangrove forest, and the water, too deep for the trees to root, allowed a channel back into a shallow lagoon. Orlando Valle was to have the lighters hidden at the end of the channel.

In a low voice, he said, "Have Gib keep an eye on my wife. I want the glg alongside and the mast rigged. If anything happens he's to take her off in the gig, and get her down the coast to Puerto Hondo." Going below, he found Corazon was reading by lamplight. "I'll be heading in to fetch Orlando's boats. If there's a problem, I want you to get into the gig with Gibbon. I don't want to worry about you."

She stood with a look of concern, about to speak.

He held up a hand. "You promised to do exactly what I said, with no argument," he reminded her. "This is only a precaution for my own peace of mind."

She gave him a hug. There was an acid smell to his skin, and she'd learned that meant he was tense.

"I'll see you in a little while," she whispered.

The engine of the yawl boat sputtered, barked and began to run smoothly. Asher gave his wife a quick peck on the cheek. She let him pull away for it was futile to try to hold him at such times. She watched his back disappear.

Coming out of the hatch, Asher had to let his eyes adjust for a moment as shadows took form. Hans, Green Billy and Grasse were in the boat. He took his pistol from the chart house and climbed down with them. Grasse pushed off as Asher put the tiller over.

"Put her in gear."

The engine began to make its high popping sound and the boat moved. The trees rose up ahead; surf broke on either side. The schooner was a dim shadow astern as they entered the channel, its tangle of roots walling them in, trees beginning to overhang as it began to narrow. Green Billy lit the lanterns, blue and yellow, the signal, and they slowed the engine. Mosquitoes became thick, covering their clothes, and the sour odor of rotting vegetation filled their nostrils.

"Talk about mosquitoes, dis a hell of a place, I tell you,"

Grasse grumbled, slapping at himself, continuing to mumble under his breath as he splashed water on his clothes.

"Those boys been back here long, Cap'n, dey be sucked dry," Hans mumbled and turned his collar up, then pulled the shirt over his head.

At a fork, Asher held to the right and ran aground on an oyster bank. They backed and pushed off with oars, rocking the boat until it backed clear. Green Billy now began to swear. He cursed, loud and pitiful, at the insects, which had no opposition as the men worked.

"Throw a tarp over yourself and shut up," Asher ordered. "Whining doesn't suit a man."

Abruptly, a mass manifested itself directly ahead, and as the engine went in reverse, Asher turned. With a solid thump, the yawl boat slid alongside a fifty-foot lighter barge. A canvas pitched back and Valle's head popped up, his face swollen from bites.

"By the saints, you've finally come," he uttered wretchedly. "Satan's hell is not flames," he cried, his voiced strained. "Hell is mosquitoes."

"Are you alone?" Asher asked.

"There's two men with me; the others are dead," he said wiping insects away.

"You were attacked?" Asher said apprehensively, looking side to side for danger.

"No! We could not agree. There," Valle pointed at the middle boat. "It has an engine. They tried to leave in it; we disputed. It is on their own heads;" he crossed himself.

"Hans, you and Grasse get that thing fired up," Asher said, pointing at the boiler on the lighter barge. He spit bugs. "French, get this tow line on while I pole the boat around."

There was mud on the pole, and stinking as it was, they spread it thickly on their clothing and bare skin. Asher

303

breathed through his mouth and again spit mosquitoes.

"Cop'n," Green Billy French said, "y'all gonna tow all this mess together?"

"Just the first boat, we'll come back for the other if Hans has trouble getting steam up. Cast the line off that tree there," Asher pointed. "We'll be back in about thirty minutes," he said and kicked the clutch in.

Overloaded, the lighter was dangerously low in the water, but except for an easy swell that broke on the reef, the sea was near flat. He put the lighter alongside to port, and called Goose down onto the yawl boat before running inshore again. When they neared the end of the bight, Asher could see sparks coming out of the lighter's stack. He eased alongside the second barge, a forty-footer and made-fast.

"You got enough pressure to move?" he called to Hans.

"Got plenty, Cop'n, and got a swelled up dead man, too. He's 'bout to pop," Hans complained.

"Grasse," he snapped. "Cast off there and help him dump that body. Let the crabs clean up the mess. Follow me out, but come up on the port side of the ship," he ordered.

By the time he put the second lighter barge alongside, the crew had a start at emptying the first. He secured the falls to the yawl boat and went up them hand-over-hand to the aft deck where he found the three Cubans. Ruez stood smoking, while Valle and Silva both lay under a lantern. Corazon was bandaging Silva's arm, and looked up with a disapproving expression as her husband came over the rail.

"Perhaps," she said testily, "you will attend Señor Valle, as his britches will need to be removed, and you are as filthy as the rest." She finished with Silva and stood. "I suggest you all wash. I'll go get them something to drink," she said dispassionately and left without a backward glance.

Asher cleaned the mud off his hands and forearms; he knelt

304

to look at Valle's wound. The belt was already undone, and he pulled the trousers down to Valle's knees. The bullet had passed through the inside of the thigh about six inches below his crotch entering and exiting about three inches apart.

"Was he trying to kill you or geld you, Orlando?" Asher smirked.

"*No es importante*," Valle mumbled, unappreciative.

He poured iodine on his hands, on the gauze, then poured some on the wound.

"Ayy yi yi yi," Valle howled. "By the mother of whores, that burns," he swore.

"Orlando, it appears my wife was less than sympathetic," he mentioned as he began to wrap a bandage around the thigh.

"She asked about the wounds. Silva told her what happened," Valle, said this through gritted teeth. "Silva was honest. Honesty is seldom a wise thing with women. She thought it insufferable that men should kill each other over mosquitoes." Valle chuckled. "They could have waded ashore and good riddance, but we could not let them take the boat and you see, they insisted on keeping their feet dry." The chuckle was the old Machado.

"I understand entirely," he admitted.

Corazon came up with liquor and glasses, pouring both men large drinks. Silva went forward to the foc'sle, and Valle went to sleep in a cabin forward of the chart house.

By midnight the lighters were riding high, their loads hauled over the rail and stowed. The forty-footer was winched aboard, using the heavy fore and main masthead blocks and lashed athwart ship over number one hatch. They rigged hawsers to tow the others. The mizzen was set; the anchors heaved, and the foresail went up quickly, followed by the staysail and jibs. Helm over, *Miss Fay Gibbes* backed to port. Her bows fell to starboard; she shuddered; she took the wind. Blocks squealed as the sheets were hauled. She heeled, crabbed to lee, and bubbles rose up from under her counter as she made way!

He gave MacArt a course to clear Garden Bank, and remained on deck long enough to see the mainsail set. Tired to the bone, he went below. Corazon looked up from her book, and rose to meet him, doing a little half step to the side as the ship felt the swell.

"Oops!" she uttered with amusement.

He smiled and closed the door. "Couldn't sleep?" he asked as she came to hug him, but then stopped short, holding him off with an outstretched hand.

"Oh, ugg, waiting for you is all. Uuck! the stench, give me that shirt," she ordered, wrinkling her nose and backing away. "Give me everything," she said, wishing for one of the many servants she'd once had.

She had a pan of water sitting next to the bunk, and as the schooner cleared the land, the wind put her over more. The schooner heeled, and the water began to spill.

"Oh, pooh!" Corazon cried, grabbing it. She stuffed a towel under one side to level it, and took his smelly clothes from him as he stripped. "Sit here," she indicated, pointing at a stool next to the pan. He sat with a sigh, and she scraped his back, and wiped with a wet washcloth. She pointed at the tub, part filled with scented water. "You do the rest," she said. "You smell of sulfur and rotten fish."

As he washed, Corazon turned the bed down and began to undress. Finally, she climbed between the sheets and propped on one elbow, waited for him.

"You're tired, Ash."

"Yeah, I am kitten."

He opened the valve letting the water down the scuttle,

and as he climbed into bed, Corazon wiggled herself against him. She tossed her hair to one side and nipped his ear. He gave her a kiss and she squirmed around, adjusting herself, making the kiss longer and more satisfying than Asher had planned. One thing led to another and when her knee brushed up over his groin, she giggled.

"Why, darling," she whispered, "I thought you were tired."

He rolled over, pulled her nightgown over her head, and drew her against him. "I'm tired but I'm not dead," he mumbled against her flesh, and pounced on her in the most lascivious manner.

Chapter 34

One hundred miles northeast of Vera Cruz, the *Miss Fay Gibbes* ghosted, rolling gently in the northerly airs. Her massive booms strained first against the sheets then the preventers, causing a rhythmic creak, squeak and clatter with the changing strains. It being their last evening before landfall, Corazon had invited Asher's officers and the Cubans to dinner. She had given Crow instructions for a portion of the meal, and then driven him from his galley while she made pastries and sauces. The meal, for all its lengthy preparation, disappeared quickly and Corazon received the compliments of her guests.

Crow Tibbs made a clumsy job of serving, muttered an oath under his breath, and spilled soup on Banks but had no problem pouring brandy. Gib excused himself after the meal to take the watch and the company was pleasant. During a break in the conversation, Corazon took the opportunity to apologize to Silva and Valle for being short with them.

307

"I had no right to question your morality, to speak in such an overweening manner," she confessed. "I'm ashamed to admit, gentlemen, that although I've a bias against violence on the moral plain, I'm ill-tempered and own to an emotional propensity for it." She dropped her eyes, appearing a model of feminine gentility as she spoke her apology.

Asher sniggered. "I could tell you about her temper," he said, grinning playfully.

"Asher Byran," she cried, admonition in her voice.

He held up his hands, signaling a promise of discretion, and his wife's face softened and reddened all at once.

Silva chuckled. "A toast," he offered, raising his glass. "*Women and gun powder, may men handle both with care.*"

"You're married?" Asher asked.

"These fifteen years," Silva said. "My wife is in St. Petersburg. One day I shall bring her home to Cuba, but only when it's safe. Her home was in the city of Trinidad."

"She's been gone long?" Corazon asked her head tilted with the question.

"Since the first months of '95," he said.

"My father, he also sent us to the mainland in '95," she said reflectively. "We departed only days after the first shots. I was fortunate to be on the mainland during the war."

"I wish I had been so wise," Valle said, reproving of himself. "War is bad, but revolution is worse. Both are impossible for women and children. All people must make certain adjustments in their minds to become survivors," he said, and seeing he had his companion's interest, he continued. "I made this adjustment far too slowly you see. I had studied in France and married my Madeline there. When the violence began, I believed we were above it. When the Spanish retreated from Holguin, we remained. We remained when they took it back. What was the violence to me? I was a neutral, unconcerned. When they began dragging people from their houses, I became concerned. I armed myself. Another pistol I put in our bedroom. You see, my friends, I had weapons but not the determination to use them. To survive one cannot hesitate to act.

When they kicked in my door, I could have killed them and saved my family. There were only four you see, volunteers. Young gentlemen," he laughed. "Instead I spoke logically, then I threatened and I took a bullet here," he said, pointing to his face. "Madeline came from behind them with the other pistol, but she did not shoot either. You see, we were civilized —. They grabbed her pistol and two of them took her on the floor while another shot our children. When they had finished with Madeline, they strangled her. Me—I appeared to be dead. I was, for a time, paralyzed but I witnessed all of it. Having been taught a cruel lesson, I recovered by mere chance. The lesson is this: ' *Any creature that hesitates to instantly flee or kill when threatened, it will not survive*'. This truth is known to the lowest beast of the jungle."

Valle smiled meekly and looking from face to face said, "Civilization is but a thin paint. Reasons are not important, for men find endless reasons to threaten and to act with violence. The men with us in the boats had weapons. They caused Ruez, Silva and myself to choose between life and death. We did not hesitate in our choice to survive. Life is hard." He shrugged. "It calls for ruthless choices, made without hesitation."

Conversation was halting after Valle spoke. Banks excused himself to go to the head, while Silva and Valle went on deck for a smoke. Asher went to his charts.

Corazon straightened up and went on deck. She sat at the lee rail, looking out toward the invisible coast. A colorful tropical bird rushed out of the dark. She watched it spoon water off a barrel, and preen, stretching its wings. A hatch slammed; the bird launched itself into the air, fluttering south. Voices came from below where Corazon sat, the sound of men shooting craps at the foot of the mizzen, the roll and slide of the dice, grunts, the occasional "Yessss!" or "Come to me."

A man passed gas loudly. Others complained. A voice said, "Dreamed white last night, white ship and white clouds. Saw white bird, Ibis be on de galley top dis night. Dat bad luck—De omens dey is plain."

"That's shit."

"Oh yes, dreams be certain sign. Dey mark of good fortune, dey mark of woe."

"That may be but you's got's de color wrong. My grand-mama, she says, it is marked That black is de sign of evil: black cat, black horse, storm and night, dey all black, all bad luck."

"You's a black mon, black Goose. Spose you's bad luck to youself?"

"To every man, the luck, she is a different thing. I carry mine here", a deep voice threatened.

"Don't need to be flashing no blade there, Green Billy."

Silence, only the clatter of the dice, sighs, groans and Corazon stood. Softly, she walked aft of the chart house. Banks and Valle, with Asher now, bent over a chart of the coast. She slipped into the chart room unnoticed, reclined on the settee. She listened to them speak, listened as she always had listened to men. Drawn to their dialog, she at the same time felt the alien strangeness of their world, a world she had always been curious of, yet could not reconcile.

"All the trigger mechanisms will go with the ammunition, and field pieces in the steam lighter. The rifles in the other two," Valle explained. "If we conceal them in separate locations, one is no good without the other, and if they cheat it will do them no good."

"Can't trust these Mexicans," Silva said. "Double-cross

their mothers over a peso." He puffed on his cigar, pointed with it toward the deck. Be wise to put one case of those Mausers in your arms locker, Captain. These men have no honor."

"We won't have anything aboard for them to take," he said unconcerned. "Besides, I've four rifles, some shotguns and a couple pistols as is." He pointed to a place on the chart, to a place on the coast southeast of Vera Cruz. "We drop the steam lighter off here tomorrow. It runs into Alvarado Lagoon after dark and hides at the northwest end. We continue on past Punta Lazario, and cast off the other two lighters in tow of the yawl boat. It tows them up into the Jamapa River. The yawl boat will be back before dawn. We'll be a few miles off the port. Anyone who sees us will believe we're waiting for a pilot to take us in at dawn, which by then, we will." Asher thumped the chart table with his fist, and declared, "The rest will be up to you, gentlemen. I'll discharge my cargo and leave. If possible, it would be better if you book passage home on another ship."

"Yes," Valle said. "We have no intention of remaining here longer than necessary."

"Whatever you're going to take ashore," Asher said, "put it in the boat after it's loaded. An offshore breeze blows at night, and it's generally mild this time of the year. Light swell unless there's a norther blowing. Mr. Banks has been on this coast before, and I have a seaman who knows Alvarado Lagoon. He'll leave the steam lighter with Ruez and walk into Vera Cruz. Banks will take you into the river, Orlando."

"Agreed then," Valle said, "tomorrow."

It required three days to discharge the manifested cargo from the *Miss Fay Gibbes*. The crew spent another day loading exotic woods, which Asher acquired on speculation. Corazon purchased several parrots, and was determined to have a small monkey. The sulfurous sweet odors emitting

311

from an area occupied by monkey vendors hastily eroded that determination. With Ben Bodden carrying her packages, she shopped her way along a street made narrow by vendor's stalls, and was in the process of purchasing a jacket done in Indian embroidery. She felt a tug on her skirt. Hiding in the alleyway, was a much-disheveled Orlando Valle.

"Please," he hissed, indicating a door behind a display of straw brooms. "Come."

Bodden was bargaining over a belt, and she motioned, indicating for him to follow her. A dozen steps and she ducked through the door to where Valle waited in the dim light.

"What's happened to you?" she asked her face full of apprehension.

"Much! All bad! The dogs tried to play us for fools. First a refusal to pay; they laughed until they found all the trigger assemblies were missing. Then they approached Silva a second time. They paid us then, paid us in silver and gold coin, the bastards! It was too heavy to move without a cart. They caught us yesterday, on a side street when we went to board our steamer. I ran two men down with the mule cart when they tried to block the street. Silva, Ruez, both shot dead. *Mierda*! All those years of war and killed by thieves. I dumped the chests off the sea wall, but no one saw. They know I am near. They watch. Pure luck, you shopped on this street. More that I saw you."

Corazon's mind raced. She looked at Valle, and sucked her cheeks in for a moment. "Bodden," she said, "bring that package. "Is your knife sharp?"

"Yes um! It razor sharp."

"Mr. Valle," she said, "may he shave your chin and mustache?"

Valle looked at her with an empty stare.

She smiled coquettishly and said, "For a little while we'll make a woman of you."

"Ah," he gasped. "I see."

Corazon slipped into a closet space, and removed her dress, putting on the skirt and lace blouse she'd purchased. She tied up her hair with a scarf. A different woman stepped out placing her dress on the table. Bodden took only moments to clean Valle's face.

Looking at the scars on Valle's face, Bodden said, "Going to be an ugly woman."

"Mr. Valle," she said, "take no offense, but you're not a large man. You should fit into my dress. If you'll put it on, I shall do the rest."

He wiggled into it and although it was three inches short and tight in places it looked presentable. She stuffed the bodice; put her hat on him with a scarf holding it down, and a fine gauze veil, ladies used to keep flies from their face. Her gloves had to be split down the palms to fit his hands, but Corazon decided the illusion was sufficient.

"A woman in that dress entered this street. A servant, a large Negro, accompanied her. A woman will be seen leaving with that servant. It shouldn't cause any suspicion," she announced, with a smug look. "Am I not clever?"

"Brilliantly so Señora," Valle said in his deep baritone.

Bodden picked up the packages. "Best not talk," he advised. "You gots ah voice like some bullfrog."

Corazon went out first; examining some leather goods, as she waited, then

followed the men along the crowded streets. At the cathedral, Bodden hired a carriage. To a casual observer he appeared to assist a matron and her maid into it. Bodden climbed up next to the driver and pointed. They were aboard the ship within ten minutes.

Asher was preparing to leave port, when the trio came aboard. He stared at Corazon in her Mexican clothes, and puzzled at the ungainly woman wearing his wife's dress. A word from Valle as he passed was all Asher needed to end amusement on his part. He followed them below and learned of disaster.

"Its worse," he told Valle. "Estefen's drunk; his tongue was loose while ashore. Grasse and Smithe knocked him upside the head and dragged him back aboard, but rumors will be flying concerning this ship. I wanted to be gone this afternoon, but we can stretch our stay until dusk, sail out on the land breeze."

"Let me out of this thing," Valle said disdainfully plucking at the rags stuffed in the front of the dress. "I'll point to the place on the sea wall where the chests are."

Asher pondered while Valle changed his clothing. He rose and sat three times in the course of a minute in order to look outside. Corazon moved behind him. She placed her hands on his shoulders, rubbing his neck. "You're worried," she said.

"We stayed a day too long Cori." He said this with apparent unease,

"Officials here could cause us trouble if they suspected us of gun running, but its Valle's customers I'm concerned with. If they hear this ship brought in the guns, they may assume it's going to take out the money. They've already proved to be ruthless." Asher became silent.

Bending, Corazon wrapped her arms around him hugging his back, her cheek pressed to the side of his head. He put his hands up over hers; the scent of her hair filled him.

In a gentle voice he said, "Could I persuade you to stay at a hotel Cori, take a steamer up to New Orleans?"

She kissed his ear. "No!" she whispered with finality.

"You'll give me gray hair."

"Look who's talking."

"Let me go, darling," and standing, he un-wrapped her arms with agitated energy, "I've things I must attend."

He found Banks and told him to send Bodden, Grasse and Chop Davis aft. He waited, impatiently checking his pocket watch, as hats in hand they shambled aft to the chart house. He produced a purse with some Mexican silver and tossed it to Bodden.

"I've a task for three of you. You go down there, to that beach," he said pointing. "You bargain for one of those little fishing boats. Sixteen to eighteen feet is all you need and do not dally. Take along some of that old cargo net, and a few fathoms of one-inch manila line." Pointing across the harbor, Asher said, "You see that old seawall? Its there where the town runs down to the water—near where all those fishing boats are moored?"

"See it, Cop'n," Bodden said.

"By that blue house, the alley, Mr. Valle lost something there."

"Dat for sure," Bodden said, round-eyed.

"Chop, you're a fair diver. I've heard it."

"Go deep, stay long, Cop'n," the islander bragged.

"You're going to rig that cargo net under the boat. Slack it to the bottom. There are two heavy chests, and they may be in the mud. Chop," Asher instructed. "Once you find those chests, if you can't get them into the net, get Ben in the water to do it. Main thing is you have to find those boxes." Asher picked up his binoculars. "Chop, come below here. Look through the porthole and mark the place.

Valle waiting by the porthole pointed, "There by the blue wall, where the alley comes out."

Chop looked through the glasses. "See de place sir."

315

"Well, that's where they are, two steel boxes, black," Valle said.

Asher went up the steps with a canvas bag and Chop followed him. "There's a Colt .44 and extra bullets in here," Asher said, passing the bag to Grasse. "You keep it out of sight. Don't use it unless the situation becomes desperate. Understood?"

Grasse grinned wickedly and nodding, said, "I got it, Cap'n."

"So, you don't draw attention, get some old straw hats to wear. Grasse, you speak the language, you talk, and the other boys keep shut. To have what's in them boxes, why every soul in this town would gut you, and leave you for the crabs," he warned, "Don't pull for the ship straight away. Go on up the dock a little; mix in with the bum-boats, then ease on back. We'll keep an eye on you, in any case. Understood?"

The three men nodded, started to walk

"And boys," he called causing them to pause, and turn. "There'll be a little something extra in it," he promised with a grin. "Now get!"

The three men went, Bodden and Chop smiling, Tom Grasse with his somber scowl. Asher watched them walking along the waterfront until he lost sight of them in the bustle. Banks was sitting on the port rail, and Asher told him to get the yawl boat over, hawser rigged, and all the ship's mooring lines in but two. Those two were to be on bites.

"Cop'n you thinking about leaving in some kinda hurry?" the mate inquired.

"Yep, and anybody that's not on board's going to get left," he grumbled. "We'll be lucky to get out of here without trouble, Tros. He looked up into the rigging, contemplative. "Might be a good idea to dry a couple sails, hoist them, and brail them up, Mr. Banks," he said winking.

Banks nodded, grinned and went off to attend to his order.

316

Asher went below where he found Valle cleaning his pistol, a hard look on his face.

"This has not gone well," Valle apologized unhappily. "The blame must fall to me."

"You know something of them, Orlando. Would they come after us?"

"In port, certainly," Valle shrugged, "away from the dock, only God knows."

Asher rubbed his chin. "I'm going to arm some of the crew. I'll pick the ones, who can shoot," he said. "I've things to do now." In his cabin, he took the key from his desk. Opening the gun locker, he laid the weapons side by side on the deck as his wife watched.

She pressed back against the door. "Has it come to this?" she asked soberly.

"I hope not," he said lightly, trying to convey an air of confidence, "but it's best to be prepared. I have my *Zarpe* ' clearance' and I'm hoping to cast off before dark or a little after," he said, beginning to load a shotgun. "Once we're at sea, we shouldn't have anything to worry about."

With two rifles and four of the pistols, Asher went topside to the chart house. He'd give the carpenter and Mr. MacArt the rifles; Mr. Banks, Green Billy, Bodden and Swallow pistols. Two rifles he would reserve for Valle and himself. The chart house and his cabin would do for the shotguns. He picked up his binoculars again. A skiff with three men was rowing across the upper harbor. He placed the binoculars in their case and called Mr. MacArt, who was sounding the bilges just forward, the mizzen. Asher gave him the glasses, and told him to watch the skiff. To do it through a port so as not to be seen watching it. If the skiff pulled away from the seawall or anything happened, he should call him. Forward, he saw the chief mate was rigging out the hawser. The bos'n was coming up the dock with Goose and the cook in tow. These were the last of the crew ashore. When, finally, the skiff eased up under the counter, Asher glanced nervously down the dock and thought, "almost there."

A smoky haze blurred the town as the air began to move seaward. The ship began to swing out from the wharf. As the yawl boat strained on the hawser, it pulled the bow through the eye of the wind. Cast off, she motored under the stern to pick up the falls. Above, they clewed down the lower topsail and braced it round. One by one the sails went aloft, soft round billows, pushed out by a weak breeze, until sheets were hauled home, hardening them to their work.

Corazon stood beside the binnacle, clear of activity, and watched the harbor slip astern. Outside, the broad horizon swept wide and opened to the smooth expanse of the Bay of Campeche. Mr. Banks, his eyes aloft, shouted orders to slack or tighten this line or that. Asher, to right of the helmsman, spoke the courses. "To wind a point, steady there," she heard. His voice was calm, measured. The tension in her, the threatened feelings, they diminished with the freshening air; the rise and fall of the deck assured her. The pilot went over the rail to his skiff, and the city with its murky fear, its perfidious intrigue, fell off astern.

Chapter 35

Banks climbed up from the waist, reporting. "Cop'n, de anchors are on de claws, hatches secure, bosun say de bilge show three-inch. She secure for sea."

"Very good, Mr. Banks." He looked over the side, and said, "Were only making steerage. Hold her north-northwest with the wind on the port quarter. Hold that for as long as this land breeze lasts."

"Will do it, Cop'n."

"And Mister Banks, keep a couple men on lookout while we're inshore. Pass the same to Mister MacArt. I'll want to know if anyone sees anything," he instructed.

"Looking squally, Cop'n; we being in ballast."

"Yeah, you shorten if the wind blows cool, Mr. Banks, and scandalize her if you're caught napping."

Pork Davis nodded to Corazon as he climbed out of the yawl boat. Asher motioned him over, told him to send the cook aft with whatever dinner was. The deck, taken by Mr. Banks, was all in good order. Asher smiled, acknowledging his "other wife." She took his arm possessively, accompanying him below, satisfied now, the temporary transition had been made, from captain to husband.

"Strange," she thought. *"It was like sharing him with another woman and each having her turn at his attention."* She smiled wistfully. She supposed, children eventually took much of a woman's attention from her husband, but she had no children, and the ship at times seemed a rival. She wondered, *"Would he be jealous of his children?"*

Speaking little in the heat, they ate, their perspiration dripping in their food. With the schooner in airs from astern, the cabin was sticky warm. Shedding their clothes, they sponged off and lay across the bed, letting the water cool their skins.

Corazon must have napped for she woke alone. She heard the sound of rain blown under the skylight, spattering the deck. From outside the shouts of the crew came to her, and sail beating as they shortened it. Hurriedly, she put on a skirt and blouse. Reaching the crank on tiptoes, she screwed the skylight down, and was about to wipe up the water when there was a loud thump against the hull.

Immediately, she heard yelling and several shots fired. There was a great deal of shouting, and feet pounding on deck. Asher's shotgun lay on the shelf and she grabbed it, pulled it to her as adrenaline coursed through her body. She looked at the two steel chests lashed in the corner. "God help us," she thought. They've come for it after all."

Clutching the shotgun, she cracked the door into the passageway leading to the chart house. A man sprawled on the floor, feet over the steps, his toes curling, as someone kicked him savagely. A Mexican, in a short black jacket, had Asher by the hair, holding a pistol under his chin. Several others were shouting at once, demanding to know where the strongbox was. They would kill the man on the floor, they promised. Where are the chests? They yelled it, repeatedly.

Corazon eased the door shut. Here—they would come here next. She and everyone would be killed. By going up the stairway, she could do nothing but die. She must conceal herself and wait for her moment . Her eyes fell on the settee that covered the bathtub. In three steps she crossed the deck, threw the top up, and placing the shotgun in the tub, she climbed in after it. On her knees, she closed the cushioned lid. Bent forward, she could see through the one-inch finger hole. Trying to breathe evenly, she peered out, hands on the shotgun.

The cabin door splintered and burst inward, as Asher was thrown through it. He landed on his side and slid across the deck. The first man in shouted with glee, "aqui! *Es aqui,* 'here, its here'." Four more crowded into the cabin, and one began to hammer at the latch with his pistol butt.

Corazon shuddered; clutching the shotgun, her finger had found the trigger. She remembered Orlando Valle's wife had been behind armed men with a gun. In that instant, she had possessed neither the heart nor the courage to save her loved ones. Madeline Valle, gun in hand had trembled, hesitated and lost all.

A voice in the cabin hissed, "Kill him; kill them all."

Corazon straightened, lifting the seat with her head and shoulders, and heard a click as the hammer as the pistol was cocked. The pump shotgun was at her waist, and she pulled the trigger. The twelve-gauge bucked, almost enough to tear away from her. The pistol and parts of the man's hand flew against the locker. She pumped the lever and fired again, fired into the astonished men clustered before the strong box, and again at a man's back going through the door. A pistol flashed in front of her, as she fired toward it. The breath flew from her lungs, and she fell sideways. The lid slammed down on her head. There were other shots then, furious shouting and running feet. She heard Orlando Valle cursing and a croaking in her own throat as she tried to suck in a breath, and then blackness.

Pouring rain rinsed the blood from the *Miss Fay's* decks even before the bodies drifted clear of her. Twelve had come on a steam launch. Masked by the squall, they had closed the ship unseen, and by chance or by plan, they had boarded as the crew were engaged in shortening sail. The first warning was a thump, then the bullet that killed Urias Estefan. They took the stern then, and in that instant, half the crew. Four of the Fay's crew clutched pistols and hid in the dark, waiting their chance.

The eruption of gunfire below gave them that chance. Those that were able among the boarding party went over the side as lead flew in both directions. Seven of their number died aboard in the fighting, but they in turn wounded four of the schooner's people. Tom Grasse was hit in the side, MacArt in the calf, and the bos'n had part of his ear shot away. Valle,

321

he was creased across his stomach.

Below, Goose mopped blood from the cabin deck, while Asher sat on the settee, cradling his wife. Corazon shivered, feeling the need to vomit. She wished to scream and to crawl into her bed, pulling the covers over her head. Now that it was over, she was in horror of what had almost happened, and of what she had done.

Valle held a three-inch chunk of porcelain-coated cast iron out to her as Asher dabbed at the cut on her scalp. "You should keep this for luck," he said. "Better to have your breath taken for a few moments than lose your life." He looked at the splintered wood. "You won't be able to put much water in your bath, of course." He said these things in an attempt to lighten the moment for her. A poor try at levity, but his best.

She sniffed, trying to smile, turned her face to Asher's chest and wept again, thinking, "My God, is the guilt this terrible for men when they kill, or are men different? Are they born to cruelty? Perhaps they harden themselves somehow."

When she looked again, Valle was gone as was Goose. Asher picked her up and placed her on their bed. He poured a brandy and made her drink. "Don't go," she begged as he moved toward the passageway.

He came back and kissed her forehead. "Only for a moment," he swore, and guilty to his core, returned to the deck.

Banks, standing at the starboard rail, nodded as Asher came on deck. He said, "How de Missus, Cop'n?"

"She'll be fine, Mr. Banks. How is everything here?"

"Doing fine now, just fine, but Grasse, he be down awhile. Dat bullet, it go in, it go out, but it not touch nothing but fat. He be fine," Banks assured. "Dat MacArt, he be needing off he leg for a bit. Dat Bos'n is some pissed. Lost a gold ring wit' a diamond dat was hung on he ear, you see. Estefan, he forward, wrapped in canvas."

"Service for him in the morning, and I'll be up to take MacArt's watch," Asher said. "Call me in three hours, before, if you need me."

Valle watched as Asher went below. Unbuttoning his bloody shirt, he crossed the deck, lit a cigar; he offered another to the mate.

Thank'ee Señor," Banks said taking it, biting, and spitting the end over the rail. As Valle struck a match, he cupped it to the cigar and puffed.

"How dat belly, there?" he said, indicating Valle's stomach.

"Burns like fire," Machado admitted, "but when you feel pain, you should rejoice for you are still alive. This is good," he chuckled. "The captain has gone back below?" he asked.

"I spect de Missus, she be a mite upset. He be looking to her."

"She is weak now Mister Banks. This is because she can now afford to be weak," Valle said. He drew on his cigar, its glow giving his lean scarred face a cruel cast. Blowing smoke, he said, "When it was required, she had the courage of the bravest man; and more, she had the intelligence to choose her moment." Valle breathed deeply, "A rare thing *señor*, rare among men, far more so among women. I know this to be true."

"Truth be sure," Banks said with resolution, and drew deeply on his own smoke.

"I would wonder," Valle, asked pensively, "Does our captain

knows what a rare prize he has? Few men know the value of the things they possess."

Banks moved to the rail, blew smoke while observing the luff of the main. He looked back to the Cuban lawyer. "Cop'n Asher, he ain't no fool, but den, like ya say, few men know just what dey got when it comes to dere woman. Dey just too close to see it, ya know."

****

Corazon fell into a torpid slumber; she quaked occasionally, and drew herself against her husband, as if to reassure some ragged part of her unconscious mind that he was with her. Sometime before the mid-watch, she awoke to an overpowering need. A lust that consumed her, and she passed it to him as she silently urged him to use her. Finally, that wild passion became a warmly serene sleep.

He brushed sweat, damp curls from Corazon's face. He watched her breathe, and in the dim light, watched the glitter of perspiration as her breasts rose and fell. "She is mine," he thought pulling the sheet up to cover her. After dressing, he stood beneath the skylight, unwilling to leave.

He had seen his death tonight. Not a foot from his forehead the finger had squeezed inexorably downward on the trigger of a pistol. An explosion swept both hand and gun away, and he was stunned that he was alive. He saw her after the second blast, firing toward the door as he, himself, scrambled for a pistol. A man bloodied and peppered with buckshot aimed at her from the floor, but Asher hadn't been able to bring his pistol around to fire in time. It seemed as if the Mexican's pistol and the twelve-gauge had erupted at

324

once. She had jerked back and collapsed with surprise.

Asher had shot a man and emptied his pistol into the bodies on the floor. It took an immense will to look beneath the lid, for in his heart, he assumed that she was dead. Yet she was alive! He had died twice in a space of four seconds, and though he did not show it, Asher Byran was shaken far worse than his wife. He feared her loss. She was a gift. He knew this beyond any reason. She was his because she chose to make the gift of herself. The only authority he had over Corazon was what she herself gave him, and he must take more care with her. If she insisted on sharing dangers, he must in the future avoid dangers. He would end his involvements in hazardous ventures. Corazon was a blessing beyond price, and he was resolved to remember.

Chapter 36

For general maintenance and bottom paint, the *Miss Fay Gibbes* went on a railway above Jacksonville. Again, Pappy MacArt was employed to oversee the work, and the crew were released for the haul out. For a two-week holiday, The Byrans took the Florida East Coast Express south, arriving in Miami in time for the Independence Day celebration. They spent the night at the Royal Palm, watching fireworks bursting over the bay and dancing in the ballroom.

Corazon, impatient to see the progress on her new house, woke Asher at dawn. She harried him mercilessly, until he agreed to dress and drive her to Coconut Grove. Paint fumes were strong as they approached, noticeable even before they reached the porch. To her delight, not only were the walls up, they had been plastered and the moldings were nailed in place. The house wasn't a mansion but it was roomy. Tiled in the Spanish style, it had three bedrooms on the second floor and a porch on three sides. The ground floor was over twice the size of the upper, and included a guest room and small study off the parlor. Corazon ran from room to room, describing ideas for decoration. Asher sat on a sawhorse at the base of the stairs where he could watch. She was a child delighted with a new dollhouse.

"We must have a name for it before we move in," she told him. For days afterward, he found lists of possibilities, but no name seemed to appeal to Corazon beyond a moment's consideration.

To Asher, the house did not seem grand enough to own a name. It was his intention to build Corazon a much finer home, although at one thousand eight hundred, this one was dear enough, and furnishings must increase this figure. When he did provide for her, the kind of place she had been born to, a place she could entertain and invite guests there with pride. The structure, he would someday build, would be a home that would outlive them, and be in time an anchor for their children.

Talking to Dick Talbot, he was surprised to see how fast the value of property was rising. The price of choice land was at times, hundreds of dollars an acre. Even marsh and mangrove was worth something. When he took Corazon sailing a few days later, he carried a map to look at property farther down the bay called Cuttler Ridge, but the insects were so thick they dare not go ashore. He bought the land anyway, fifty acres at four dollars an acre, feeling that if the value increased just a little, it was better than having the money lying in the bank.

The July heat was oppressive, and the insects insufferable -- they chose an early return to Charleston. Corazon arrived armed with a list, prepared and looking forward to the choosing of furniture. She was in possession eight hundred dollars, a coveted sum that she longed to exchange for beautiful things. By her second day, treasures began to pile up in Fay's coach house, but a telegraph from their Miami contractor put a sad face on the shopping. A hurricane, passing just to the south, had taken out windows and a striped off a part of the new house's roof.

"It is entirely unfair," she announced when Asher returned home. She thrust the offending telegram toward him and said, "According to this report the entire house is a sodden mess."

"I'll have the roof repaired and the walls plastered again," he said as he read the telegram.

"This will set back all my plans," she complained.

"When you choose to live along the great hurricane road, you're bound to be visited from time to time," he said as a wide grin spread over his face. "We'll rebuild."

An expression of absolute delight transformed Corazon's face. "That will be the name. Let Commodore Monroe have his *Barnacle*; the name of our home shall be *Hurricane Road*.

To raise her spirits, he suggested they go riding on Saturday and that they have a picnic. To his surprise, she insisted on going in a buggy instead of riding her mare. With a picnic basket behind the seat, they took the ferry across the Ashley River, and drove south along the old oak-draped roads toward Folly Island. On a low mound overlooking the water, they set out the picnic. Corazon had taught him to play dice and cribbage. He was teaching her chess. She had packed three kinds of pie for his sweet tooth, also ham and potato salad, wine and grapes. As Asher pondered his move, she cheated by feeding him grapes, and brushing against him in all the ways she had learned to be most effective.

"Do you really want to continue?" he finally asked, becoming just a little sour.

"U mm, yes," she said, sweeping the board, and pushing him off balance onto his back. She grinned, climbing over him on hands and knees, with a bit of wanton glee in her eyes giggling, "I do—really—wish to play."

To Asher's astonishment, she began unbuckling the front of his britches, and what she found sprang to life with amazing rapidity. He complained, prudishly looking out toward the road.

"Shush—be a good boy," she crooned, leaning forward to kiss him. "My sweet, you just lie still and relax. My darling," she breathed against his ear.

The skirt was pleated and spread out around her as she rocked back and with a little wiggle and adjustment, she slipped down on him in a moment of satisfied concentration.

"Ah, Jesus," Asher sighed. His eyes became wide for a moment. "Where's your pantaloons?" he blurted, both surprised and pleased.

"Didn't wear any," she admitted wickedly.

"You planned this!"

"U mm hmm," she admitted, beginning to move up and down in a leisurely manner.

"Hussy."

"And you love it, don't you," she said, squeezing him internally.

"Aahh yes," he moaned.

"This too," she said, changing pace and doing something entirely new.

He was able to stand it for only a few minutes before he rolled her over and exposed his bare butt. The horse saw it, birds saw it, critters saw it, but fortunately, no one passed on the road before she had finished her cries of passion, and Asher had buckled his pants back.

"Where did you learn that?" he whispered stroking her through the dress.

"I shouldn't tell."

"Oh! Come on," he urged twirling a strand of her hair, nuzzling her neck.

"Well, I've acquired this book, and—well, it was somewhat ambiguous on certain matters, so I inquired—discreetly of course, of an older, far more experienced woman."

"No!" Asher said, incredulous.

"Oh, yes," she giggled, "and there are some very interesting things I'd like to try when we get home." She whispered this while nibbling his ear in a way that suggested an enthusiastic interest in exploration.

He was speechless but his other hand went to her back and pulled her closer. She kissed him once lightly then again enticingly, pressing her parted lips to his.

"I have been advised all my life that proper ladies ought not to do this or that. Never admit to certain things, or submit to others, yet Ash, you men all seem to have a great deal of fun with the not-so-proper women who do." She blushed a little despite herself and said softly, "I want you to have whatever you desire, my darling and have it right at home."

Feverish minutes followed her speech, during which their kisses left little breath for conversation and then a long ride home. Monday morning Corazon rose early. She had Tess make up a large breakfast, and brought up to him in bed. There she sat, cross-legged, cutting and feeding him a bite at a time, while he held and sipped his coffee.

"What is it you want?" he finally asked with a sly grin. "Out with it, Cori me-love."

She leaned, placed the tray on the table, and sitting back on her heels, she said, "I'm hoping you'll forgive me for not sailing with you Friday. I plan to get the house ready."

"How long do you plan to be in Coconut Grove?" he asked, a little disappointed.

"I'd meant to tell you properly, darling, but—well—at least six months."

"Six what?" he sputtered. "How long does it take to move furniture?"

Corazon cocked her head. "You are so obtuse," she told him, hands on hips. "As long as men are getting what they want, well! You never notice a thing," she laughed. "Hasn't it struck you odd, my love, that there's been absolutely no interruption in your pleasures, none, not a day for more than two months?"

Asher's face held a dumb blank look, for he'd not quite gotten the hint.

She reached for his hand, and pulling it to her stomach, said, "I want your promise to be in port, at home for Christmas. I expect your first child will be born within a week or two of Christmas."

He pulled his hand back, overcome with the most unsettled feeling. Corazon's expression was that of the 'very pleased with herself sort' that came over her when she'd been very clever or gotten her way over someone's objections.

"Asher, you look so stunned. You did want children—didn't you?"

"Of course," he choked, "but you might have hinted a little first, you know, to get me past the shock. And do you think you should be alone down there?"

"I won't be alone," she explained. "Jenny's coming down to help me set up the house, and I will hire a maid. Aunt Fay will be there. She's promised to take the train down in October and stay during my confinement."

"What about a doctor?"

"Eleanor Simmons practices in the Grove, and Dr. Jackson in Miami. I'm healthy as can be, and none of the women of my family have had problems making babies," she declared.

"It sort of scares me," he said sheepishly.

She smiled, "Poor darling! It's a good thing I'm the one to have it, then, isn't it?"

"Cheeky, aren't we," he said grasping a handful of her gown.

"I am going to miss you, though," she said, and walking on her knees, came and slipped herself under his arm. "I can't imagine sleeping alone. You'll try to come home often," she sniffed.

"From everywhere I can catch a train," he promised. "Maybe I can even carry freight into Miami."

"U mm, nice," she sighed, and shifted, making herself more comfortable.

"I'll be back as often as possible," he joked, "before you're too large to get at."

"Humph," she grunted, refusing to rise to his baiting. "We'll just have to attack the problem from another angle," she suggested and pinched his nipple.

"Hey," Asher yelped and wrestled her hands to her sides.

"Beast!" she hissed.

"Yeah!" he bragged, parting her gown, and sticking a warm tongue in her navel. "Oh, God, Asher," she cried, thrashing, "Stop it, Ah, u mm, baby no—shussh, mm, oh! Oh God, that's—Ash, please—Asher, lock the door."

Chapter 37

Standing south at dawn on a brilliant blue sea, *Miss Fay*, appeared before the rising sun as three pale towers of white. Preceding the fresh east wind, which created them, came the long swells. Advancing like rows of hills, spaced two hundred yards apart, they marched ponderously westward. Upon their blue mass, the schooner lifted slowly, bodily along her length; was silhouetted against the hazy red sky, and dropped, hidden in the valleys between.

Gliding on still wings, birds out from San Salvador and Cat Island watched from above the mast. Crow Tibbs dumped the slops alee, and the birds came screaming down into the wake, diving, plunging for morsels as the ship sailed on and abandoned them to their salvage. A weak dawn squall intercepted the course and dissipated as it crossed the bow. It wet the sails and washed salt rime from the deck, leaving the ship sparkling as it reached southeast.

At the port rail, captain and mate stood side by side, each with his sextant, bringing down the sun. Asher checked his watch and went into the chart house where he compared it to the chronometer and wrote the time. They took the average of the angles and Asher quickly worked a problem for his line of position. The sun observed almost due east would provide a longitude. He carefully plotted the line, and ran up the pre-dawn latitude by Polaris for a running fix. He studied the chart and frowned, taped the barometer, and entered the time and position in the log.

"October twenty-fifth, 1899, 0730 + 5, Position, 24^0 30' N. 74^0 12' W. Wind North East, 14 knots, long swell and dropping glass, high haze."

He went out of the chart house. The mates and bos'n

standing in muted conversation, turned to face him. "Two hundred twenty miles to Banes, day and a half, but the glass is still dropping fast." Asher looked up at the high-altitude haze. Concern and indecision wrinkled his brow. "I'm not at all comfortable about getting down among the islands with a hurricane bearing down," he confided. "What do you think, Mr. Banks?"

"Ah spec you's right, Cop'n," Banks said gesturing to port. "Dese swells, de coming from de East and dis wind, she veering round east. Hurricane east dere someplace and she a Cape Verde storm by de size dose swells."

Asher nodded. "I'm thinking of putting about," he said. "Hell, no, I'm going to put about," he declared. "Hate to lose on our cargo rate, but — he didn't finish, instead he looked east again, grimaced and shook his head.

"Get no argument from me," Banks said palms up.

"Well, let's put her about then, run back north, get over the top of the Bahamas Bank and gain more sea room," he was decided now. "I'll take the watch once we're about. I'll want everything secured and I'll have that new lower topsail bent to the yard Mr. Banks. Have the bos'n lay out the storm try-sails."

"It be done, Cop'n. Think we get de main and mizzen topsails down also?" he asked.

"Yes! Get the main topsail off before we tack about, we'll let the mizzen topsail lay across the gaff peak halyards until we get to it. Call all hands."

Banks hurried forward. Asher sent below for the second mate, who appeared on deck, sleepy eyed, tucking his shirt with one hand, and carrying his shoes in the other.

"Mr. MacArt, we're putting about shortly," he informed. "Looks like weather. Soon as we're about, extra lashings on the yawl boat, and haul inboard on the longboat and gig. After that, get with Mr. Banks."

The crew was on deck now; Asher stepped to windward, to the helmsman he called, "Full and by," And the ship fell off three points, heeled another ten degrees and picked up speed.

From forward, Banks bawled, "Stand by for stays," and the crew moved to their stations, each knowing his place and the line to be handled.

Asher yelled, "Ready about," then to the helmsman, "Helm down."

"Aye! Hard alee, Cop'n," Chop answered and spun the wheel.

The schooner arched gracefully up into the eye of the wind. The fore topsails rippled, luffed and thumped aback. The jibs collapsed and bellied against the stays. Starboard sheets were cast off, jibs hauled to port.

Asher yelled above the rumble of thrashing canvas and banging tackle, "Fore yards, let go and haul."

Five men hauled at the braces, and the foretopsail yards began to pivot about the mast; the topsails bucked filled, they bellied tight, and with the command of, "Full and bye," the *Miss Fay* fell off. Beam to the wind, she heeled, gaining speed.

"Bring her up three points, Chop. See if she draws at ten degrees."

"Ten-degree, aye, Cop'n," the helmsman answered.

The bow crept up into the wind two points then three to, ten degrees. The luffs shivered and held; Banks adjusted a sheet here and there.

"She holds ten, Cop'n."

Asher waved forward and Banks cried, "Belay all, boys."

Asher gazed toward the east. Faint below the rising sun,

great humps of cumulonimbus spread out beyond the horizon. "A hard gamble," he thought, running north on the track of a hurricane, possibly running into the dangerous quadrant. However, the Bahamas lay to the west and south, and there resided only the low islands, reefs and the narrow passes. The storm approached from the east. He must run north, gaining sea room, and hope to be clear of the worst. If the worst came, they must trust to the ship, and to providence.

He hated losing time, for on this cargo, a higher rate was paid for a rapid delivery. On the average, though, he had no room for complaint. Since July, he had full cargoes and better-than-average weather. He had arrived in Matanzas in August to find a hurricane had passed south of the island, and in September, three storms had struck the mainland behind him. The *Miss Fay Gibbs* had happily been elsewhere in every case. Now, near the end of hurricane season, their luck seemed to have run out.

Asher logged the course change and its reason. He went to the windward rail and looked up into the rigging. She was going well, breeze up to about seventeen knots, and stiff, with a cargo of steel rails for the new railroad lines under construction in Cuba. His mind drifted to home. He'd been to the Grove only three weeks past. A yellow fever epidemic in Miami had kept Corazon in Charleston until mid-September. Considering she'd only three weeks to put the place in order, Hurricane Road looked wonderful. She now had men carting coral rock from where they blasted the new channel, to build walls and a walkway around her flower garden.

Corazon bulged out a bit in front now, and seemed uncommonly proud of it. If anything, his wife had become increasingly lusty in her pregnant state, something that went in the face of everything Asher had heard about women in the family way. Not to say he minded, only that he was a little surprised.

Building was booming in Miami and he was considering purchasing a small steam tug. He'd saw it in Jacksonville, along with a couple of barges. The idea of a lightering contract, and hauling building materials seemed profitable. He was doing well but there were many opportunities, and he knew it was possible to do better. He might even spend more time at home. He missed having his wife aboard—her favors certainly, but more importantly, her companionship.

About 8:00 a.m., with the mizzen topsail sent down and a single reef taken in the mizzen, Banks reported all secure. The wind was up to twenty-five, and the schooner was making a good twelve knots. Asher turned the watch over and went below to sleep.

"Cop'n! Cop'n!" Bodden called, thumping on the door.

"Yes," he croaked, drunk with sleep. What time? Where? A storm, he remembered.

"De mate, he says come see, Cop'n. De weather, she is picking up."

"Coming," he said and heaved himself out of his bunk.

He glanced at his watch, forty past noon, five hours when he'd only intended to sleep a couple. He hurried on deck looking up through the rigging. The sky was overcast, low racing clouds, and behind them blackness. A squall was passing a mile astern. Another showed to windward. *Miss Fay* was double-reefed, reaching now as the wind had veered to the east. Asher approached the mate, leaning toward the pressure of the wet wind.

"Logging thirteen knots, Captain," Gibbon MacArt reported through cupped hands, "but these swells are starting to crest and winds increased more than ten knots in the last thirty minutes."

Asher nodded, looked aloft and said, "Get the upper topsail in, the jibs next. After that I'll want to rig storm the trysails and manropes. Call out the watch below. I want it done quickly while we have it easy."

The wind had begun to drive a heavy chop over the swells, battering the ship with regular thumps and bangs. The men had to shout over the wind, "Let go, clew up," the Bos'n howled. "Lay on, lay on." The upper topsail yard lowered, pulleys squealing, sinking down to the top as six men laid out on the yard, to fist and furl the sail. It whipped and bellied out between the bunt-lines like a row of fat buttocks. They heaved and fisted, dragged it in, passed the gasket man to man, and wrapped it tight. They laid into the mast, getting down to the deck with relief.

Two men, sent onto the bowsprit, gathered the jib into its own belly as it lowered away. They furled and frapped it to the stay, and lashed it again with a series of half hitches. The second jib, they secured in the same manner, while the mizzen was lowered and fought into submission by Mr. MacArt and five men. The mizzen storm trysail was set, and the crew moved to the main as the wind rose through forty knots or better. Between intermittent squalls, a clear patch of sky showed. Seas building atop the long swells began to board *Miss Fay*, and water streamed across her waist. The crew managed the fore trysail with difficulty.

The bos'n yelled, "Come on, run it up now. Way ho—way ho—way ho," they chanted as they heaved it board hard across the wind. "Belay there and coil down," he bellowed, finally satisfied.

"Bos'n," Gib called over the wind, "Lay the watch below, and sound the bilges. I'm going aft to report."

In the lee of the cookhouse, the men gathered. The cook was dishing out food: tins of beans and rice, ham, hard bread and coffee. They sat braced and squatting, eating quickly, leaning over the food. A sea slammed against the bow, burst upward, with spray driven across the deck in a heavy horizontal sheet, as the cook sliced ham.

"Dat what I call a cook."

"Crow?"

"Ship jumping all round," Grasse said, "still got good food."

"Cap'n knows, can't keep no steady crew, ain't got no good cook. Man got to know his job, got to do his job."

Men grunt in affirmation, some go back for more. A squall bore down on *Miss Fay*, with blinding rain and sixty-knot gusts that staggered the ship. The boatswain, Swallow, dragged himself into shelter and demanded his food. As the off watch filtered into the foc'sle, Swallow ate in silence, drank his coffee and glowered into the dark chaos.

MacArt reported, "Four inches in the well, Cap'n." Leaning close and speaking loudly, "Staying dry and all buckled down."

He nodded, "Good, that's good! Lay below Gib. Mr. Banks will be back up shortly."

The cook, Crow was weaving his way aft with the captain's food; Tom Grasse, holding to the manrope, assisted him with a grip of his belt. A cross-sea put three feet of water on deck, wetting them to the waist. As it receded, Crow pulled himself up the quarterdeck stairs, and with a look of triumph, presented Asher with his dinner. Banks arrived in oilskins and took the watch, while Grasse relieved Bodden on the wheel.

Asher ate in the chart house, slipped his dishes into a net. He took his dividers and walked off his estimated course and run, estimating their position to be near, 26^0 30' N. Latitude - 74^0 00' W. Longitude. That was a hundred eighty miles east of the Abacos and the Little Bahamas Bank. He had his sea room now. Forty more miles and he'd be north of the Bahamas. The wave crests were rising to twenty-five feet and the schooner lay over, laboring, as he stepped out of the house.

He yelled with cupped hands, "Mr. Banks, put the wind a

point aft the beam. Let's run off a little for more speed."

"Cop'n, she like to take charge of de helm. She will broach and sheer up to de wind if she got too much way on. Happen with dis kinda sea on de quarter — Ah see it happen more than once."

"Need the speed, need to try for more northing," Asher argued stubbornly. "Just watch her close and we'll hold her up if she gets unmanageable."

"You de Cop'n," Banks grumbled, for he'd had her heel over on him and sheer madly up into the wind. Twice it had happened when old Enriquez had owned her out of Roatan. She buried the foc'sle four feet under and flooded the entire waist to the caps. Well, it took seeing to believe, Tros Banks guessed.

Off two points, the *Fay* increased her speed by half, but now Grasse grappled with the wheel, which kicked, jolted and tried to tear the spokes out of his hands. Banks yelled forward where the watch huddled in the lee of the cook shack, "Another man to the wheel." Wallace hurried aft, sheltering behind the mainmast for a moment when the seas burst against the starboard side, then dashed for the quarterdeck stairs. He tied the safety line about his middle, and stepped to the lee side of the wheel, bracing himself and catching a spoke. Together they held her, though at times she raced angling down the face of a sea, until like a hard-mouthed mare, she took the bit in her teeth and charged three points to windward with the helm hard alee.

Past nine, a strong squall howled down on them, blasting the *Fay*. She staggered, heeling fifty degrees and slid alee, burying her port rail and twelve feet of deck. Banks grasped the binnacle as his feet went out from under him; the wheel spun right, lifting Wallace from his feet and slamming him down on Grasse, who had the spokes torn from his hands. Asher grasped a turnbuckle of the starboard mizzen shrouds and his feet swung clear of the deck. Up the bow came, into the wind she soared, high on a towering crest she hung, poised, then plummeted down, sticking her bows under the next short steep sea. The forestaysail went to ribbons, riven by weight of wind and water, its pieces flying downwind like frightened birds. Slowly the schooner leveled, water pouring from her sides. Wallace hung to lee of the wheel, doubled by his line. Grasse, bloody-faced, grunted, fighting the wheel back alee. Asher stepped over Wallace and threw his strength into the battle and slowly the bow fell off a bit.

"Dat's what I saying, Cop'n," Banks yelled. "She gets to going, den she runs right up to de sea, and pitch she bows under. Be best to hold her close hauled on a starboard tack, slow and slipping off to lee, wit' her nose in de wind."

Convinced, Asher nodded . "Get two more men for the wheel," he shouted over the winds rush. "We're going to go watch on watch, four hours, and get the fore storm trysail in. We'll see if she likes this angle."

Wallace was on his hands and knees, blood dripping from his nose. Asher grabbed him under the arm and hauled him up to the wheel. He grinned red and grasped the spokes again. Goose and Smithe, trying to frap the fore trysail, were being bucked nearly off the boom as the sail was slacked off. The block and halyard blew to lee, throwing sparks where it ricocheted off the rigging.

The wind had become a solid drone, and the men had sunk to hand signals and mouthing to communicate. The relieving watch stumbled out of the foc'sle. The wind buffeted them, propelled them toward the lee bulwark before they grasped the power at hand. Bos'n Swallow took Bodden by the shoulder; he pointed to Chop Davis, and gestured aft. As Banks sounded the well, the battered Wallace and Grasse, now relieved of the wheel, passed him. There were eighteen inches in the well, and he ordered two men put on the pump at the base of the mainmast. He dragged himself wearily up into the quarterdeck.

MacArt, swathed in oilskins stepped on deck and as he moved from the shelter of the house, was blown, sliding, to the mizzen shrouds.

"God Jesus," MacArt swore, his words blown away. He hauled himself back into the lee of the chart house where Banks gave him a brief summary of the ship's condition.

Banks, having been relieved, clutched a manrope, and hand over hand pulled himself past the helm to where the captain stood at the wheel box. He reported eighteen inches in the well and being pumped. It was a little wild on the foc'sle deck; to bend a new stay-sail that is, but Banks said it could be done if the captain wished. Asher thanked him, told him to get some rest if he could.

The *Miss Fay's* bow fell off a wave, and she was boarded by a cross sea. It just rose up and surged over her lee rail with no real force, submerging the men at the pump to their armpits. The others piled up onto the fife rail and main boom. The bows lifted slowly and water rushed aft and back over the port rail like a flood over a spillway.

"Blowing worse before," Crab Sanchez puffed, "and by Jesus, was not less than seventy knots, de last squall. Blowed de hair out of me head, it did."

"Hope we got plenty of sea room," Green Billy said. "In a press of wind like this—ain't no way for a ship to work to weather. Her heads up; she's up, but we just slipping off to lee. Ain't no kinda weather to have white water to lee."

"Get light tomorrow," Bodden said. "We see better; we fall off, and sail out of this some, man. Can't see to do much in de night; take you's beating in de night, but even if de weather be just as bad in de day, least you can see, and dat put you high in the mind, you know!"

341

"You boys got breath to yap—spell me—on this her pump," the carpenter gasped.

Green Billy swung down off the boom, and eased into the rhythm of the handle, pumping with Sanchez in short, jerking strokes. The flywheel spun, spinning the impeller far below, driving the water up the casing and ejecting it from the spout. The wind caught the gushing stream, carrying it to leeward with hardly a drop touching the deck. The carpenter, still breathless, sounded the well.

"Ten inches boys keep her spinnin'."

"Steamship have steam pump, more easy," Sanchez complained.

"Ain't no steamship," Bodden said.

Near midnight, a squall came out of the gloom; it bore down on the ship like a gray curtain, and slammed her, as a thirty-foot comber collapsed over the starboard bow. She took a sidewards lurch and heeled with full decks. The full blasts of the squall roared down, pressing her to port; the main storm trysail exploded into threads, leaving only the clews and bolt-ropes streaming in the wind. Another sea took her and the port shrouds' turnbuckles disappeared below the sea. Green water rose past the hatch coamings to the fife rail. The foresail yard nearly touched the sea, and the boatswain standing on the side of the chart house bellowed.

"She flounders, Cop'n; should we cut de mast?"

Asher stood on the side of the wheel box looking forward. The cookhouse, torn from its foundation, drifted mostly submerged, fifty feet to lee. Shapes, whose he couldn't say, crawled up toward the foc'sle ladder, hoisting themselves on cleats and deck rings. Two men had reached the weather shrouds, and lay on them pinned by the wind; others huddled against the capstan and samson posts. One waved aft. Grasse dragged himself up onto the poop, and sat gasping on the side of the house next to the boatswain. All eyes looked aft toward Asher, waiting for a saving command that would deliver them. A true understanding of what a captain must be chilled his soul.

"Cut away, Cop'n," the Boatswain entreated.

Asher looked alee, looked at the masts stretching out into the rain; masts inclined more toward the horizon than the sky.

"No," he shouted, thinking she must be brought around. "Get the mizzen trysail off her; see if she'll fall off."

MacArt hauled himself onto the side of the skylight, and jumped, landing across the boom. "Come on," he called, motioning to Grasse. Challenged, the seaman leaped out onto the mass of the furled boom and gaff at the mast.

Asher motioned to the boatswain, "Slack off the halyard."

The peak flew outward, the block and shackle whipping madly, sparks and splinters flying, as the gear began to beat itself to pieces. Legs wrapped, gripping the boom, the two men fought the heavy canvas. Swallow, a line in his teeth, scrambled out joining them, lashing the sail a few feet at a time. A great sea struck and the yard touched the water. Every man grew still, waiting for the *Fay Gibbes* to roll her masts under, but she rose back. Again, the blast caught her, holding her pinned between wind and wave. Another sea struck and exploded like surf against a cliff.

"Gotta cut de mast, Cop'n," the boatswain beseeched again.

"Not yet," Asher yelled. "Cut away the lashings on the number two jib. More pressure forward to bring her round. The wind will almost blow the sail up the stay. Haul in on the weather sheet first and hoist her up in a hurry."

Asher knew he had ordered a desperate thing.

The boatswain looked forward at the deck that was inclined more than a steep roof, like a waterfall as seas broke aboard.

343

With a reluctant sigh of courage, he turned to Asher. "Ah give it mah best, Cop'n."

They watched Swallow disappear over the break, reappear crawling along the side of the hatch coaming. He hung from the manropes, moving hand over hand, gaining the main. They lost him in a great rush of water, again in the spray, and saw him finally at the edge of the fore hatch, climbing up to the foc'sle deck. He lay for a moment, exhausted, he waved and soon men could be made out moving about the foc'sle deck. One crawled outward, embracing the bowsprit, inching toward the jib boom.

Asher looked out at the mizzen topmast and called, "MacArt," He pointed at the shrouds shouting, "Cut away the topmast shrouds, cast off the flag and topsail halyards."

"Will she break sir?"

"If she doesn't, we must cut her at the cap. She should slip her collar if she goes, but if not, we must cut the mizzen top forestay when she swings into the main mast."

"Aye!" MacArt said.

He motioned to Smithe and spoke to him with cupped hand. Smithe hoisted the young mate down to the port gear locker. He removed a bolt cutter and hacksaw, and passed them up to Grasse. Smithe pulled the mate back up the steep deck.

"Cut 'em away boyo," MacArt shouted, pointing at the marline wrapped steel cables, and drawing a sheath knife, he went for the topsail halyards himself.

The two shrouds went, but the spar held. MacArt sighed, looked aloft and nodded at his shipmates. He began to climb. Grasse, ax slung at his back, followed the mate up and out over the sea toward the mizzen tops. Finally, in place, MacArt straddled the mast, one knee hooked round the topping lift block, and reached for the ax. Grasse passed it and anchored

344

him against the wind. He swung. Once, twice, three cuts, and the spar splintered and fell away to the seas. It jerked around once, and the collar twisted and slipped from the spar.

On the bow, canvas was whipping. Asher shielded his eyes, staring. Four men on the foc'sle head heaved from sitting positions, and the inner fore topsail jib jerked up its stay. Slowly, imperceptibly the bow began to fall down wind. The port turnbuckles were visible for the first time in an hour, and the top of the gig's davits.

"Mr. MacArt," Asher bawled as the mate reached the deck, "stand by the braces as she falls off. Square the yard a little, and then to the pumps, we must man the pumps."

The *Miss Fay* fell off slowly and began to move ahead. Smithe wove his way to the wheel when Asher called for him to attend the helm. The cap of the bulwark showed, and the whole deck creamed white with swirls, and eddies as she began to drag herself forward, shedding the tons of dead weight. Another great sea reared up on the quarter, broke over the poop three feet, and submerged the waist, again sweeping the men who were clearing the braces from off their feet, and washing them forward to the foc'sle head.

"She's answering her helm," Smithe yelled.

"Put the wind a point aft the quarter," Asher hollered.

He was now convinced they would live to witness another dawn, as long as the foretopsail did not blow out. The boatswain and mate had the brace manned again. The yard swung twenty degrees and stayed. *Miss Fay Gibbes* wallowed as her decks cleared. A great wave, racing up, lifted her as she turned, and rising to a great height, she was propelled by it, thrust ahead, beginning to show a wake. Smithe struggled with the wheel and Asher backed him on the lee side, calling for another man to the helm.

When finally, MacArt came aft, he clung, arms hooked about the mizzen shrouds, he asked, "Anyone lost?"

"No sir, but fearsome battered about. The cooks with an arm broke; Mr. Banks, he's broken a leg, and all have been banged about some."

A sea humped up over the poop and swirled about their knees, cascading over the break.

And the ship?" Asher asked.

"Three feet in the well sir, four men pumping, rends in the deck where the cookhouse went, and the foc'sle she's a wreck. Hatches appear tight, God be praised."

Asher nodded. "We've been lucky," he said. "But it takes good men to do what needs done, all good men. Now we must hold what we've won. Bend on a new fore stay-sail, and everyone takes his turn at the pumps. Get Mr. Banks aft when you can so we can splint him properly."

Asher stepped to the wheel box and tied on a safety line. He watched another towering crest advancing, half as high as the mizzen top, it loomed up, threatened and collapsed short of the counter. Foam and spray burst around and over the poop and blew forward.

Through black night and white froth, the ship ran ragged, fleeing blind before the elements. It seemed an endless time of pumping and patching, eyes drawn to the two pieces of rigid canvas forward. Again, the wheel was relieved, and again the pump and Asher felt some of the tension going from his body. A band of squalls came an hour after dawn, blowing with a vibration beyond sound, gusts that pinned the helmsman to the wheel and made raindrops strike like bullets. It created vacuums that hurt their ears, and sucked the breath from them. The jib went to ribbons, and the ribbons to threads. Asher could have cried for the ship and its crew, as

346

they were swept, over and over by the endless westward marching gray beards.

The wind did not relent noticeably by force, but by tone. It was less when they could hear one another, and when it ceased to be milky blown froth, becoming water that could be seen. The great waves again stepped in ordered rows, rather than chaotic, leaping cross-seas. The wind had veered southeast, and the *Miss Fay* ran dead before it with her decks nearly clear of water.

On the second day, Asher got his longitude at dawn and had a running fix by noon. The *Miss Fay Gibbes* now carried sail on all masts, though it was double reefed, for she was so strained, her pumps could barely stem the flow. In 36 hours, they had gained only six inches. Three hours past noon, the schooner hove to off May Port, flying signals for a tug. Seven days and they were returned to where they'd begun, only badly mauled. Asher looked shoreward at the smoke of an approaching tug. From forward came the ceaseless rattle of the pump. "Life is hard," he thought.

Chapter 38

A steam pump took the place of men that night, and most of the ship's crew embarked on a drunken binge somewhere off Main Street. *Miss Fay* discharged her cargo. It passed into another ship and she towed directly to the shipyard where the surveyor crawled through her, deck to keel. What he found caused him to order the schooner onto yard railway for fear she would sink at the dock.

Asher read his report the following day. Strained and racked, estimated over forty percent of her tunnels sheered, knees split, and beams sagging. Foremast and bowsprit sprung. Repaired, she might find use as a barge, little more. Short of spending a fortune, the hull could not take the strain of sail. He ordered scanty repairs to her bottom and had her gear stripped. The *Fay* was abandoned on the mud flats off Green Cove Springs where he had bought her eleven months before. He presented a copy of the log, and the surveyor's report to the underwriter and paid off the crew.

With the broken-legged Banks in tow, he caught the train for Miami and home, and found his house full. It contained his wife of course, and her maid, and his Aunt Fay, and her maid Tess. Nothing, it seemed, melted away a mother's frigid displeasure with a daughter more than the imminent birth of a first grandchild. Isabel O'Ryan, in all her protective glory was also in residence.

Finding his home crammed with female relatives did not influence Asher's intention to provide a place for Tros Banks to recover. He hired a carpenter to knock together a room, a sort of cottage lean-to off the carriage house. Before long, he found himself in the backyard more than in the house. He and Tros spoke for hours, sometimes sat silent over a game of checkers or dominoes. Shrill female voices carried out to them, on occasion perfectly clear. Often one voice overlaying the other in passionate disagreement or laughter. Isabel's strident voice often made Asher wince. When Asher made a wry face, Tros Banks shrugged his shoulders; after a moment, he smiled laughingly across at Asher.

"You's marries ah woman, you's marry her mama. Dat is de law of human kind. One day de other daughter, she gone to have a child, then mama she go." Banks raised his eyelids knowingly. He said, "Gots to have patience; gots to have things to be busy with. Women, they makes a man crazy otherwise."

"Yeah," Asher agreed. "Seems, I'm fondly received but not much needed."

"You have done de deed, ha, ha! Now de time for other things," Banks smirked and moved a pawn. "Sides, a woman—she ain't de same with her man, not when her mama round."

"Is that so?" Asher mumbled. Dejected he took the pawn.

"Dat de fact, I sposed you see it by now, Cop'n. Checkmate!"

Asher had nothing to say on the subject. He had come home, perhaps expecting a certain amount of special attention. He would not call it pity; actually, heartfelt concern might be a more apt term. The near-destruction of his ship and crew had discouraged him. Perhaps better to say the near destruction of his crew. For most useful purposes, the storm destroyed the *Miss Fay Gibbes*, and he was unsure of what the underwriters would pay. He paid the stevedoring costs to transfer the cargo to another ship, and the cost of the marine railway. He should be thankful, he supposed. He had, after all, paid for his home and now had more money than he'd begun with. However, he'd worked hard and taken great risks in the past twelve months, only to see his profits battered into junk by a single hurricane.

It was both pleasing and infuriating that his wife should have such confidence in him; that she should be so sure of his ability to overcome adversity, as to give it no thought. Asher found himself in a situation impossible to complain of. He wanted to commune with her and discuss ideas for the future, but her entire focus was on the baby she would bear. It was only natural, Asher assumed. Again, he could not complain, nevertheless, he did feel as if the ground beneath his feet was unstable.

"Banks is a wise old dog," Asher thought. "At least I can talk with him."

By the first week of December, Asher made a decision to purchase the *Bull*, a steam tug he'd looked at in September. It would cost him a third his capital, but he figured on working it around Miami and the upper Keys. Banks convinced him with the suggestion that it was suitable for salvage along the Florida Reefs. He found a pair of scows for sale cheap, and with them in tow; he departed for Biscayne Bay a week before Christmas. The two-day trip took six, and would have taken longer if they hadn't carried sail. At times, the tug broke down hourly. Twice they'd been forced to anchor and pull for shore in a small boat in order to secure parts for the repairs. The only redeeming quality was, the *Bull*, powered with a steam engine of the railroad type and pressured by a marine boiler, was easy to fix.

They limped in the day before Christmas and tied off to a wharf at the mouth of the Miami River. Asher abandoned the *Bull* and her disheartened chief, to a leaking stern gland, and a steam reciprocation pump that dare not be stopped. He'd barely made it home for his first Christmas.

Corazon ran to him, awkwardly. She kissed him with warm affection, if not passion, and holding him by both hands, led him to the tree. She bubbled with a pride in their home and a tenderness that went straight to his heart. She was relieved, delighted. "Where had he been? Had he been wrecked again? He could not imagine how pleased she was that he'd kept his promise . Oh, and come taste the Christmas cake she'd made—how wonderful, he was home—she hadn't slept for missing him—and the baby's moving—Asher! Feel him kick!"

"I missed you, too," he whispered, "and you are beautiful, darling, and big, big."

She was, too. She had a blooming glow. Astounded by the

size of her belly, Asher could not help comparing it to the rest of his slender wife. It was huge. Her hair was done up under a scarf, but some had escaped, and those vagrant wisps pleased him. It particularly pleased him when she absently blew one of the dangling curls away from her nose. By the Christmas tree, he took her in his arms, sideways, and began to kiss her, but she pushed him away, lightly turning.

His mother-in-law had walked in. Conversation immediately switched to Spanish, and what attention Asher received amounted to hand-holding. He poured himself a drink, then another. Fay entered, gave him a hug; Mrs. Simons dropped by and the women promptly forgot him. He went out the kitchen door, intending to visit Tros Banks. From the sounds, as he approached the room, obviously Banks was engaging with a more welcome visitor. Asher returned to the parlor, sat in the corner and pouted. He sipped his drink and glowered. "Merry Christmas," he mumbled to his wife's cat.

With repairs, and the condensers cored the tugs steam engine ran well, and she stayed busy into the New Year. Asher had several small jobs hauling building materials in the bay, difficult due to the shallow water, but lucrative. He towed a load of shell into the river three days into the new year. Afterward, he took a nap. He woke with Bodden shaking his foot.

"Cop'n Asher! Wake, Cop'n!"

"What now?" he complained.

Bodden was big-eyed. "You's to come home," he blurted excitedly, "de missus, she is having de baby. She having it Cop'n, she having it dis very minute."

Bodden's message had his attention. On a borrowed horse, he galloped for the Grove, covering the six miles in a jiffy. He hurried into his house, only to be stopped at the stairs, and told to wait in the parlor. Women hurried back and forth, fetching; Fay smiled at him as she went past, but mostly, they ignored him. He stood and sat several times, and found himself twirling the hair on top of his head, a nervous habit he had been broken of at the age of ten.

Doctor Jackson came down a little after, and told him all was well, and that his wife had been in labor for five hours. Six to eight was about average for a first baby and he should not be concerned. Asher kept wincing and looking up at the ceiling. There was a great deal of noise coming from upstairs, mostly from Corazon, and it did not sound to Asher that things were going well at all. During the next hour, she shouted out words that he had no idea she was acquainted. His nerves jangled, and he went to sit on the porch. Sometime after dark, he fell asleep. When Tess woke him, it was past nine.

"It's a boy," she said.

Asher jumped up, with every intention of rushing the stairs.

"Sir! Captain Byran, sir!" she said, grasping his coattail, "Dr. Jackson said he'd be a few minutes yet. He'll be down, sir."

He waited by the stairs tapping his fingers on the banister post. He fidgeted, scratched, he paced. When the young doctor appeared, descending the stairs with his bag, he calmed himself.

"She's well?" he asked worriedly.

"Yes! She's well but very tired. First births take longer generally, but this was a breech birth and a big baby," said Jackson, smiling wanly. "It's not at all uncommon. I regret having to say she's had a very hard time."

"Is there anything I can arrange?"

"No," said Jackson. "I've given her some laudanum, and she will sleep very soundly. She'll be in bed for several days, and I'll return to attend her." He chuckled, "There are certainly enough women here to look after things. Your wife is in good hands Captain Byran. Relax! Congratulations on a fine strong son."

Asher nodded. He shook the doctor's hand and hurried upstairs, almost sneaking into the room. Fay and Isabel were fussing over the baby; Tess was bundling some soiled linen. She was exhausted, indeed limp on her bed. Face pale and hair matted and wild, Corazon lay seeming barely to breathe. It was not pain he read on her face, but wear, a fatigue so profound that it had wiped away all feeling. Asher sat next to the bed and reached for a limp hand. Her eyes followed him, but she had neither the will nor the energy remaining in her to speak or turn her head. He leaned close and kissed her forehead.

"I love you," he murmured.

The slightest flicker of a smile showed at the corner of her mouth, and then her eyes closed.

"What are you doing here?" his mother-in-law asked, in a tone that was appropriate on discovering a base burglar. Quietly, but with a stern indignation, she hissed, "Out! She must rest!"

Frowning darkly, Asher put a finger to his lips and turned away, ignoring her. Isabel fumed silently for some time. Fay whispered to her diplomatically, and they let him be. During the next days, Asher left Corazon' side only when the women attended her or when Dr. Jackson called. Soon, Isabel engaged a wet-nurse, and slowly, Corazon came back to herself. It was a week before they let her out of bed. As before, Asher found himself separated from the domestic activities of the house.

Tros Banks, now hobbling around with a cane, had taken to handling the tug while Asher was home with Corazon. Business had become brisk enough for the men to work opposite each other. Asher had just finished moving a small dredge owned by the railroad, when Banks came tearing up in a buggy, whooping and waving his hat. There was a ship on Triumph Reef.

With a barge in tow, it took five hours to reach the *Latti Bloom,* but they beat both the Key West and Bahamian wreckers by half a day. The ship had misjudged her set, and struck during a squall. Though she had not bilged, she was stuck fast. Banks, an old hand at this, advised Asher of the proper wording of the salvage agreement with her master. Before dusk the barge had been warped into the shallow water alongside, and the *Bull* had two of the *Latti Blooms* anchors set in deep water. They were able to lighten the ship by two feet. At high tide the next day, she floated. The *Bull* escorted her to Key West, where they filed the papers and registered the wreck. The entire operation had taken only a week. The estimated salvage claim was over five thousand, and after the crew's shares and expenses, Asher hoped to clear over three thousand.

At home he suggested a party to celebrate, but was rapidly discouraged by his mother-in-law. Instead, he got drunk at the Peacock Inn, where talk of salvage led to treasure, and treasure to wrecks and maps of treasure wrecks. Jean d'Hedouville, who researched these things, seldom tired of speaking of them. Banks related he'd seen coin from the *Santisima de Leon* in the ragged Keys. That led to talk of the *Asotoca* off the Marquesas, and the entire treasure fleet, which had wrecked off the mouth of the Saint St. Lucie River. Treasure fever is something akin to malarial fever, in that once contracted, it returns throughout the life of the victim, striking when his resistance is down.

The salvage claim on the *Latte Bloom* settled in February, although no agreement had been determined with his underwriters on damages to the *Miss Fay.* His towing work had borne profit of over two hundred a week and Asher decided to search for a second shallow draft tug. He found a suitable vessel in the Cedar Keys, and bought it for five thousand dollars. The *Cyclops* was sixty feet by twenty, iron-hulled, and drew only five feet, so shallow that at high water she could navigate most parts of the bay or the Keys. Her engineer stayed with her, and Banks became her captain A crew of two stokers, a fireman, a cook and two deckhands were hired, and they brought her around with a coaling stop at Punta Rassa.

Asher arrived in Miami to find another tug at work. A competitor had brought a third tug into the bay and work for three became slow.

They had a party for Fay and on February 15, she returned to Charleston. Without her as a buffer, Asher found himself continuously at odds with his mother-in-law. Never approved of by Isabel and used to having his own way, had he fallen into a routine of petty warfare. Isabel was a woman accustomed to dominating a household, and for the present, Corazon seemed pleased with her mother's dominion. Asher discovered that trying to hold onto his money with Isabel O'Ryan administering the house was like clutching water. Never introduced to a need for thrift, Isabel had no reason to consider it. Asher, though not a cheapskate, found himself short of funds, and began to chafe at the waste of hard cash. All these matters came to a head at a time when business was at low ebb, and Asher had begun to feel the threat of failure.

Two weeks after Fay's departure, Isabel discovered Candice, her servant in the throes of passion with Tros Banks. After discharging the poor woman, she advised Banks that he was to be off the property by dark. This usurping of authority was a step too far in Asher's present state of mind.

She had told him of Banks' banishment in a moral fit of anger.

"How dare you bully my associates, order my guests to leave this house," Asher had growled, sounding far from civil. "It's not enough that you stick your over-sized nose where it's not wanted, and at all hours of the day, but now you overstep yourself completely."

"Guest!" she screamed. "You consider your nigger *secoundo* a guest! You bring him into this hovel, this hovel in which you force my daughter to reside, so that he might seduce my servant. You have no right to enjoy the company of gentle people," she hissed, now red-faced. "What she sees in you I will never understand."

"Madam," Asher said through clenched teeth, but with volume that could carry the length of a ship, "feel free to remove your fat ass from my hovel at your first convenience."

Anger so choked the woman, her lips flapped with hardly a sound emitted. Then she spat out a string of words, so venomously acid as to remove paint from the woodwork. Asher followed with a few choice words of his own, at which Isabel rounded up and vanished into her room, slamming the door. The voices, not at all faint, carried upstairs. Isabel's, not so well defined, overlaid by Asher's naval bellow. Most of what was clear came from Asher.

Putting Fred into his cradle, Corazon rushed downstairs in time to hear the last few of her husband's well-chosen adjectives concerning her mother, and to witness the slamming of Isabel's door.

"How could you!" she wailed, her lips beginning to tremble. Snatching the first thing her hand fell on, a bronze figurine, Corazon let fly catching her astonished husband squarely on the nose. "My mother, after all she's done these last months!"

A humidor came next and still blinded by the bronze, it caught him in the forehead. Somehow, her hand found the fireplace shovel, but Asher managed the front door before she hit him more than a half-dozen times. Numerous were the things uttered by Corazon during the assault. Other things she yelled after her husband, as he walked east toward the bay, words that were regrettable.

Afterward, as is often the case with overwrought women, angry with their husbands, Corazon had no complete idea what she said. Husbands, just as often, are unaware that the not remembered words are not really meant.

Chastened, feeling unworthy, and with a deep sense of failure, Asher arrived at the dock and ordered the *Bull* provisioned. On the following day, he ran away to sea.

Chapter 39

Light expanded above the eastern sea. The bow rose and fell, rolled, extending shadows with each lift. The anchor rode lifted, creaked and stretched as the water rushed off the banks and funneled, ripping through the cut. The tug, Bull, sat alone in the center of the cut, waiting for the current to slack. The cay was lonely and barren, an empty place on the earth. It owned only sand, rock, thorns, and cactus. Life was comprised of birds and small things that scurried just out of sight. The wind howled, mewed, wailed and moaned through and around the limestone bluffs, and sand invaded everything when it blew. Water Cay was marked as a place of duppies and restless spirits, an abandoned place avoided by sensible men. Asher's crew had found ballast rock, cannon, and several gold coins. They were no longer men with sense.

Between weather and current, not much was accomplished in the first month after they arrived. They did learn that nothing lay in the shallows around Water Cay, only in the depths. With this knowledge, Asher had steamed south to Cuba, where he re-supplied and bought a better diving suit and pump compressor. For a month, they worked the deeper water but the current was strong. So strong that an hour or two during each day's slacks was all, they dared. Additional time was lost when the seas were up, as they had been a few days earlier, for the *Bull* must shelter behind the island when waves went above five feet. At that time the longboat had sailed north to Long Island and the Clarence Town market in order to secure fresh produce.

Presently, the crew sat or squatted near the galley door, each with a mug of coffee at his feet, each scooping eggs and grits into his mouth. Asher stepped out of his cabin behind the pilothouse; the engineer pointed upward with his fork, and the cook hurried to fill another plate.

"Smell de food and de cop'n, he is waking right quick" Wallace said, grinning.

"He, he, wind, she blowing dat way. Ain't no mon gots to wake de Cop'n if he smells de rations"

"I heard that, Ben Bodden," Asher grumbled. He scratched and reached down off the bridge deck for his coffee. "At least I don't wake up when the first pot rattles in the galley," he countered and disappeared into the pilothouse.

"Got more dose eggs dere, Patsy?" Bodden asked, thrusting out his plate.

"You want more, you get you ass out dere on de Cay and do some egging," the cook said, dumping a glob of grits on the plate. "The last of dem was for the Cop'n."

"Listen to dat pink-eyed Jamaican instructing me what I must do to eat."

Wallace set down his plate, sipped his coffee. "Man can't cook what he ain't

got," he pointed out.

"Y'all boys skerd of going ashore. I recon I can come long, and protect y'all," Griggs teased. "Bring long my fly swatter,

358

take care those ghostees."

"You's take care de boiler, we take care de rations, old man," Bodden said, good-naturedly. "Got three hour yet fore de current slacks, get some eggs, some conch."

"See any crayfish, y'all be sure to grab them up now," the old engineer wheedled.

"We do dat; do dat sure, there, Griggs. Ain't gonna chew em for you now."

Griggs smiled a near toothless smile, and turned to blow his nose over the side as Bodden led Wallace and Goose into the skiff. Asher looked down as they piled in. Bodden smiled up. His broad face held a wide, open grin.

"Gonna do some egging, Cop'n. Dat and gather some conch," Bodden called.

"Be back before the slack," Asher said.

"Be here, Cop'n."

Goose set the rudder in just dandy, but as he stepped the mast, its sail bellied, wrapping around him, and the boat heeled against the tug, shipping water.

"Dom! Dat a poor job and I thinking you do better in dat, Goose—drown us all," Bodden chided. "Let go de line now, if you's can do dat and keep dry."

Wallace pushed off and they fell back with the current, until the wind caught the sail. The gaff-rigged skiff reached inshore on the sparkling green water, skimming the coral shelves, rising, falling on the swell. A quarter mile in, she doubled the point, and dropped Wallace in the shallows with a basket for eggs. Birds rose in waves, wheeled, alighted, and rose again, all screaming at the thief.

Sailing out onto the bank, Bodden tossed the twilly into a white sand hole, its coral shelf almost surrounding the boat. Taking a gig and sack from the bilge, he prepared to dive. Herons landed a hundred feet away, wading over the shallow coral as Goose furled the sail.

"Strange, dose birds out here. Where there be mangrove it likely you find them most. Not natural," Goose complained, hinting at the possibility of bad spirits.

"Ain't no duppies," Bodden said. Tired of his shipmate's superstitions, he dropped over the side.

Giving the heron a last hard look, Goose followed. He plunged deep to begin the hunt. They dove steadily, surfacing, and tossing conch into the skiff. Antenna protruded from holes in the coral, giving away the hiding places of crayfish. Using a pole with a barb, the men went after them. Bodden rolled a rock to expose a nest and something glittered through the cloud of coral marl. He broke the surface with a whoop.

"Gots another gold coin," he shouted triumphantly, waving it above his head. "Gots it right here."

The long boat, loaded with sweet potatoes, beans, pineapples, some mangoes and a hundred pounds of rice sailed in from Clarence Town, arriving no more than forty minutes after Bodden's discovery. Everyone was for diving in the hole. Despite their complaining, Asher put the crew to storing the fresh food and the preparations to dive the deep water.

Before noon, Airi was suited up and put over the side. He worked for over an hour in ten fathoms of water, until the flooding current made controlled moving near impossible. Looking up he signaled to start his assent. He found no sign of treasure, only clumps of coral rocks, and dangerous crevasses, leading down slope toward the abyss.

Five hours past noon, the current died the slack before the ebb. The Greek sat on his stool as they placed and locked his helmet. Wallace tapped the metal; Airi stood and clomped to the ladder. Two men began to pump and the Greek descended. Moments later, he was twelve fathoms down; a thin stream of bubbles trickled to the surface. He jerked the hose and line to him, as he moved across the bottom. Two men with a glass box watched him from the skiff. Forty minutes into the dive, twenty feet of hose went out suddenly, and Bodden belayed the line. Goose shouted from the boat; the early stages of the current had swept him into a crevasse.

Goose yelled from the skiff, rapidly pulling for the *Bull,* "He in a crevasse and de helmet jammed. Current taking de hose, it hold him in."

"Damn," Asher swore. He pulled twice at his chin, took a half step toward the side and turned back. "Anybody here can dive to eighty feet?"

"Been down sixty, Cop'n," Wallace offered.

"Ain't been down no thirteen fathom Cop'n Asher," Goose said, "I try it."

"Take a ballast bar, get the skiff over him but a tad up current, and let the iron carry you down fast, boys," Asher advised. "Go together and hope one of you makes it. Kick the helmet loose, but be careful of the glass."

They nodded and went into the skiff with Patsy at the oars. Two hundred feet and well up current of the bubbles, they jumped over and clung to the gunnels. The cook gave each a twenty-five-pound pig of iron, and they hung breathing deeply. At last they nodded to each other and let go, plummeting into the depths, each drawn downward by the pig of iron he grasped. It was a long two minutes.

Goose broke the surface first, with a long, harsh gasp. Wallace was ten seconds behind, and sixty feet down current. Patsy pulled for him and they lifted him aboard the skiff. His nose bled for a few moments, but he was smiling. Airi, hauled up in stages, came aboard Fifteen minutes later. "I quit," were his first two words. "Cigar," was his third.

They gathered around him, getting his suit off, everyone arguing with the stubborn Greek. Griggs took the hose loose from the compressor, coiled it, and hauled in the basket line. It was heavy.

"Gimme hand here, boys," he called to Patch and Rummy, his stokers.

They hoisted it, a mass of coral caught in the web. Patch yanked it clear, and started to roll it back over the rail.

"Wait!" the old man shouted, pushing him aside.

Griggs gave the coral a crack with a hammer and gold glittered. He hit it repeatedly and as it shattered, hundreds of gold coins revealed themselves to glitter in the sun.

"Where'd you get it?" Asher asked the Greek excitedly.

"I didn't," he said; "the basket went over the edge with the current; it caught. I slipped over trying to get it loose." He was smoking a cigar now, his hand shook. Blowing smoke, he added, "And it's deep. The edge of the world. Go off the edge of that, and I get the squeeze, and when you pull me up, you can just bury me in the helmet. All of me, pushed up in the helmet. Gold, she's no use to a dead man!"

The obvious danger sobered everyone, but the gold glittered as they separated it from the coral. It was right beneath their feet, wealth for the taking, but Aristotle was done with it.

Within the hour, low-racing clouds covered the setting sun, they swept out of the west with rain before the wind; the wind chilled, veered rapidly northeast. The sky went starry clear and it blew a gale. The *Bull* got steam up and slipped behind the island, nudging bottom a few times in the dark. They anchored her against the steep sand beach and waited the storm out. Three days it blew, sand and spray coming off and over the Cay. The wind moaned, calling to them from the rocks, and it made even Griggs nervous.

Asher chafed at the weather, at the delay. He cleaned and polished the coins, counted over two hundred. He twiddled his thumbs weighed and counted again. He had a small fortune. He knew he was close to a great fortune. The main mass of the wreck must have gone into the deep underwater valleys and crevasses. Enough gold to make a dozen fortunes. He wanted at least one fortune, and that fortune required only the courage and the will to harvest it. If Airi refused to dive, he would dive himself, how hard could it be?

He turned down the lamp and lay back on his bunk. Restless, he tried to sleep, but his mind moved from the gold to his family. He was a husband and father after all, with responsibilities. His mind was more on Corazon though, more so than on his son or the work at hand. She was a treasure of far greater value to him than what was below the reef. She was not a common girl. He felt himself compelled by that awareness to succeed. He was not stupid. He knew what the risk entailed, but it would be fast. To make that kind of money, by ordinary means, could take years. He gazed out over the reef, studied the breakers.

Perhaps slow and steady was preferable. He had considered returning home without the gold often enough. Hourly at times when things were difficult. However, he detested the thought of being branded a quitter on top of his other faults. He refused to admit to his fears.

When his wife drove him out of the house, she had named any number of his faults for him. Perhaps he was not a fit husband by the O'Ryan's measure. Perhaps he was not enough of a businessman to become a success by their standards; nevertheless, he hoped he was by Corazon's.

He was willing to accept that he had too much liking for low and common company, and that he searched out employment at what pleased him. It was conceivable that a few tons of gold would not hurt his standing with the O'Ryans, nor would it displease his wife. If wealth were required to gain respect, he would acquire wealth. He knew where to find it.

During the night, wind had gone east and dropped off some. The first useful slack water would be at late afternoon. He'd not be able to dive tomorrow, but he could set and buoy the anchors from the longboat. This would allow the tug to be on the spot at dawn. "I'll dive the day after tomorrow," he decided. Choices were what life was about. *"Don't weaken"* he told himself and repeated his mantra, "fear is beneath you. Life is hard."

Chapter 40

Through the day, clouds threatened rain, but at dusk, the sky over Charleston cleared to a soft blue, and the sunset was a hazy gold. Burdened as she was with the objects of her shopping trip, Corazon chose to walk back to her Aunt Fay's house. Her arms had ached; many of her muscles ached, but the walk had given her time to analyze her thoughts once more, and her behavior. Again, she considered the atmosphere of the last months, before Asher steamed out of Miami on the *Bull*.

Corazon put her packages on the bed, and walked lightly to the corner of the room. Fedrico Douglas Byran lay sleeping in his crib. Tess had just put him down after another day of wailing and spitting up. *"Better she than I,"* Corazon thought, and felt an immediate twinge of guilt. She had only Maude to help with the baby since her mother had left. Between the sleepless nights and Fred's constant demands for attention, she was worn to a frazzle.

She knew that society expected mothers to worship their babies, but children were not all that she wished for in life. That is, if maternal devotion meant never ending streams of soiled diapers and nights spent pacing. To see her firstborn lifted bloody from her body and laid across her breast, had at the time, seemed more a relief than a joy. Fourteen hours of wracking agony had left her too weak to hold him or even gaze at his furious little face. She tried to nurse him, but had been far too ill those first few days, and her breasts had somehow clogged. They had become so tender and inflamed that his lusty attempts to suckle had been a frustration to him and an excruciating ordeal for her. Mercifully, Fay had hired a wet nurse.

How horrid she had looked! Puffy and swollen, the tone gone from her body, her breasts so ponderous, she seemed off balance. It had been so confusing. She looked at her devastated body in the mirror one moment, fearful the sight of her would repulse her husband. The next moment, remembering the trials of childbirth, she was terrified at the thought of being put through it again. It had taken weeks for her depression and the odd lethargy to pass. It had been so easy to leave everything to her mother. The activity of the last month had made a vast difference. She had planted a garden, gone to town, and taken walks. She was going riding again. She began to look, and feel herself, and to want her husband.

Corazon bent down and brushed Freddie's head with her lips. He was bathed and clean, and smelled of powder and oil and that sweet mustiness only babies have. All things aside, he was hers, and she loved him desperately. He was beautiful, with his father's features and her blue-green eyes; a volume to his voice that was certainly Asher's, but he howled out with temper that was unfortunately her own.

She tiptoed out and carefully eased the door shut, selfish for an hour of peace, before he woke again. She heated milk for cocoa. Its aroma was as comforting as the drink itself, and sat with it by the fireplace in Fay's parlor. She remembered how Asher had kissed her on this couch a few nights before their wedding. She remembered what the thrill of those kisses, those first caresses, had been like, and wickedly admitted to herself that he could have had her right there on the sofa if he wished. The memory of it caused similar sensations to trickle through her body and she hugged herself.

"My God, what a fool I was," she told herself, or perhaps it's just something that a woman goes through after producing a child. Only in retrospect did she realize what had taken place. She had shut her husband out without thinking. Her mother had been a buffer. "Poor Asher," she thought, remembering only a few of the things she had yelled at him. It was only much later, after talking to Aunt Fay that Corazon first began to realize why her husband was so taken with making money. Asher was never truly affected by money; rather, it was the game more than the gain. Now he felt driven to provide her a style of living akin to what her father had provided. After the loss of the *Miss Fay,* he must have been uncertain of their future.

No small wonder her mother had set him off. Isabel had inadvertently found the chink in Asher's armor, and had sent her dart straight for it. Corazon could understand his being angry and stomping off for a few days, or even a week. She was ready to accept his getting drunk, or any of the ridiculous things' men did when their feelings or pride were injured. Asher had been gone nearly two months, though, and her pity and remorse were changing to anger.

She had sent her mother home a week after he left and waited. She had taken care of decisions with the towing business. She'd dealt with lawyers and settled his claim on the schooner, all the time dealing with her home, her baby and her loneliness. Through invoices, she discovered the purchase of diving suits and compressors. After the interrogation of friends and employees, she discovered the reason for the equipment, which was sunken treasure. Her husband had gone off to seek their fortune on a fool's treasure hunt. Enough was enough, Corazon had decided. Fay agreed to look after Freddie. Tomorrow Corazon intended to leave for the Islands. If her husband thought he could abandon this wife for months on end, she was about to prove him mistaken.

Her southbound steamer had arrived in Nassau thirty hours out of Savannah. Corazon, with the mail and other passengers, had been ferried ashore before lunch. Visiting the harbor-master's office, she learned it would be two days until the next scheduled mail boat for Georgetown, Exuma. An administrator with the ports colonial office was kind enough to recommend a hotel, where she had stayed the two days. Her accommodations were pleasant, and there were those among the many guests, who were good company. Under other circumstances, she could very well have enjoyed herself. However, having deserted her baby—even though Freddie was in the best of care, caused Corazon to suffer guilt of every sort. The more she worried about Freddie, the more impatient she became. Even though the mail boat was a nasty, smelly little schooner with box-like cabins, she boarded without hesitation.

The first port-of-call was Spanish Wells, and then on south to Governor's Harbor. The fare on board consisted of well spiced rice and peas, or rice and fish twice a day but with the luxury of coffee in the morning. This food was horrid and the boat packed with all description of cargo and livestock. In Governor's Harbor, Corazon purchased cheese, crackers, a ham and some wine to supplement her rations.

The schooner, *Ellie Blessing,* had no sooner cleared Cape Eleuthera than a norther struck, forcing her to seek shelter on the banks behind Allen's Cay. A banjo played, and some of the boys took to singing and stomping. Soon the crew and some of the passengers took to cards and drinking. As the boisterous group grew ever noisier and more pleased with their' diversions, Corazon latched her cabin door, and enduring the humid heat of the stuffy box, went to sleep with her pistol.

Quite late, she woke to a rasping noise, very close. The door was wiggling; she could see a crack of light expand and shrink as someone tried to jimmy and pry the lock. At many points in her life Corazon might have been frightened, but at this instant, she was merely irritated beyond words. She was sweaty hot, cramped, hungry, tired; she was guilty at having abandoned her baby, and she missed her husband. She brought up the pistol and fired through the deck over her head. The explosion in the confined space was deafening, and instantly followed by the panicked squealing of an unfortunate pig penned directly over her cabin. Shouts came from forward.

"No more playing about," she called; "the next bullet comes through the door, you dog. If you have rape in mind, you will have nothing to rape with when I'm done shooting, and I will aim low. Do you hear?"

"What the bloody hell," the Captain's voice shouted over the squeals of the dying pig. "Avery, you hound! I'll have you in irons."

"For mistaking my cabin door, Captain?" the guilty planter blustered.

"For attempting to enter a proper lady's cabin uninvited," Whippet growled. "Get forward and sleep on deck, you drunken fool."

Corazon heard murmurs and words spoken beyond hearing,

a scuffle then a knock on her door.

"You all right, ma'am?"

"I will be fine, Captain," Corazon said crossly, "if only you'll do something to quiet that unfortunate pig."

"Yes, um, and sorry for the trouble, ma'am. You'll not be bothered again."

"I should think not," she mumbled. Stuffing the pistol under her pillow with a sharp motion, she plopped down on the lumpy mattress.

Dawn arrived, bringing fluffy cream clouds and a brisk fair breeze. Underway with the first light, the mail boat made excellent speed, and hove too off the Bight at Cat Island that evening. The offensive Mr. Avery was put ashore with the mail, and the *Ellie Blessing* fell off for Georgetown, Great Exuma. The schooner raised Channel Cay at dawn, and berthed at the city wharf by mid-morning. The Captain, in a courteous attempt to make amends, saw to inquiries, and early on the following morning, an old man came up from Rollytown, asking after a Mrs. Byran at the George and Crown.

Stephen Rolly was a slender man in his early sixties, a former slave. His hair was near white, and his feet broad and gnarled. His face had a sweetness that Corazon warmed to immediately, and soft eyes gazed out from a mass of leathery wrinkles. They were on the veranda of the small Inn, and Corazon moved to the shade of a cassarina.

"Was telled you's want to hire a boat, Missy. I hass ah sloop south ah Rollytown," he announced softly. "Ain't but twenty-four foot, but she's ah goody. Take you's down to de Jumentos, right smart."

"How far to Water Cay, Mr. Rolly?" she asked, holding her hat from blowing.

"Bout thirty mile south, Missy," he said, gesturing with one hand. "Be 'bout six hour if de weather holds. Wind in de so-west, you's see, might get to blowing strong afore de night come."

"Would we reach the island this afternoon?" she asked excitedly, paying no attention to such abstract notions as weather.

"Yes'um! Take ah carriage down Rollytown, be going now, be there if de weather allows, for dark!"

"If you could arrange transport, I would be so grateful, Mr. Rolly." She smiled. "I'll get my things directly."

What he got was a donkey cart, and though she felt ridiculous, bouncing along trying to keep her hat from blowing away, she was far too excited to be concerned with appearances. Only six hours and she would be with Asher, and this entire miserable journey would have been worthwhile.

The sloop, named *Gull,* was an ordinary leg-a-mutton rigged Bahamas boat. She had a hold forward of a tiny cutty cabin, and a cockpit with benches aft. A young boy began to run up the sails as they approached.

"Dat my gran boy, Kip," Rolly said with a proud smile. "Be ah fine sailor mon one day."

A path of planks led out across the mangrove roots, and old Stephen took her bag and walked unconcerned out to the sloop, while she followed carefully after. The *Gull*, though simple, was clean and neat. The old man handed Corazon aboard, and put her bag in the little cabin. She unlaced her shoes, pulled them off wiggling her toes, and put the shoes in her bag. She squirmed out of a petticoat, and tied her dress up between her knees. Comfortable, she sat down out of the way of the sloop's tackle.

"Cast off ah here, boy," Rolly yelled, and reached for the sheets.

The bow spun round off the wind, the boom swung and the

sail snapped taut against the hoops. She heeled and water foamed at her bow. The *Gull* began to fly south. The water was amazingly shallow, only four feet for the first couple of miles, and then it became deeper, and filled with dark coral heads. Two hours and Exuma sank astern, first as a waving mirage, then gone; the horizons were empty. The old man cut a coconut, and gave it to her to drink. The boy slept on the fore hatch.

"Your grandson lives with you?" Corazon inquired.

"Oh yes, Missy, only us, you's know. He parents, they dead. He doddy lost right out there," Rolly, pointed to the empty horizon. "East Pear Cay! When de' *James Ware* lose her mast and strike de reef," he said nodding, as if affirming the truth of it. "He mama, she wake up and see Joe in she room. Joe, he talk to her, tell her where he lays out there on No Bush Cay— saying he want to be buried for to have peace. He not want he spirit to wander out dere on de empty Cays.

I be off at sea, and dat daughter mine, she took wild. Got some skiff and row those miles she self, for weren't no one dat want to go out there after what she tell. Five-day after, they finds my Melly dead from thirst, finds her down off Hog Cay, wit' Kip's doddy Joe. He dead body in de boat with her. She know ware find she mon, but don't got de strength bring him home." The old man smiled. "Dey both in Christian ground now. Dat Melly, she give she mon de peace he ask for. Dat grand boy mine, he have good parents, both them."

Corazon shivered, touched by the strangeness and the loyalty within the story. Could love reach beyond life? It was as if Kip's mother had traveled alone, into what for her was a sort of hell, to rescue her mate's spirit. That they conceived of the spirit to be of equal importance to the living being, it touched her. How often it was that one heard of such supposedly uncommon things, these bonds between men and women, soul mates, whose love went beyond the physical, beyond the normal.

She napped until spray wet her face, waking her. The setting sun was gone, and low black clouds raced over a sea, gray-green and white-streaked. The wind began to whine. The boy and his grandfather struggled to reef the mainsail, as the cast-off jib whipped madly. Two islands loomed, perhaps a mile off, steep and barren, with a small strip of sand on the near one's west side. The old man hauled the jib sheet, tucked the tiller up to his chin, and the boat shot for it, puffs of spray sweeping over her.

"Gonna beach de sloop, Missy, for this wind put she on some coral."

He laughed in the face of the elements, and the boy, hiking out on the windward rail, he laughed too. The sloop flew shoreward. Rain began to spatter and lightning fell with such frequency the clouds seemed to walk on electric legs. Sheeted tight and heeled hard, the little sloop ran over the shallows and into a cove. Her stern touched, rose up on the keel, and she slid up into water no more than eighteen inches deep. The boy jumped, splashing up the short slope, and set the anchor on the beach, as the old man dropped the sail.

"Dis ain't de Water Cay, Missy, but this be where we is," he hollered over the wind, expressing in these words, his natural acceptance for the power of the elements.

A limestone ledge with a shallow overhang faced the beach. The boy built a fire and they sheltered under it. The sky cleared but the wind blew even stronger from the northeast. The great waves that struck the island's windward side shook the earth.

"Dat be de north end of Water Cay, Missy," Stephen Rolly said, pointing across the cut, now become a raging maelstrom.

"So close," she said, peering through salt mist at the cliffs only two hundred yards away.

"She 'bout two-mile-long, little more," Rolly described, drawing in the sand. "Your mon, he be down south end of there, near to Melita Cay. Dat where de Sponish ship strike."

"You know about it," She blurted.

Rolly laughed, a deep easy laugh, like a parent enjoying a child's foolishness.

"Missy, every mon in de Exumas know 'bout dat Sponish treasure. They knows 'bout de deep-water current and de sharks. Many mon, he go there, not so many mon, they come home. Dat gold, it gots de curse just like dat island, it got de curse." He threw his stick on the fire. "This mon don't need no Sponish gold to live good. Got de fish and de garden. Build a boat; build a house, life is good."

"Is it really so dangerous a place?" she asked.

The old man leaned back on the sand and pointed, saying, "Climb up on de rocks dere. Look at how de current, she rush to sea, how she fight de waves. Sharp coral dat fall off into de abyss." He closed his eyes. "Why, dere nothing here but duppies, Missy."

Bent to the wind, Corazon climbed, climbed up to the crest of the little cay. She observed the fury of the sea, thundering against current that roared off the banks. She was both terrified and fascinated by it. It was like a great waterfall or rapid. A person could watch and watch and the power of it never failed to have an effect.

For two days, the storm blew, and on the afternoon of the third day, it fell calm. The current was slack, but there was no wind to drive the sloop. Corazon persuaded Rolly to scull the sloop across the cut. She would walk the length of the island and reach her husband's camp before dark. When she took out her pistol, Kip looked alarmed. Rolly grinned, cackled with amusement.

"Ain't nothing, but them spirits on dat Cay, Missy, lest you's

373

planning to shoot some poor mon."

She smiled sweetly, for a wild woman. Her hair was tangled and her face sunburned. The sand fleas were vicious, and she covered herself with silk scarves.

"Some men require shooting," she joked, and with a wave, started up the slope.

The going became far more difficult than she expected, with ravines and beds of cactus, offering impassable barriers. Often, she could walk the beach. Just as often, low cliffs forced a detour inland over the barren, crumbling rock. At dusk, with the sun already down, the wind blew once more. She saw the tug's shape in the twilight, outlined against a campfire, and she hurried down the beach toward the glow.

Chapter 41

Before dark, the longboat had put out from the cay with the anchors, but a good swell was rolling in. Getting anchors set and buoyed had taken time. Both breeze and the current were against the boat as it returned, and the boys sat watching in the dim light as their chums pulled long and hard for the point. Patsy had cornbread baking and thick chowder bubbling. Heat filled the small galley, sweat ran rivulets off his skin and ducking outside he walked across the plank, wiping his face with a towel.

Patch's head jerked round at the cook's first squeaky scream. He saw Patsy fall into the water then scramble up, running toward the point. He was watching Patsy, dumbfounded when Rummy and Goose shrieked and fled after him. Patch Ross stood stiff, prickly skinned and turned his head.   The pale duppie was drifting down the beach, surrounded by blowing veils. It had no face. Patch ran into the chief, who swallowed his chaw and tore after the younger man with astonishing speed for his age.

Arriving at the point at the precise moment the longboat doubled it, the five rushed wild-eyed into the water, half swamping the boat as they clambered aboard. The whole sodden mess broached, and swept back out into the cut, while their captain cursed.

Corazon, somewhat mystified, stood by the fire unwrapping herself. She thought to follow and see where everyone had run off to, but there was coffee on the fire, and the smell of something good coming from the tug's galley. She crossed the deck, heard running water and jumped back red-faced. Airi, who had come on deck, was relieving himself over the side.

"Excuse me," she mumbled, blushing.

He buttoned his britches. "Who you, lady?" he asked, looking abashedly over his shoulder.

'I'm Captain Byran's wife," she answered. "Where is everyone?"

"Ah! Mrs. Byran. Sorry," he said, extending his arms and looking down. "Didn't know a lady was here." He pointed, "They're out in the cut, making ready for the captain to dive."

"The captain," she said, puzzled.

"Too dangerous, I quit," the Greek, proclaimed. "No more, too bad here. Aristotle Mickelos is not crazy enough to go down again."

Corazon's hackles rose. "Are you insinuating my husband is crazy," she said archly.

Airi looked confounded. "What is insinuating?" he inquired

humbly.

"Never mind," she mumbled, unsure of the subject herself. "Why would you be crazy to dive?"

He pulled his yarn hat off; he wrung it nervously in both hands and said, "Too much current, sweep you off into deepwater or trap you in the rocks. I am almost killed. I know, everyone knows. " He shrugged. "Have wife, children." He shrugged, "why die?"

Corazon considered what the Greek said. Simple enough, anyone stubborn enough to dive in that cut would ultimately be killed. Her husband was definitely, and without question obstinate. She considered reasoning with him. She looked at the diving suit and the polished brass of the helmet, and twisted her mouth to one side in contemplation of a suitable solution.

Finally, she put down her pistol, and pulled an axe from its place adjacent the tow bits. Airi stepped back in alarm. The first blow knocked the faceplate out of the diving helmet; the second bounced off, so she chopped up the hose, and knocked the fittings off the pump. She dropped the axe, picked up the pistol, and put three rounds through the helmet, then another through the pump casting. The reports echoed off the sandstone cliffs disturbing birds. Satisfied, she looked around to find herself alone. Airi was running up the beach. Corazon surveyed her work and smiling, went into the galley to see what there was to eat.

When the longboat arrived alongside, some forty minutes later, she had bathed, washed her hair, and was reading the *Bull's* log by candlelight. In confused disbelief, and with a ridiculous sensation of guilt, Asher gawked at her. Wanting to take her in his arms, he leaped over the rail, but before he had the chance, she raised the empty pistol between them aiming directly between his wolfish gold eyes. The blue-green of her own sparked as she backed him to a bulkhead.

"Asher Byran," she declared with an even and very certain voice, "I'm entreating your understanding, begging your forgiveness for treating you as I did. You are my husband, and I had no right taking my mother's part against you. I was wrong and I regret the way I behaved."

Asher smiled uncertainly. Having spent a year with Corazon, the concept of being threatened and apologized to at the same time did not seem out of character. Asher felt wood press against his backside.

"But," she continued, "You had no decent cause, no true excuse to go off, leave me, to abandon me like that, Asher. None at all," she complained, "and seeking to salvage some treasure, why that's no excuse for these long months and with no word." She tossed her head to attend a wayward lock of hair that had fallen over one eye, "And if I'd wished to live alone, I'd not have married. If I'd found servants and residence in a mansion more precious than your companionship, I'd have remained in my father's house." I chose you over wealth and I'll not lose you to the pursuit of it.

"And," she added, squinting until she was steely eyed, "If you can't see reason, if I'm to become a widow over some desperate scheme to raise treasure, you just tell me. I swear, much as it pains me, I will shoot you now Asher Byran. If it is only to save myself the anguish of worry, the uncertainty of waiting for it to happen, I will shoot you now."

She paused, thumbing back the hammer of the pistol knowing full well it was empty, and said, "Shall we go home Asher, or shall I pull the trigger?"

Asher swallowed wearing an expression much like a boy caught out of school. Out of the corner of his eye, he recognized the wreckage of what had been a fine diving rig. He saw the faces of his men, some amused, some concerned.

"I can't do much diving now kitten," he mumbled half disgusted, "but I guess that's not so bad." He cocked his head

377

to one side and shrugged. "We'll have steam up in half an hour if you could lay off scaring the boys with that thing," he said pointing.

"No more treasure hunts?" she bargained, tilting her head.

"None," he promised and as she stepped forward, he took her in his arms. The empty pistol thumped on the deck, and as their lips touched he mumbled, "Where's Freddie?"

Epilogue

The voyage home was idyllic, a fair weather run across the empty banks below Andros. The Byrans enjoyed two weeks together at *Hurricane Road*, before traveling north to collect Freddie. Rumors that Flagler would push his railroad south through the keys proved true, and the Byrans recognized opportunity. Fortune is amassed through enterprise, and the Byran's were enterprising people. Storms, man-made and natural, came and went. Wealth came at it's own pace, and the bay shore was settled around them. The modern world had arrived at Coconut Grove. That quiet part of Florida was changing, becoming both more and less than it had been, but life is change.

In 1902, twin boys, James and Connor, were born; and 1903 brought a daughter, Cathleen, to the household. With Cathleen's birth, an unspoken truce formed between Asher and his wife's family. Biscayne Shipping was operating four ocean going vessels, and several tugs by 1910, and the Byrans, feeling the security of modest wealth, built a new home, a finer Hurricane Road on their Coconut Grove property. It was a structure, which would never be described as a hovel.

On an evening in the library of Hurricane Road, Corazon found her husband gazing at ancient doubloons, displayed in a glass case. Asher offered up a guilty grin. Corazon frowned and lead him up bed.

Sixteen fathoms deep and east of Water Cay, a treasure lay waiting as it had for centuries. That gold — the Great War, the lives of the Bryan's and their children asleep in their beds, are all parts of stories revealed in other novels.

The next in the series is **Florida Straits.** This novel follows the characters if **Hurricane Road,** from the years of the Great War to the onset of the Great Depression, and the Roaring Twenties in between. Women get the vote and everyone loses their Booze. It's bootlegger's heaven. Be ready for a wild read.

Titles in this series:

1 Hurricane Road *******
2 Florida Straits
3 Valuable Things
4 A Change of Times
5 Lies and to the wall
6 Implausible Deniability
7 Paths of War

.

Made in the USA
Middletown, DE
02 October 2020

20940841R00210